THE SPEARWIE...
by R. A. S...

**Thrilling fantasy and adventure from R. A. Salvatore—
bestselling author of *Siege of Darkness*, *The Legacy*,
The Halfling's Gem, and other acclaimed novels!**

THE WOODS OUT BACK

The adventure begins as Gary Leger stumbles upon the
fantasy world of Faerie in the woods behind his home . . .

"Fantasy . . . with literacy, intelligence, and a good deal
of dry wit."   *—Booklist*

THE DRAGON'S DAGGER

Gary travels back to Faerie to battle a fearsome dragon that
is burning up the countryside . . .

"Looking for a pot of gold? Read this book!"
    —Margaret Weis, *New York Times* bestselling author

"A classic tale . . . certain to retain its predecessor's
audience."   *—Booklist*

Now the adventure continues with Gary Leger's
final journey to the mystical realm—one which will
determine his fate, and the fate of all Faerie . . .

DRAGONSLAYER'S RETURN

Ace Books by R. A. Salvatore

THE WOODS OUT BACK
THE DRAGON'S DAGGER
DRAGONSLAYER'S RETURN

SPEARWIELDER'S TALE

DRAGONSLAYER'S RETURN

R. A. SALVATORE

ACE BOOKS, NEW YORK

This book is an Ace original edition,
and has never been previously published.

DRAGONSLAYER'S RETURN

An Ace Book / published by arrangement with
the author

PRINTING HISTORY
Ace edition / August 1995

ISBN: 0-441-00228-5

ACE®
Ace Books are published by The Berkley Publishing Group,
200 Madison Avenue, New York, NY 10016.
ACE and the "A" design are trademarks
belonging to Charter Communications, Inc.

PRINTED IN THE UNITED STATES OF AMERICA

10 9 8 7 6 5 4 3 2 1

To Susan Allison,
my editor, my friend,
with all my thanks for letting me write this tale,
so very dear to me, and with the sincere hope
that we will work together again

FAERIE

pass
GONDABUGGAN
the
FIVE SISTERS

AMAL

BULDRE

the CRAHGS

LOCH TULLAMORE
(DRY)

the witch's
teats
GLEN DRUITCH
GIANT'S THUMB

RUINED FOREST

DREADWOOD

N

W · E

S

Ann Meyer Maglinte

† Prelude

The October wind bit hard, tossing leaves, yellow and brown and red, into a swirling vortex and sweeping them past the man standing solemnly at the top of the hill, near to the road and the spiked green fence that marked the boundary of the cemetery. Cars buzzed along Lancaster Street just beyond that fence, the bustle of the living so near to the quiet cemetery. White flakes danced in the air, an early-season flurry. Just a few flakes, and fewer still ever seemed to reach the ground, carried along on the wind's continual ride.

Gary Leger, head bowed, hardly noticed any of it, the snow, the wind, or the cars. His black hair, longer now than usual for lack of attention, whipped about into his stubbly face, but that, too, he didn't notice. The *feel* of the day, that classic New England autumn melancholy, was in Gary, but the details were lost—lost in the overwhelming power of the simple words on the flat white stone set in the ground:

Pvt. Anthony Leger
Dec. 23, 1919–June 6, 1992
World War II Veteran

That was it. That was all. Gary's dad had spent seventy-two years, five months, and fifteen days alive on this Earth, and that was it.

That was all.

Gary consciously tried to conjure memories of the man. He remembered the cribbage games, remembered the great blizzard of '78, when his dad, the stubborn mailman, was out at five in the morning, trying to shovel his car out of the driveway.

Gary snorted, a sad chuckle at best, at that recollection. The weatherman had forecasted a few inches, and Gary had awakened with the hopes that school would be canceled. Yeah, right. Gary peeked through the side of his shade, and saw that it had indeed snowed. Perspectives were all askew that February morning fifteen years before, though, and when Gary looked down to the driveway beneath his window, trying to gauge how much snow had fallen, all he saw was a black circle a few inches in diameter. He thought it was the driveway, thought his car, his precious '69 Cougar with the 302 Boss and the mag wheels, had been stolen.

Gary ran downstairs in just his underwear, screaming, "My car!" over and over.

The car was still there, the embarrassed young man soon learned, standing practically naked in front of his mother and older sister; the black spot he had seen was not the driveway, but the vinyl roof of his car!

And there was his father, stubborn Dad, at the end of the driveway, plunging the shovel upward—up above his shoulders!—into a snowdrift, trying to get his car out so that he could get to work. Never mind that the city snowplows hadn't even been able to climb up the Florence Street hill; never mind that the snowdrift went on and on, down the street and even down the main road.

Gary could see it all so clearly, could even see the cemetery, across the street and across their neighbor's yard. Even in that memory, Gary could see the statue marking his father's family grave, the virgin with her arms upraised to the gray sky.

Just like now. Just like forever. The plaque that marked his father's grave was a few feet behind that same statue, and Gary's eyes wandered to the virgin's back, followed its lines and upraised arms into the sky, full of dark clouds and white clouds, rushing along on the westerly breeze. Gary's chuckle was gone, replaced by a single tear that washed from his green eye and gently rolled down his cheek.

Diane, leaning on the car twenty feet away, noted the glisten of that tear and silently bit her bottom lip. Her eyes, green like Gary's, moistened in sympathy. She was helpless. Totally helpless. Anthony had been gone four months and in that short time, Diane had watched her husband age more than in the seven years they had been together.

But that was the thing with death, the helplessness. And as much as Diane felt it in looking at wounded Gary, Gary felt it ten times more in looking down at the simple words on the simple stone in the wind-strewn cemetery.

Gary had always been a dreamer. If a bully pushed him around at school, he would fantasize that he was a martial arts master, and in his mind he would clobber the kid. Whatever cards the real world had dealt to him, he could change his hand through his imagination. Until now, looking down at the grass covering his father.

There were no "conquering hero" daydreams for this reality.

Gary took a deep breath and looked back to the stone marker. He didn't come to the cemetery very often; he didn't see the point. He carried his father's memory with him every minute of every day—that was his homage to the man he had so loved.

Until June 6, things had been going well for Gary Leger. He and Diane had been married for almost two years, and they were starting to talk about children. Both were building careers, following the paths that society said was proper. They had lived with Gary's parents for a short while after their wedding, saving for an apartment, and had only been out on their own for a few months.

And then Anthony had died.

His time had come. That was the proper cliche for it, the most fitting description of all. Anthony had always been the most responsible of men; Anthony would dig at that towering snowdrift because by doing so, he was making progress towards fulfilling his responsibilities. That was Anthony's way. Thus, when Gary, the baby of the family, youngest of seven, had moved out of the house, Anthony's responsibilities had come to their end. His children were out and on their own; his daughters and his sons had made their own lives. The time had come for Anthony to sit back and relax, and pass the time in quiet retirement.

Anthony didn't know how to do that.

So Anthony's time had come. And though he felt none of the I-wish-I-had-told-him-while-he-was-alive guilt, for his relationship with his dad had been truly wonderful, Gary couldn't help thinking, in the back of his mind, that if he had stayed at home, Anthony would have stayed responsible. Anthony would have stayed alive.

Gary felt that weight this chill and windy autumn day. But more than that, he felt pure and unblemished grief. He missed his dad, missed having him down at third base, coaching softball, missed watching TV, sharing grumbling sessions at the always bleak daily news.

As that summer had begun to wane, Diane had talked about children again, but her words seemed ultimately empty to Gary Leger. He wasn't ready yet for that prospect, for the prospect of having children that his dad would never see.

All the world was black to him.

All the world, except one sliver of hope, one memory that could not be dulled by any tragedy.

When the grief threatened to engulf him, overwhelm him and drop him listless to the leaf-covered ground, Gary Leger turned his thoughts to the mystical land of Faerie, the land of leprechauns and elfs, of a dragon he had slain and an evil witch who would soon be free—or perhaps already was free, bending the land's independent people under her iron-fisted rule.

Gary had been there twice, the first time unexpectedly, of course, and the second time after five years of wishing he could go back. Five years in this world had been just a few weeks in Faerie, for time between the lands did not flow at the same rate.

For a fleeting instant, Gary entertained a notion of somehow getting back to Faerie, of using the time discrepancy to come back to a living Anthony. If there was some way he could get back on the night Anthony's heart had stopped, some way he could be beside his father, so that he might call the emergency medics . . .

Gary dismissed the wild plan before it could even fully formulate, though, for he understood that the time discrepancy did not involve any backward time travel. Anthony was gone, and there was not a thing in all the world that Gary could do about it.

Still, the young man wanted to get back to Faerie. He wanted to get back to Mickey McMickey the leprechaun, and Kelsey the elf, and Geno Hammerthrower, surly Geno, the dwarf who never seemed to run out of fresh spittle. Gary had wanted to go back, off and on, in the four years since his last adventure, and that desire had become continuous since the moment he saw his dad lying on the hospital gurney, since the moment he realized that there was nothing he could do.

Maybe his desire to return was merely a desire to escape, Gary fully realized.

Maybe Gary didn't care.

1 † Crumbling Bridges

The three unlikely companions—leprechaun, elf, and dwarf—crouched behind a vine-covered fence, watching the ranks of soldiers gathering to the south. Five thousand men were in the field, by their estimate, with hundreds more coming in every day. Infantry and cavalry, and all with helms and shields and bristling weapons.

"Kinnemore's to march again," said Mickey McMickey, the leprechaun, twirling his tam-o'-shanter absently on one finger. Only two feet tall, Mickey didn't need to crouch at all behind the brush, and with his magical pot of gold safely in hand (or in pocket), the tricky sprite hardly gave a care for the clumsy chase any of the human soldiers might give him.

"Suren it's all getting tired," Mickey lamented. He reached into his overcoat, gray like his mischievous eyes, and produced a long-stemmed pipe, which magically lit as he moved it towards his waiting mouth. He used the pipe's end to brush away straggly hairs of his brown beard, for he hadn't found the time to trim the thing in more than three weeks.

"Stupid Gary Leger," remarked the sturdy and grumpy Geno Hammerthrower, kicking at the brush—and inadvertently snapping one of the fence's cross-poles. The dwarf was the finest smithy in all the land, a fact that had landed him on this seemingly unending adventure in the first place. He had accompanied Kelsey the elf's party to the dragon's lair to reforge the ancient spear of Cedric Donigarten, but only because Kelsey had captured him, and in Faerie the rules of indenture were unbending. Despite those rules, and the potential loss of reputation, if Geno had known then the ramifications of the elf's quest, from freeing the dragon to beginning yet another war, he wouldn't have gone along at all. "Stupid Gary Leger," the dwarf grumped again. "He had to go and let the witch out of her hole."

"Ceridwen's not free yet," Kelsey, tallest of the group—nearly as tall as a man—corrected. Geno had to squint as he regarded the crouching elf, the morning sun blinding him as if reflected off Kelsey's lustrous and long golden hair. The elf's eyes, too, shone golden, dots of sunlight in an undeniably handsome and angular face.

"But she's soon to be free," Geno argued—too loudly, he realized when both his companions turned nervous expressions upon him. "And so she is setting the events in motion. Ceridwen will have Dilnamarra, and likely Braemar and Drochit as well, in her grasp before she ever steps off her stupid island!"

Kelsey started to reply, but paused and stared hard and long at the dwarf. Unlike most others of his mountain race, Geno wore no beard, and with a missing tooth and the clearest of blue eyes, the dwarf resembled a mischievous youngster when he smiled—albeit a mischievous child bodybuilder! Kelsey was going to make some determined statement about how they would fight together and drive Kinnemore, Ceridwen's puppet King, and his army back into Connacht, but the elf couldn't find the words. Geno was likely right, he knew. They had killed Robert the dragon, the offsetting evil to Ceridwen, and with Robert out of the way, the witch would waste little time in bringing all of Faerie under her darkness.

At least, all of Faerie's human folk. Kelsey's jaw did firm up when he thought of Tir na n'Og, his sylvan forest home. Ceridwen would not conquer Tir na n'Og!

Nor would she likely get into the great Dvergamal Mountains after Geno's sturdy folk. The dwarfish Buldrefolk were more than settlers in the mountains. They were a part of Dvergamal, in perfect harmony with the mighty range, and the very mountains worked to the call of the Buldrefolk. If Ceridwen's army went after the dwarfs, their losses would surely be staggering.

And so Faerie would be as it had once been, Kelsey had come to believe. All the humans would fall under the darkness, while the dwarfs and elfs, the Buldrefolk of Dvergamal and the Tylwyth Teg of Tir na n'Og, fought their stubborn and unending resistance. After quietly reminding himself of the expected future, the elf's visage softened as he continued to stare Geno's way. They would be allies, like it or not (and neither the dwarfs nor the elfs would like it much, Kelsey knew!).

A horn blew in the distant field, turning the three companions back to the south. A force of riders, fully armored knights, charged down onto the field on armored warhorses, led by a lean man in a worn and weathered gray cloak.

"Prince Geldion," Mickey remarked sourly. "Now I've not a doubt. They'll start for Dilnamarra all too soon, perhaps this very day. We should be going, then," he said to Kelsey. "To warn fat Baron Pwyll so that he might at least be ready to properly greet his guests."

Kelsey nodded gravely. It was their responsibility to warn

Baron Pwyll, for whatever good that might do. Pwyll could not muster one-tenth the force of Connacht, and this army was superbly trained and equipped. By all measures of military logic, the Connacht army could easily overrun Dilnamarra, probably in a matter of a few hours. Kelsey's allies had one thing going for them, though, a lie that had been fostered in rugged Dvergamal. After the defeat of the dragon, Gary Leger had returned to his own world, and so the companions had given credit for the kill to Baron Pwyll. It was a calculated and purposeful untruth, designed to heighten Pwyll's status as a leader among the resistance to Connacht.

Apparently the lie had worked, for the people of Dilnamarra had flocked about their heroic Baron, promising fealty unto death. Connacht's army was larger, better trained, and better armed, but the King's soldiers would not fight with the heart and ferocity of Baron Pwyll's people, would not hold the sincere conviction that their cause was just. Still, Kelsey knew that Dilnamarra could not win out; the elf only hoped that they might wound Connacht's army enough so that the elves of Tir na n'Og could hold the line on their precious forest borders.

"And what of you?" Kelsey asked Geno, for the dwarf had made it clear that he would soon depart when this scouting mission was completed.

"I will go back with you as far as the east road, then I'm off to Braemar," Geno answered, referring to the fair-sized town to the north and east, under the shadows of mighty Dvergamal. "Gerbil and some of his gnomish kin are waiting for me there. We'll tell the folk of Braemar, and go on to Drochit, then into the mountains, me to my kin at the Firth of Buldre and Gerbil to his in Gondabuggan."

"And all the land will know of Ceridwen's coming," Kelsey put in.

"For what good it will do all the land," Mickey added dryly.

"Stupid Gary Leger," said Geno.

"Are ye really to blame him?" Mickey had to ask. Geno had always remained gruff (one couldn't really expect anything else from a dwarf), but over the course of their two adventures, it seemed to Mickey that the dwarf had taken a liking to Gary Leger.

Geno thought over the question for a moment, then simply answered, "He let her out."

"He did as he thought best," Kelsey put in sternly, rising to Gary's defense. "The dragon was free on the wing, if you remember, and so Gary thought it best to shorten Cerid-wen's banishment—a banishment that Gary Leger alone had imposed upon her by defeating her," he pointedly added, staring hard Geno's way. "I'll not begrudge him his decision."

Geno nodded, and his anger seemed to melt away. "And it was Gary Leger who killed the dragon," the dwarf admitted. "As was best for the land."

Kelsey nodded, and the issue seemed settled. But was it best for the land? the elf silently wondered. Kelsey certainly didn't blame Gary for the unfolding events, but were the results of Gary's choices truly the better?

Kelsey looked back to the field and the swelling ranks of Ceridwen's mighty hand, an evil hand hidden behind the guise of Faerie's rightful King. Would it have been better to fight valiantly against the obvious awfulness of Robert the dragon, or to lose against the insidious encroachment of that wretched witch?

Given the elf's bleak predictions for Faerie's immediate future, the question seemed moot.

*   *   *   *   *

Gary's first steps off the end of Florence Street were tentative, steeped in very real fears. He had grown up here; looking back over his shoulder, he could see the bushes in front of his mother's house (just his mother's house, now) only a hundred or so yards and five small house lots away.

The paved section of Florence Street was longer now. Another house had been tagged on the end of the road, encroaching into Gary's precious woods. He took a deep breath and looked away from this newest intruder, then stubbornly moved down the dirt fire road.

Just past the end of the back yard of that new house, Gary turned left, along a second fire road, one that soon became a narrow and overgrown path.

A fence blocked his way; unseen dogs began to bark.

Somewhere in the trees up above, a squirrel hopped along its nervous way, and the lone creature seemed to Gary the last remnant of what had been, and what would never be again.

He grabbed hard against the unyielding chain links of the fence, squeezing futilely until his fingers ached. He thought of climbing over, but those dogs seemed quite near. The prospect of getting caught on the wrong side of a six-foot fence with angry dogs nipping at his heels was not so appealing, so he gave the fence one last shake and moved back out to the main fire road, turned left and walked deeper into the woods.

Hardly twenty steps farther and Gary stopped again, staring blankly to the open fields on his right, beyond the chain-link fence of the cemetery.

Open fields!

This fence had been here long before Gary, but the area inside it, these farthest reaches of the cemetery, had been thickly wooded with pine and maple, and full of brush as tall as a ten-year-old. Now it was just a field, a huge open field, fast filling with grave markers. It seemed a foreign place to Gary; it took him a long time to sort out the previous boundaries of the cleared regions. He finally spotted the field where he and his friends had played football and baseball, a flat rectangular space, once free of graves and lined by trees.

Now it was lined by narrow roads and open fields, and rows of stone markers stood silent and solemn within its sacred boundaries. Of course, Gary had seen this change from the cemetery's other end, the higher ground up near the road, where the older family graves were located.

Where his father was buried.

He had seen how the cemetery had grown from that distant perspective, but he hadn't realized the impact. Not until now, standing in the woods out back. Now Gary understood what had been lost to the dead. He looked at the playing field of his youth, and saw the marker of his future.

Breathing hard, Gary pushed deeper into the woods, and could soon see the back of the auto body shop on the street that marked the eastern end of the trees. Somewhat surprised, Gary looked back to the west, towards Florence Street. He could see the light-shingled roof of the new house! And he could see the auto body shop! And across the open cemetery, across the silent graves, he could see the tops of the cars moving along the main road.

Where had his precious woods out back gone? Where were the thick and dark trees of Gary Leger's childhood eye? He remembered the first time he had walked all the way through these woods, from Florence Street to the auto body shop. How proud he had been to have braved that wilderness trek!

But now. If he and Diane had kids, Gary wouldn't even bother taking them here.

He cut left again, off the fire road and into the uncleared woods, determined to get away from this openness, determined to put all signs of the civilized world behind him. Up a hill, he encountered that stubborn chain-link fence again, but at least this time, no dogs were barking.

Over the fence Gary went, and across the brush, growling in defiance, ready to pound any dog that stood to block him. He was in the back lot of the state-run swimming pool, another unwanted encroachment, but at least this section of land hadn't been cleared. Beyond this stretch, Gary came into the blueberry patch, and he breathed a sincere sigh of relief to see that this magical place still existed, though with the trees thinned by the season, he could see yet another new house to the west, on the end of the street running perpendicular off the end of Florence Street. That road, too, had been extended—quite far, apparently. Now Gary understood where the dogs were kept chained, and predictably, they took to barking again.

Gary rubbed a hand over his face and moved across the blueberry patch, to the top of the mossy banking that settled in what was still the deepest section of the diminishing wood. Here, he had first met the sprite sent by Mickey McMickey, the pixie who had led him to the dancing fairy ring that had sent him into the magical land.

He moved down the steep side, out of sight of anything but trees, and removed his small pack, propping it against the mossy banking as a pillow.

He stayed for hours, long after the sun had gone down and the autumn night chilled his bones. He called softly, and often, for Mickey, pleading with the leprechaun to come and take him from this place.

No sprites appeared, though, and Gary knew that none would. The magic was gone from here, lost like the playing field of his youth, dead under the markers of chain-link fences and cement foundations.

2 ✝ Say It Loud and Say It Often

Prince Geldion stomped across the muddy field, cursing the rain, cursing the wind, cursing the night, and cursing the impending war. Head down and thoroughly consumed by his anger, the volatile Prince walked right into one guard, who started to protest until he recognized the perpetrator. Then the common soldier stood straight and silent, eyes wide and not even daring to blink or breathe!

Geldion's dark eyes bored into the frightened man, the Prince's well-earned reputation for ferocity making the look more ominous indeed. Geldion said not a word—didn't have to—just let his imposing stare linger over his shoulder as he sloshed away.

He wished a star would come out, or the moon. Anything but these clouds. Geldion hated riding in the mud, where with every stride his horse took he felt as if they would slip sideways and pitch over. And this coming ride would be forced, he knew, driven by his father's insatiable desire to put Dilnamarra under Connacht's widening thumb.

Dilnamarra, and all of Faerie. Kinnemore had always been ambitious and protective of his realm, but now those feelings had reached new heights. Geldion wasn't sure what had changed, beyond the reforging of Cedric Donigarten's

17

spear and the slaying of the dragon. So Robert was gone, but when was the last time anyone had seen the wyrm out of his distant mountain hole anyway? And so the spear was whole, but who might wield it, and even if such a hero might be found, what grudge would he hold against Connacht? To Geldion's thinking, the politics remained the same. Kinnemore was still King and as far as the Prince knew, the people of all the communities still swore fealty to him. True, the army of Connacht, led by Geldion, had skirmished with the folk of Braemar and Drochit, but that had been an excusable faux pas, an indiscretion born on dragon wings as Robert the Wretched had terrorized the land. Diplomacy would certainly calm the realm and put all back in line.

That didn't seem good enough for King Kinnemore.

No, not Kinnemore, Geldion decided, and a hiss escaped his lips as he continued on his trek around the muddy perimeter of his encampment. Not his father, because his father made no independent decisions concerning the kingdom. Not anymore. This impending war was driven not from Connacht, but from Ynis Gwydrin, the Isle of Glass, the home of Ceridwen the witch.

"A place yous ne'er been," a raspy voice remarked, and the Prince skidded to a stop, went down into a crouch, and peered all around, his hand on the hilt of his belted dirk. A moment later, with nothing in sight, he straightened. A puzzled expression crossed Geldion's face as he came to realize that whoever, or whatever, had spoken to him had apparently read his mind.

Or had it been merely the drifting words of a distant, unrelated conversation?

"Nay, I was spaking to yous, Princes Geldion," the voice replied, and Geldion whipped out his dirk and fell back into the crouch once more.

"Above yous," croaked the voice. Geldion looked up to

watch the descent of a bat-winged monkey, its torso nearly as large as his own and with a wingspan twice his height. The creature landed quietly in the mud before the Prince and stood at ease, showing no fear of or respect at all for Geldion's waving dirk.

"Who are you, and where are you from?" Geldion demanded.

The monkey bat smiled, showing a wicked row of sharpened fangs. "Where?" it echoed incredulously, as though the answer should have been obvious.

"Ynis Gwydrin," Geldion reasoned. He saw some movement to the side and behind the monkey bat, his soldiers rushing to the scene. As the creature chuckled its confirmation that it was indeed a messenger of Ceridwen, the Prince held up his free hand to keep the soldiers at bay.

"Come from Ceridwen for Geldion," the monkey bat rasped. "The Lady would see Geldion."

"I am to ride . . ." the Prince started to ask.

"To fly," the monkey bat interrupted and corrected. "To fly with me." It held out its clawed hands towards the Prince, inviting him into an embrace.

An involuntary shudder coursed along Geldion's spine, and he eyed the creature skeptically, not replacing his weapon on his belt. His mind soared down several possibilities, not the least of which was warning him that Ceridwen, sensing his doubts and his anger at his father, might be trying to get him out of the way. He didn't replace the dirk on his belt; he'd not walk into such a trap.

But the witch had apparently expected his resistance. There came a sudden flurry from above, and a second monkey bat dropped down atop the Prince's shoulders, clawed feet and hands catching a tight hold on Geldion's traveling cloak. Geldion was off the ground before he could react, and with the cloak bundling about his shoulders, his overhead chop with the dirk did little damage.

Soldiers cried out and charged; the first monkey bat leaped away, pounding wings quickly taking it above the reach of the soldiers' long pikes and swords.

Geldion continued to struggle, freed up one arm and half turned to get into a striking posture.

"Would yous fall?" came a question from the darkness, from the first monkey bat, Geldion realized.

Those sobering words forced the Prince to look down and consider his position. He was already fully thirty feet from the ground and climbing rapidly. He could stick his captor, but a wound on this monkey bat would result in a drop that was not appealing.

"The Lady would see Geldion," the first monkey bat said again, and off they soared, through the driving rain and wind. There were more than two of the creatures, the Prince soon learned; there were more than twenty.

Ceridwen was never one to take chances.

Half the army was roused by that time, torches sputtering to life against the rain all across the muddy field. Hosts of archers bent their great yew bows skyward. But the night was dark and their efforts futile. Word went immediately to Kinnemore, but the King, apparently not surprised by Ceridwen's visitors, brushed away his soldiers' concerns and bade them go back to their watch and their sleep.

* * * * *

Prince Geldion saw little from his high perch in the dark sky. Every so often, the winged caravan would pass over a hamlet, nestled in the rolling fields east of Connacht, and the lights from windows would remind the abducted man of just how high he was.

Then the monkey bats fast descended, touching down on the wet grass, where they were met by a second group.

Again the Prince was scooped up, and off the fresher couriers flew. There came a second exchange, and then a third, and not so long after that, with the sky still dark in the throes of night, Geldion saw great looming shadows all about him.

They had come to Penllyn, the mountainous region surrounding Loch Gwydrin, the Lake of Glass. Geldion had never been here before—few had—but he knew many tales of the place. Everyone in Faerie had heard tales of the witch's home.

The sun was just peeking over the eastern rim, in their faces, as the troupe flapped through a pass between two towering peaks and came in sight of the still waters of the famed mountain lake.

Slanted rays touched upon its surface, turning the waters fiery golden. Geldion watched unblinking as the light grew and the scene unfolded. Ynis Gwydrin, the isle, came into sight, and then, the witch's castle, a crystalline palace of soaring spires that caught the morning light in a dazzling display of a million multicolored reflections.

Despite his general surliness, and his more pointed anger at being abducted, the helpless Prince could not hide his awe at the magnificent sight. No tales could do Ynis Gwydrin justice; no paintings, no sculptures, could capture the magic of this place and this crystalline castle.

Geldion took a deep breath to compose himself, and to whisper a reminder that the magic of Ynis Gwydrin was surely tainted by danger. This was Ceridwen's island, Ceridwen's castle, and a single wrong word would ensure that he never left the place alive—at least, not as a human. Ceridwen had a reputation for turning people into barnyard animals.

With that disquieting thought in mind, Geldion stepped down onto the isle, on a stone path through the sand that led to the crystalline castle's towering front doors. The monkey bats herded him towards the door, and he offered no resistance. (Where did they think he might run?) At the portal, he was met by a group of goblins, ugly hunched creatures with sloping foreheads and overgrown canines curling grotesquely over saliva-wetted lips that seemed too stretched for their mouths. Their skin was a disgusting yellow-green in color and they smelled like raw meat that had been too long in the sun.

"Geek," one spindly-limbed goblin explained, poking a gnarly finger into its small chest. The goblin reached out to take Geldion's arm, but the Prince promptly slapped the dirty hand away.

"I can offer no resistance on Ynis Gwydrin," Geldion explained. "If you mean to lead me to Ceridwen, then lead on. Else move away, on threat of your life!"

Geek sputtered and shook his ugly head, muttering something uncomplimentary about "peoples." He mentioned the name of Ceridwen, his "Lady," as Geldion had expected, and motioned for the Prince and the goblin guards to follow.

Inside the castle, they moved swiftly along mirrored corridors, and Geldion soon lost all sense of direction. He didn't much care, though, for he had no expectations of escape. He was in the lair of mighty Ceridwen, the sorceress, and in here, he knew well, he could only leave when Ceridwen allowed him to leave.

Geek stopped at a large wooden door and tentatively clicked the knocker a couple of times.

Geldion understood the goblin's nervousness. The guards shuffled uneasily behind him, and he got the distinct feeling that they did not want to be in this place.

The door swung in, apparently of its own accord, and suddenly Geek and Geldion were standing alone in the corridor, for the other goblins had taken full flight back the way they had come.

A warm glow emanated from beyond the opened door, the tinge of an inviting, blazing fire. From the corridor, Geldion could see only a portion of the room. A pair of overstuffed chairs were set on the end of a thick bearskin rug, and rich tapestries hung on the far wall. One Geldion recognized as a scene of the court in Connacht, though the work was old and Geldion did not know any of the men and women depicted.

Geek nervously motioned for Geldion to lead the way. If the Prince held any doubts that Ceridwen was in there, they were gone now, considering the goblin's truly fearful expression. Geldion took a deep breath, trying to fully comprehend what was at hand. He had never actually met the witch, though he had spoken several times to the talking crows that were Ceridwen's messengers. His father certainly had sat with Ceridwen, on many occasions, but Kinnemore rarely spoke to anyone of the meetings.

Now Geldion was to meet her, face to face. He looked down at his muddy traveling clothes, realized that in the confusion of the dragon-on-wing and the skirmishes with the eastern towns, he hadn't bathed in several weeks.

Geek made a whining sound and motioned again, more forcefully, for the Prince to go in. Without further delay, proud Geldion obliged, stepping boldly into the room (though he winced a bit when Geek pulled the door closed behind him).

At the head of the bearskin rug was a small divan and next to it a tall woman, taller than Geldion, wearing a white gown that clung to her many curves like some second skin.

There she stood, the legendary sorceress, undeniably beautiful, unearthly beautiful, her hair the color of a raven's wing and her eyes the richest blue. A simple look from those penetrating orbs sent icy chills along Geldion's spine. He wanted to lash out at the witch and fall on his knees and worship her all at the same time. Kinnemore had revealed little about the woman after his meetings with Ceridwen, and suddenly Geldion understood why.

No words could truly communicate the imposing specter of Ceridwen, no words could accurately re-create the aura surrounding this beautiful and awful creature.

"My greetings, Prince Geldion," she said in the sweetest of voices. "It strikes me as odd that we have not met before."

"Lady Ceridwen," Geldion replied with a curt bow.

"Please, do sit down," the witch purred, and she moved to the front of the divan, her shapely legs appearing through a slit in the gown. She sat and stretched languidly to the side, tucking her feet up inside one of the divan's arms and resting her arm over the other.

Geldion never took his eyes off her (couldn't take his eyes off her) as he slid into an overstuffed chair.

"Did you enjoy the journey?" Ceridwen asked.

Geldion looked at her curiously, for a moment having no clue as to what she might be talking about. With a start, he suddenly recalled the monkey bats, and the extraordinary trip that had brought him to Ynis Gwydrin.

"I prefer to ride," he stammered, feeling positively stupid. "Of course, your . . ." He paused, searching for a word to describe the monkey bats. "Your creatures," he said finally, "were faster than any horse."

"I needed to see you this day," Ceridwen explained.

"Had one of your crows called, I would have come," the Prince started to reply.

"This day," Ceridwen said again, forcefully, coming forward in the divan, blue eyes flashing dangerously. Geldion squirmed and clenched the arms of his seat, and hoped that the witch had not noticed the tremor that ran along his backbone. Geldion had fought a dozen battles, had led his army into combat without hesitation against powerful foes, including giant mountain trolls. But he was scared now, more so than ever before.

"And of course, I cannot yet go out from my island," Ceridwen went on calmly, and to the Prince's profound relief, she rested back in the divan. "Else I would have come to you. That would have been easier."

Geldion nodded, again feeling small and stupid. Ceridwen seemed to sense his discomfort, and she smiled, but did not say anything for a long while.

Increasingly uncomfortable, Geldion cleared his throat several times. Why wasn't she talking? he wondered. She had been the one, after all, to convene this meeting. So why wasn't she talking?

A few more minutes slipped by, the witch relaxing comfortably, stretching her porcelain legs (and revealing more of them with every move), while her blue eyes scrutinized the Prince's every nervous shift.

"Why am I here?" Geldion finally blurted.

"Because I wished to speak with you," Ceridwen replied, and she went silent again.

"Then speak!" Geldion cried out another long minute later, and he regretted the outburst as soon as it had come forth, thinking that Ceridwen would probably strike him down with a snap of her fingers. And sitting in that room, Geldion held no doubts that she was indeed powerful enough and wicked enough to do it!

But Ceridwen did not strike out at him. She merely laughed, heartily, and tossed her long mane of impossibly thick black hair back from her face.

Geldion had a sudden urge to fall on the floor and grovel before her, and the mischievous way she looked at him

made him think that she recognized and understood—
indeed, that she had purposely inspired—that urge. That
realization gave the Prince the courage to withstand the
mental assault, though his grip on the arms of his chair grew
so tight that his knuckles whitened for lack of blood.

Ceridwen nodded a moment later, as if in approval that
Geldion was still stubbornly in his seat.

"The army is gathered?" she asked unexpectedly, shattering the silence.

Geldion stammered, then nodded his head. "Ready to
march to Dilnamarra," he replied.

Ceridwen nodded. "Why?" she asked.

Geldion looked at her curiously. Wasn't she the one
behind all these plans of conquest? he wondered. "To put
down any potential uprising," he answered. "The people are
uneasy, speaking of old heroes and dragonslayers. King
Kinnemore fears . . ."

Ceridwen cut him off with an upraised hand. "And where
are you to go from Dilnamarra?" she prompted.

Geldion shrugged. "To Braemar, I would guess," he said.
"And then to Drochit. If the three main villages can be put
in line, then all the land . . ."

"And you will fight all the way?" Ceridwen again
interrupted. "Your wake will be messy indeed, flooded with
the blood of your enemies."

Geldion stroked his stubbly chin with his hand, not quite
understanding.

"You do not approve of the plan for conquest," Ceridwen
stated more than asked.

Geldion's eyes widened, and he worked hard to keep his
breathing steady, wondering why, if Ceridwen knew his
thoughts, she had not simply ordered her monkey bats to
drop him to his death.

"Speak your thoughts without fear," the calculating witch

prompted after a moment of silence, Geldion showing no inclination to respond to what he perceived as an accusation.

"Baron Pwyll slew Robert, so 'tis said," Geldion explained. "Or at least, he was among the group who slew the dragon. I do despise the fat man, but in the eyes of Dilnarmarra's peasants, he is a hero. I do not like the prospects of killing a hero."

"Good," Ceridwen purred.

"What game do you play?" the frustrated Prince, growing bolder by the moment, asked bluntly.

Ceridwen sat up straight, and Geldion nearly lost his breath in surprise. The sorceress seemed suddenly tired of the whole affair. "The army goes to Dilnamarra," she said firmly. "But not for conquest."

"Then why?" Geldion was neither disappointed nor hopeful, just perplexed. He managed to sit back again and regain a bit of his calm.

"You go on the pretense of a ceremony for a hero," Ceridwen said. "Baron Pwyll cannot refuse."

Geldion scratched at his face yet another time, beginning to catch on.

"To let the people view the true hero of the day," Ceridwen continued.

"The true hero," Geldion echoed. "And not Baron Pwyll."

"To let them see King Kinnemore of Connacht," Ceridwen agreed, smiling widely. "The warrior who slew Robert."

Geldion's face crinkled with disbelief and Ceridwen laughed at him. Geldion only shook his head back and forth in reply, hardly believing what the witch was proposing.

"Of course they know the truth," Ceridwen declared. "But Pwyll, that cowardly Baron, will not disagree. He will proclaim your father as the dragonslayer, for all to hear."

Geldion was still shaking his head doubtfully.

"Kinnemore killed the dragon," Ceridwen insisted. "Pwyll will say so with the prospect of war on his doorstep. King Kinnemore will become the hero, and our army will already be in place in Dilnamarra. What then, will poor Baron Pwyll do?" the witch cackled.

"What indeed?" said Geldion, and he did not seem so happy.

"From Dilnamarra, we announce the treachery of Drochit and Braemar," Ceridwen went on, and Geldion was nodding before she even finished the thought, completely expecting it. "Dilnamarra will thus be forced into an unintentional alliance, and when we march to the east, Baron Pwyll will ride between you and your father at the head of the army."

Geldion was still nodding, but he was far from convinced. The plan seemed perfectly simple and devious, and if it worked, it would bring all the land under Kinnemore's thumb in a short time and with minimal fighting. Perfectly simple and perfectly devious, but Geldion noted one serious hitch that the supremely confident Ceridwen might have overlooked. The Prince suspected that there might be more to this fat Baron Pwyll, and to the people of the land, than Ceridwen believed. By all accounts, Pwyll had faced a true and huge and terrible dragon, and not only had survived, but had walked out victorious. And Pwyll had been present on those eastern fields, beside Lord Badenoch of Braemar and Duncan Drochit, when the armies had skirmished.

Ceridwen took no note of Geldion's sour expression. Her eyes held a faraway, glassy look, as though she was basking in anticipated conquests. She would be free soon, Geldion knew, and Robert would no longer oppose her. All the land would be Kinnemore's, and Kinnemore was Ceridwen's.

The witch snapped her fingers and the door swung

open—and Geek, who had obviously been kneeling against the wood, trying to eavesdrop, stumbled into the room.

"Show the good Prince the way out," the witch purred, showing no concern for her overly curious attendant. "He has much to do."

Geldion remained silent for the rest of the time he was in the crystalline castle, and offered no resistance or no complaint when the monkey bats grabbed him up in their clawed hands and feet and set off from Ynis Gwydrin.

But Geldion was fuming, angry with Ceridwen and her malicious and dangerous plans, and, for some reason that he did not understand, Geldion was angry with his father. He had been anxious for the war, more than willing to take on the upstart Barons and put things aright. His father was the rightful King, and woe to those who did not profess undying fealty to the rightful King!

Suddenly, though, it seemed to Geldion that a righteous war had become a web of intrigue.

3 † A Sense of History

"I told you we should have come here later in the summer," Diane complained halfheartedly. She brushed back her dirty blonde hair—which was shorter now, for she had gotten into one of her I-need-a-change moods and cropped it tight about her ears, leaving the front longer than the sides and back, as was the fashion—and blew a raindrop off the end of her nose.

"It'll be raining in the summer, too," Gary assured her. "This is England. It always rains in England."

Diane could hardly disagree. They had been in London for three days and had actually seen the sun on several different occasions. The brightness had been fleeting, though. Always another dark cloud rolled in from one horizon or the other, pelting them with a cold spring rain.

What made it worse was that Gary insisted that they always be outside. Diane could think of a hundred places to visit in London, most of them indoors, but Gary was too restless for such orderly sightseeing. He wanted to walk London's streets, and walk they did—to the palace, to the tower, to Big Ben and Parliament and Westminster Abbey. But even in Westminster Abbey, where one could spend an entire day just reading the tomb markers of the famous dead, Gary had been restless. They had spent no more than an hour inside, rushing over Charles Darwin's floor stone, sliding past the great ornate caskets of the kings and queens, of Elizabeth and Mary, ironically buried side by side, romping through Poet's Corner, where lay Geoffrey Chaucer and the Brontës, and a score of other writers whose works Diane and Gary had grown up with and come to love.

Diane could have spent the entire day and the day after that just sitting in Poet's Corner, thinking of those books and those writers, feeling their ghosts hovering about her and taking comfort in the perpetuity of the human condition.

So why were they outside and walking along the wet streets again? she wondered. And in a completely different section of London? Diane sighed and looked about, watched a black cab zip past at about fifty miles an hour on the wrong side of the street. To her right was a large brownstone building, another of London's many museums, she figured— not that she'd get to spend any time *inside* one!

Gary plodded along a few steps ahead of her, and Diane had the distinct impression (and not for the first time!) that he hardly noticed that she was even there. More than once in the last three days, Diane had wondered why Gary had asked her to come along, and why he had picked London for their yearly vacation. The thought of taking separate trips, something the young woman would never have dreamed of before, was beginning to sound appealing.

"What is it?" she asked, somewhat impatiently, when she caught up to Gary. He was standing in the middle of the uneven sidewalk, staring down at a small crater in the stone.

Gary pointed to the mark.

"So?"

"It's not new," Gary remarked. He bent down and ran his fingers around the smoothed edges of the hole. "This happened a long time ago."

"So?" Now Diane's tone showed that she was clearly growing flustered. "It's a hole in the sidewalk, Gary. It's a stupid hole in a stupid sidewalk, a hole that's filling up with rainwater."

Gary looked up at her, and the pained expression on his face, as though she had just insulted him profoundly, stole some of the drenched woman's ire.

"What do you think made this?" he asked.

"What do you think?" she echoed, not really in the mood for such games.

"A V-1 rocket?" Gary asked more than stated. A wistful smile came over his face. "It was, you know," he added. "Or some other German bomb from World War II."

"Am I supposed to feel guilty?" Diane asked sarcastically, wondering if Gary was snidely referring to her German heritage.

"No," he assured her, standing once more, "but do you feel . . ." He stopped and flapped his hands in frustration, as if he was trying to physically pull the needed word from his mouth.

"Feel what?" she asked impatiently.

"The history," Gary blurted. "The sense of history."

Diane sighed. "You don't know what made that hole," she reminded him, though she did not doubt Gary's claim of the German bombing and had, in truth, thought the same thing when she first saw the crater. "It could have been a car accident, or an IRA bomb from just a few years ago."

Gary was shaking his head.

"Besides," Diane went on stubbornly, "if you want a sense of history, then why did you rush us out of Westminster Abbey? You can't get more historical than that! Every king and queen from Britain's history, and the people who wrote their stories are buried in there. But here we are, out in the stupid rain, standing over a bomb hole in the sidewalk."

"That's different," Gary insisted, and he took a deep

breath to clear his mind of the clutter. Diane did not seem convinced. "The history in there was our history," Gary explained deliberately. "Human history, purposely designed for us to go and see."

"Well then what's this?" Diane asked incredulously, pointing down at the crater. "Human history."

"It's not the same."

"Of course it's the same!"

"No!" Gary insisted. "It's . . . this wasn't put here on purpose, for us to look at it. This was an unintentional side effect of a historical event. No after-the-fact markers, just a moment in time, caught and preserved. It's like finding a dinosaur footprint out in the woods. That's different from going to a museum and seeing reconstructed bones."

"Okay," Diane readily conceded, still having no idea of the point of it all.

"That's why we're in London," Gary went on.

"I thought we were here on vacation," Diane quickly interjected, and though her words obviously stung Gary, he stubbornly pushed forward with his argument.

"That's why we're in England," he finished. "They've got more history here—without trying—than we can find back home."

"The United States was in World War II," Diane sarcastically reminded him.

Gary sighed and ran his hand over his cheek and chin. "But if we had any craters from German bombs, we would have filled them in," he lamented. "Like the Arizona Memorial at Pearl Harbor. We'd have built a bunch of new stuff around the site, explaining what happened in great detail, probably complete with movies you could watch for a quarter, instead of just letting the history speak for itself."

"I really don't know what you're talking about," Diane sighed. "And I'm really getting tired of walking in cold rain." She gave the crater a derisive look. "And you really don't know what made that," she added.

Gary had no retort; he just shrugged and started away, Diane loyally following. They soon found more craters—in the sidewalk and on the stone wall surrounding the large building—and then they spotted a small, unremarkable plaque set in the wall. It named this building as the Victoria and Albert Museum, and confirmed Gary's suspicions about the craters' origins, proclaiming that they were indeed a result of the German blitz.

The proclamation came as only a very small victory for Gary, though, for Diane still didn't understand the point of it all and didn't look too happy. He understood and sympathized with her disappointment. This was supposed to be their vacation—their one vacation of the year!—and he was dragging her around in the rain, searching for sensations that she didn't understand.

Gary, of course, had not come to England to see the typical sights. He had come in search of something more elusive, in search of one of those diminishing bridges Mickey McMickey had spoken of, a link between his world and the world of Faerie. This would be the place, he had figured. Somewhere in the British Isles.

Somewhere. But England, even London, wasn't quite as small as Gary Leger had figured. With that innate superiority so typical of third- and fourth-generation Americans, Gary had thought England and all the isles a small and rural place, a place he could thoroughly search in the two weeks he had off work.

There was nothing small or rural about London.

Three of those fourteen days were gone now, and all Gary had found was a small sense of history beside a chip in the sidewalk on a rainy London street. He was beginning to privately admit that London was too metropolitan, perhaps all of England was too metropolitan. Earlier that day, he had inquired of some Brits about the possibility of visiting Nottingham, remembering the "Robin Hood" movies and thinking Nottingham the pure English hamlet.

But the Brits assured Gary that Nottingham was not as he pictured it. It was a rough, blue-collar town, and according to those who knew, the remnants of Sherwood Forest amounted to about three trees. That notion stung Gary, reminded him of what had happened to his own precious woods in a land three thousand miles away.

It was true, as Mickey had lamented; the bridges from the real world to Faerie were fast disappearing.

The next morning, Gary announced that they would leave London, would take Britrail to Edinburgh, four hundred miles to the north. To her credit (and partly because she wanted to see Edinburgh), Diane went along without complaint. She understood that something was deeply troubling her husband, and figured that the loss of her vacation was a small price to pay if allowing him his strange quest would bring him some measure of comfort. They weren't so far away from the first anniversary of Anthony's death, and Diane realized that Gary had hardly begun to recover from that loss.

Four hundred miles in four hours, and the two walked out of the Edinburgh train station for their first glimpse of Scotland. Since they were carrying all their luggage, Gary agreed to take a cab.

"So where ye goin'?" the cabby asked, more casually than any of the stuffy gents in the London black cabs had ever been.

Gary and Diane stared blankly at each other; they hadn't booked a room.

"Ah, ye've got no hotel," the cabby reasoned, and Gary

looked at him hard, thinking how much his accent resembled Mickey's.

"Well, it's a wet time and there aren't too many visitors," the cabby went on. "We might be able to get ye something near to the castle."

"That'll be great," Diane quickly replied, before Gary could offer some other off-the-wall suggestion, and off they went.

A short while later they turned onto a wide boulevard, lined on the left by hotels, restaurants, and other shops that showed this to be a tourist section. A long park was on the right, down a grassy slope that put the widest part of the many blooming trees in the park at about eye level with the street.

"Castle o' the Rock," the cabby announced, looking to the right across the park.

Gary shifted low in his seat to get a better view past Diane and out the window. At first, he couldn't tell what the cabby was talking about, for all he saw through the tangle of trees was the park, and an occasional glimpse of the base of a hill across the way.

"Wow," Diane breathed when the trees thinned, and when Gary considered her, he realized that he should be looking up, not straight out. He leaned farther over her lap and turned his eyes skyward, up, up the hill that suddenly loomed more as a mountain. Up, up, hundreds of feet, to the walls of a castle that seemed to be growing right out of the top of the pillarlike mountain.

Gary couldn't find his breath.

"Stop the cab!" he finally blurted.

"What's that now?" the cabby asked.

"Stop the cab!" Gary cried again, crawling over Diane and grabbing at the door handle.

The cabby skidded over, and before the car had even

come to a full stop, Gary was out of it, stumbling forward to the edge of the park.

Diane rushed to join him and took his trembling arm as he continued to stare upward, transfixed by the specter of Edinburgh Castle. Gary had seen this place before, this mountain and this castle. He had seen it in a different world, in a magical place called Faerie.

There the mountain was known as the Giant's Thumb, and this castle, Edinburgh Castle, was the home of a dragon named Robert.

A wyrm that Gary Leger had killed.

* * * * *

"Your father . . ." the soldier began, but Geldion waved a hand to silence the man. Though he had only been back on the field for a few minutes, the Prince had been told already—a half dozen times, at least—that his father was looking for him. And the last soldier, a friend of Geldion's, had added that King Kinnemore was not in good humor this day.

Neither was the exhausted Geldion, flustered from his uncomfortable flights to and from Ynis Gwydrin and even more so from his encounter with devious Ceridwen. The witch had made Geldion feel small, and Prince Geldion, forever fighting for respect in his father's cold eyes, did not like that feeling. The guards standing to either side of Kinnemore's tent apparently recognized the volatile Prince's foul mood, for they stepped far to the side, one of them taking the tent flap with him, offering Geldion an opening large enough for several men to walk abreast.

"Where have you been?" the scowling, always scowling, King Kinnemore asked before his son had even entered the tent. "I have an army sitting dead on a field." Kinnemore stood behind a smallish oaken desk, making him seem even taller and more imposing. Few men in Faerie reached the height of six feet, but King Kinnemore was closer to seven. His frame was lean, and yet he was broad-shouldered, and obviously physically powerful. He had seen fifty years, at least, but was possessed of the energy of a twenty-year-old. A nervous energy that kept him constantly moving, wringing his hands or stroking his perfectly maintained and regal goatee. His gray eyes, too, never stopped, darting back and forth, taking in all the scene as though he expected an assassin behind every piece of furniture.

"Ceridwen summoned me," Geldion remarked casually, and Kinnemore's continuing tirade came out as undecipherable babble. He finally slammed a fist down on the table, its sharp bang giving him a moment of pause (and opening a crack in the wood) that he might regain his always tentative edge of control.

"You above any should know that we must jump to the witch's call," Geldion finished, and there was a measure of sarcasm in his voice. He couldn't resist goading his father just a bit more. Geldion rarely pushed the King, knowing that he, like any other fool who opposed Kinnemore, would likely wind up with his head on a chopping block, but every now and then, he could not resist the opportunity to offer up a slight tweak.

His father, eyes set in the midst of widening crow's feet, jaw so tight that Geldion could hear the man's teeth grinding, looked very old to the Prince at that moment. Old and angry. Always angry. Geldion could not remember the last time he had seen Kinnemore smile, except for that wicked smile he flashed whenever he ordered an execution, or whenever he talked of conquest. Had it always been like this, always so filled with hatred and blood lust? Geldion couldn't be sure—all his clear memories fell in line with Kinnemore's present behavior.

But the Prince sensed that something had indeed changed.

Perhaps it was only wishful fantasies, and not true memories, but Geldion seemed to recall a time of peace and happiness, a time of innocence when talk was not always on war, and play was preferred above battle.

A low growl escaped the King's lips, a guttural, animal-like growl. How could anyone be so horribly and perpetually angry? Geldion wondered.

"What did she want?" Kinnemore demanded.

The Prince shrugged. "Only to speak of Dilnamarra," he replied. "Of how we will use Baron Pwyll to anoint you as the slayer of Robert."

A sweep of Kinnemore's arm sent the small desk sliding out of the way, and the King advanced.

"If you are plotting with her against me . . ." Kinnemore threatened, moving very close to his son, his long finger poking the air barely an inch from Geldion's nose. Geldion was more than a foot shorter than his imposing father, a fact that was painfully evident to the Prince at that moment.

Still, Geldion didn't bother to justify the threat with a denial. He could be rightfully accused of many less than honorable things in his life, but never once had he entertained a treacherous thought concerning King Kinnemore. Geldion's loyalty wasn't questioned in the least by any who knew him. By all his actions, he was the King's man, to the death.

He didn't blink; neither did Kinnemore, but the King did eventually back off a step and lower his hand.

"What else did Ceridwen have to offer?" he asked.

"Nothing of any consequence," Geldion replied. "We force Dilnamarra into an alliance, and march east. Little has changed."

Kinnemore closed his eyes and slowly nodded his head, digesting it all. "When Braemar and Drochit are conquered,

I want Baron Pwyll executed," he said, calmly and coldly.

"Baron Pwyll will be an ally," Geldion reminded him.

"An unintentional ally, in an alliance he will surely despise," Kinnemore reasoned. "And he will know the truth of the dragon slaying. That makes him dangerous." The King flashed that wicked smile suddenly as a new thought came to him. "No," he said, "not after the conquest. Baron Pwyll must die on the road to Braemar."

"Ceridwen will not approve."

"Ceridwen will still be imprisoned upon her isle," Kinnemore retorted immediately, and then Geldion understood his father's reasoning. By the time Drochit and Braemar fell, Ceridwen would likely be free, and then, unless the witch was in agreement with the double-dealing, Kinnemore would have more trouble striking out against Pwyll. But Ceridwen could do little to prevent the treachery while on her island.

Geldion smirked, marveling at the misconceptions the people of Faerie held concerning his father. Most of the commoners believed that Kinnemore was no more than Ceridwen's puppet, but Geldion knew better. Ceridwen might indeed be the power behind the throne, but that throne held a power all its own, a savage strength that scared Geldion more than the witch ever could.

"And what will that bode for the alliance?" the Prince asked as forcefully as he could.

"You will do it," Kinnemore went on, so entranced by his line of thought that he seemed not even to hear Geldion's protest. "You will make it appear as an assassination by one of the eastern towns. Or if you are not wise enough to follow that course, you will make it appear as though the fat Baron had an accident, or that his poor health simply overcame him."

Geldion said nothing, but his scowling expression re-

vealed his sentiments well enough. He wondered of his own
fate, should the truth come out. Would his father stand
behind him if he was named as Baron Pwyll's executioner?
Or would King Kinnemore wash his hands of Geldion's
blood, brand him an outlaw and execute him?

Kinnemore just kept smiling, then, suddenly, snapped his
hand down to grab Geldion by the front of his tunic. With
horrifying strength, the older man easily lifted Geldion into
the air.

Purely by reflex, the Prince put a hand to his belted dirk.
His fingers remained on the hilt for only a moment, though,
for even in defense of his own life, Geldion knew that he
could not muster the nerve to strike out against his father.

"Get my troops moving," King Kinnemore growled.
"You let Duncan Drochit and that wretched Lord Badenach
escape once. I'll not tolerate another failure from you."

Geldion felt the man's savage power keenly at that
moment. Felt it in his father's hot, stinking breath, the
breath of a carnivore after a bloody kill.

He left Kinnemore's tent obviously shaken and walked
across the field, trying to summon those distant, fleeting
memories of his younger years, when Kinnemore had not
been so angry.

4 † The Hero

The meager forces of County Dilnamarra, some two hundred men and boys, and a fair number of women as well, stood quietly about the perimeter of Dilnamarra village and watched helplessly as the flood that was the Connacht militia, rank after rank, flowed across the rolling fields towards their village. The Dilnamarrans would be no real match for the trained and well-armed soldiers of the southern city, but they were ready to fight and to die, in defense of their homes and their heroic Baron.

Still, more than one sigh of relief was heard when a small contingent rode out from the swollen Connacht ranks under two flags, one the lion and the clover symbol of Connacht, the other a scythe in a blue field, Dilnamarra's own standard. The horsemen trotted their mounts into the town unopposed, stopping and dismounting by the main doors of the square and squat keep that anchored the village proper.

Rumors ran along the Dilnamarran ranks that it was Prince Geldion himself who had ridden in, and there was quiet hope that the fight might be avoided—especially when the stone building's iron-bound door was opened and the Prince and his men admitted.

For the little boy (who was really a leprechaun in disguise) sitting atop one of the unremarkable houses, news of the Prince's arrival did not bring optimism. Mickey had

43

dealt with Geldion before, had been chased halfway across Faerie by the man and his soldiers twice in the last few weeks. In Mickey's estimation, Geldion's apparently peaceful foray into Dilnamarra did not bode well.

In Mickey's estimation, nothing concerning Prince Geldion boded well.

*   *   *   *   *

Baron Pwyll met the Prince and his entourage in the main audience room of the keep's first floor. The fat Baron rested back easily in his chair, trying to appear composed, as the always cocky Geldion briskly strode in.

"Good Baron," the Prince said in greeting, and he jumped a bit when the heavy door slammed closed behind him. There was only one window in the room, barely more than a tiny crack, and two of the four torches set in the sconces at the room's corners weren't burning—and the two that were aflame were burning low.

Geldion glanced around knowingly, guessing correctly that Pwyll had arranged for the darkness. In the dim light, the obviously nervous Baron's true feelings might be better disguised, as would any of Pwyll's henchmen, lying in wait in case of trouble. Geldion did not doubt for an instant that at least one loaded crossbow was trained upon him at this very moment.

"Back in Dilnamarra so soon, Prince Geldion?" Baron Pwyll asked sarcastically. He was playing with one of the long and straggly hairs on his bristling beard, pulling it straight and twisting it so that it would stand out at an odd angle.

"And I was not expected?" Geldion slyly replied. "Really, good Baron, you should set better spies out on the road. Our approach was more than a little conspicuous."

"Why would we care to set out spies?" Pwyll asked,

matching sly question for sly question, trying to get Geldion to play his hand out first. He had not missed the Prince's reference to the sheer size of Connacht's army, though he did well to hide his fears.

"I am not alone," the Prince said gravely and bluntly.

"Ah, yes," Baron Pwyll began, straightening his large form in his seat. "Yes, you have brought your army. Really, my good Prince, was that such a wise thing to do? The dragon is dead, the land is again at peace—and long live the dragonslayer!" he added, simply for the sake of his guards standing tall behind him and for the other secret allies, men hiding behind the room's many tapestries. As far as the soldiers of Dilnamarra knew, their own Baron had taken on mighty Robert and had won out; at this dangerous time, Pwyll thought it a good thing to remind his soldiers of the reasons for their loyalty.

"But considering the unfortunate incident on the eastern fields," the Baron went on, trying to turn the situation back on Geldion, "parading around the land with your army on your heels might be considered tacky, at the very least."

Pwyll thought he had the Prince at a disadvantage with the reminder of the unnecessary skirmish, a battle facilitated by Geldion. He expected an explosion from the volatile Prince, a tipping of the man's true intentions. He expected it and hoped for it, for Pwyll was not unprepared. If he could wring the truth from Geldion in here, then he and his men would simply not honor any pretense of truce. Geldion would be taken prisoner and ransomed to force the army back to Connacht.

So Pwyll hoped, but Geldion's next statement caught him off guard.

"The dragon is dead," Geldion echoed, and he bowed low. "But that is the very reason that brings us to Dilnamarra."

"Do tell," said an intrigued Pwyll.

"Robert is dead," Geldion reiterated with a grand sweep of his arm. "And we of Connacht are indeed 'parading,' as you so eloquently described it. We have come for celebration, in honor of the dragonslayer. Faerie has few too many heroes in this time, wouldn't you agree?" As he spoke, Geldion looked over to the fabulous armor and reforged spear of Cedric Donigarten, in place on its rightful pedestal in Dilnamarra Keep. The fabulous and shining shield rested in front of the suit, facing Geldion, and it seemed to the Prince as if its embossed standard—the mighty griffon, a legendary beast, half eagle, half lion—was watching him suspiciously.

Pwyll didn't miss the look, and he narrowed his eyes at the clear reminder of Geldion's treachery. Geldion, by the edict of his father the King, had tried to prevent the quest to reforge the spear. When that had failed and the spear was whole once more, the Prince had come back to Dilnamarra and had tried to forcefully remove the artifacts. That, too, had failed, for the items had been stolen away by Mickey McMickey before Geldion had ever gotten near to them. Was that the point of all this once more? Pwyll wondered. Was Geldion back in Dilnamarra, at the head of an army this time, in yet another attempt to remove the artifacts?

"And so we have a new hero, that we might place on a pedestal, that we might sing his praises," Geldion began again, excitedly. He looked back to Pwyll, stealing the Baron's private contemplations.

Pwyll didn't know how to react. Why was Geldion and the throne in Connacht ready to give him any praise? He was among Kinnemore's most hated rivals, and certainly, with his newfound mantle of dragonslayer (whether that mantle had been truly earned or not), Pwyll had become among the largest threats to Kinnemore's apparent quest for absolute rule.

There was another possibility, one that Baron Pwyll's considerable vanity would not let him ignore. Perhaps his fame had become too great for Connacht to openly oppose him. His name was being loudly praised in all the hamlets and all the villages of Faerie. By the actions and manipulations of Gary Leger and Mickey McMickey, and several others, he, Baron Pwyll of Dilnamarra, had been elevated to the status of hero. Did King Kinnemore need him? he dared to wonder. Did the smug ruler of Connacht fear that all the people of the kingdom would rise behind their newest hero and threaten Kinnemore's rule?

The thought intrigued Pwyll more than a little, and, try as he might, he could not hide that intrigue from his expression.

Geldion fully expected it, and did not miss the superior look.

"We may ride in, then?" the Prince asked. "To pay honor to one to whom honor is due?"

Pwyll, in spite of his vanity and his hopes, remained more than a little suspicious. But he was on the spot. How could he rightfully refuse such a gracious request?

"Ride in," he agreed. "We will do what we might to make your stay comfortable, but I fear that we have not the lodgings . . ."

Geldion stopped him with an upraised hand. "Your generosity is more than we ever expected," he said. "But the King's army will be back on the road this very day. We have been too long from Connacht."

Pwyll wouldn't disagree with that last statement. He nodded, and Geldion bowed.

"I will arrange the ranks about the platform in the village

square," the Prince said, "and return with a fitting escort for the heroic Baron of Dilnamarra."

Again Pwyll nodded, and Geldion was gone. The soldiers behind Pwyll bristled and whispered hopefully at the unexpected turn—one even reached down to pat Pwyll's broad shoulder. But Pwyll did not acknowledge their relief. He sat on his throne, fiddling with his wild beard, trying to peel away the layers of possible treachery and figure out exactly what Prince Geldion truly had in mind.

The significance of the appointed site, of that platform in the square, didn't bode well, either. It had been erected a few weeks before by Geldion's men as a gallows for Pwyll, and only the last-minute heroics of Kelsey and Gary Leger had freed Pwyll from the noose.

But that was before the skirmish on the eastern field, before the slaying of Robert. Might it be that Connacht would try a new approach to their rule, a softer, more insidious touch? Might it be that Connacht would indeed pay Pwyll the honors due him, trying to wean him into their fold with coercion instead of force?

Baron Pwyll, like his men behind him, wanted to believe that, wanted to believe that Faerie might know an end to the warfare, and that diplomacy might again be the rule of the day. For the man who had spent many years battling Kinnemore's iron-fisted and merciless rule, that was a difficult thought to swallow.

*   *   *   *   *

"What is Geldion about?" Kelsey asked Mickey a short while later. The elf, Mickey, and Geno were holed up in a barn, a quarter-mile north of Dilnamarra proper. Geno had meant to go straight on to the east, to Braemar and Drochit, but Mickey had convinced him that he should stay around a bit longer. If the Connacht army meant to roll over Dilnamarra, then why had they hesitated? Certainly Baron Pwyll's ragtag militia would offer them little resistance.

Mickey looked out the barn's south window, to the squat keep in the distance, and shrugged.

"You did not overhear?" Kelsey questioned.

"I'm not for certain what I heared," Mickey replied. "Prince Geldion went in to speak with Pwyll, and so he did. I seen it meself from the keep's small window. It's what I heared that's got me wondering. By the Prince's own words, the army's come to honor the dragonslayer."

"King Kinnemore has come a hundred miles to honor Baron Pwyll?" Geno asked skeptically, and Kelsey's expression showed that he, too, doubted that possibility.

"That's not what I said," Mickey replied after a moment of thought. Geno's incredulous question had sparked another line of reasoning in the leprechaun, made him recall all that Geldion had said to Pwyll, and more pointedly, what Geldion had not said.

"By all accounts, Baron Pwyll killed Robert," Geno argued, but Mickey was hardly listening.

"Ye know," the leprechaun remarked, more to Kelsey than to Geno, "not once did the Prince mention that his father had come along for the ride."

Geno, of the rugged and secluded Dvergamal Mountains and not well schooled in the etiquette of humans, didn't seem to understand any significance to that point, but Kelsey's golden eyes narrowed suspiciously.

"Aye," Mickey agreed.

"Enough of this banter!" Geno protested. "I'm for the eastern road, to tell Drochit and Braemar to prepare for war, and then to my own home, far away from foolish humans and their foolish games."

"Don't ye be going just yet," Mickey warned. "By me

thinking, things aren't all they seem in Dilnamarra. The day might grow brighter yet."

"Or darker," Kelsey added, and Mickey conceded the grim point with a nod.

* * * * *

They came into Dilnamarra to a chorus of blowing trumpets and the hoofbeats of two hundred horses. Prince Geldion rode at their lead, the proud army of Connacht. No longer did he wear his stained traveling cloak, but was rather outfitted in the proper regalia for such a ceremony. Long purple robes flowed back from his shoulders, and a gold lace shoulder belt crossed his thin chest. Even so, he wore no sword, only that famous dirk, tucked into his belt, not far from reach.

"And still there's no showing o' Kinnemore," Mickey remarked suspiciously. He, Kelsey, and Geno had moved closer to the village, to a hedgerow not far from the square (despite Geno's constant grumbling that he was getting more than a little tired of hiding behind hedgerows and fences).

Kelsey shook his head and had no practical response to the leprechaun's claims. Normally the King led his forces. It could be that Kinnemore feared a potential assassin, but that didn't sit well with Kelsey's understanding of the fierce King. Kinnemore was Ceridwen's puppet—all in Faerie knew that—but despite that fact, he was not known as a cowardly man.

The brigade formed into neat semicircular ranks about the perimeter of the platform that centered the square, while Geldion and a group of armored knights again went to the keep. They were admitted without incident, to find Baron Pwyll and a handful of his closest advisors waiting for them inside.

The Prince put a disdainful look on the fat Baron. Pwyll

was wearing his finest robes, but even these were old and threadbare, reflective of the difficult times that had befallen all of the baronies in the last dozen years of Kinnemore's reign. The Baron held himself well, though. He seemed neither intimidated nor exuberant, had settled into a confident calm.

Geldion's expression changed when his gaze went from the threadbare clothes to the Baron's resolute features. The Prince's doubts about Ceridwen's plans came rushing back.

"I am ready," Pwyll announced.

"Are you?" Geldion asked slyly. He nodded to his knights, and as one they brought out their great swords and shifted about, each moving within striking distance of one of Pwyll's associates.

"What treachery is this?" Pwyll demanded. "What murder?"

"Fool," Geldion said to him. "There need be no spilling of blood. Not a man of Dilnamarra need die."

Pwyll raised a hand to keep his men from reacting, then to stroke at his bristling beard. He changed his mind before his fingers touched the woolly hair, not wanting Geldion to recognize his growing nervousness.

"We will march out of here as planned," Geldion explained. "To the square, between the thousands of my army. There, you will announce the dragonslayer."

"King Kinnemore," Baron Pwyll reasoned.

Geldion nodded. "My father awaits your call," he said, and he stepped back and to the side, turning to the door and sweeping his arm for Pwyll to lead.

"I should not be surprised by your treachery," Baron Pwyll retaliated. "We have come to expect nothing less from the throne of Connacht. But do you really expect the people to believe . . ."

"They will believe what they are told," Geldion interrupted. "A man at the wrong end of a sword will believe anything, I assure you." As he spoke, he looked around to the grim faces of Pwyll's helpless advisors.

Baron Pwyll, too, glanced about at the fuming men. They had no practical chance against the armed and armored knights—even the two crossbowmen whom Pwyll had strategically placed behind tapestries in the room could do little to prevent a wholesale slaughter by Geldion's men.

The Baron motioned again for his men to be at ease, then stepped forward, moving past the Prince. Geldion's hand came up to block him.

"I warn you only once," the Prince said. "If you fail in this, the price will be your life, and the lives of all in Dilnamarra."

Pwyll pushed past. When he exited the keep, he had no intentions of failing the task. What harm was there in granting King Kinnemore the honors for slaying Robert? he figured. Surely the cost would not approach the massacre Geldion had promised.

Pwyll and Geldion moved out through the parting ranks, Geldion's knights close behind. Pwyll's men drifted apart and scattered into the crowd.

"I'm not liking the fat Baron's look," Mickey remarked when Pwyll, Geldion, and three of the knights emerged above the crowd, climbing the steps of the platform.

Geno grumbled something and sent a stream of spittle into the hedgerow.

The group shifted about on the platform, with Geldion finally maneuvering Pwyll forward. Pwyll glared at him, but the stern Prince, always loyal, did not relent, did not back down an inch.

Baron Pwyll surveyed his audience, saw how vulnerable

his people were with two hundred cavalry in the town and thousands of soldiers camped just outside Dilnamarra's southern borders.

"Good people of Dilnamarra," the Baron began loudly. Then he paused again, for a long moment, looking out over the crowd, looking to the hedgerow wherein hid Mickey and the others, the same hedgerow that they had used to get near to the action on that day when Pwyll was to be hung.

Hung by the edict of an outlaw King, the same King that Pwyll was about to announce as the hero of all the land. How could he do that? Baron Pwyll wondered now. How could he play along with Kinnemore's continuing treachery, especially with the knowledge that wicked Ceridwen, the puppetmaster, would soon be free of her island?

The Baron sighed deeply and continued his scan of his audience, looked at the dirty faces of the men and women and children, all the people who had been as his children, trusting in him as their leader, looking to him for guidance through the difficult years. Geldion had more trained soldiers in and about the town than all the people of County Dilnamarra combined. Images of carnage worse than anything he had ever seen before rushed through Pwyll's mind.

"Go on," Geldion whispered, nudging the Baron with his elbow, a movement that sharp-eyed Mickey and Kelsey did not miss.

"It was not I who slew the dragon," Pwyll began. Immediately there arose from the gathered folk of Dilnamarra a crestfallen groan and whispers of disbelief.

"So there ye have it," Mickey remarked. "With Pwyll and Dilnamarra in their fold, nothing will stop Ceridwen and Kinnemore."

"Time to go east," Geno growled, and he spat again and turned from the hedgerow. But Kelsey, who knew Pwyll better than anyone, perhaps, saw something then, something in the look of the fat man. He grabbed Geno by the shoulder, roughly turned him about, and bade him to wait a few moments longer.

Baron Pwyll had reached the most crucial test of all his life. Just as he was about to announce Kinnemore—and he saw the King then, out of the corner of his eye, bedecked for the ceremony and sitting astride a white charger at the back of the cavalry ranks—he came to consider the full implication of his words. He came to understand that by so proclaiming Kinnemore, he would be pledging fealty to the King, he would be surrendering Dilnamarra without a fight.

What would that imply for the people of Drochit and Braemar, and all the other villages? What would that bode for the Tylwyth Teg in their forest home not so far from Dilnamarra Keep? These were Pwyll's allies, friends to the Baron and to his people.

"In truth, the dragonslayer was . . ." Pwyll saw the smug look come over the advancing King, a superior look, an expression of conquest.

". . . Gary Leger of Bretaigne!" Pwyll cried out. Geldion turned on him, shocked and outraged. "And Kelsenellenelvial Gil-Ravadry of Tir na n'Og, and famed Geno Hammerthrower of Dvergamal, and Gerbil Hamsmacker, a most inventive gnome of Gondabuggan!"

Pwyll's body jerked suddenly as a crossbow quarrel entered his chest.

"And a leprechaun," he gasped. "My friend Mickey. Beware, people of Dilnamarra!" Pwyll cried. "They will kill you with weapons if they cannot snare you with lies!"

Geldion grabbed him roughly, and only that held Pwyll upright on his buckling legs.

"Do not hear the hissing lies of a serpent King!" Pwyll

roared with all the strength he had remaining. "These I have named are the heroes. These are the ones who will lead you from the darkness!"

Pwyll groaned in agony as one of the knights came over near to the Prince and plunged a sword into the Baron's back.

"My friend Mickey," Pwyll said, his voice no more than a breathless whisper, and he slumped to his knees, where the darkness of death found him.

"Where did that come from?" a stunned and obviously appreciative Geno wanted to know.

"From Baron Pwyll of Dilnamarra," Kelsey declared firmly.

"Me friend," added Mickey, and there was a tear in the leprechaun's eye, though he knew that he had just witnessed Baron Pwyll's finest moment.

Geno nodded and without another word ran off, knowing that the road east would surely soon be blocked.

All about the platform erupted into a sudden frenzy. The people of Dilnamarra could not hope to win out, but their rage consumed them, and they pulled many soldiers down.

Through it all, Geldion stood on the platform, holding fast to the dead Baron. He felt a twinge of sympathy for this man who had so bravely died, felt as though his father, and that wicked Ceridwen, had underestimated Pwyll all along.

King Kinnemore and his bodyguards pushed through the throng to the platform, the King rushing up to stand by his son. Geldion glared at him as he approached, and Kinnemore had no words to deny the Prince's anger.

Kinnemore tried to call for calm, but the riot was on and out of control. Flustered, Kinnemore turned to Geldion, and smacked his son hard, trying to wipe that I-told-you-so look from Geldion's face.

Geldion started to blurt out a retort; then his eyes went wide as a long arrow knocked into Kinnemore's breastplate.

"Ye just had to put yer thoughts in," Mickey said to Kelsey, the elf's great bow still humming from the incredible shot.

"I thought the voice of the Tylwyth Teg should be heard at this time," Kelsey said easily.

Mickey looked back to the platform, to King Kinnemore, still standing, looking with surprise upon the quivering shaft.

"I think he got yer point," Mickey snickered.

To their amazement, to the amazement of Geldion and all the others who had noticed the arrow, Kinnemore calmly reached down and snapped the shaft. He took a moment to study its design, then casually tossed it aside. "Find the elf and kill him," he calmly ordered some of his nearby men, pointing in the general direction of the hedgerow.

"He's a tough one," Mickey remarked, his voice full of sincere awe. "And we should be leaving."

Kelsey didn't disagree with either point. He scooped Mickey up to his shoulder and ran off to the north, towards Tir na n'Og, where he knew that his fellow Tylwyth Teg would be waiting to turn back any pursuit.

As soon as the initial shock of the riot faded, the skilled army of Connacht systematically overran the village. Dilnamarra was secured that very night, with more than half the populace slain or imprisoned.

Refugees, more children than adults, came to the southern borders of the thick forest Tir na n'Og all that night, where the normally reclusive Tylwyth Teg mercifully allowed them entry.

"Ceridwen might get her kingdom," Mickey remarked, standing by Kelsey's side and looking south from the tree line. "But by the words o' Baron Pwyll, suren she's to fight for every inch o' ground!"

Kelsey said nothing, just watched solemnly as another group of young boys and girls ran across the last moonlit field to the forest's dark border, pursued by a host of soldiers. A hail of arrows from unseen archers high in the boughs turned the soldiers about, and the youngsters made it in to safety.

The war for Faerie had begun.

5 † A Call on the Wind

The tour guide was full of good cheer, all in all a remarkably entertaining old Scottish gent, complete with a button-top cap and a plaid quilt. Even Gary, not thrilled that he had to tag along with a group of tourists, couldn't hide his chuckles at the man's continuing stream of humor as they moved past the outer walls towards the castle proper.

"Pay no attention to these doors," the guide ordered in his thick brogue as they passed between two massive open portals, iron-bound wooden doors with an iron portcullis hanging overhead, each of its imposing pegs as thick as Diane's arm.

"They're not old," the Scotsman went on. "They were made when I was a boy, just two hundred years ago!"

The wide-eyed people of the tour group were so intrigued by the sight of the portals, and of the castle that lay beyond them, that it took every one of them many long seconds to even figure out the joke.

And Gary, transfixed as he stared at the lower courtyard of the castle, of Robert's castle, missed it altogether.

Diane, laughing, looked to him, but her mirth was quickly washed away by his firm-set features, that same determined and wide-eyed look that had led them to England, then to Scotland, in the first place.

"Two hundred years ago," she echoed, grabbing Gary's strong arm.

"What?" he asked, turning to regard her.

Diane let it drop, with only one final sigh of surrender. She took Gary's arm in tow and halfheartedly followed the group around the lower courtyard, its stone wall overlooking the city of Edinburgh. Antique cannons, preserved museum pieces showing the twilight of the years of castles, sat at regular intervals along the walls. The guide was speaking of them, but Gary didn't bother to listen. He thought it curious that cannons lined the castle wall, yet it was the cannon that made the castle an obsolete defense. More than curious, though, Gary thought it terribly wrong to see cannons in this place. There had been no cannons in Robert's castle, of course, no guns at all. Gary preferred things that way.

"They don't belong," he whispered.

"The cannons?" Diane asked.

Gary looked at her curiously. He hadn't been speaking to her, hadn't been speaking to anyone. "The cannons don't belong—especially that one," he said, pointing to the farthest edge of the curving wall, to a modern Howitzer standing silent vigil in a roped-off area that indicated it was not for show, and certainly not a piece for children to climb upon.

"I think it's neat," Diane argued. "You can see how this castle evolved through the ages. They've got a chapel up there that's from the fifth century! You can see how this place was built, and expanded, and modernized to adapt to the changes in the world around it." She was growing noticeably excited, reveling in the fun of it all—until she looked again at Gary, and that determined smirk of his.

"What?" she asked sternly.

"I'd like to show you this place before the cannons," he said. "When the only sentries were lava newts and . . ."

"Are you going to start that again?" asked a flustered Diane. She turned away, and noticed that the tour group was ascending a flight of exposed stairs up to the higher level, the inner bailey.

"Are you coming?"

"I can tell you everything that's up there," Gary boasted, following her lead. "Except for the newer changes."

"You're starting to get on my nerves."

"You've been saying that for a week," Gary pointed out.

Diane spun about, halfway up the stairs, and glared down at him. He fully realized that his obsession was ruining her vacation, but he simply could not let go of it. Gary needed to get back to Faerie, but if the Howitzer was any indication, those tentative bridges between the worlds were crumbling faster than he had expected.

Still, he realized that it wasn't fair for him to play out his frustrations on poor Diane, and he apologized sincerely.

By the time they got to the courtyard atop the stairs, the tour group was moving through a door to a tall tower.

"We'll go there later," Gary explained as he grabbed Diane's hand and rushed off diagonally across the courtyard, to an open door at the far end of a long and lower building.

Diane went along without complaint, sensing the urgency in her husband. They rushed through the door, into a dimly lit short corridor. Just a few steps in, they turned to the left, into a massive hall.

This was the place where Gary had first met Robert. It seemed very much the same, with spears and other weapons arranged on the walls, empty suits of armor standing guard in pretty much the same positions as Robert's lava newt sentries had been.

"This is it," Gary breathed.

"Come on, Gary," Diane said quietly. "Tell me what's going on."

He could tell by her tones that his cryptic words and actions had gone beyond simple annoyance. He was beginning to frighten her.

"This was Robert's hall," he explained. "Just like this. It looks the same—it feels the same. Even the gigantic interlocking beams of the ceiling."

Diane looked up along with Gary to that fabulous ceiling—more wondrous still when the two took a moment to realize how high it actually was, and thus, the true width of those supporting beams.

"Incredible," Diane mouthed.

"And I've seen it before," Gary assured her. She looked to him as he turned away, moving out from the wall.

Diane didn't reply, just followed Gary as he crossed the great hall, turning with every step to take in the view and the feel of the place. Suddenly he stopped, as if his gaze had fallen on a new and brighter treasure. Diane followed the line of that stare to an immense sword, leaning from a pedestal base against the far wall.

"Robert's?" she asked, following the logic.

Gary tentatively moved up to it. Without even bothering to look around, he grabbed the weapon's massive hilt in his two hands and tilted it against his chest.

"Mickey," he called. "You have to hear me now, Mickey." By Gary's reasoning, this sword had to be deeply connected with Faerie. It had to be.

"You're not supposed to touch it," Diane whispered, glancing about nervously, expecting a host of police to run up and arrest them on the spot for disturbing a national treasure.

"Mickey," Gary called again, loudly, defiantly.

"Robert," a voice corrected, and for an instant Gary thought he had made an otherworldly connection. Then a hand crossed in front of him and gently eased the sword back to its original place. "The sword of Robert," the guard explained.

Gary's mind swirled at the possibilities that name evoked. He realized that he was still in his own world, but in that case, how could this modern-day man know of Robert?

"Robert the Bruce," the guard clarified, pointing to a plaque on the wall. "And ye should'no' be touchin' it."

Gary fell back, nodding, and Diane caught his arm in her own. Robert the Bruce was one of Scotland's legendary heroes, a man of Gary's world and certainly no dragon in Faerie. Still, Gary was sure there was some connection between this sword and the sword Robert the dragon had used when in his human form, the same sword that Gary had stolen to lead the dragon into a trap.

And it was connected to Faerie; Gary had felt that keenly when he touched it. But he had heard no answer to his call to the leprechaun, and whatever magic had been in this place was gone now, stolen by the mere appearance of the guard.

Gary and Diane didn't finish that castle tour.

* * * * *

"What do you hear?" an observant raven-haired elf asked Mickey, seeing the leprechaun's faraway look.

Mickey glanced over at Kelsey, who was sitting across the campfire, talking with some friends and smoothing the burrs from the edge of his crafted sword.

As if he had felt that gaze, Kelsey stopped his talk and his work, and stared hard at Mickey.

"It was not a thing," the leprechaun answered the elf standing beside him, though he was still looking across the fire to Kelsey. "Just a song on the wind, is all. A bird or a

nymph." The other elf seemed satisfied with that, and he
took no notice as Mickey walked away from the fire and
into the thick brush. Kelsey caught up to the leprechaun
twenty yards away, the elf's stern golden-eyed expression
demanding a better explanation.

"Not a thing," Mickey said and started to walk by. Kelsey
grabbed the leprechaun's shoulder and held him in place.

"What're ye doing now?" Mickey asked, pulling free.

"It was no bird, nor Leshiye the nymph," Kelsey said.
"What did your clever ears hear?"

"I telled ye it was nothing," Mickey replied.

"And I asked you again," Kelsey retorted and again
grabbed a firm hold on the elusive sprite's shoulder.

Mickey started to argue once more, but stopped, figuring
the better of it. They were in besieged Tir na n'Og, Kelsey's
precious home, with Kinnemore's army forcefully knocking
on the door. Kelsey would grab at any hope, at any hint, and
he would not be dismissed by avoiding answers.

"It was the lad," Mickey admitted. "I heared a call from
the lad."

Kelsey nodded. This time, the call must have been closer,
for the leprechaun was visibly disturbed.

"Gary Leger wants to return," Kelsey reasoned.

"Only because he doesn't know," Mickey quickly added,
shaking his head. "We were all thinking that things'd be
better with Robert gone and Pwyll named as hero. Ye seen
it yerself—when the lad left, he left with a smile."

The leprechaun paused and closed his eyes, and it seemed
to Kelsey that he was hearing that distant call once more.

"No, Gary Leger," Mickey whispered. "Ye're not wanting
to come here. Not now."

Kelsey let go of Mickey, and let the leprechaun walk off
alone into the dark forest night. He didn't dismiss what

Mickey had revealed, though, and he wasn't so sure that Mickey's answer to that call was correct.

Kelsey and a handful of stealthy elfish companions left Tir na n'Og later that night, after the moon had set. The quiet elfish band had little trouble slipping through the Connacht lines and making its way to Dilnamarra Keep.

* * * * *

Gary leaned his head against the window of the tour bus, watching the countless sheep as the rolling fields of the Scottish Highlands drifted by. He had planned to stay in Edinburgh, so he could return to the castle and to the sword as often as possible, seeking that tentative link to Mickey.

Diane had other ideas. As soon as they had returned to their hotel, she had secretly booked a three-day bus tour of Scotland. Gary, of course, had resisted, but Diane, so patient with him all these weeks, had heard enough. He was going with her, she said, or he would be alone for the rest of the vacation. She hadn't said anything more outright, but Gary believed that if he didn't go on this tour, he might find himself alone longer than that.

Diane sat in the seat next to him, very close to him, chatting with a Brazilian couple across the aisle. Music played over the bus's intercom, pipers and accordions, mostly happy and upbeat, but every so often a mournful tune.

They were the perfect tourists, riding along the winding roads in the majestic and melancholy Scottish scenery. All Gary saw were the sheep.

His mood brightened, to Diane's sincere relief, as the day wound on and the bus approached their first stop, Inverness. Gary was thinking of Faerie again, of Loch Devenshere, nestled in the Crahgs, where he had seen a sea monster. Perhaps Loch Ness would show him the bridge.

They didn't get to the legendary loch until the next day,

and Gary was in for a disappointment. He saw a monster, a plaster replica of Nessie, sitting in a small pond (a large puddle) next to the Drumnadrochit Monster Exhibit, but despite the dark waters of the cold loch across the highway, and the stunning view of the mountains across the long lake, there was little magic here, little sensation that Mickey would hear his call.

"Two more days," he said as the bus rolled west, towards the next stop, the Isle of Skye.

"Then we're going to Brighton," Diane announced.

"Brighton?"

"South coast of England, near Sussex," she explained. "It will take us about six hours from Edinburgh. We'll go right from the bus drop to the train station."

Gary's first instinct was to protest. He had gone along with the bus tour, but planned to spend some time back in Edinburgh after the three days. He bit back his retort now, though, seeing no compromise in Diane's green eyes.

When he spent a moment to consider that determined look, Gary found that he couldn't really blame Diane. She had been wonderful about his obsession with Faerie over the years, listening to him without complaint or ridicule as he repeated his wild stories at least a hundred times. Before this trip, Diane had allowed him his many nights sitting in the woods out in back of his mother's house, had even gone and sat by his side on several occasions.

And Diane really didn't believe in Faerie, he knew. How could she? How could anyone who had not gone there? Diane had compromised—even the first half of their vacation. Now it was Gary's turn to compromise.

"Brighton," he agreed, and he settled back in his seat and tried very hard to enjoy the highland scenery.

6 † Isle of Skye

High in the boughs of a pine tree, Mickey awoke from a restful sleep to the twang of bows and the screams of men later that night. Truly the leprechaun was bothered by what was going on in the woods all about him, and by the turmoil that had become general in Faerie, but he meant to stay out of the battle. He had gone on the quest to fix the spear, had recovered his precious pot of gold, had helped to put the dragon down, and had even done a bit of spying for Baron Pwyll and the others resisting King Kinnemore, but now Mickey was back in Tir na n'Og, the forest he called home, and by his sensibilities, all of this had become someone else's problem.

He rested back on the pliable pine branch, pulled the front of his tam-o'-shanter down over his eyes, and dreamed of running barefoot through a field of four-leafed clover.

Then Mickey heard someone cry out for Kelsey, and the image of the clover field disappeared in the blink of a mischievous gray eye. "O begorra," Mickey muttered, realizing that he could not dismiss it all, not with friends as loyal as Kelsey in danger down below. He popped open an umbrella that conveniently came to his hand, used the pine branch like a spring board and leaped out into the night air, floating down gently to the forest floor.

On the ground, the leprechaun tried to figure out from

which direction the noise of the fighting was coming, but there were apparently several separate battles raging all at once.

Mickey tapped his umbrella (now appearing as a small and carved walking stick) atop a mushroom. "Good toadstool," he asked of the fungi, "might ye know where Kelsey the elf's hiding?"

Mickey listened for the answer, and got one (because leprechauns can do those kinds of things), then he politely thanked the mushroom and moved to a crack at the base of the pine in which he had been sleeping. He politely asked the tree for permission to enter, then did, magically traveling along the root system from tree to tree (because leprechauns can do those kinds of things) until he stepped out of a crack in a wide elm near to the fighting.

To Mickey's surprise, he saw not an elf in the small clearing ahead of him, but a human, a Connacht soldier, clutching tightly to a sword and glancing nervously about, as though he had gotten separated from his fellows.

How the man's eyes widened when he turned about and saw a leprechaun standing before him! It seemed as if some craziness came over the soldier then, and all fear flew away, his eyes bulging and his face brightening with a smile. He tossed his weapon aside and dove down at the leprechaun, thinking his fortune found and all the life's prayers answered. The soldier came up a moment later, clutching his prize, eyes darting this way and that in case any saw.

Then he peeked at the catch—and found that he was holding a dirty mushroom. He took off his helmet and scratched at his head.

"Ye got to be quicker than that," he heard, and he spun about to see the leprechaun leaning easily against a tree.

Cautiously, still holding tight to the mushroom, the soldier approached. "How'd you do that?" he asked.

Then he blinked, seeing that the leprechaun on the ground was really a mushroom. He looked back to his catch, still a mushroom, and scratched his head again.

"Behind ye," Mickey said.

The soldier spun about, and saw the leprechaun once again. The man's hungry grin lasted only the moment it took him to realize that the sprite was sitting atop the shoulder of a very angry elfish warrior.

"Have ye met me friend Kelsey?" said the leprechaun's voice, and though this newest illusionary image of Mickey disappeared, the very real Kelsey remained.

The soldier threw the mushroom at Kelsey, and the elf promptly batted it aside and advanced—pausing and wincing only when he heard the slapped "mushroom" groan.

The soldier looked all about for his weapon, spotted it on the ground and dove for it. But Kelsey's foot stamped upon his fingers as they closed about the swordhilt, and Kelsey's deadly sword came down, stopping with its keen edge against the side of the soldier's neck.

"Don't ye kill him," the disheveled Mickey, who was not a mushroom anymore, said to Kelsey. "It's not really his fight."

The soldier turned his head to nod his full agreement with the plea for mercy, but when the man looked upon the stern elf, he fainted away, thinking his life at its end.

Kelsey growled and lifted his sword as if to strike.

"By me own eyes," Mickey moaned from the side. "And here I be, thinking the Tylwyth Teg're the good folk."

Kelsey winced and let the sword slowly come back to rest against the man's neck. The elf narrowed his golden eyes as he regarded the smug Mickey.

"Candella is dead," Kelsey said, referring to a female elf,

a good friend to Kelsey, and more than a mere acquaintance to Mickey.

Mickey shook his head slowly, helplessly. "And what o' yerself?" he asked, pointing to Kelsey's arm, the elf's white sleeve darkened with fresh blood.

Kelsey looked down at the wound. "A crossbow," he explained. "Just before you appeared."

Mickey glanced about. They were fully a hundred yards inside the border of Tir na n'Og, and it suddenly struck him as odd to see a soldier so deep in the wood. "Is he the only one left alive?" the leprechaun asked, realizing that many other soldiers must have accompanied this one for him to get so far in.

"The only one of two score," Kelsey answered grimly.

Something seemed very wrong to Mickey, very out of place. "They tried to get in, then," the leprechaun reasoned. "But why would soldiers, human soldiers who do'no' see so well in the dark, try to get into Tir na n'Og under the light o' the moon? Why would they come in at night to fight the elfs that do see well in the dark?"

"They were pursuing us," Kelsey explained. Mickey shrugged and seemed not to understand.

"On penalty of their deaths, were we to escape," Kelsey went on. "Since King Kinnemore prizes the armor and spear of Cedric Donigarten above all other treasures in his realm."

"Ye stole the spear and the armor?" Mickey gawked.

Kelsey nodded gravely.

"Then Candella died for the sake o' the spear and armor?" Mickey asked incredulously.

Kelsey didn't flinch.

"But ye got none to wear it or wield it," the leprechaun reasoned. "Ye all got yerselfs shot at and chased for the sake of a treasure that's only for show!"

The leprechaun continued his tirade for a few moments

longer, until he realized that Kelsey wasn't blinking, wasn't even listening to the arguments. Mickey stopped with a loud huff and stood trembling, hands on hips, one holding the umbrella-turned-walking-stick.

"Well?" the leprechaun demanded.

"You said that Gary Leger wanted to get back," Kelsey answered, as though that should explain everything.

It took Mickey a long moment to digest this unexpected turn. In their two adventures side by side, Kelsey had come to trust in Gary, and even to like the man, but Mickey could hardly believe that any member of the haughty Tylwyth Teg would risk his or her life for the sake of any human!

"But I didn't say I'd bring him in," Mickey reasoned. Kelsey didn't flinch.

*   *   *   *   *

Gary stood transfixed at the end of a bay, staring across the dark waters of the North Atlantic to the westering sun, its slanted rays skimming the waters about the many pillarlike rocks that stood like gigantic sentinels, silent and proud testaments to ancient times, to times before men and science had dominated the world. The wind was constant and strong, straight off the water, blowing the salty mist into Gary's face. Its bite was fierce and chill, but Gary didn't care, couldn't pull himself away from this place.

A hundred yards out in the bay lay a rock island, triangular and imposing. How many ancient mariners had tried to sail in past that rock? Gary wondered. How many had braved the winds and the cold waters to come to this shore, and how many more had died out there, their feeble boats splintered against the timeless rocks?

It seemed likely to Gary that more had perished than had successfully navigated this stretch. There was a power here far greater than the wood of boats, one that transcended even the human spirit. A preternatural power, a sheer strength that had not been tamed by the encroachment of civilization.

Standing near that bay, in Duntulme, on the northern rim of the Isle of Skye, Gary Leger felt at once insignificant and important. He was a little player in a great universe, a tiny drop of dye on the great tapestry of nature. But he was indeed part of that tapestry, part of that majesty. He couldn't tame these waters and these pillars, but he could share in their glory.

That was the most important lesson Gary had learned in the land of Faerie. That is what the Buldrefolk living amongst the mighty peaks of Dvergamal, and the Tylwyth Teg, so at home in the forest Tir na n'Og, had shown to him.

"It's incredible," Diane whispered, standing beside him, her arm in his. In full agreement, Gary put his hand over her forearm and led on, picking his way across the sharp rocks and wet sand.

The land climbed steeply along the left side of the bay, coming to a high point where the somewhat sheltered water widened into the North Atlantic. On that pinnacle stood the ruins of a small castle, an ancient outpost. Diane resisted as Gary made his way along the curving beach, to the narrow trail that topped the edge of the cliff face.

"Most of the others are going up there tomorrow," she explained, for the trail seemed treacherous in the fast-dying light. She noticed, too, that Gary had his small pack with him, and she worried that if he got up on that cliff, it might be a long time before she could coax him back down.

"That's why we're going up there today," Gary replied calmly, and moved on.

Despite her very real fears, Diane didn't argue. The sight was spectacular, to say the least, and her heart was pulling at her to go up to that pinnacle, that lost outpost, almost as much as Gary's was pulling at him. She pictured what the sunset might look like from the high vantage point, realized that she would glimpse an eternal scene, the same view as that of the men who had once manned that outpost. As was her habit on this trip, Diane carried two cameras with her: her reliable old Pentax 35mm and a Polaroid. All along this trip, whenever Diane spotted what looked like a reasonable shot, she'd click one off with the Polaroid. As that picture developed before her eyes, she would get a better idea of the effect of the lighting and the scenery, and then she'd go to work with the Pentax, often clicking off two rolls at a stretch.

The worst part of the climb was the ever-present sheep manure on the trail, slimy and slippery. A rope had been strung to the right side of the path, offering some protection from a drop into the bay, and a sturdier fence (though it was broken in many places) had been erected on the left, portioning off a sheep field. Diane had always thought that sheep were cute little beasties, but when they came towards her now, on that narrow and slippery trail, she was more than a little nervous.

Gary would have been nervous, too, if he had been paying any attention to the sheep. His eyes were squarely focused, transfixed, on the ruins up above. He felt the energy of this place more keenly with every step, felt the tingles of magic building in the air about him.

The wind increased tenfold when the pair crested the hill, and they could both understand what had so battered the walls of this ancient bastion. Men had come to this place and built their stone fortress, and had probably thought themselves invulnerable up on that cliff, behind thick stone walls and surrounded by the treacherous and rocky waters.

Gary couldn't imagine that any enemy humans had conquered this fortress, or destroyed its walls, that any hostile ships (the longships of Vikings, perhaps?) had put up on the beach. But the fortress had been defeated. It had been taken down by the incessant and undeniable power of nature. Like the men who had manned it, the constructed castle had been taken down and turned to crumbling dust, a temporary bastion in an eternal universe.

Gary found a high perch on a fallen slab. He looked to the low sun, then spread his arms high and wide above him to catch as much of the wind as he possibly could, to feed off its strength.

Diane milled about behind him, clicking away with her Pentax. So entranced was she, so alive at that moment, that the normally sensible woman crawled out through a hole in the wall to a precarious perch on the very edge of the northern cliff, simply to get a good angle on a shot. Then, when she came back within the boundaries of the fortress, she braved a trek into a small and dark tunnel, though a plaque on the stone warned against entry.

Gary noticed some flickers of light, and turned to the side curiously as Diane emerged from the other end of the tunnel, her camera flash in hand and her smile from ear to ear.

"You're not supposed to go down there," he remarked.

Diane's smile was infectious, made Gary picture her as a little girl with her hand in the proverbial cookie jar. He was glad that she was so entranced by this place, because he had already made up his mind that the sun would be long gone before he made his way back down to the bay and the inn.

It got cold after sunset and the two huddled together behind a fallen slab of rock.

"It will probably rain," Diane remarked, a reasonable guess in this perpetually gloomy land. There were stars shining up above them, but both had been on the isles long enough to realize that could change in the matter of a few minutes.

They talked and they cuddled; they kissed and they cuddled some more. Gary spoke of his adventures in Faerie, and Diane listened, and under that enchanting sky in that enchanting place, she could almost hear the song of the fairies and the rhythmic ringing of the Buldrefolk hammers.

Gary realized that Diane's patience with his wild stories was a precious gift. In all the years since his first trip, Diane had been the only one he had told. Even his father had not known.

"Were there any unicorns?" Diane asked him at one point, a question that she often asked him during his recountings.

Gary shook his head. "None that I saw," he replied. "But I wouldn't bet against it."

"I'd love to see a unicorn," said Diane. "Ever since I was a little gir . . ." She stopped abruptly and Gary turned to her, hardly able to make out her features in the dark night.

"What?" he prompted.

There came no reply.

"Diane?" he asked, nudging her a bit. She rolled with the push and let out a profound snore.

Gary laughed, thinking it cute how quickly she had fallen off to sleep.

Too quickly, Gary suddenly realized. How could she possibly be talking one instant and snoring the next?

Gary went on the alert, rolling up into a crouch. "Where are you?" he asked into the quiet night.

He fully expected what came next, but still found that he could hardly draw his breath. A tiny sprite, no more than a foot tall, stepped up onto the rock slab, small bow in hand.

The same bow the creature had used to shoot Diane, Gary knew, remembering well the sleeping poison of the sprites.

"Mickey wants me back?" Gary reasoned.

The sprite gave him a smirk and half turned on the slab, leading Gary's gaze to a small clearing just beyond the back edge of the ruins. A glow came up, a ring of soft lights, accompanied by a sweet melody, tiny voices singing arcane words that Gary did not understand.

With a disarming smile on his face, Gary lifted his small pack and started to rise. His hand reached into the pack and shot out suddenly, and the sprite, quick as it was, could not avoid the wide-spreading reach of the hurled net. The creature thrashed and scrambled, but Gary was on it, quick as a cat. He grabbed it up in one hand, cried out as it drove a tiny dagger into his palm, then closed his other hand over its head.

"All I want is for you to take her along with me," he explained to the suddenly calm sprite. "Just take her to Faerie. You can do that."

The creature uttered some response, its high-pitched voice moving too fast for Gary to decipher any words.

Gary closed his hand a bit tighter over the sprite's head. "Tell them to dance around her," he said, suddenly grim. "Or I'll squish your little head." It was an idle threat, of course; Gary would never harm one of Faerie's fairies. But the sprite, engulfed by a pair of hands that were each nearly half the size of its entire body, was in no position to take any chances. Again came its squeaking voice, and a moment later, the fairy ring broke apart, the soft lights flickering away into the darkness.

Gary didn't know if he had been deceived, and he clutched the sprite a bit tighter, fearing that it too would fade away into the night. He breathed easier when the lights and the song reappeared, encircling Diane with their magic. Gary let go of the sprite and removed the net and quickly joined his wife in the ring. He winced when a not-unexpected little arrow stung him in the butt—but he figured he had earned that.

Gary didn't fall asleep immediately, though, felt no tingling poison coursing through his veins. He looked back to the sprite, on the slab still, bow in hand and glaring wickedly his way, and he realized that the arrow had not been poison-tipped, had not been fired for any better reason than payback. Gary started to say, "Touché," but stopped and fought hard to hold his balance as all the world blurred around him, blurred and begin to spin, slowly and smoothly, like the soft lights of the fairy ring.

And then they were on a ridge in Tir na n'Og, under a beautiful starry sky and with a very confused Mickey McMickey staring open-mouthed at the sleeping Diane.

Gary tossed a mischievous wink and a smile at the leprechaun's unusually stern expression, but Mickey just shook his head slowly, back and forth.

7 † Into the Fire

They charged in fiercely, every man carrying a sword, axe, or spear and a blazing torch. By Prince Geldion's assessment, the thick edge of Tir na n'Og was akin to a castle wall, and the assault on the elfish stronghold was on in full.

Bows hummed in retaliation from every bough. A deadly rain of arrows cut deep into the Connacht ranks, leaving men sprawled and screaming. But many were Geldion's soldiers, and whether out of loyalty to the crown or simple fear of Geldion, their line would not waver. Their voices raised in a singular battle cry, they reached the forest's edge and hurled their torches, hundreds of torches, into the thick underbrush.

Flames, the forest's bane, sprouted in a dozen places, two dozen, and through all the openings between the fires, the Connacht soldiers flowed into the wood, hacking at the trees themselves for lack of any apparent elfish targets.

Kelsey, commanding the guard, looked down from his high perch in a tall elm and knew immediately that the perimeter had been overwhelmed. He heard a rumble of thunder overhead and took hope, for the elfish wizards had gone to work, using their magic to try to counteract the fires.

"Down!" the elf-lord called to his ranks, a cry echoed from tree to tree. The elfs had miles of forest behind them and could easily escape the clumsy humans in the darkness. But Kelsey had no intention of running, not yet. If the Tylwyth Teg allowed Connacht any foothold into Tir na n'Og, their greatest advantage, the open fields surrounding the forest, would be lost.

Kelsey verily ran down his tree, bow ready in his hands. He spotted the black silhouettes of three men in front of the nearest fire, and fired as he stepped lightly down to the ground, dropping one of the soldiers in his tracks. Out came Kelsey's magical sword, gleaming with elfish magic in the flickering light.

He was hard-pressed almost immediately as the two trained soldiers rushed to meet him. One snapped off a series of cuts with his sword, and Kelsey parried each one, while the other jabbed ahead with a long spear, keeping the elf on his heels, preventing him from launching any counterattacks.

Though the fires reflecting in the golden eyes truly revealed his inner rage, the elf suddenly wondered if he could win out—especially when he saw two more soldiers rushing in from the side.

He heard a bow from somewhere behind him, once and then again, and both the newcomers skidded down, one dead, the other curled in a ball, clutching at his bleeding belly. Kelsey took heart in the unexpected help, while his attackers eased up cautiously, as if they expected the next shots to be aimed at them.

The cat-and-mouse game went back and forth for several minutes. Kelsey working a defensive dance and every so often snapping off a thrust of his own. Always that long spear kept Kelsey's strikes measured, though, the tip of his marvelous sword whipping across short of its mark as the elf was continually forced back on his heels.

And no more bows sounded from the trees. The fighting

was all about them by then, the ring of steel on steel, graceful elfish blades smacking against the heavier and thicker weapons of the burly humans. Melodic elfish songs joined in the chorus of the Connacht battle cries, and Kelsey took heart again. This was his home, the elfish home, beautiful Tir na n'Og.

A bolt of lightning split the dark sky, followed by a sudden downpour, rain pelting the fires of the invaders.

"You cannot win!" Kelsey screamed at the two men he was fighting. "Not here!" His sword darted ahead, three times in rapid succession. He slashed it out to his right, knocking aside a halfhearted counter by the human swordsman, then brought it back hard and down to his left, catching the shaft of the thrusting spear, bringing its tip down to the ground and cutting right through its thick wood.

The spearman cried out and threw his hands up in front of his face, thinking the elf's ensuing backhand aimed at him. But Kelsey's sword cut short of that mark, whipping back to his right to knock aside the swordsman's next thrust. Kelsey stepped ahead and jabbed, quicker than the swordsman could react, and the man grasped at his punctured breast and stumbled to the ground.

The spearman had turned to flee by the time Kelsey came back the other way, but he wasn't fast enough to get out of range of Kelsey's deadly sword. The thrust started for the man's back and would have easily slipped right through his meager armor and into his lung. But Kelsey thought of Mickey then, and their earlier encounter with the pitiful human. He remembered Gary Leger, his friend. Candella had given her life in retrieving Donigarten's armor and spear, for the sake of Gary Leger, and ultimately, for the sake of all of Faerie.

The adventures of the last few weeks had taught haughty Kelsenellenelvial Gil-Ravadry many lessons; had, in many ways, allowed the elf to rise above his xenophobic kin. He was Tylwyth Teg, and certainly proud of that, but the world was a wide place, big enough to share with the other goodly races.

His sword caught up to the fleeing human, but dipped low, taking the soldier in the back of the hamstring. The man fell to the ground, crying in agony, but very much alive.

That was why the defenders of Tir na n'Og were better than their attackers, Kelsey told himself. That measure of mercy was why the goodly folk of Faerie would, in the end, win out over the evil that darkened Faerie's clear skies.

On ran the elfish warrior, leaping burning brands, the fires already lower, and many of them sputtering from the drenching rain. Kelsey boldly rushed in wherever he saw battle, his ferocity and deft swordplay quickly turning the tide in the favor of his kinfolk. And then he ran on to the next battle, sweeping those elfs in his wake, spearheading an undeniable force. With every skirmish Kelsey joined, more elfs came into his fold and more of the Connacht army was turned away. Soon the whole line of elfish warriors was moving as a singular unit through the darkness, silent as death on the soaked leaves.

By contrast, the Connacht assault was scattered, the small groups of soldiers wandering disoriented. They heard the cries of the wounded, and more and more of those cries were human and not elfish. Any of the soldiers who found the edge of the forest ran off across the fields, seeking to regroup with Geldion's rear lines halfway to Dilnamarra, or merely to flee altogether, wanting no part of Tir na n'Og and its staunch defenders. Other groups wandered aimlessly in the forest, lost without their fires to guide them, until Kelsey and his warriors fell upon them.

Several of the Tylwyth Teg died that night, most in the

first furious moments of battle. Many more humans died, and many more than that were taken captive. Kelsey took note of how readily many of the humans surrendered their weapons. It seemed to him as if their heart was not in this fight. In contrast, not a member of the Tylwyth Teg would surrender, no matter the odds, nor would their likely allies, the tough Buldrefolk of Dvergamal, Geno's folk. Kelsey had once seen Geno fighting wildly in the midst of a dozen huge trolls, outnumbered and with no chance of winning. But fighting on anyway, with no thought of surrender.

This, too, was the strength of the outnumbered opposition to King Kinnemore. Their strength, and the Connacht army's weakness.

*   *   *   *   *

"Ye should'no' have brought her," Mickey remarked, and his words were accentuated by the distant sounds of the raging battle. They were in Tir na n'Og, Gary knew, just by the smell of the place. He looked around, his eyes adjusting to the darkness. They were in a small empty gully edged by dirt and moss walls, and both sides capped by tangles of birch. The night sky weighed low with thick clouds, and the heavy rain sent rivulets of water streaming down the gully's side.

"It's not a good time in Faerie, lad," the leprechaun remarked.

"Unlike the other two times I've been here," Gary replied sarcastically. He skipped up to a high bluff and peered into the distant blackness, trying to catch a glimpse of the action. "Geldion?" he asked.

"Who else?" Mickey replied.

"Ceridwen is free, then," Gary reasoned.

"Not yet," answered the leprechaun. "She's another couple o' weeks to go, but she's sent her calling card, first to Dilnamarra, and now to Tir na n'Og."

Gary paused to consider that for a moment, always amazed at the different rates at which time passed between the worlds. He had been on two adventures in Faerie, each lasting weeks, and yet, on both occasions, he had awakened back in his own world barely hours later than when he had left. This time, years had passed in his own world, while only weeks had gone by in Faerie. Mickey had explained it as depending upon which way the sprites were turning in their dancing ring when they opened the portal between the worlds. Gary could only hope they had danced correctly again—else he and Diane might well miss the turn of the century!

With that thought tucked behind him, Gary considered the leprechaun's words. "First to Dilnamarra," Mickey had said, but what did that bode for Gary's friends in the muddy hamlet?

"Baron Pwyll . . ." he started to inquire, but he stopped when he turned to look upon Mickey, the leprechaun slowly shaking his head, his cherubic features more grim than Gary had ever seen them.

"No," Gary breathed in denial.

"He died a hero, lad," was the best that Mickey could offer. "He could've saved his skin by giving praise to King Kinnemore, but he knew what that praise—and Dilnamarra's unintentional alliance with the Connacht army—might mean for the folk o' the other towns."

"Where's Geno?" Gary asked immediately, fearing that he had lost more than one friend in his absence. "And Gerbil?"

"The dwarf's halfway to Braemar by now, would be me guess," Mickey answered easily, glad that he could deliver some good news, as well. "And there, the gnome's waiting for him, so he said."

Gary breathed easier. Down in the gully, Diane groaned

and shifted, wakened by the stream of chilly water rushing past her prone form.

"I'll be expecting a proper introduction," Mickey announced.

Gary nodded. He had every intention of letting Diane get well acquainted with Mickey. By the sound of that battle, the war was not so far away, and Gary couldn't afford to have Diane wandering about in a state of denial. She would have to be "convinced" that Faerie was very real in a short time.

An agonized cry split the night. Gary looked down upon Diane and wondered if he had been wise to bring her to this place.

*   *   *   *   *

Despite Mickey's claims to the contrary, Geno Hammer-thrower was far from all right, and a lot farther from Braemar than the leprechaun believed. The dwarf had camped in Cowtangle Wood, a small forest along the eastern road, two days before, after making fine progress out from Dilnamarra.

A short nap was all the sturdy dwarf allowed himself, rising long before the dawn and running off. More than once, Geno slammed face-first into trees in the dark wood, but the impact hurt the trees more than the dwarf. He cleared the eastern edge of Cowtangle with the breaking dawn, but skidded to a quick stop after climbing over the first rise in the rolling fields.

There sat Connacht soldiers, twenty at least, their spear-tips gleaming in the morning light, their horses blowing steam into the brisk air with every snort.

Geno paused for a split second, trying to decide whether he should turn back, or walk on calmly, feigning ignorance of the events in Dilnamarra. He had just dismissed the latter course, and was turning back to the wood, when one of the soldiers spotted him and cried out.

"Stonebubbles!" the dwarf grumbled, perhaps the very worst of dwarfish curses. The thunder of hooves sounded behind him, one soldier called out for him to halt, and Geno suspected that this was no chance encounter.

He figured that he had a chance if he could get within the protective thick boughs of Cowtangle. If he could keep the soldiers scattered, their horses moving slowly through the heavy underbrush, he could outmaneuver them and hit at them individually.

That plan was lost almost immediately, though, when the dwarf saw riders flanking him, outdistancing him back to the tree line. Geno veered for a hillock instead, and got to the high ground at the same time as a rider, coming up the back side.

The soldier lowered his speartip as he closed on the dwarf, but a second later, he was rolling over backwards in his saddle, knocked unconscious by a spinning hammer. He tumbled heavily to the ground, and Geno tried to catch hold of his horse. But the beast was too tall for the dwarf, and for all his frantic efforts to leap onto the nervous beast, all Geno got was a horseshoe-shaped bruise on the side of his chest.

"Stonebubbles!" the dwarf growled again, planting himself firmly in the center of the high ground, looking around at the tightening ring of soldiers.

"You cannot escape, Geno Hammerthrower," one man asserted, and the dwarf growled again at the sound of his name, at the confirmation that he had been expected all along. He cursed Kelsey and Mickey for convincing him to follow them back to Dilnamarra before turning east; cursed Kinnemore and Geldion, those two upstart pretenders who knew nothing about ruling and nothing about the land; cursed Ceridwen, and Gary Leger for ever letting the witch out of her hole; cursed Robert for forcing all of this; cursed Gerbil for not going along on the scouting mission to the fields near Connacht; cursed everything and everyone, except for his Buldrefolk kin and the stones they lived among.

Geno was not in a good mood, as the next soldier who tried to scale the hill found out. The rider came up slowly, talking calmly, explaining to the dwarf that it would be better for all if he simply surrendered and went along with them back to Dilnamarra, "where all would be explained."

Geno's first hammer spun between the ears of the ducking horse, and caught the man full on the chest. Before he could even try to draw his breath again, Geno's next shot nailed him square in the faceplate of his great helm, bending the metal against the man's nose and crossing his eyes. If he had been a wise man, the soldier would have fallen over, but he grasped the bridle tightly and stubbornly held his seat.

Geno's third hammer got him in the head again, and all the world was suddenly spinning.

Geno cursed himself for being so foolish as to throw three hammers at one target. With four on the ground, he only had six remaining. Six for twenty enemies.

The dwarf just sighed as the charge came on. He spun a complete circuit, launching hammers at equal intervals so that all sides of the hillock got one. Three of four shots took down riders; the fourth knocked a horse so silly that it began turning tight circles, hopping up and down, despite its frantic rider's tugs and cries.

The ring closed about Geno, but only a few riders could get up the hillock at one time. Holding his last remaining hammers, one in each hand, the dwarf looked for the area of most confusion and boldly charged, his muscled arms pumping away at rider and horse alike. He couldn't reach up high enough to strike at any vital areas, but found that a hammer smash on a kneecap more often than not drained an enemy's desire for the fight. One horse, confused as its rider lurched in agony, turned sideways to the dwarf, banging into him. Geno growled and grabbed, and heaved with all his strength, turning the beast right over on the uneven ground.

Geno saw his break and meant to charge ahead, meant to leap right over the fallen man and beast and plunge through the surprised second ranks, using their confusion to give him a head start back towards the wood.

He couldn't ignore the speartip jabbing through the back of his shoulder as a soldier caught him from the other side.

Geno spun wildly, hammers chopping. One got hooked under the tip of the bloody, waving spear, the other slapped against the shaft.

"Hah!" Geno roared in victory. "No dwarf made that child's weapon!" In Geno leaped, smacking the broken shaft free of the man's grasp. The soldier threw his arm out to block, and Geno's hammers snapped upon the outstretched hand, one on either side.

How the soldier howled!

Geno crashed into the side of the horse, but bounced away, hearing another enemy approaching from behind. He turned his shoulders down as he hit the ground, falling into a roll at the approaching horse's feet.

The horse kicked and skipped, but Geno had the leverage. Ignoring the punishing hooves, the dwarf pressed onward, barreling under the steed, bringing it to a halt so abruptly that the rider pitched over the horse's head, crashing face down to the ground.

Up came Geno, spitting dirt and laughing wildly. A rider dove upon him and wrapped him in a bear hug, but Geno grabbed the man's thumbs, turned them outward, and simply fell to his knees, using his tremendous weight (it was said in Faerie that a dwarf weighed as much as an equal volume of lead) as a weapon. The man's hand bones broke apart and Geno was free, scooping up his hammers once more and darting back the other way, again into the area of most confusion.

A spear prodded towards him; he snapped off a hammer throw, caught the spear just below its tip and tugged, bringing the rider forward, bringing the man's face right in line with the spinning hammer.

Geno caught the hammer on the rebound, and paused, staring curiously for a moment, for the man's helmet had turned right about on his shoulders and Geno wondered if his head had turned with it. With a shrug, the dwarf hopped about.

And caught a flying spear right in the belly.

"Now that hurt," Geno admitted. One hammer fell from the dwarf's hand, and he clutched at the spear's shaft.

Using that moment of distraction, the nearest rider charged right for Geno, trampling the dwarf under his mount's pounding hooves.

Another man dismounted and cautiously approached. "He's out," the soldier announced, reaching down to see if the battered dwarf was still alive.

Geno bit that reaching hand, bit it and held on like a bulldog, growling and crunching even after a handful of soldiers fell over him, punching and kicking, battering him with their spearshafts and shields.

The beating went on for many minutes, and finally Geno fell limp. But even then, it took the Connacht soldiers a long time to extract their comrade's hand from the vise-grip that was the dwarf's mouth.

*   *   *   *   *

Diane yawned deeply and stretched, her eyes still closed and the thick slumber of sprite's poison still dulling the edge of her consciousness. She groaned and rolled over onto her belly, and finally managed to crack open one eye.

It took some time for the image to solidify in her thoughts, for her to appreciate that she was staring at the strangest, curly-toed little pair of shoes she had ever seen. She rubbed both her eyes and forced them open, then locked her gaze on those shoes and scanned upward.

"Mickey?" she asked, her voice cracking with the effort. This was a leprechaun in front of her—this had to be a leprechaun in front of her!—and she was no longer in Duntulme.

"Ah, good lad," Mickey replied, looking up the side of the muddy gully to Gary. "I see that ye've told her about me."

Diane shrieked and rolled away. She scrambled up to her knees, would have risen altogether and run off, had not Gary caught up to her and stopped her with an embrace.

"So good to know ye're speaking highly o' me," Mickey remarked dryly.

"She's just scared," Gary tried to explain, and he leaned his weight onto Diane, trying to hold the trembling woman steady. "This is all so different to her, so . . ."

"I'm knowing that better than yerself, lad," Mickey assured him. "I've seen more than a few of ye first awaken in Faerie. And, by yer stories, it seems she's already knowing it's no dream."

Diane pulled away, but the effort cost her her balance and she fell on her rump against the soft banking, skidding down in the loose mud and winding up seated squarely before Mickey. "This can't be happening," she whispered.

"Did you think that I was lying?" Gary asked her sharply.

Diane looked to regard him, was embarrassed that her reactions had wounded him. "I thought . . ." She searched for a way to complete the answer. "I believed that you believed," she stammered, "but that didn't mean that I believed!"

Gary's jaw dropped open as he tried to decipher that one.

"She'd be one to talk a gnome into a corner," Mickey put in, and he tossed a wink Diane's way, thinking that she needed a friend at that moment.

"I mean, this can't happen," Diane blubbered on. "Those stories . . . your adventures . . . they couldn't have been real. I mean . . . oh, hell, I don't know what I mean." She put her head in her hands, staring down at the ground.

"I know what ye mean," Mickey said reassuringly.

"Oh, shut up," Gary said to the leprechaun.

"And let yerself take care of it?" Mickey was quick to respond. "Rest yerself easy, lad, but it's not seeming to me that ye're taking much care of it."

Gary started to retort, but stopped, mouth open and one finger pointing accusingly Mickey's way. In thinking about it for that instant, though, Gary realized he had nothing to accuse Mickey of.

"Is it so bad that the lad's stories were true?" Mickey asked Diane in all seriousness. The leprechaun waved his hand and a rainbow-colored flower, each of its soft petals a different hue, appeared in Diane's hand. She looked at it incredulously, sniffed its delicate aroma, then turned a questioning gaze upon Mickey.

"Is it?" Mickey asked again. "Wasn't there just a bit o' ye that wanted to go where the lad said he'd gone?"

"More than just a bit," Diane admitted. "But that . . ."

"But that's all ye need," Mickey interrupted. "And so ye've found yer way. Be happy with that, and happy with this. Tir na n'Og's a beautiful place, I tell ye, though ye could've picked a better time to come."

Diane sat staring, from Gary to Mickey, and back to Gary again. She looked to her cameras, the Pentax in its case at her side and the Polaroid bouncing in front of her, and then turned her gaze back to Mickey again.

"Here then, what'd ye bring?" the observant Mickey asked.

Diane's green eyes narrowed.

"Not now," Gary said to her. She turned to him, her expression revealing her surprise.

"Not now," Gary said again. "You'll have plenty of time for your pictures later."

"Pitchers?" Mickey asked, not understanding.

"Pic-tures," Gary clarified. "A bit of magic from our world."

"Oh, that I'd dearly love to see," said Mickey, to which Diane snickered and Gary emphatically reiterated, "Not now!"

Both Diane and Mickey turned a sour look upon Gary.

The man snapped his fingers. "But I did bring you these," he explained, pulling off his small book bag and fumbling with the tie. He produced a boxed set of four books, *The Hobbit* (but not the copy that Mickey had changed) and *The Lord of the Rings* trilogy.

"The rest of the story," Gary explained to the beaming leprechaun. "For you to keep."

Mickey waved his little hand, and the boxed set rose into the air from Gary's hand and floated gently across the empty space to Mickey's waiting fingers. Obviously thrilled, Mickey waggled those fingers and the boxed set seemed smaller suddenly, then smaller still, then no more than the size of a postage stamp.

"I'll be keepin' this safe," Mickey remarked, tossing another wink Diane's way, and he tucked the shrunken treasure into one of his gray waistcoat's many pockets.

Diane found that she was laboring to find her breath again. It wasn't only the leprechaun's telekinesis that astounded her, but the way Mickey had accepted the books. Diane remembered keenly that time Gary had shown her his special copy of *The Hobbit*, the book that he claimed had been altered by a leprechaun's magic. According to Gary, Mickey McMickey had cast a spell over the book so that its type had transformed into the flowing Gaelic-looking script that now adorned its pages. It was the most solid evidence that Gary had ever shown to Diane concerning his journeys to this magical land, and the one piece that she had always found difficult to rationalize in her logical doubting of Gary's tales.

Now that book, and the others in the series, seemed a link to reality for the young woman. Everything fit together too perfectly to be denied. She was in Faerie, in this land that Gary had told her about for all these years. She was sitting before a leprechaun!

She broke out in laughter, wild laughter, and both Gary and Mickey looked at her with more than a little concern, fearing that the shock of it all had driven her to hysteria.

Diane was flustered, overwhelmed, but she was not hysterical, and she gulped down her laughter, sobered in the blink of an eye, when a beautiful, golden-haired and golden-eyed creature, too delicate to be a man, walked into the sandy gully from the trees behind Gary.

Gary turned, and a smile widened on his face to see Kelsey once again.

"Well met, Gary Leger," the elf greeted, walking over to clasp arms with the man. "You are needed now, perhaps more than ever before."

Gary nodded, and Kelsey's remark took on a suddenly greater significance when the man noticed the blood staining the elf's boots, as though Kelsey had been standing in a deep puddle of the crimson liquid.

Diane came up to Gary's side, staring blankly as she studied the elf from head to toe.

"This is Kelsey," Gary explained.

"Kelsenellenelvial Gil-Ravadry," Diane quickly corrected, remembering the proper name Gary had given to his elfish companion.

Kelsey did not blink at the surprise correction, but gave a slight approving nod—Diane could not have said anything else to make a better first impression.

Watching the three, hearing Kelsey's greeting, Mickey was beginning to believe that maybe the elf had been right in insisting that Gary be brought back to Faerie. After Pwyll's startling defiance, and subsequent demise, the people of the land might be looking for a hero—a living hero—to lead the struggle, and it just so happened that this would-be hero fit perfectly into the armor of the legendary Cedric Donigarten.

Mickey didn't know where Diane might fit in, but considering the way she had just handled (indeed, the way she had charmed) the stern elf, she seemed resourceful enough.

"Oh, begorra," the leprechaun muttered, and a snap of his fingers brought his long-stemmed pipe floating from a pocket to his mouth, lighting as it went.

8 † An Oath to Sir Cedric

The overcast dawn came quietly, with no more fighting along Tir na n'Og's southern border. Many men had been slain the previous night, and only a few elfs, but with Connacht's overwhelming odds, the Tylwyth Teg could hardly claim a victory.

Mickey spent the early morning with Diane, talking to her in great detail about the events of the last few weeks, and particularly about Gary's role in those events. While they were chatting, Gary and Kelsey wandered off. At first Diane was nervous about being left by Gary in this strange world, but Mickey's charming manner soon put her at ease.

She began to think about leprechauns, about the stories in her own world. Images of rainbows and pots of gold came to mind, and she fixed an intent stare upon Mickey, hardly hearing his words.

Mickey understood that look, had seen it from humans for years and years. He said nothing, figuring that she'd just have to learn for herself, and confident that if the woman came after him, he could easily evade her.

To Diane's credit, her expression gradually softened and she relaxed back, the moment of greedy weakness passed. Mickey didn't miss the point, and he silently applauded the young woman.

Gary and Kelsey returned soon after, bearing heavy

bundles and Gary holding the most incredible spear Diane had ever seen. She got up to her feet and moved near to him, running her hands over the flat part of the magnificent weapon's wide head.

"This is for you," Kelsey explained, putting down his bundle and turning it over so that a coat of fine, interlocking links of chain rolled out onto the grass.

Gary overturned his bundle as well, and the bulky plates of Donigarten's armor spilled onto the ground.

Diane was staring open-mouthed at the fabulous armor— of course Gary had described it to her in great detail, but seeing it was something altogether different!—when Kelsey approached her, the chain mail coat in hand.

"Put this on," he bade her. "Tir na n'Og has ever been a safe place for those whom the Tylwyth Teg name as a friend, but in these dark times, we cannot be sure."

While Kelsey turned to help Gary in strapping on the bulky pants, Diane slipped the metal jacket over her head. It was surprisingly light, no more encumbering than a winter coat, and though it was a bit tight about her chest and shoulders, the fit was acceptable.

"Suits ye well," Mickey remarked, and he gave a wink as Diane looked over to him.

Kelsey came over just long enough to offer Diane a belt and scabbard, holding a slender sword. The woman eyed it suspiciously, nervously.

"Take it," Kelsey instructed.

"Just in case," Mickey added, seeing the woman's dilemma.

Diane did as she was told. She handled the sword tentatively, strapping on the belt and eyeing Gary all the while. For the first time, she began to understand that they might be given specific assignments by the leaders of the elfish resistance, that they might be separated. And with a

sword strapped around her waist, Diane could hardly ignore
the possibility that she might see battle.

Gary had most of the armor on by then, and he returned
Diane's stare, almost apologetically. Gary knew how Diane
felt about violence, knew that she thought of war as an
incredibly stupid exercise in futility. Whenever he had tried
to tell her of the battles he had seen in Faerie, she had only
half listened, waiting for him to get past the violence and
back to the story.

"You will be shown to a guard position," Kelsey explained to Diane. "We have many prisoners, and can spare
few of our warriors to watch over them."

Diane didn't stop looking at Gary, and didn't blink.

"Gary Leger will accompany me," Kelsey went on,
understanding her questioning look. "His presence will
bolster the defense of the forest and bring fear to our
enemies."

Diane's look quickly turned sour, and Gary flinched.
Diane was wondering why he was apparently being given a
more important role than she, he knew.

"I wear the armor of Cedric Donigarten," he said, as
though that should explain it all.

"So I'll sit back here while you go off to fight," Diane
retorted. "Like a good little wife."

Gary flinched again, suddenly more afraid of the next
time Diane got him alone than any horrors he might
encounter on the battle lines.

"Be reasonable," he said. "You've got no idea of how to
fight with a sword."

"What about you?"

"I have the spear," Gary replied. "It talks to me, and has
told me how to fight. I explained all of that to you a long
time ago."

"Then let me use it," Diane stubbornly replied, though

she knew that to be impossible, and didn't really want the blasted thing anyway.

Young sprout! came the sentient spear's telepathic scream of protest in Gary's mind.

"I think it's a chauvinist," Gary explained with a helpless shrug.

* * * * *

"She is strong-willed," Kelsey remarked after he, Gary, and Mickey had left Diane with the other guards, the three heading back to the south, where the fighting had renewed. The rain, too, had begun again, a heavy drenching downpour. Kelsey understood the implications of the storm; elfish wizards were in control of the weather over Tir na n'Og, and they were using the rain to douse fires set by Kinnemore's men. Given the strength of this storm, Kelsey figured that the assault on Tir na n'Og must be on in full.

"Lucky me," Gary answered, but his sarcasm was apparently lost on Kelsey.

"Indeed," the elf said sincerely.

Gary regarded Kelsey for a moment, then chuckled softly. Of course the Tylwyth Teg valued the role of the elfish females, he realized, and precisely because there was no defined "role" for elfish females. They fought alongside the males, led and followed. They went out on life-quests, as serious as the one Kelsey had undertaken to reforge Donigarten's spear. In fact, that very morning Gary had learned that the King of the Tylwyth Teg was not a "King" at all, but a Queen, an elfish female who had ascended to the rather informal seat of power in Tir na n'Og through her leadership and battle prowess in a war a century before.

And it struck Gary, too, how complete a person Kelsey was. The elf could be the fiercest of warriors (Gary had seen that side) or the quietest of poets. Kelsey seemed equally at ease to Gary with a sword in hand or a flower. Gary nearly laughed aloud at the notion, thinking that the elf, without even trying, would surely fit into the "political correctness" of his own world. Within the society of the Tylwyth Teg, there were none of the preconceived notions, the barriers, sharply defining gender roles, and yet, their existence was certainly more primitive and harsh than Gary's society.

He'd have to spend more time thinking about that issue, he decided. It seemed to Gary that Kelsey held the answer to the frustrations of feminists and the confusion of men in his own world.

But he'd have to think about it later, a cry of pain from somewhere not too far ahead pointedly reminded him. The business now at hand was battle.

Kelsey went down into a crouch and signaled for Gary to hold steady. In an instant Kelsey was gone, disappearing into the heavy brush without a whisper of sound. Gary tensed, went down to one knee, then breathed easier as Mickey appeared atop his shoulder.

Mickey, whose senses were by far the keener, nodded ahead a moment later, signaling Kelsey's return.

Again, Kelsey came through the brush without a whisper of sound. He looked to Gary, nodded, and held up six fingers, then motioned for the man to flank to the left.

Gary eased up and moved slowly and deliberately, though he felt awkward and noisy indeed compared to the graceful forest dance of Kelsey. He stopped when he felt the burden on his shoulder lighten, and a panicked look came over him at the thought that Mickey wouldn't be by his side.

"Easy lad, I'll be about," Mickey promised from a low branch just behind him.

Gary adjusted his great helm, which was far too loose-fitting, and moved on through the thicket, coming to the edge of a small and shady clearing beneath the thick boughs of a wide elm.

Patience, young sprout, came the spear's call in his head, and Gary agreed with the assessment and crouched low in the brush, waiting.

There came a groan from not so far away.

Patience, the spear reminded him once more, sensing Gary's desire to rush off and investigate. A few moments later, Kelsey came running through the brush, to the edge of the clearing to Gary's right. A leaning log marked that border, about waist high, but hardly a barrier to the nimble elf. Bloodied sword in hand, Kelsey dove headlong over the log, touched the ground with his free hand and ducked his head so that he rolled right over and right back to his feet. He crossed the clearing with a few graceful strides, lifted his arm and leaped up, catching the elm's lowest branch. He was gone in the blink of Gary Leger's astonished eye, rolling up around the limb and disappearing into the cover of the trees' thick boughs.

"There's only one!" came a cry, a human voice, not so far behind.

"Flank to the right!" called another.

Gary watched as three men came to the log. They slowly crossed the barrier, two crawling under, readied crossbows in hand, and the third scrambling over. These were trained soldiers, Gary realized, from the way they complemented and covered one another's movements. They entered the clearing cautiously, looking all about, particularly to the sheltering elm. The fully armored crossbowmen kept the lead, holding close to the brush and easing around to their left, towards Gary. The third man, wearing only a leather jerkin and holding no weapons that Gary could see, took up the rear, quietly directing.

The man looked to the right more than once, and Gary figured that his companions would soon be coming around the clearing, probably entering from the other side.

Gary wrung his hands nervously over the metal shaft of the great spear. His stomach was in knots; he felt like he had to go to the bathroom.

Easy, young sprout.

So nervous was he that Gary almost replied to the spear's reassurance out loud! He didn't know where Kelsey had gone off to, didn't know what Kelsey expected him to do. The soldiers were close to him then; he could leap out and likely take one of them down.

He wondered how good Donigarten's armor might be against a crossbow fired point-blank.

Gary's relief at seeing Kelsey's return lasted only the moment it took him to realize that the elf had just walked out from around the elm's trunk, right into the open! He opened his mouth and almost called out, then fell back and winced as the crossbows fired and Kelsey fell.

Now! the sentient spear implored him, and purely on instinct, Gary leaped from the brush, right before the two armored soldiers. He slashed the spear straight across in front of him, taking the blocking crossbow from the hands of the nearest man, crunching the crosspiece on the bow of the second man.

Back across came the slicing spear, and Gary blindly thrust straight ahead. The soldier almost dodged, but got hit on the shoulder. A normal weapon would have done little damage, would have merely deflected off the metal plating of the man's armor to ride high to the side. But Donigarten's hungry spear bit hard and the soldier's armor melted away, the spear's wicked tip diving deep into the man's shoulder. He fell to the ground, clutching the wound, writhing in pain.

Overbalanced to the right, Gary stopped his momentum and jabbed straight back with the butt end of the spear. He was aiming for the second soldier's belly, but the spear came in a bit low.

The new angle proved even more effective, though, and the soldier groaned and lurched, his eyes crossed with pain.

Gary retracted and whipped the butt end straight up, slamming the man under the chin, under the faceplate of his helm. He straightened and staggered back a step, but not out of range of the long weapon as Gary butt-ended him again, squarely in the faceplate.

Down he went, flat on his back, his feet skidding out from under him on the slippery grass.

Gary came up straight, spinning to his right to face the third man squarely. He screamed out and tried frantically and futilely to dodge the sliver of metal spinning his way.

The man's shot was near perfect, the dagger coming point in at Gary's faceplate. Its tip sliced through the slits in the great helm and gashed the side of Gary's nose and his cheek. He screamed again and fell away, and purely out of fear, purely on a survival reflex, he hurled the spear.

The man in the leather jerkin, another dagger in hand, threw his arms out defensively in front of him.

The soaring spear crossed between them, though, and blasted right through the pitiful leather defense, right through the man's chest and back. He flew backwards, staggering many steps until he slammed against the log, where the spear tip bit again, through the dead wood, holding the dead man upright against it.

Gary, on the ground, one eye closed because of blood, the other teary, didn't see the hit. He was looking the other way, to the tree and beyond, where the missing two soldiers had entered the clearing and were looking over the fallen body of the elf, prodding the corpse with their swords.

At that moment, the real Kelsey dropped down from the boughs, right between them.

Gary didn't understand—until the image of the fallen elf dissipated into nothingness and Gary remembered that

Mickey was not far away and that the leprechaun was especially proficient at crafting illusions of Kelsey.

The soldiers were not caught unawares. Kelsey's sword darted straight ahead, but was turned aside. It came streaking right back in, at a lower angle, but was slapped downward by a perfect parry.

Left, right and left again, Kelsey snapped his sword, now on the defensive and blocking the press of the two soldiers. Back to the right came the elf's fine weapon, steel rang out against steel, and Kelsey thrust straight ahead, aiming low. The soldier recovered quickly enough to parry, his sword again coming down atop Kelsey's, driving the elf's blade harmlessly low.

Kelsey expected the block and went with it, moving his sword down and to the right, towards the tip of the blocking sword. Kelsey stepped right, as well, just out of the reach of the other soldier's lunge. A subtle twist of the wrist brought Kelsey's sword around the soldier's, and the elf promptly stepped ahead.

The soldier snapped his angled sword upward, trying to throw Kelsey's weapon high and wide. The elf's forward thrust was too quick, though, and Kelsey's fine sword cut into the man's breastplate, drawing a deep red line up his chest and forcing him to fall back.

The other soldier came in furiously and Kelsey just managed to free up his blade and snap it across, deflecting his enemy's prodding sword when it was barely an inch from his side. Kelsey spun on his heel and launched a weak two-strike combination that had no chance of hitting. The maneuver bought him enough time to square up, though, putting his parries in line as the outraged soldier came forward once more.

The wounded soldier stubbornly stepped ahead, and

worse, Kelsey heard the heavy footsteps of another enemy approaching from behind him. He plotted an evasive maneuver, a ducking spin that would allow him to swipe at the legs of the man coming in from the back and roll away from all three attackers.

But then the healthy fighter pressing the elf stepped back suddenly and dropped his weapon to the ground. He fell to his knees, swearing fealty to the memory of Sir Cedric Donigarten!

Kelsey batted away the weak swing of the wounded man, and looked back over his shoulder to see Gary Leger, weaponless and with blood running out from under his great helm. Obviously dizzy, Gary staggered stubbornly to join his friend.

"And what of you?" the quick-thinking Kelsey demanded, spinning back and thrusting his sword viciously at the wounded man. He batted the weak attempt at a parry aside and stood firm, his swordtip a foot from the man's wounded breast.

The soldier looked to his kneeling comrade, to the other two on the ground behind Gary and to the man standing limp, impaled against the log.

"Donigarten," he said quietly.

"On your word of honor!" Kelsey snarled, lunging ahead, closing the distance between swordtip and breast. "Swear fealty."

"To Donigarten," the man said again and dropped his sword to the dirt. "An oath to Sir Cedric."

Kelsey eased his sword away, his golden eyes continuing their unrelenting stare at the man. Finally, convinced that this one would cause no more mischief, Kelsey turned a sidelong glance at Gary.

"I'm all right," Gary assured him, lifting his arm to keep the concerned elf at bay.

Kelsey nodded and looked beyond him. "We have five prisoners," he explained. "For I injured but did not kill the man back in the woods."

Gary didn't have to look back to the log for the grim reminder that his spear throw had apparently claimed the only kill.

Mickey appeared then, atop the low branch just above them.

"A fine deception," Kelsey congratulated. "But temporary. My enemies would have been held longer off their guard if the illusion had held."

"I do what I can," Mickey replied, somewhat sourly.

"I have come to expect more of you," said Kelsey.

"And so ye got it," the leprechaun explained. "I was not so far away, turning aside another dozen o' the enemy. Suren the forest's thick with Kinnemore's army! And ye got four prisoners, not five, for the others found the man in the woods and took him off with them."

"Where are they now?" Kelsey demanded.

"Chasing yerself," Mickey explained. "Back the other way. Don't ye worry, I told a fair amount o' yer kinfolk they'd be coming."

Kelsey nodded, Gary swayed, and the elf stepped over and offered him a supporting arm. He helped Gary sit down against the elm's thick trunk and gently removed the helm. The wound was superficial, though bloody and obviously painful. Kelsey reached into a pouch for some healing herbs, but Gary stopped him.

"They need you more," Gary explained, indicating the Connacht soldiers. The one healthy man was trying to tend the other three.

Kelsey agreed with the observation and left Gary with a clean cloth and a vial of clear water. He started to clean the wound, and nearly swooned from the sharp pricks of pain. Mickey walked up next to him and took the cloth.

"Nasty nick, but not so deep," the leprechaun assured him. Despite Mickey's comforting words, Gary noted a good measure of tension in Mickey's voice. He studied Mickey closely, with the usually perceptive leprechaun too involved to even notice.

"Are there that many enemies in the forest?" Gary asked, thinking that to be the cause of Mickey's distress.

"What's that?" Mickey asked, startled by the unexpected question. "Oh, no, lad, not too many for Kelsey's kin to fight off."

"Then what is it?" Gary demanded.

"There's some fires burning," Mickey answered.

"In this rain?" Gary could hardly believe it; the ground was near to flooding, and the tree branches sagged low under the pounding and unrelenting downpour.

"Our enemies got their means," was all that Mickey would say, and he went back to his work.

A group of Tylwyth Teg entered the clearing a few minutes later, a handful of human prisoners in tow. They immediately went to help Kelsey with the wounded, and to speak with the elf-lord, and by their grim expressions Gary realized that they had learned what Mickey had learned. The young man pulled himself up from the ground and walked over to join them. By the time he got there, Kelsey too wore a grave look.

Gary was about to ask for an explanation when he got his answer. A flaming ball of pitch soared through the gray sky, slamming the high top of a tree not so far away. Despite the rain, the burning pitch clung to the tree's branches.

"Catapults," one of the elfs explained. "Across the field and out of bowshot, and with ranks of soldiers dug in between them and the forest."

"They'll not take Tir na n'Og," Kelsey added. "But surely they mean to despoil it."

The targeted tree exploded as the pitch burned its way to the sap core. Flames shot high into the air, defying the rain.

9 ✝ The Oldest Trick in the Book

The determined group was in agreement that the Tylwyth Teg had to get to the catapults—what else might these creatures of Tir na n'Og think with their beautiful forest being despoiled right before their eyes? Kelsey and two of the other older elfs spoke of gathering as many warriors as they could spare to launch a full-out attack through the Connacht lines.

They were desperate, and, by Gary's estimation, so was their plan. How many elfs would die for the sake of stopping those catapults? And if the cost to the Tylwyth Teg was high, what would stop Kinnemore from simply constructing new ones? Gary told Kelsey and the others just that, and though, to their credit, none of them responded with the "Have you got a better idea?" cliche, resourceful Gary did indeed have a better plan.

"Our targets are the catapults," he explained. "And only the catapults. There's no reason to fight Kinnemore's men all the way to them."

"We have no time to flank the long lines," Kelsey interjected. Despite the fact that Kelsey was the sole elf voicing any doubts, he alone among the gathering was listening intently to Gary's ideas. The young man from

Real-earth had proved his worth and his ability to improvise several times over the last two adventures. Gary Leger was the one who had devised the plan that allowed them to escape from imprisonment on Ceridwen's isle; Gary Leger was the one who had figured out a way to beat the dreaded dragon.

"No need to go around," Gary calmly and confidently explained.

"You mean to walk right through the enemy?" another elf, a noble-looking, black-haired creature by the name of TinTamarra, asked skeptically. Thinking he had solved Gary's puzzle, TinTamarra turned a suspicious eye, a green eye that seemed to burn with inner fires, on Mickey. "The leprechaun is good with tricks, but he cannot fool so large a concentration of men, not when they are lined in battle trenches, expecting danger."

"Mickey's role will be minor," Gary assured the elf. "But those two"—he pointed to two of the men who had sworn fealty to the memory of Cedric Donigarten—"will perform the deception."

Every elf in the clearing wore a sour expression—every elf except for Kelsey, who was beginning to catch on.

"Prisoners?" he asked, and Gary nodded, understanding that Kelsey was not referring to the captured Connacht soldiers.

"Caught by the men," Gary answered. "Caught by those two soldiers and by the wearer of Donigarten's armor."

"Kinnemore, or at least Prince Geldion, knows your allegiance to Kelsenellenelvial," TinTamarra put in.

Gary was shaking his head before the dark-haired elf even finished. "The Prince knows only that I accompanied Kelsenellenellenell . . . Kelsey on the quest to reforge the spear and in the matter of defeating Robert. If Kinnemore is as close to Ceridwen as everybody says, then he likely knows that it was I who banished her to her island, but also that it was I who released her from her bondage. Even more, by the King's own words, it was said that I came along only to steal the armor and spear and make for Bretaigne, for my own purposes and without the blessings of the Tylwyth Teg. They don't know my true allegiance, and I would bet that they'll be thrilled to learn, and eager to believe, that I have come to join their cause."

It sounded somewhat reasonable, but more than a little dangerous, and most of the elfs were shaking their heads as they whispered among themselves.

"Perhaps it would be best if you remained behind," Kelsey offered at length to Gary. "I, and two or three of my kin will go, along with the two Connacht soldiers. If we get through to the catapults, they'll not fire again against Tir na n'Og."

"I'm thinking it's a bit more believable if ye take the lad," Mickey interjected, drawing the attention of all in the field. "It'll take more than a trick to make Kinnemore's men— who've battled the Tylwyth Teg these last few days and heared tales of elfish warriors all their lives—believe that the two o' them catched any of ye. But if Gary Leger's along, and the men say he helped, it'll look more believable. He's wearing Donigarten's armor, after all, and has been named as the one who beat the dragon."

Kelsey stared hard at Gary, trying to determine which was the better reasoning.

"It's my plan," Gary said with a smile, and Kelsey appreciated that loyalty, appreciated that Gary would be so willing, even eager, to undertake such a dangerous venture for the sake of Tir na n'Og.

"He goes," Kelsey announced, and there were a few grumbles, but no elf spoke openly against the trusted elf-lord.

Just a few minutes later, Gary, Kelsey, Mickey, two other elfs including TinTamarra, and the two soldiers left the field. On Mickey's suggestion that it would add credibility both to the illusion and to Gary's stature, and reasoning that it would allow them to travel more easily, Kelsey called one of the magnificent white-coated Tir na n'Og horses for Gary.

Magnificent indeed did the wear of Donigarten's armor look, sitting tall upon that steed! And, of course, with the mount, Gary could more than keep up with the others.

Another benefit of Mickey's plan, one that the leprechaun didn't bother to mention, was that he too, cuddled in his customary nook at the base of the steed's neck, might enjoy the comfort of a ride.

They left Tir na n'Og in a line, Gary at the head, the four "captured" Tylwyth Teg behind him, and the two armed soldiers behind them. Gary appreciated how great a leap of faith Kelsey, and particularly the other two elfs, were making at this point, to allow armed Connacht soldiers at their backs. Their trust was a wonderful thing, Gary decided, and he was confident that they would not be betrayed.

The group was surrounded immediately when they neared the Connacht line. Mickey's illusion at this point was a simple one, the leprechaun merely masking the fact that Kelsey and the other two elfs carried weapons and were not nearly as wounded as they appeared.

"What is this about?" the field commander of the Connacht forces demanded, bypassing Gary and speaking to one of the traitorous soldiers. More than once he looked suspiciously at Gary Leger; by all previous accounts, the stranger from Bretaigne was no friend to Kinnemore's throne.

"It is about prisoners," Gary answered boldly. He swung

his mount about and walked it right before the field commander, demanding an audience.

The man eyed him dangerously. "I was speaking to . . ." he began, but Gary, sitting tall on the shining white stallion, looking magnificent indeed in his unrivaled armor and holding the legendary spear, cut him short.

"You will address me!" Gary growled. "It was I who saved your pitiful soldiers, and I who captured the three Tylwyth Teg."

"And left a dozen more lyin' dead in the woods," one of the traitorous soldiers unexpectedly replied. In truth, the man had not spoken at all; the words had been thrown by an invisible Mickey McMickey, still nestled comfortably in the crook between Gary's saddle and his mount's strong neck.

The field commander continued to eye Gary suspiciously, unblinking. "It is rumored that you are allied with Tir na n'Og," he remarked and looked to his bristling soldiers, standing ready a short distance away.

"Would you prefer that I was?" Gary asked. "You impertinent insect! How many weeks will you lie here in the mud, while those wretched Tylwyth Teg dance free under the stars? Have you no desire for order?"

The man seemed truly perplexed, as Gary had hoped, but if he was convinced then of Gary's friendship, he did not show it.

"Stand your men aside and let us pass," Gary demanded.

The field commander straightened and narrowed his eyes. "Prisoners are to be kept in a barn to the east, not behind the line to the south," he said.

"These prisoners are not to be 'kept' at all!" Gary roared back. Mickey crinkled his brow at that one, though, of course, nobody saw the movement. Kelsey too seemed concerned, for Gary was obviously improvising, trying to wriggle around the soldier's unexpected declaration. Next to

Kelsey, TinTamarra closed his hand tightly about the hilt of his masked sword, ready for trouble.

"I have a surprise for the defenders of the forest," Gary went on, and he put so wicked a glare over Kelsey and the other elfs that they, for an instant, honestly wondered if he was betraying them. "Let us see how the elfish morale holds up when the living, screaming missiles crash in!"

The field commander swayed, overwhelmed by the unexpected announcement, and several of his soldiers began whispering and smiling at the devilish plan.

"By whose order?" the obviously shaken field commander asked.

"By my order!" Gary yelled at him. "By order of the dragonslayer, of the knight who defeated Redarm on the field of honor, and who now plans to take that fool's place by Prince Geldion's side.

"Bring them!" Gary instructed the two traitors, and he walked his steed forward, and, to his ultimate relief, the Connacht ranks parted.

"You may tell Prince Geldion that I await his presence at the catapults," Gary boldly called to the field commander. "Tell him to hurry, before I change my mindset and my loyalty!"

Kelsey and the other elfs could hardly believe how easily Gary had played on the man's fears. The other two looked to Kelsey for some explanation, and the elf-lord smiled and nodded, convinced again of this one's resourcefulness. Truly, the bluff had been perfect, as had the lie about launching living elfs from the catapults.

"Ye got a set on ye, not to doubt," Mickey praised when the group of seven moved beyond the ranks, not a word of dispute filtering from the soldiers they had left behind.

"A set?" Gary asked, not understanding.

"A set to make a heeland bull cry for envy!" Mickey laughed.

Gary chuckled and did not reply, not even to tell Mickey that, in truth, he had nearly wet his pants.

They came in sight of the catapult batteries a short while later, two of the war engines sitting low behind a ridge, each manned by a crew of half a dozen soldiers. Even as the companions watched, mesmerized by the workings, the closest catapult fired, the flaming pitch ball soaring high into the air towards Tir na n'Og.

On the second catapult, the men strained at a heavy crank, bending down the great beam.

"Hold!" Gary cried to them, kicking his mount out ahead of the others. "Hold and clear that basket!"

Twelve curious expressions turned on the armored man, the man from Bretaigne, they thought.

Gary walked his shining white steed down at a slow and comfortable pace, formulating his lies as he went. He meant to keep up the façade that they would launch the elfish prisoners into Tir na n'Og, to break the morale of the Tylwyth Teg. If the deception worked, Gary and his friends would be within the enemy ranks before the soldiers ever suspected anything amiss. If the deception worked, the fight might be relatively painless, the catapults quickly taken out of action.

Kelsey and the other proud elfs, watching the first pitch ball soar towards their precious forest home, watching the second catapult readied for another strike, had no more patience for deception and intricate plans. Gary was halfway to the enemy then, with more than one of the Connacht soldiers holding a weapon, when a volley of arrows raced in.

Gary's eyes widened in surprise. He heard the charge of Kelsey and the two other elfs (and of the two men, as well) coming behind him, and searched for some way to calm things back down, to put the situation back under control.

It had already gone past that, the young man realized. Two of the Connacht men lay in pools of blood, and the fight was on.

Gary kicked his steed into a run just as Kelsey came up even with him. Lifting his great bow, Kelsey skidded to a stop, and Gary charged on, screaming wildly. His scream changed in timbre as he saw one of the Connacht soldiers raise a loaded crossbow his way. But Kelsey saw the man, too, and the elf's arrow took him down before he could fire the crossbow.

The soldiers scattered before Gary's pounding charge. Another went down, an arrow in his side, and then a fifth, catching an arrow in the back as he scrambled to get over the bulk of the catapult.

Gary's mind raced frantically as he tried to pick out a target, looking from one fleeing group to another. A quick turn of his horse would have put him in line with one nearby man, would have allowed him to easily run the man down.

Gary missed the opportunity, and truly had little heart for killing these pitiful soldiers. He realized his best target a moment later, when he heard again the ominous clicking sound of the catapult bending to ready.

"Use all of your magic!" Gary cried aloud.

Throw well, young sprout! came the sentient spear's telepathic reply, the weapon reading Gary's thoughts and in complete agreement with the plan.

Gary lifted the spear in one hand as he came around the front of the closest catapult. He had to shift suddenly, though, when a form leaped out at him from the wooden base of the great war machine. The man crashed against Gary squarely, and Gary tightened his legs about his horse's flanks, just barely managing to hold his seat. One of the reins slipped from his grasp, and Mickey came visible holding tightly to it, hanging from the side of the horse's neck, his curly-toed shoes kicking frantically in the air. Gary let go the reins altogether, forced to hook his arm under the shoulder of his thrashing adversary.

The soldier's arm whipped across, his small axe slamming hard into Gary's chest. Cedric's armor turned the brunt of the blow and Gary heaved the man across his lap, laying him out straight over the saddle. They fumbled and struggled, and Gary freed up his arm just as the stubborn man started to rise, trying to pivot and bring his axe to bear once more.

Gary's metal-plated sleeve slammed hard against the back of the soldier's head, and he fell limp across the saddle. Gary grabbed him by the seat of his breeches and heaved him all the way over, then took up the reins again, and the spear, and turned his attention back to the catapult.

The great bending beam was only a few yards away by then, and Gary had no time to consider the implications of his actions, no time to consider that he would then be weaponless in the midst of armed enemies. He ignored Mickey's continuing cries for help for the moment, and hurled the spear. Its enchanted tip flashed like a lightning stroke as it hit, and then bit deeply into the neck of the bent beam. Energy surged from the powerful weapon, and cracks widened along the side of the beam.

The crew manning the weapon had no way of understanding the extent of the spear's damage, though, and they fired the catapult. The beam broke apart under the sudden jolt, the flaming ball lifting straight into the air, perhaps a dozen feet, then falling right back down, squarely into the framework of the disabled war machine.

Gary grabbed hard at the reins, reached desperately for Mickey, and swung his mount sharply to the side, smiling in grim satisfaction. That smile melted into horror as one man, covered with flames from the splattering pitch, ran screaming out from the other side of the catapult.

As he passed behind the bulky machine, Gary's horrified expression became one of fear. He pulled Mickey in close to him and tugged hard on the reins, and the Tir na n'Og steed responded by rearing onto its back legs at the same instant that the two crossbowmen fired. The evasive movement saved Gary's life, and Mickey's, but the horse, intercepting both bolts, was not so fortunate. The beast came back down to all four hooves, then continued down, headlong, throwing its riders straight to the ground.

Gary's breath blew away as he hit and started to roll, and that momentum was abruptly halted as his horse came all the way over, slamming against his twisted back. A blinding flash of pain exploded along the side of the man's neck and down the side of his back. The horse rolled right off him an instant later, lying dead on its side on the ground before him.

Only Gary's right arm came to his mental call that he had to get up and get out of there. He propped himself out of the muddy grass on his elbow and looked back to his left—to see his shoulder far out of place, far to the back of where it should have been. Waves of pain rolled out of that shoulder, washed over the fallen young man, and left him bathed in thick sweat. He stared incredulously at his twisted limb for many seconds, then looked beyond it, to Mickey, sitting on the grass and straightening his tam-o'-shanter.

A moment later, Gary felt the curious tickle of grass sticking through the slits in his helmet as he lay facedown on the field.

All six of the men on the first catapult, and one of the second crew, were downed by arrows before Kelsey and his kin got near the machine. Those losses, plus the man Gary had beaten and thrown from his saddle and the one who had died covered in fiery pitch, left only three soldiers remaining.

Three soldiers against three Tylwyth Teg.

Kelsey intercepted one, a large man wielding a two-headed axe, right beside Gary, the man apparently of a mind to finish Gary off. He swiped his axe across at Kelsey instead, but the elf nimbly jumped back out of range, the heavy weapon cutting the air an inch from Kelsey's sucked-in belly. Kelsey came forward a quick step, then retreated again as the axe came across in a furious backhand cut.

The action repeated, across and back, again, and then a third time, and with each swing, the growling soldier advanced a step, forcing Kelsey back. The man thought that he had the elf in trouble, thought he could back Kelsey all the way to the other catapult, where he would catch the elf, where he would cut the skinny elf in half.

But his swings were inevitably slowing, his arms fast tiring under the weight of the heavy weapon. Kelsey acted the part of a troubled adversary, feigning fear, even looking back nervously over his shoulder more than once. He had the man's measure, though, and only allowed the façade to continue because each swing slowed a bit more, ensured his victory a bit more.

"They're coming behind us!" one of the traitors who had accompanied Kelsey's band cried from the platform of the still-intact catapult. Kelsey heard chopping begin, the two men going to work on the machine.

The axe swiped across in front of the elf again, the growling man stubbornly coming on. But Kelsey had no more time for the game. The man reversed his grip, beginning the backhand, but suddenly the fierce elf was in his face, and the elf's fine sword was through his belly.

Kelsey caught the weakening swing of the axe in his free hand, eased the weapon, and then its wielder, to the ground.

Looking ahead, he saw TinTamarra take down a second soldier, near the burning catapult, and saw the third elf chasing the remaining enemy away.

But suddenly there came from behind Kelsey a ticking sound, almost like the pounding of a hailstorm, and he spun to see a shower of arrows descend over the intact catapult. One of the men got hit a dozen times, stumbled off and staggered a few steps and fell to the ground dead at Kelsey's feet. The other, after taking a grazing hit in one shoulder, used the great beam as a barrier and continued his chopping.

Kelsey looked back the other way, trying to formulate some plan for retreat. Could he get to Gary Leger? he wondered. Was Gary Leger even still alive? And where had Mickey gone off to?

Kelsey's whirling mind was stopped in place as he turned, as he focused on his kin who had run off in pursuit of the last enemy. The elf floundered on the field, squirming and turning. His body jerked as another arrow plowed into him, and then again.

He continued to squirm, continued to take wicked hits.

Kelsey looked beyond him, up to the crest of the rolling hill, where sat a line of Connacht cavalry.

A hand signal from the man in the middle—Kelsey recognized him as Prince Geldion—and the archers lowered their bows. Behind Kelsey, the wounded man stumbled down from the catapult.

"I am sorry," he began, for the catapult still appeared operational.

Kelsey cut the man short with a curt wave of his hand. There was no need for any apologies; both this man and his dead companion had proven themselves worthy, despite the failure.

A second figure, a giant of a man, rode up beside Geldion, and the horsemen began a slow and steady walk down the hillock, the Connacht ring closing tight about the companions.

Thirty yards away. Twenty.

"What tricks have you, leprechaun?" Kelsey whispered to Mickey, the sprite still sitting on the grass near the groaning Gary Leger.

"Even if I made it look like we'd escaped, we'd not get this one far," Mickey replied. "I'm thinkin' that ye're catched."

Kelsey did not miss Mickey's choice of words, did not miss the fact that the leprechaun had said that Kelsey and the others, but not the leprechaun, were apparently soon to be captured. The elf-lord was not surprised as Mickey faded away into nothingness.

A commotion started almost immediately to Kelsey's right, the Connacht horsemen jostling, one even swiping with his sword. The elf understood that Mickey was involved, probably making it appear as though Kelsey's band was trying to get out that way.

Kelsey looked to TinTamarra; was this the time for them to try to make their break?

The tall man seated next to Geldion raised his arm and called for calm.

"Hold tight your ranks!" Geldion called on cue. "This group is known for trickery. Hold tight your ranks, and do not let what you see deceive you!"

The tall man was King Kinnemore, Kelsey now realized, though he hadn't seen the man up so close in many years, and did not remember him as being quite so large, and did not remember his face as being so . . . feral was the only word Kelsey could think of to describe Kinnemore's snarling features. Even viewing him on the platform in Dilnamarra, Kelsey hadn't realized quite how imposing a figure Kinnemore truly was. He towered over Geldion as the two made their way down, looked cleanly over his son's head as easily as if it had been a young boy sitting next to him.

Kinnemore closed his eyes as he did this, and then began turning his face deliberately from side to side. Kelsey's eyes widened with curiosity as he realized that the man was sniffing the air like some animal!

The King's eyes widened soon after, and a smile broke out on his stern face. "There is a leprechaun about!" he declared.

"Now how might he be knowing that?" the invisible Mickey, now perched on the base of the catapult behind Kelsey, quietly asked.

The Connacht ring tightened even more, the King and Geldion sitting no more than a dozen yards from Kelsey and TinTamarra, the two defensively flanking the fallen Gary Leger. Geldion smiled and whispered to his father when he came to recognize the elf-lord, long an adversary.

"I have lost one of my catapults," King Kinnemore announced a moment later. "In exchange for an elf-lord, another of the Tylwyth Teg, the stolen artifacts, and the pretender from Bretaigne. I'd call it a favorable trade. What say you, Kelsenellenelvial Gil-Ravadry?"

Kelsey held fast to his sword. He thought of grabbing for his bow, of trying to put another arrow into Kinnemore, or perhaps one into that wretched son of his. He had to admit that he wouldn't get near to readying the weapon, though. At least a dozen crossbows were trained upon him, and a dozen on TinTamarra and on the human traitor, as well.

"What say you?" Kinnemore demanded again. "Do you yield?"

Kelsey looked to his elfish kin and nodded, and both of them dropped their bloodstained swords to the grass.

The soldiers rolled in about them. "A thousand gold pieces to the man who captures that leprechaun!" King

Kinnemore asserted, and every soldier who was not assigned a specific task began a wild search of the area.

The surviving raiders were bound by their wrists and ankles, Kelsey, TinTamarra, and Gary Leger together (though Gary was still far from cohesive). On Kinnemore's orders, the traitor was taken in a different direction, to the one working catapult.

"You sang a fine lie to walk through my ranks," the King explained to Kelsey, his face just an inch from the elf's and his smelly breath hot on Kelsey's face. "I do thank you for the idea."

Kelsey wasn't sure what the evil King was talking about, until Kinnemore ordered the catapult readied and the traitor placed in the basket.

A cry from the side stole everyone's attention a moment later, and a soldier ran in, holding a frantically kicking Mickey McMickey. "I got him! I got him!" the man shrieked, moving to stand before his King.

Kinnemore grabbed the kicking leprechaun from the soldier's hands. Again came the curious sniffing. "Smells like a mushroom to me!" Kinnemore roared, and he squeezed with all his considerable strength.

"Oh, begorra," the real Mickey, still invisible and still by the catapult, muttered under his breath. Kings were supposed to be better at seeing through illusions, but this guy was uncanny.

Another soldier came running in, making a similar proclamation and holding a similarly kicking leprechaun. And then a third man cried out from across the way, and a fourth near the ruined catapult. Before King Kinnemore could sort it all out, a dozen men were standing before him, each holding a likeness of a very animated Mickey.

Prince Geldion couldn't bite back his chuckle—and Kinnemore promptly slapped him across the face, so hard that he tumbled to the ground. He sat there for a long while, staring unblinkingly at his surprising father.

"Send him flying to Tir na n'Og!" the embarrassed King roared at his soldiers manning the working catapult. "Show the Tylwyth Teg, and our own ranks, how King Kinnemore deals with those who oppose him!"

The poor man in the basket began a pitiful whining.

"Easy, lad," came a whisper from the invisible leprechaun who had secretly crawled in next to him.

Kelsey and TinTamarra, many of the Connacht soldiers, and even Prince Geldion gave a unified groan as the beam creaked into place and then launched with a great *whoosh* of air. The man's horrified scream diminished quickly as he flew away through the rain.

High over Tir na n'Og, arching down, the man felt a sudden drag, a sudden slowing, and Mickey, holding tight both to him and to an umbrella, came visible at his side.

"Easy, lad," the leprechaun said again. "I got ye."

Below Mickey's magical umbrella, they floated down slowly into the thick canopy of Tir na n'Og. By the time they got to the ground, they were both scratched and bruised in many places.

But far better off, in Mickey's estimation, than Kelsey, TinTamarra, and Gary Leger.

10 † Witch for a Day

The dreary weather seemed fitting indeed to poor Diane as she sat on the wet grass of a small, cleared hillock in Tir na n'Og, not far from the continuing battle.

"We should be getting ye back to the prisoners," Mickey, sitting beside her and honestly sympathetic, remarked. "Even though most o' the prisoners seem to have a heart to be joining our side instead of fighting with Kinnemore, and even them that don't join with us aren't showing much spirit for keeping their fighting for th'other side."

The leprechaun blew a ring of blue smoke out of his gigantic pipe. It floated up into the air, then descended over Diane, encircling her like some magical necklace. Mickey blinked his eyes alternately and the ring shifted hue, moving right through the rainbow spectrum of colors. "'Course, that might be soon to be changing," the leprechaun finished glumly.

Diane understood Mickey's reasoning. Many Connacht soldiers had sworn fealty to Tir na n'Og, or more particularly to the hero wearing the armor of Cedric Donigarten. But now that hero was gone, taken captive, perhaps even killed, and the armor was in Kinnemore's hands.

Diane sniffled back a wave of emotion. "I want to go home," she whispered. "If Gary's dead, then I want to go home."

Mickey had explained to her the ramifications of death in Faerie. If Gary or Diane died here, then dead they would be, in both worlds. If Kinnemore had killed Gary, and Mickey and Diane could not retrieve his body, then he would, as far as people in the other world were concerned, simply vanish.

Diane wondered how she might explain that one to her mother-in-law. Even if they found the body, returned to the ruined castle on the hill in Duntulme, how was she going to get back to the United States and explain sword wounds?

"He's not dead yet, lassie," Mickey remarked.

Diane turned sharply on the sprite. "How do you know?"

"Kinnemore'll make a show of it," Mickey reasoned. "Gary Leger was hurting, but not too bad, when I left him. If Kinnemore means to finish the job, he'll do it in grand style, an open hanging in Dilnamarra—or might be that he'll take Gary all the way back to Connacht, where a hundred times the number might watch. He was always one for crowd-pleasin'."

Diane thought it over for a moment. "If you get me beside him, can you just beam us out?" she asked.

"Can I what?" Mickey responded, eyeing her curiously.

Despite the awful predicament, Diane gave a small snort. With the accent, Mickey did sound a bit like Scotty. "Can you send us away?" she explained. "Back to our own world?"

Mickey took a deep draw on his pipe and nodded his understanding. "Only through a bridge," he replied. "And suren there's few o' them left. And truth be telled, I cannot do it. That's pixie work." Mickey studied Diane's crestfallen look for a moment, then his voice took on an angry and frustrated edge. "I telled ye ye'd not want to be here," he accused. "Not now, not at this time!"

Diane looked away, but she did not blame Mickey.

"I'm not thinking that Kinnemore'll kill Gary and Kelsey

at all," Mickey went on, trying to offer some comfort at least. "Ceridwen's coming free soon, and the witch'd not be pleased to learn that her puppet King stealed such pleasure from her."

Diane started to respond, but stopped short, her mind working furiously down a new avenue of thought. "Is Kinnemore afraid of Ceridwen?" she asked.

"Ye'd be afraid o' her, too, if ye knowed her," Mickey was quick to respond.

"How often does he speak with her?"

Mickey shrugged, having no way to know the answer.

"And you told me that Gary was the only one who could shorten her banishment," Diane rolled on, taking no further notice of Mickey's responses. "And he did shorten it, when the dragon was alive and loose. So he could shorten it again, right?"

"Lassie, we're in enough trouble now," Mickey said dryly.

But Diane's smile did not diminish; the weight had been lifted from her shoulders. She felt suddenly like she was in the middle of a delicious novel and, for the first time, like she might have some control over the pen.

*   *   *   *   *

They crouched at the corner of a small building, the sunlight fast fading behind them. Getting into Dilnamarra had not been much of a problem, as Diane's plan had worked wonders on the badly informed common soldiers of Kinnemore's army.

"There's Kinnemore," Mickey whispered, indicating the area before the door of the town's squat keep. "With Prince Geldion beside him."

"I thought you said that Gary was brought to Faerie in the first place because he was big enough to fit Donigarten's armor," Diane whispered. "Kinnemore's got to be a foot taller than him!"

"Aye," Mickey replied. "And bigger than I'm remembering him. But he's too big for the armor—and ye think we'd have had a chance o' persuading him to go, anyway?"

Diane nodded. King Kinnemore seemed indeed an aberration. Diane, at five-foot-eight, was taller than any man she had met in Faerie, except for the giant King.

The two remained in place for some time, watching Kinnemore and Geldion, and the King did not seem very pleased with his son!

Diane, carrying all of her otherworldly equipment with her, glanced back to the westering sun, then took out a small meter. Nodding happily, she brought her Polaroid around from her side and lifted it towards the King.

"Here now, what're ye up to?" Mickey wanted to know. "We can't go starting a fight in the middle o' Dilnamarra."

"No fight," Diane promised and clicked off the picture. The exposed film ejected and she took it away. "You'll see."

Geldion stormed away from the meeting and leaped atop his horse, thundering out of town, his father's scowl on his back and his own scowl set on the road before him. Then Kinnemore spun about, knocking one of the guardsmen to the ground, and entered the keep.

"Come along," Mickey instructed, wanting to get this over with quickly, before the King had the time to relax and sort things out (and, possible, to make some sort of contact with Ceridwen!).

The leprechaun, who looked like a spindly-armed goblin, skittered out, and Diane began to follow. She took one quick look at the developing photo, meaning to tuck it into a pocket.

"Hel-lo," she said in surprise. She looked to Mickey, who was too far ahead, and decided this newest "development" would have to wait. She tucked the picture safely away and rushed to catch up.

If Diane had any doubts about the power of Mickey's latest illusion, they vanished the moment the two guards standing beside the iron-bound door to Dilnamarra Keep noticed the pair coming. They bristled about and readied their weapons at the sight of Mickey, in goblin guise, and how they blanched, falling all over themselves in a feeble attempt to come to rigid attention, when they noticed Diane!

Mickey walked right up to them boldly, daring them. Neither dared to look down at the little goblin; neither dared to move his eyes at all, or even to breathe.

"Whereses is Kinnemore?" Mickey rasped in his best goblin imitation. "The Lady wantses to see Kinnemore!"

"The King is inside the keep," one of the guards was quick to answer. "I will announce —"

"Stop!" Diane said, and the man nearly fainted. "Where is Prince Geldion?"

The guards looked nervously at each other. "He went to the prisoners," the first answered. "Then he was off to the battlefield to direct the next attack."

"Ah, yes, the prisoners," Diane remarked, trying to hide her overwhelming relief that Gary and Kelsey were apparently still alive. "You have caught that wretched Gary Leger, and an elf-lord of Tir na n'Og. Pray tell me, where has Geldion put those two?"

"In a secluded barn," the guard promptly answered. "West of Dilnamarra, beside an abandoned farmhouse. They . . ."

"I'm for knowin' the . . ." Mickey interrupted, and he caught himself, and his unwelcome change of accent quickly and looked to the guards to make sure they had not caught the slip. "Geek knowses the place, lady," he corrected. "Geek knowses the place!"

Diane stood as if in deep thought. "Come along, Geek," she said at length, her tone wicked with thick sarcasm. "We will visit with Kinnemore later—for now, let us go and tell Gary Leger how fine it is to see him again!

"And you!" she snapped at the pale guards. "Say nothing to Kinnemore of my coming. Ceridwen needs no announcement." She rose up, tall and terrible, completely amazed at the power granted her by this disguise. "If your King has even a hint that I have been here," she warned, "you will live out your pitiful lives as barnyard animals!"

She held her hand up and out towards the men, drawing their attention, and then with a *pop* there came a blinding flash, followed by clouds of leprechaun smoke, and when it cleared, Mickey and Diane were gone, leaving the bewildered and terrified guards to their uncomfortable watch.

"Fine trick, lassie," Mickey remarked as he and Diane skittered across the field west of Dilnamarra. "How'd ye do it?"

Diane held up the flash for her Pentax. Mickey eyed it curiously, his keen ears picking up the faint whining sound as the batteries brought the flash back to the ready.

"Fine trick," the leprechaun said again, and he let it go at that, having no time, with the barn prison now in sight, to search out the details. "Are ye ready?"

Diane nodded. "We go in hard and furious," she said, paraphrasing the leprechaun's earlier plans. "Intimidation is our ally."

"Aye," Mickey agreed. "And a bit o' luck wouldn't hurt."

Diane looked at the sprite's grim expression.

"I'm hoping Prince Geldion's not about," Mickey explained. "I've seen a lot o' that one, and he's seen a lot o' me, and suren he'll be harder to fool!"

Diane skidded to a stop, as though she had just realized

the potential implications of failure. "Should we wait?" she asked nervously.

Mickey nodded ahead, to the dilapidated wooden barn and the many Connacht guards standing about it. "Yer Gary's in there," he grimly reminded her, and Diane said no more.

*   *   *   *   *

The door to the keep swung open and King Kinnemore rushed out, his expression curious. He looked from one guard to the other (and both silently agreed that they were not having the best of days!), then began sniffing the air.

"Who has been about?" Kinnemore demanded in his most commanding voice.

One of the guards cleared his throat; his knees went weak.

"No one, my King!" the other guard quickly put in, fearing the prospect of viewing the world through a pig's eyes. "Er, just some beggars—there are so many beggars in this filthy . . ."

"Silence!" Kinnemore demanded, and he sniffed the air again, his face crinkling as though he had smelled something utterly foul.

"Be on your best guard," he said to his men, as he continued to glance all about. "I smell leprechaun, and that can only mean trouble."

Now the two guards were in a terrible dilemma. They looked to each other, exchanging unspoken fears about their previous encounter. If that was a leprechaun's trick, then they had played into their enemy's hands. But if they told Kinnemore of the incident and that last visitor was truly Ceridwen, then the consequences would be horrid.

"Look alert!" Kinnemore roared, not understanding the silent exchange. He pushed between the men and back into his keep, slamming the door behind him.

"What are we to do?" one of the guards asked his companion.

The other guard hushed him, but had no answers. He didn't want to betray his King, but he didn't think he would look so good sporting a curly little tail.

There came the sound of a galloping horse, and a moment later Prince Geldion came charging through Dilnamarra, heading for the keep.

"That witch didn't say nothing about telling Geldion, now did she?" the first guard said slyly.

His companion smiled broadly, with sincere relief, thinking they had just been let off the hook.

*   *   *   *   *

Walking up the dirt path to the barn, by the stone skeletal remains of the farmhouse, the pair met a small horse-drawn cart coming the other way. A dirty soldier drove the cart, one of his shoulders heavily wrapped in soiled and bloody bandages. The man widened his eyes in shock at facing the illusionary Lady Ceridwen, and he coaxed his horse to a near stop and pulled far to the side.

"Geek, see what he is carrying," Diane instructed, and Mickey rushed over and climbed the side of the cart.

"Ooo, Lady!" the leprechaun exclaimed in perfect goblin voice. "He's gotses the armor and spear! And an elfs's armor, too!"

"Turn that cart around," Diane said without hesitation.

"But the King has ordered the armor to Dilnamarra Keep," the poor soldier weakly protested. He started to go on with the explanation, but his next words, with help from a ventriloquist leprechaun's trick, came out sounding like the croak of a bullfrog. Predictably, the man's eyes widened in shock.

"A frog, Lady?" Mickey happily squeaked. "Can Geek eatses the frog?"

"Patience, dear Geek," Diane replied coolly. "Let us see if this one is ready to obey." She hadn't even finished talking before the cart swung about on the road and rushed off the other way, back for the barn.

"Well done," Mickey congratulated. "Just a bit more o' the tricks, and we'll all run free."

Diane nodded determinedly, but in truth, she was actually enjoying this charade. She, and not Mickey, led the rest of the way to the barn, passing among the dozen or so bewildered soldiers with a confidence that defeated any forthcoming words of protest before they were ever uttered. She stalked right up to the man holding a spear across his chest as he blocked the barn door, and, with a simple swish of her head, sent him dancing aside.

He turned on her as she started to enter, but the camera flash fired in his face and he shrieked and stumbled backwards, tripping over his own feet and falling to the ground.

"Leave us," Diane ordered the two men inside the barn, and she did well to keep her voice firm and steady at the sight of Gary, Kelsey, and TinTamarra, obviously beaten. They stood in a line, their arms chained above them, their feet barely touching the floor. One of Gary's arms was cocked at a curious angle as it went up above his head, held fast by the chains, and was paining him greatly.

Diane's gaze never left her love, and she jumped when the barn door banged hard behind her, swung wide by the fleeing men. A bit of leprechaun magic brought the door swinging closed.

"So you're free," Gary Leger growled defiantly at Diane, which confused her for just an instant. "Give me back the spear, witch, and I'll put you back in your hold!"

Kelsey, standing beside Gary, eyed Ceridwen and Geek

curiously for a moment, then, to Gary's confusion, both he and his elfish companion began to laugh.

"Aye, none can see through tricks better'n the Tylwyth Teg," Mickey remarked, using his own voice.

Gary's eyes widened.

"Dear Geek," Diane said. "Do go out and have the good soldiers bring the equipment into the barn."

Gary, figuring it all out then, tried to laugh, but the attempt brought waves of stinging pain shooting through his shoulder. Diane was beside him immediately.

"Dislocated," she said after a quick inspection.

"Get away," Gary whispered, and Diane moved back just as the door opened again and Mickey entered, accompanied by three soldiers bearing piles of equipment.

"They broughtses the dwarfs's things, too," the illusionary goblin explained.

"The dwarf?" both Gary and Kelsey mouthed silently.

Diane was trying to figure out how she might convince the guards to leave the keys for the shackles as well, without making them too suspicious, but to her surprise, Mickey forcefully dismissed the men, practically chasing them out of the barn.

She met the leprechaun just inside the door. "We need to get the keys," she started to explain, but Mickey smiled wide, put a hand into a deep pocket, and produced a ring of keys.

Diane was back at Gary's side in a moment, carefully freeing him and helping him to a sitting position. She hugged him tightly, taking care not to press the dislocated shoulder.

"Get to Kelsey!" Mickey sharply reminded her. "We've not the time."

Diane fumbled with the ring, finally finding the right key, and Kelsey, too, was free. He rushed for the pile and quickly began donning his fine armor, while Diane went to the still-chained TinTamarra.

"Hurry," Mickey prodded her, but there were a score of keys on the chain and she fumbled about.

The leprechaun's declaration that they had little time rang painfully true then, as the barn door swung open.

"Out a bit early, aren't you, Ceridwen?" Prince Geldion remarked.

11 † Every Desperate Chance

The slender man looked ominous indeed, silhouetted in the barn door, his soldiers at his back and his worn traveling cloak billowing in the stiff breeze.

Gary forced himself to his feet, Diane holding him by his good arm until he regained his balance. Kelsey dropped his armor—he had no chance of donning it—but held fast to his fine sword, its tip gleaming furiously in the slanted rays of light coming through the open barn door.

"You will drop that weapon," Prince Geldion said to him matter-of-factly.

Kelsey didn't flinch.

"Kill the chained elf," the Prince calmly ordered, and the two soldiers closest to him, both holding crossbows, stepped up to the threshold and took aim at TinTamarra.

Gary, Kelsey, and Diane all cried out denials at the same time, but it was Mickey's voice, his magical voice, raised in an illusion outside the barn, that saved the chained elf. Several soldiers cried out warnings of the ambush, and the crossbowmen, seeing a host of fierce elves coming at them down the dirt road, instinctively loosed their bolts in that direction.

Mickey couldn't witness the flights of the quarrels from

inside the barn, of course, and so his illusionary force did not properly react, tipping the Prince and his men off to the truth of the matter.

"A leprechaun trick!" Geldion yelled above the general commotion. "My father said that a leprechaun was not long ago outside the keep. He said he smelled the foul thing!"

"I'm meaning to ask him how it is that he keeps doing that," Mickey replied, coming visible (and looking like a leprechaun again) and perched on a beam above where Gary had been shackled.

Before Geldion or his crossbowmen could react to the appearance of the sprite, Mickey waved his hand, and Cedric's mighty spear lifted from the pile near Kelsey and floated across the room, to Gary Leger's waiting grasp. Gary held the thing tentatively in his good hand, his other shoulder throbbing with pain.

Well met, young sprout! the spear emphatically greeted him.

"If you say so," Gary replied, a deep sense of hopelessness evident in his voice.

Geldion was fuming by this point. "Take them!" he cried. "Take them all, and if any die in the event, then so be it!"

The soldiers bristled about, but did not immediately advance. Some glanced to the side again, to the continuing, and unnerving, illusion of an elf host. Others looked to Mickey, their expressions revealing both greed and trepidation, and still others looked to Kelsey, and mostly to Gary, the spearwielder, supposedly the dragonslayer. He had been captured out on the field near the catapults, and had been taken easily, but on that occasion, Geldion and Kinnemore had more than ten times this number of soldiers surrounding him.

"Aye!" Mickey yelled unexpectedly, and unexpected, too, was his apparent agreement with Geldion's call. "Take them, as the foul Prince has spoken! Kill the wielder of Donigarten's own, he who slew Robert and saved yer precious town, and any other town in all the land. Take him now, this hero who's come from far off to show us the way!"

Whispers erupted among the soldiers; Geldion called again for a charge and drew out his dirk, and the men did come on—at least, most of them came on. There was some commotion near the back of the ranks, and before any Connacht men got near to Kelsey or Gary, the sound of steel against steel rang out, along with a call for "Sir Cedric!"

"That's me noble soldier," Mickey whispered, and the sprite faded away again to invisibility, honestly wondering how many tricks he had left. Diane's disguise went away as well, then, the leprechaun trying to conserve his magical energies—energies he had already depleted considerably.

Kelsey ran to the side, around a ladder and under the barn's loft. The closest two soldiers came fast in close pursuit. Kelsey dashed around a hay bale, turning to ambush the men, but they did not follow the course, stopping instead and rolling the bale aside.

As soon as the obstacle was out of the way, Kelsey charged ahead, right into the two, his sword slashing and hacking mightily as he tried to score a quick kill.

He got near one man's face, and struck the other's shield hard enough to break one of its straps and leave it hanging awkwardly on the man's arm. But he drew no blood in that initial flurry and the trained soldiers, well armored in thick leather jacks that were sewn with interlocking metallic rings, moved a few steps apart, measuring their strikes.

Diane rushed back to TinTamarra, still hanging limply from the shackles. She fumbled frantically with the key ring, going through several keys before finding the one that fit. She got it in place, but before she could turn it, she yelped in pain and moved away, the key still hanging in the elf's shackle, as a swordtip pinched her side.

Two soldiers stalked her, and she fell back against the wall, stumbled along it. The chained elf lifted his feet from the floor and kicked one of the men hard in the thigh. The soldier grimaced and turned, slapping the still-kicking legs aside with the flat of his sword. "Get the woman!" he told his companion, and he moved in on TinTamarra, punching hard with the hilt of his sword repeatedly.

Mickey exerted some magical energy then, trying to telekinetically push the key all the way in and turn it. To the leprechaun's dismay, though, the soldier coincidentally reached up and pulled the key free of the shackle, throwing it to the hay-strewn ground.

Not far away, Gary's only thought was to get back to Diane's side, to protect his love. But he too found two men facing him, circling him, feigning thrusts and swipes, one with a sword, the other with a club.

Gary jabbed with the sentient spear, waved it across in front of him frantically to keep the men at bay. As balanced as it was, however, the nine-foot-long weapon was unwieldy when used in one hand, and Gary spent a long time recovering from the momentum of each swing. Soon both the soldiers were smiling, then even laughing openly at Gary's feeble attempts to fend.

Across came the sword, and one of the men, instead of his typical retreat, stepped ahead, inside the slashing tip, dropped his own weapon, and caught the spearshaft in both hands.

"Here now, mighty dragonslayer," he taunted. "What are you to do now?"

The end had come, so Gary thought, as the other man lifted his club and advanced, while the man holding the spear gave a great tug. Gary held on stubbornly, though he didn't know what good that would do.

"What are you to do now?" the man chided a second time.

Cedric's spear answered for Gary.

Gary felt the telltale tingles an instant before the spear's magical energy gathered along the shaft and blasted into the man. His hair stood on end, and off he flew, across the barn, to crash into a fork and scythe and wheelbarrow. He came up on his elbows, staring incredulously, his hair still flying wildly and his whole body trembling from the jolt. Then his eyes crossed and he fell back to the ground, out of the fight.

The soldier's companion watched the flight in disbelief, but Gary wasted no time. As soon as the spearshaft was free of the man's grasp, Gary whipped it across, tucking it tight against his side for support. The powerful weapon easily cut through the remaining soldier's armor, gashing his side, and the man cried out in pain and fell back. He ran a hand over his wound, then stared at the blood in his palm.

"Son of a Bretaigne pig!" he roared at Gary. "You're to die for that one!" On he came fiercely, his club banging away at the blocking spear. Gary fought hard to keep the long weapon up between him and the man, not doubting the threat in the least, but each clubbing blow sent a shock wave of pain coursing up his side, and he feared that he would surely pass out.

Diane was in trouble, Gary was in trouble, and Kelsey was fighting two against one without any armor. Even worse, the fighting had ended back at the door, leaving two men dead, but Geldion remained, his dirk dripping blood and four more soldiers ready at his side.

And Mickey could do nothing to help any of those situations, for TinTamarra was in truly desperate straights.

The chained elf was helpless, and the soldier meant to kill him—that much the leprechaun knew for certain.

"Here now, laddie," Mickey called from his perch, and he came back into view. "When ye're done with him, ye think ye might take a try for me pot o' gold?"

The bait didn't work quite as the leprechaun had expected, for, though the man pushed away from the battered elf and lunged for him, he did so with his long sword leading. Mickey was nearly skewered. He skittered back along the beam as the soldier pressed onward, up on his tiptoes and poking eagerly. Stubbornly, the man leaped up and grabbed the beam with his free hand, determined to skewer the leprechaun, or to chase the troublesome sprite away.

How his hungry expression changed when the open shackles, shackles that had been used to hold Gary Leger, seemed to come to life, grabbing at his wrists, locking fast about his wrists!

The soldier fell from the beam to a hanging position (for he was not as tall as Gary). He held fast to his sword, but the weapon would do him little good with his hands so tightly bound.

"Where are ye to run, pretty lass?" the pursuing soldier asked Diane, and it took all her courage to steel her emotions against the implications of his lewd tone. More ominous did he seem, for his face was dirty, his beard several days old, and judging from the abundance of dried blood on his tunic, he had seen quite a bit of fighting at the front lines.

She continued her slide along the barn's back wall, hoping to get under the loft, where she might dart around some of the hay piled in there and get to Kelsey's side.

That plan disappeared in an instant, though, first as Diane

bumped into something hard protruding from the wall, breaking her momentum, and a moment later when she heard one of the newcomers to the fray call out to her pursuer.

"I've got her this way!" the second soldier declared.

The pursuing soldier stopped and held his arms out wide, spinning the heavy club in one hand. "You got nowhere to run," he chided. "So come along easy."

Diane glanced over her shoulder and saw the second man coming out from under the loft, smiling as wickedly as her pursuer. She glanced farther over her shoulder, to see what had stopped her retreat, to see what inanimate object had so deceived her.

A small windlass was set into the wall, running a rope to a pulley over the loft, and to a bale of hay, suspended near the loft's edge. Diane needed luck, couldn't stop to measure the angle or the timing. She grabbed at the windlass crank and pulled free its pin.

"What?" her closest pursuer asked as the rope spun out. The suspended hay bale dropped five feet to bonk the man's oblivious reinforcement on his thick head.

The man went down under the bale.

Kelsey worked magnificently, his sword darting so quickly from side to side and straight ahead that neither of the soldiers he faced scored as much as a nick on his unarmored body. But the few hits that Kelsey managed were not significant, his thrusts pulled short for fear of a counter, and the solid armor of his opponents absorbing most of what was left.

The elf went on undaunted, too angry at Geldion and Connacht to let the odds dismay him, too angry at Ceridwen and at the despoiling of Tir na n'Og to think of anything but his fury.

His sword banged hard off a shield, whipped back across to intercept a thrust from the other man, then snapped back again, this time slipping past the shield to deflect off the first man's shoulder.

Back the sword came again, and Kelsey stepped ahead, prodding and poking. The soldier worked desperately to counter, his sword flicking back and forth as he stumbled into a short retreat, but Kelsey would have had him cleanly had not his companion recovered from the stinging nick in time to come ahead and force the elf to relent.

Kelsey narrowed his golden eyes, his frustration finally beginning to build. These two were practiced swordsmen, and had fought side by side before, and Kelsey realized that he had little chance of scoring a fast kill.

The three were near to the loft's ladder then, Kelsey still forcing back his adversaries. For a moment, the elf thought himself tiring, thought that his vision was blurring. Then he understood. He held his smile and his hopes, and pressed the attack.

The soldier nearest the ladder reached for it, thinking to make use of its offered support and defensive advantages. His eyes deceived him, though, and he grabbed only air.

He lurched sidelong, through Mickey's illusionary ladder, to bang into the real one, a foot farther to the side.

On came Kelsey, before the man or his startled companion could recover. Wisely, the off-balance soldier twisted so that he would fall all the way around the ladder, farther from the elf's wicked reach, but Kelsey's move at him ended short anyway; it was only a feint.

The second man, sliding across to block the elf from his companion, widened his eyes in shock as Kelsey pulled up short and cut sharply to the side. The soldier got his sword up for a block, but Kelsey's blade was too swift, sliding past the parry to jab deeply into the soldier's belly. Kelsey did not have to fear a counter by the other man this time; there was nothing to stop his deadly progress.

Nothing but his expanding conscience.

The soldier fell away, grasping his wounded belly. He went to the floor, writhing, but very much alive, and totally confused as to why the fierce elf had pulled up short, had not finished him with a simple twist of the wrist, a simple change in the angle of the penetrating blade. In any case, the man was out of the fight.

Diane spun back, but her pursuer was upon her, his club right over his head and coming to bear. Again the woman's reaction was purely instinctual, a simple movement she had learned in basic self-defense classes her work office had offered a year before. She brought her open hands up in front of her and stepped ahead and to the side, pivoting on one foot and turning her upper body as she went. Predictably, her attacker shifted the angle of his descending club, but Diane's nearest hand was too close for the weapon to strike effectively. She caught it right above the man's hands and continued her turning retreat, absorbing the energy of the blow and putting the man off balance.

At the same time, Diane tugged fiercely at the club and stomped hard on the man's instep.

"You witch!" he protested through a groan. He was stumbling forward, and let go of the club with one hand, trying to grab onto something for support.

Diane reversed her tug into a hard shove, and the butt end of the club smacked the soldier in the face, crunching his nose.

"You witch!" he shouted again, sputtering with warm blood.

Diane pivoted back in to face him squarely, only a few inches away, and up came her knee.

And up the groaning man went on his tiptoes, his eyes crossing.

"You witch," he tried to say again, but suddenly he had no breath for the words.

Diane yanked the club free of his grasp and stepped back, thinking to hit him. But there was no need. His nose broken, his breath nowhere to be found, the soldier fell hard against the wall and to the ground, curling into a fetal position.

"Ooo lassie, well done!" Mickey, finished with his latest trick, congratulated her.

Diane looked at the leprechaun in disbelief. She looked to the club, as though it might offer some answers. Then she looked back to the crumpled soldier and shrugged, embarrassed and apologetic, and sincerely amazed at the effectiveness of her self-defense tactics. The situation was pressing, and far from won, but Diane made a mental note then and there that if she got out of Faerie alive, she would enroll in more martial arts classes.

Gary winced repeatedly as the soldier's club slammed hard against his spear, jolts of energy coursing along the vibrating shaft. He hardly thought he could hold out against this single adversary, yet when he looked past the man, he saw two others steadily advancing, their swords already bloody from their fight with the traitors at the barn door.

Gary had no time to even think about those two, though, as his current opponent kept up the pressure. A few more parries, a few more stinging hits, and a distracted Gary wondered where the man's reinforcements might be. Why hadn't they come in yet to strike at him?

He glanced over the soldier's shoulder once again—and saw, to his disbelief, that the two others were battling each other!

Gary thought about it only long enough to come to the

conclusion that Mickey was somehow involved. His relief did not last long, however, for his spear was slammed on the side, and wavered across his body. He instinctively reached for it with his other hand, and the sudden throbs of agony from his wounded shoulder nearly overwhelmed him.

Gary somehow managed to put the mighty spear back in line before his opponent, who was justifiably wary of the weapon, dared to advance. But Gary was still wobbly when the next hit came, and then the next, both clubbing straight down atop the spearshaft.

Gary hardly even realized that he was no longer holding the weapon. More from exhaustion and agony than from any set plan, Gary tumbled backwards and to the floor, his good hand coming to rest on the very end of the fallen spear's shaft.

Gary understood then his doom, realized that the soldier was fast advancing. He clutched the spear but, holding it so near to the back end, had no hope that he could even lift it.

Now, young sprout! the spear cried in his head.

A blast of energy came out from the sentient spear's tip, scorching the ground and blasting the tip upward. At the same moment, Gary pulled with all his strength, and to his amazement (for he had not seen the energy release), its huge tip rose up from the ground.

To the amazement of the approaching soldier, as well. The man caught the flying tip in the hip, the spear's hungry head biting hard through the meager padding of his armor, through his flesh and bone. He toppled to the side, screaming, taking the embedded spear from Gary's weakened grasp.

Gary was on the verge of unconsciousness, but he heard those pitiful screams, and surely they tore at his heart.

Diane heard them too, and was equally horrified. She wanted to run over to Gary, then, to offer support and to get some, but she had her own problems. The man she had clobbered with the bale was crawling out, more angry than hurt.

Fuming with unfocused rage, mad at all the violent world, Diane charged and leaped atop the rising man, bearing him to the ground. She whacked him with the club across the shoulder blades and told him to lie still, and when he did not, she whacked him again.

She hoped he would fall unconscious; she feared she would have to kill him.

Kelsey would have finished the remaining man at the ladder quickly, but then Prince Geldion was at the soldier's side and it was two against one once more.

The elf fell back in despair and went to the defensive, fending off the sword attacks and Geldion's surprisingly adept strikes with his long and nasty dirk. Even worse, Kelsey noticed that the other man, the one he had wounded in the belly, was starting to rise, and the elf wondered if his mercy had been misguided.

"He had me!" the wounded man cried breathlessly. "Liam, he had me. I tell ye!"

The man fighting beside Geldion eyed his wounded companion curiously, then turned his confused gaze upon Kelsey.

"Too many have died for an unlawful King!" the elf growled, seizing the moment and the possibility for further dissention in Geldion's shaky ranks. Kelsey had already seen enough evidence that the Connacht army's heart was not in this conquest to guess what his adversary might be thinking.

Geldion apparently understood the sentiments, too. "Fight on!" the Prince roared. "For the glory of King and country!"

"He had me dead, Liam!" the wounded man, staggering for the door, said again.

Liam looked to Geldion, his expression truly horrified. The Prince snarled in response and lashed out with his dirk—for Liam and not for Kelsey!

But Liam was quick enough to sidestep, and he ran off, grabbing his wounded friend and shuffling for the barn door.

Geldion threw a hundred empty threats at his retreating back.

"Now it is as it should be," Kelsey said grimly, stepping aside to momentarily break the melee. "You and I shall decide this, Prince Geldion, a course you began those weeks ago when you unlawfully tried to prevent my quest."

"Kinnemore is law!" Geldion spat. "And the Tylwyth Teg are outlaws all!" On came the bold Prince, his dirk slashing.

Kelsey hardly understood the tactic; with his longer yet equally wieldy weapon, he could easily defeat any of Geldion's thrusts.

But Geldion was not out of tricks. His dirk shot forward, and as Kelsey's sword moved to intercept, the Prince uttered an arcane phrase and the dirk elongated, its blade thickening, but holding still its razor edge. The angle of Kelsey's parrying sword was all wrong as the blade elongated, and the magical weapon slipped past the defense.

Kelsey threw his hips out behind him, scampering with quick steps to be out of the Prince's surprising reach. He only took a small hit on the thigh, but his troubles came from behind, where Geldion's last soldier stood ready, club in hand. The soldier had left the barn when the Prince had joined the fight with Kelsey, and had subsequently crawled back in through a side window, behind the hay at Kelsey's back.

His club connected solidly on Kelsey's lower back, and the elf straightened, his arms falling weakly at his sides.

Geldion waded in, fist balled over the hilt of his dirk-turned-sword, and slammed Kelsey in the face, and Kelsey toppled. Geldion's soldier hit the elf again, on the back of the neck as he rolled, and Kelsey knew no more.

"Mickey!" Diane's call was purely frantic. She moved beside Gary and helped him back to his feet. The realization of what had just happened stunned Diane; in the space of a few minutes so many men lay dead or wounded on the floor.

So many men, and Kelsey.

And Diane did not like the prospects now facing her as a grim Geldion and his soldier came out from under the loft and steadily advanced.

"Mickey?" she called again.

"I think he's gone," Gary answered. He nodded to the door. "The two that were fighting each other ran out— probably chasing Mickey."

"Well, imposter, what have you to say for your treason?" Geldion asked, drawing them from their private conversation.

"Nothing, to you," Gary spat back.

"But I am judge and jury," Geldion calmly explained. With no response apparently forthcoming, the Prince began to laugh aloud, a wicked laugh indeed.

He stopped abruptly, studying Gary's wounds. "See to the woman," he told his soldier. "I will settle the lie of the spearwielder, the imposter hero who claims the defeat of the dragon Robert."

"I did kill Robert," Gary insisted.

Geldion laughed again. "Then a mere Prince should pose no difficulty for you."

Driven by a sense of honor, Gary nudged Diane aside. She stared at him, somewhat disappointed, and thinking his honor misplaced. He was still holding the long spear in only one hand, his other arm too weak to do much more than help guide the weapon's swipes.

He was surely going to get himself killed, Diane decided, but she couldn't spend too much time thinking about that now, not with the club-wielder, a powerfully built man, his smile more filled by gaps than stained teeth, steadily approaching.

She readied her own club, putting her feet wide apart, feeling her balance. In stalked the soldier, casually snapping off a series of blows. Diane blocked and responded in kind. Each hit sent a shock wave along her arms, but she stubbornly held on, her confidence returning, her survival instincts washing away her fears.

But then the man's club hit hers down low, near the handle, and hit, too, Diane's lead hand. Her fingers went strangely numb, a wave of pain rolled up her arm, and the man's next solid hit knocked the club from her hand.

And he was still smiling wickedly.

Geldion showed Gary, and that legendary spear, great respect for the early passes of their fight. The Prince could see the fatigue and the pain in Gary's eyes and in his every movement, and the dislocated shoulder was evident enough.

Geldion did not think that there could be much power behind the spear pokes and swipes, but he had no intention of learning the truth firsthand—obviously this badly wounded man had found enough power to knock two of Geldion's men from the fight already. So the Prince would play defensive, would bide his time and let exhaustion force that heavy speartip to the ground.

Geldion's logic was obvious to Gary as well, and he tried to conserve his energy as much as possible. But that was no easy task with Diane in a fight against a trained soldier barely twenty feet away.

"Shall you watch her die?" Geldion asked, smiling wickedly.

Gary saw the bait for what it was—but could not ignore the image Geldion's words had conjured in his mind. He roared in protest and started ahead.

No, young sprout! came the sobering cry in his head.

Geldion sidestepped the awkward attack and slapped at the speartip, knocking it farther aside. Gary was already backpedaling, though, and the Prince got no clear strike.

"Easy," Gary whispered over and over to himself. He needed to keep his control.

He looked over his shoulder, though, ready to explode, when Diane cried out.

She took the only course left open to her.

She ran.

Diane cut around a hay bale, sensed her enemy's movement and reversed direction, coming back out the same side as the soldier circled the other way. He was still on her heels, though, and his swishing club clicked off her ankle and nearly tripped her up.

"Mickey!" she called, but the leprechaun was nowhere about. She went under the loft, cut around another bale, and came right back out. She hopped over the man she had clobbered with the hay bale and nearly tripped again as the semiconscious soldier grabbed at her ankle.

Off balance, head low, she cut a straight line across the barn, past the man Mickey had tricked into the shackles, past the beaten TinTamarra, hanging limp at the end of his chains. The eager Connacht soldier came in close pursuit, ignoring the pleas of his trapped comrade, pushing the hanging elf roughly aside.

He did not notice that TinTamarra was watching him under half-closed eyelids, and his surprise was complete when the elf's legs came up suddenly and wrapped about his neck, pulling him off balance.

Diane heard the commotion and dared to look back—just in time to see the soldier snap his club up above his head for a solid hit on TinTamarra's chest. Still the stubborn elf held on, and the man hit him again, and lowered his club to begin a third strike.

Diane barreled into the soldier, wrapping him in a tight bear hug, pinning the club down low. The soldier and Diane pitched right over, but held fast in the grasp of the elf's strong legs, they did not fall all the way to the floor. They hung there, weirdly, the soldier's neck twisted and his air cut off.

Geldion saw the turn of events by the shackles and pressed furiously, his magical dirk/sword throwing sparks whenever it struck the metal tip of Cedric's spear.

Gary matched the Prince's intensity, though the effort pained him greatly. He swiped with the spear, accepting the jolt as Geldion's sword connected, and when the Prince sidestepped one thrust and rushed in, Gary promptly retreated, turning as he went.

He crashed into one of the barn's supporting beams.

Gary, and Geldion too, heard the crack as Gary's shoulder popped back into place. Nausea and agony swept over the man; he thought he saw Diane, entangled with the soldier and the hanging elf. But the dazed Gary couldn't be sure of what he saw at that awful moment.

He thought the floor was up in his face, thought one of the barn's walls was falling outward.

He heard the ring as Geldion's sword slashed the speartip once again, saw the sparks igniting.

But they, too, were tilted weirdly, falling and spinning like all the world.

*   *   *

The man went limp under her. TinTamarra, his energy expended, let go, and Diane pulled herself from the pile. She knew that Gary was in trouble, knew that she had to help, and so she got right back to her feet and turned about, nursing her swollen hand but stubbornly searching for a weapon.

The soldier's club was not far away, but Diane found suddenly that she had no time to even go for it. Geldion's sword slashed across, connecting solidly on the shaft of Cedric's spear. The weapon flew out wide, out of Gary's grasp. He caught it with his other hand, winced with the shock of pain, then grabbed it again.

But his grip was reversed, his defensive posture shattered, and Geldion, sword up high, surely had him.

"Gary!" Diane cried, running desperately, reaching into the belt pouch Mickey had given back to her in Tir na n'Og, looking for anything that might save the moment.

Geldion snapped his head around, shifted as though he would strike Diane down first. His sword remained up high, at the ready, and Diane's hand came up as well—to block, the Prince figured.

She pushed a little button on the strange black box she held, and there came a flash, the likes of which the startled Prince Geldion had never before witnessed. Blinded and thinking some evil sorcery had befallen him, Geldion stumbled backwards, and Diane, ever the opportunist, rushed into him, both her hands locking desperately on his weapon arm.

Geldion caught his balance quickly and pushed back, whipping his arm about to pull it loose. He grabbed a handful of Diane's thick hair and tugged viciously.

"Gary!"

Diane's cry seemed distant, but her husband did not miss

its intensity. He fought through the nausea and the dizziness, forced his eyes to focus, and jabbed straight out with the butt of the spear, popping the Prince in the side of the head and sending him and Diane tumbling to the ground.

Diane hung on like a pit bull, and to her surprise, Geldion let go of his sword, which immediately reverted to its dirk form. She understood when she looked up—to see Gary standing over the man, speartip pressed to Geldion's throat.

12 † As the Gentle Rain from Heaven

Diane had never seen Gary's face so twisted with rage. He meant to finish Geldion—she knew that he meant to plunge the spear deep into the helpless Prince's throat.

"The quality of mercy is not strained," she said suddenly, grabbing at a desperate thought.

Gary glanced sidelong at the unexpected remark, and his sudden confusion halted his progress. A small line of blood began to run from the side of the penetrating speartip. "Shakespeare?" he whispered incredulously.

"It droppeth as the gentle rain from heaven," Diane stubbornly went on, closing her eyes and trying to remember the lines. "Upon the place beneath: it is twice blest; it blesseth him that gives and him that takes." She looked up and relaxed a bit, seeing that Gary had eased his grip on the spear.

"'Tis mightiest in the mightiest!" came a cry from the door. All three, Gary, Diane, and even Geldion, turned to see Mickey enter, disheveled and banging the dust from his tam-o'-shanter. "And suren it becomes the throned monarch better than his crown." The leprechaun paused to take in the scene, then nodded in satisfaction. "Yer father might be taking a tip from the Bard," he remarked to Geldion.

"The Bard?" Diane whispered, trying to sort through the illogic. She turned a confused glance on Gary. "How does he know about Shakespeare?"

Gary mulled it over for a moment, then chuckled aloud, remembering what Mickey had told him about others of his world passing over into Faerie. Mickey had claimed that J.R.R. Tolkien had obviously come over, else where would he have learned so wondrous a tale as *The Hobbit*? Could it be that some of Shakespeare's work, possibly something like *A Midsummer's Night Dream* was more than an imaginative piece of fiction?

"Don't ask," Gary said to Diane, remembering that they had more important matters to tend to. Gary looked fearfully to the area under the loft, where Kelsey had struggled to prop himself up on his elbows. Never relinquishing the trapping pressure of the spear on the Prince, Gary continued his scan, all about and back to the door, where Mickey was straightening his disheveled and dusty clothes.

"Where have you been?" the man demanded.

"Them two was better at seeing through things than I figured them to be," the leprechaun explained casually.

"And where are they now?"

"One's down the well, th'other's running back for Dilnamarra," Mickey replied. "And I'm thinking that we should be on our way."

By this point, Diane had retrieved the key and let down the wounded TinTamarra.

"What are ye meaning to do with him?" Mickey asked Gary, indicating the Prince.

"I guess he's coming with us," Gary replied.

"Kill him," came a reply from under the loft. Kelsey limped out, one hand pressing tight against his lower back. "Geldion would have shown us no mercy, and deserves none! We are wounded and weary, and will not have an easy time of getting back to Tir na n'Og with him in tow."

It was truly a horrible moment for Gary Leger. Kelsey's logic was solid, but Gary couldn't imagine finishing off the helpless Prince. Yet what might Gary do if Kelsey decided to walk over and cut Geldion down? He looked down to Diane, whose expression was unyielding.

"Don't you dare," she warned.

Gary growled in frustration, retracted the spear, and roughly reached down and pulled the much smaller Geldion to his feet. "Not a bit of trouble from you," Gary snarled into the Prince's face.

Gary looked over to see Kelsey glaring at him. The elf said nothing, though, just moved to the pile of equipment and once again began donning his suit of mail.

Gary pushed the Prince past him, prodding him for the door, but suddenly Kelsey was there, his sword snapping to a stop just an inch from Geldion's already bleeding throat.

"No!" Diane and Gary said together, thinking that Kelsey would kill the man.

In response, Kelsey held up a curious bandolier, strung one end to the other with hammers.

"Geno," Gary whispered, recognizing the belt.

"Where is the dwarf?" Kelsey demanded.

Geldion smirked as though he had no idea of what Kelsey might be talking about.

Kelsey belted him across the face.

"I ask you only one more time," Kelsey said sternly, his voice deathly even and controlled. "I will have an answer, or I will have your head."

"When did the Buldrefolk become the concern of the Tylwyth . . ." Geldion began obstinately, but his words ended in a groan as Kelsey slugged him again.

"Stop it!" Diane demanded, coming up beside them,

dragging TinTamarra, who was leaning heavily on her shoulder.

Gary held her back, knowing Kelsey better than she. He understood the unlikely friendship that had developed between the elf and Geno, and knew that neither he nor Diane could stop Kelsey in this matter. Geldion would speak, or Kelsey would kill him.

The Prince stared long and hard into Kelsey's golden eyes, matching the elf's intensity. Then Geldion nodded to the side, to the area under the loft. "In a hole," he spat. "Where dwarfs belong."

Kelsey moved under the loft and soon found the wooden slats of a trap door, pinned under a huge cask of water. With great effort, the elf picked the cask up on its edge and rolled it aside—and found that the trap door had been chained and padlocked three different ways. Not waiting to see if Geldion could be coerced into producing any keys, Kelsey called to Gary to give him the mighty spear. Diane immediately had a sword poised near the Prince, and with a nod to her, Gary moved under the loft and handed over the spear. Three hits later, all the chains were free.

Gary took note of the elf's frantic movements, further confirmation of the bond that had been forged between Kelsey and the surly dwarf. Kelsey grabbed the rope for the trap door and took a deep breath to steady himself—like Gary, he feared that Geno would be in tough shape, perhaps even already dead.

Up came the door—Geno was nowhere to be seen.

Kelsey dove down to the floor for a closer look, but the pit was only a few feet deep and a few feet wide, and encased in bare and solid stone. A bit of water had gathered at the bottom of the hole, but it was only an inch or two deep, and concealing nothing but more stone.

"He is not in here!" Kelsey growled at Geldion.

The Prince seemed honestly perplexed. "Impossible," he protested. "The pit is solid stone."

Kelsey and Geldion kept up their banter, accusations flying fast from the angry elf. Gary joined in as well, even promising Geldion severe consequences if he did not produce the dwarf.

Mickey was not so judgmental, though. More wise in the ways of the Buldrefolk than the others, and more wise in their tricks, Mickey believed that Geldion's incredulity was sincere. He calmly walked under the loft and pushed past Gary and Kelsey, peering knowingly into the hole.

"Come along, Geno," he called softly, tap-tapping the stone along the pit's side with his huge pipe. "We've not the time for games." Mickey's face brightened an instant later, when he noticed a small crack running along the wall of the pit. He tapped his pipe in that spot and called for the dwarf again.

For a moment, nothing happened, and then suddenly the ground began trembling so violently that Gary thought they were in the midst of an earthquake. Across the barn, near the opposite wall, the flooring planks broke apart and the earth erupted—and out hopped Geno, covered in dirt, his wrists and ankles tightly and heavily shackled, though he had bitten through one of the wrist chains and had done considerable damage to the other.

He shook his head, launching a spray of sand and roots, and spat out a stream of munched pebbles.

Then he spotted Geldion, and no chains in all the world could have held him back. He half ran, half hopped across the barn, bearing down on Diane. To her credit, she held her ground until the very last moment, then fell aside. Geno leaped high into the air, tucked his stubby legs under him, and slammed down atop the Prince.

Kelsey was on him in an instant, Gary and Diane helping

as much as possible. The elf finally wrestled Geno off
Geldion, a break in the action long enough for Gary to
reason with the dwarf that Geldion would make a valuable
prisoner.

Geno stood trembling and staring at the battered Prince,
on the very edge of an explosion. "Get these off," he
growled, lifting his shackles toward Geldion.

The obstinate Prince snorted and turned away.

Geno rolled his tongue around in his mouth, digging out
another pebble he had pinched between his cheek and gum.
He spat it with the power of a high-end BB gun and it
bounced off the back of Geldion's head, nearly laying the
Prince out flat.

"I told you to get these off," Geno said as the outraged
Geldion spun about. "Now do it," the dwarf warned, "or my
next spit-stone will be a piece of your crunched skull."

Not a person in the room doubted Geno's claim.

It was Mickey who relieved the tension, the leprechaun,
an expert lock-picker if ever there was one, rushing over and
quickly freeing the dwarf of the shackles.

"Don't ye kill him," Mickey whispered to Geno as he
worked the locks. "He's the treasure that'll stop the war."

Kelsey apparently did not agree. As Mickey freed the
dwarf, the elf stalked over to Geldion, his sword dangerously close to the Prince's neck.

"Easy, Kelsey," Gary remarked. "We need him."

Kelsey turned to Gary, his expression both angry and
incredulous. "You have taken command of the actions of the
Tylwyth Teg?" the elf asked.

Gary thought the question utterly stupid, and was too
surprised by it to answer.

"You have become quite the hero," Kelsey remarked.

Gary winced and Kelsey turned away.

"I do all right," Gary answered suddenly, to Kelsey's

surprise, and to his own. The elf stopped but did not give Gary the consideration of turning to face him squarely. "I've more than my share of luck and better friends than any man deserves!" Gary answered anyway.

Kelsey remained silent and still for a moment, then walked away. Gary didn't know what to think. He understood that Kelsey was frustrated and afraid—afraid for Tir na n'Og and all his world.

Diane was at Gary's side then, her arm in his, lending him support.

By the time they had donned their armor and left the barn, two more of the Connacht soldiers were up and in tow. Kelsey forced Geldion to carry the wounded TinTamarra, and Geno walked only a stride behind the Prince, telling him how much he liked the Tylwyth Teg, and promising him all sorts of pain if the elf should die.

Kelsey led them to the west, farther from Dilnamarra and farther from Tir na n'Og. They were a sorry-looking troupe, to be sure, even though Gary's shoulder, knocked back into place during the battle, was already feeling somewhat stronger. They encountered only one Connacht patrol, a group of five, who surrendered at Geldion's command (since Geno was nibbling on the Prince's ear at the time).

That night, they camped along a hedgerow. The Connacht soldiers were put in a line, with grim Kelsey and TinTamarra, who, like Gary, was fast recovering, walking a tight guard. Geldion was not with them, though. He was farther along the makeshift encampment, speaking with Diane, while Gary, Mickey, and Geno lay back on the grass not far away, staring at the stars and the occasional rushing cloud.

More than once, Kelsey came up near to the group and shot a dangerous glare Geldion's way. It was obvious to the others that the elf would have preferred to leave the Prince dead in the barn.

"Not a good time," Mickey remarked after one of Kelsey's visits, in effect apologizing for Kelsey's behavior.

"I thought he wanted me here," Gary asked.

"So he did, and does," Mickey replied. "He's just afraid, lad, and with good cause."

"What has she to say to that Prince?" Geno put in, motioning to Diane and Geldion. The dwarf had been cordial to Diane, and actually glad to see Gary again, and so his words did not sound so much like an accusation.

"She's just looking for information," Gary replied.

"Aye, that one's a thinker," Mickey agreed. "Suren she's asked me more in the short time I've known her than yerself has asked in all yer three visits to Faerie!"

"She's your wife," Geno grumbled. "She cannot be too smart."

Gary elbowed him hard in the ribs, but if the stonelike dwarf felt it at all, he didn't show it.

"I been meaning to ask ye," Mickey put in. "I heared ye calling me many the time. What made ye want to come back so badly? I mean, I've heared yer call before, now and again, but the last day, ye just wouldn't stop."

Gary, still rubbing his elbow from the contact with the dwarf, wondered how he might explain his emotional turmoil, how he might tell them about the loss of his father and his frustrations with Real-earth. These two had played such an important role in Faerie, how might Gary convey to them his sense of utter helplessness to change the bad things, in his own life and in the world around him?

As it turned out, Gary didn't have to say much. As soon as he told about his dad, both Mickey and, unexpectedly, Geno were honestly sympathetic. Geno even told the story of how he had lost his own father—to a mountain troll and an avalanche.

"But being here won't get ye away from the grief, lad,"

Mickey was quick to warn. "Not-a-thing can get ye from the grief."

Gary nodded, but he wasn't so sure that he agreed. He felt better just being in Faerie, despite the desperate situation surrounding him. He felt again like he was part of something larger than himself, like his potential death, or even the death of his father, was, after all, a very small part of a grander scheme. Far from making him feel insignificant, though, that knowledge made Gary feel invulnerable.

He lay quiet, looking at the enchanting canopy of Faerie's nighttime sky, looking at the eternal stars and the endless, rushing clouds.

And feeling as though he was truly a part of them.

13 † Worth a Thousand Words

The group got back into Tir na n'Og the next day, entering the forest far from the battle lines. All through that morning's hike, there seemed to be a measure of tension growing between Kelsey and TinTamarra. More than once, Gary saw TinTamarra turn an angry glare Kelsey's way, though it didn't seem to Gary as though Kelsey had noticed. Or at least, if the elf-lord did notice, he was feigning disinterest.

TinTamarra would not let go of that glare, though, and finally, with the safety of the thick trees all about them, the tension burst.

"You will take the prisoners, except for Prince Geldion, to the holding area, where their wounds might be tended," Kelsey informed TinTamarra. It seemed a perfectly reasonable command, spoken with all respect.

"And what, then, of the Prince?" TinTamarra retorted, his lips thin with anger.

Kelsey appeared honestly caught off guard by the sharp retort. He spent a long moment scrutinizing his fellow elf before answering. "He remains with me until I can decide what worth he might prove," he said.

"You make many decisions on your own, Kelsenellenelvial," TinTamarra replied.

"To what do you refer?" Kelsey asked, still calm, still of a mind to defuse the situation. The last thing the besieged Tylwyth Teg needed now was dissention in their ranks.

TinTamarra turned his sour expression alternately on all the prisoners, then settled it back on Kelsey. "And we left more wounded humans in the barn," he said, as though that should explain everything.

"They could not travel," Kelsey answered, missing the point.

"I think he's meaning that ye should have killed the men," Mickey interjected.

TinTamarra said nothing, but his expression confirmed Mickey's guess readily enough. To the side, the prisoners shuffled uneasily, to a man wondering if their fate suddenly hung precariously in the balance.

"That's stupid," Diane was quick to put in, pushing her way past Gary as he, more familiar with the stern and dangerous demeanor of the proud Tylwyth Teg, tried futilely to hush her.

"Why would you kill wounded men?" Diane insisted, moving near TinTamarra—too near, by Gary's estimate. He went right along beside her, though, and immediately decided that if TinTamarra lifted a weapon against her, the elf would feel the bite of Donigarten's spear. Gary wasn't confident, however. The Tylwyth Teg were fast with their blades, and he sincerely feared that any counterstrike he made would be in revenge for the murder of his wife.

Still, the stubborn woman pressed on, fearless, oblivious.

"Are you no more than a murderer?" she said, and even Kelsey, who was on her side in this argument, clenched his fist.

Geno, standing watch over the prisoners, chuckled softly, thinking that the trembling elf was about to knock the woman to the ground.

"Easy, lass," Mickey implored. TinTamarra remained silent—Gary pictured a fuse burning short atop his raven-black hair.

Diane started to speak again, but Gary hooked her with his arm and forced her away, loudly interrupting every sentence she began.

"She speaks the part of the fool," TinTamarra remarked.

"The fool that saved your life," Kelsey quickly reminded him.

TinTamarra's glare fell full over the elf-lord. "They are enemies of the wood," he said. "We will waste many warriors, having need to stand guard over the growing number of prisoners."

"What would you have us do?" Kelsey asked.

"As we always have done to enemies of the wood," TinTamarra replied grimly.

"Then we would be killing potential allies," Kelsey argued. He knew that the elf was not sharing his sympathies for the humans caught under King Kinnemore's unlawful rule, and so he tried to reach his kin on a more pragmatic level. "Many have come over to fight beside us, to fight beside the spearwielder," he reasoned. "Kinnemore's hold is not so tight, or perhaps he grasps at his army too tightly, squeezing men through his fingers. We have found allies among his ranks—was it not two Connacht soldiers who led us to the catapults? They died for our . . ."

"Only one died," Mickey corrected. Both Kelsey and TinTamarra looked at the leprechaun curiously.

"I went along for the other's ride," Mickey explained. "He got a bit o' shaking, that's all. And he's in the forest now, talking to his kin, bringing more to the spearwielder's— and the Tylwyth Teg's—side. Another week o' fighting and I'm thinking that ye'll have as many men guarding Tir na n'Og's borders as elfs."

With that said, Mickey hopped off to join Gary and Diane, who had moved some distance away. TinTamarra had no reply, to Mickey or to Kelsey.

"Bitter times," Kelsey remarked, trying to alleviate his honorable companion's obvious embarrassment. "But we must not forget who we are, and why ours is the just cause. Kinnemore will call for truce soon, by my guess. He is losing soldiers and now"—Kelsey glanced over at Geldion, looking perfectly miserable as he sat among the handful of prisoners—"he has lost his son."

TinTamarra nodded and bowed, a sign of concession, then turned towards Geno and the prisoners. Kelsey stood quietly, musing over his last words. He did indeed believe that King Kinnemore would soon call for a truce, and that truce would undoubtedly spare Tir na n'Og the scars of further war. Ceridwen was not so convinced that she could ever conquer the proud Tylwyth Teg, Kelsey knew, and so she would likely be glad just to have them out of her army's way.

For Tir na n'Og and the Tylwyth Teg, the prospects seemed bright. But Kelsey, with his increasingly worldly view, his growing compassion for those who were not of his race, truly feared that the elders of Tir na n'Og would accept that truce.

*   *   *   *   *

"I always wanted to meet a Prince," Diane said disarmingly. She sat down in the clover next to Geldion, who pointedly shifted and looked away.

"I've brought some food," Diane explained and held forth a bowl of porridge.

Despite his desire to remain aloof to his captors, Geldion could not ignore the offering. He hadn't eaten in nearly a day, and his stomach was surely grumbling.

Shortly after noon, the group had encountered another

band of Tylwyth Teg and had separated, TinTamarra and the common prisoners going with the elfs, while Kelsey led the others on a more southerly route, towards the battlefield and the elfish leaders. The group had separated again late in the afternoon, with Kelsey, Mickey, and Gary leaving Geno, Diane, and the Prince in a clover-filled meadow, lined by a row of tall and thick pines. Twilight was upon them now, the slanting rays turning all the clover orange and casting long shadows of the western trees across the field.

"You took the food, so you have to talk with me," Diane said cheerily. Geldion kept his face low, to the bowl of porridge, but his beady dark eyes turned up to regard her from under furrowed brows.

"Don't waste your breath," Geno, a short distance away, offered to Diane. "That one has little to say that is worth hearing."

Diane thought differently. She dropped her hand into her belt pouch, feeling the snugly packed cameras and the quite remarkable picture she had slipped between them.

"What's it like to be a Prince?" she asked.

"What is it like to be a pestering wench?" Geldion answered coldly. Behind him, Geno grunted and hopped to his feet, hammers ready in his hands. But Diane scowled and waved the fiery dwarf back.

"Fair enough," she conceded to Geldion. "I was just curious about your father and your life in Connacht."

Again Geldion eyed her, but he seemed a bit less sure of himself.

"He is the King, after all," Diane went on casually, glancing all about (though in truth, her focus ever remained the Prince). "And from what I've heard, he plans to rule all the world. I though it would be wise to learn more about this man."

Geldion went back to his porridge.

"And more about his son," Diane went on slyly. "This Prince who would one day be King."

"Not while he's sitting chained in an elfish forest," Geno was happy to put in. Geldion turned a glare on the dwarf, and Diane did too, not appreciating the interruption. There was a method to the woman's remarks, a design so that she might measure Geldion's responses, whether he answered verbally or not.

"What kind of a King will Geldion be?" she asked.

The Prince snorted incredulously, and Diane quieted, considering the reaction. Was Geldion brushing off her question because he believed that he owed her, the simple pestering wench, no explanation? Or did the concept of him being King at all seem preposterous to him?

"Will he be a kind man, who cares for the needs of his subjects?" Diane pressed. "Or will he . . ."

Geldion smacked his half-empty bowl of porridge away, stopping the woman in midsentence. He eyed Diane contemptuously for a moment, then pointedly turned away.

His anger told her that her second line of reasoning was on target. Geldion did not believe that he would ever be King. But why? Diane wondered. The Tylwyth Teg would not kill him—he knew that. They would bargain with him and return him to Kinnemore when the deal was struck.

Then it was Geldion's father who would stop him, Diane realized, and she dropped her hand to that telling picture once again.

Across the way, Geno snorted loudly. "King of what?" the dwarf demanded, moving near the fuming Prince. "King of a burned-out town that was once called Connacht? For that is all that will remain when the peoples of the land rise in unison against Kinnemore!"

The dwarf's boast brought Geldion out of his silent brooding.

"Kinnemore will rule the land!" he proclaimed. "And all the Buldrefolk will be slain, or driven deep into their filthy mountain holes!"

Diane thought that Geno would surely beat the man down, but the dwarf only blew away Geldion's threat with a simple and heartfelt burst of laughter.

"Kinnemore will rule the land," Geldion grimly said again.

Geno huffed. "You are to feel the same grief as Gary Leger," he replied, and he snapped his fingers (which sounded somewhat like the report of a heavy-caliber rifle) and walked away, laughing with every step.

Geldion hurled no retorts at the dwarf's back. In the course of conversation over that last couple of days, he had overheard talk of Gary's loss, and so he understood what Geno had just implied.

It struck Diane as more than a little curious that the Prince did not seem bothered at all by the dwarf's grim prediction.

*   *   *   *   *

Gary, Kelsey, and Mickey returned to the small meadow the next morning. The forest was calm this day; for the first time since the taking of Dilnamarra, Tir na n'Og had not wakened to the sounds of battle. Diane took that as a good sign, as did Geno, and even Geldion seemed more comfortable.

Diane thought that the Prince appeared relieved by the apparent turn of events, and her insight was confirmed an instant after Kelsey made his announcement.

"The King will not bargain for the life of his son," the elf explained.

Geldion's expression told Diane so very much. He was crestfallen, certainly, but not surprised. Not surprised! With everything else Diane had confirmed, by Gary's tales of Ceridwen, by her own talks with Mickey and with Geldion, and by the picture in her pouch, Diane nodded her understanding and believed that all the pieces of this puzzle had fallen neatly into place.

"Then why is the forest quiet?" Gary asked Kelsey.

"The envoys have just recently returned," the elf-lord explained. "Kinnemore will not bargain for the life of his son," Kelsey said again, pointedly looking wounded Geldion's way, "but he may yet bargain. The potential for loss has grown for King Kinnemore. His army is bogged down at the edge of the forest. His fires scar the trees, but do little damage when countered by the magics of the elfish wizards. And he is losing his soldiers, by the sword and by their consciences."

Kelsey's smile was smug indeed when he looked again to Geldion, the Prince looking perfectly miserable. "Every one of the men who were brought into the forest at your side has sworn fealty to Tir na n'Og and the Tylwyth Teg. Many of my people have been slain, yet our ranks are larger now than when the conflict began. Can your father make the same boast?"

Geldion turned away, and Diane winced in sympathy.

"So the forest is quiet," Kelsey finished. "And King Kinnemore considers the options for truce."

Geno kicked hard at a small stone—which was really a large stone buried deep in the turf. The depth of the dwarf's anger became quite obvious as the rock overturned, popping up from the ground.

Kelsey understood the source of that anger. "The options presented to Kinnemore call for a complete cessation," he assured Geno. "The Tylwyth Teg have not forsaken the eastern lands. We have not forgotten Braemar and Drochit, nor the Buldrefolk of Dvergamal, nor the gnomes of Gondabuggan."

Geno nodded. He knew the Tylwyth Teg well enough,

and knew Kelsey well enough, to realize that the inclusion of anybody outside of Tir na n'Og's precious borders in the bargaining was Kelsey's doing. But though Geno truly appreciated the loyalty of Kelsey, he also understood that the Tylwyth Teg would likely agree to Kinnemore's counteroffer, a set of terms that did not extend beyond the borders of the elfs' precious forest home. The Tylwyth Teg would accept any truce that saved Tir na n'Og, even at the price of the eastern lands.

Kelsey was smiling, trying to assure his dwarfish friend, but that smile was strained, for the elf, too, could not deny the aloof attitude of his people.

To Diane's relief, the others pretty much left Geldion alone after that. She feared that surely Geno might bring the Prince harm, or that, since his father would not bargain for him, Kelsey would send him away with the other prisoners. Certainly the elf had ample opportunity. Bands of the Tylwyth Teg, repositioning their forces as they awaited Kinnemore's reply, were all about the shadowy borders of the meadow, and more than one group came in to speak with Gary, the spearwielder.

Diane took little note of them, though. She again spent her time with Geldion, and noticed Gary's concerned, and perhaps jealous, glance her way more than once.

She was back with her four companions for lunch. Kelsey continued to be optimistic, as did Gary, but Mickey remained quiet (for a leprechaun) and Geno did not seem convinced that the skies of Faerie would soon brighten.

As soon as the opportunity presented itself, Diane turned the topic of conversation to Ceridwen. Kelsey didn't want to talk about the witch, Geno didn't want to talk about anything, but Gary, knowing his wife well enough to understand that she thought she was on to something important, was quickly becoming intrigued, and Mickey was willing to talk.

"I heard that she could change herself into a raven," Diane said. "And a snake."

"And anything else she's a mind to change herself into," Mickey assured her. "Not so much a trick to one of Ceridwen's powers. Ye've seen the elfish weather-magic fighting Kinnemore's fires and ye've seen a bit o' me own illusions . . ."

"She was a bit o' yer own illusions," Gary interjected, mimicking the leprechaun's thick accent, and drawing a much-needed smile from both Diane and Mickey.

"But ye should know that Ceridwen's powers are beyond both those magics together," Mickey continued, his smile vanished and his voice suddenly grave. "She's a wicked one, and not all the magic-spinners of Faerie together could break one o' her spells."

Diane nodded knowingly.

"We have heard enough of the witch," Kelsey said suddenly, sternly. All three, and Geno too, turned to him, wondering what had prompted his outburst. Kelsey started to elaborate, started to explain that talk of Ceridwen only destroyed what little morale was left, but stubborn Diane cut him short.

"Not so," she insisted. "We have not heard enough of the witch. Ceridwen, and not Kinnemore, is the key to our problems, and if I'm going to help at all, I'll need to know everything I can about her. Know your enemies—that is the greatest weapon in any war!"

Kelsey's amazed expression fast shifted into one of respect.

"She's adjusting well, lad," Mickey remarked to Gary.

"She's been hearing about Faerie for more than seven

years," Gary, obviously proud of his strong wife, replied. "And she believed my stories all along."

"Sure I did," Diane added with more than a little sarcasm.

They spent the next hour discussing Ceridwen, without any further complaints from Kelsey. Then the meal was finished, and Kelsey asked Geno to accompany him to the area where the elfish elders would be gathered. It was more than a simple courtesy, Geno realized; Kelsey wanted him in plain sight of the elders if and when Kinnemore's response came. The decisions of the Tylwyth Teg had implications far beyond Tir na n'Og's borders, and Kelsey wanted his elders to understand the weight of that decision fully, wanted them to appreciate the allies they might soon abandon.

"Wait," Diane bade them as they rose to leave. The sudden urgency in her tone startled the others, even Gary.

Diane took a deep breath and looked straight at Mickey. "Kinnemore is not Ceridwen's puppet," she announced.

No one spoke against her claim, but their expressions revealed their doubts clearly.

"I don't know that Kinnemore is even alive," Diane went on.

"I have seen the King," Kelsey argued.

"And so've I," Mickey added.

Diane was shaking her head before they ever finished. "That's not him, not Geldion's father," she replied confidently.

"What are you babbling about?" Geno, in no mood for cryptic games, demanded.

"I don't know who, or what, the King is," Diane explained, reaching into her pouch and taking out the picture she had snapped of Dilnamarra Keep's front door. "But I know that he . . . it is not human."

She held out the picture and the others crowded around.

There stood the two Connacht guards, and between them their King—or at least, something dressed in their King's clothes. The face was not human, with a mouth spread from pointed ear to pointed ear, and shaggy hair everywhere, seeming to sprout even from the sides of the thing's nose.

"What the heck is that?" Gary asked, having no idea of what was going on.

Geno and Kelsey seemed equally disturbed, though whether the sight of the picture alone was the source, Diane could not guess.

Mickey, the only one who had been at Diane's side, remembered the scene when they had approached the Keep, remembered the guards and the man standing between them. And the leprechaun, with his greater knowledge of the machines of Real-earth, was not so taken aback by the mere sight of a photograph.

"What is it?" Gary asked again, more emphatically.

"King Kinnemore," Diane answered evenly.

"No, lass," Mickey corrected. "This one I've seen before, and wearing the trappings of the King don't change who and what it is."

"Who?" Gary cried, growing even more agitated by Kelsey and Geno's continued disbelief, by their blank stares and by the fact that even sturdy Geno hardly seemed able to draw his breath.

"Ye've not seen it, but ye've heared it before, lad," Mickey answered. "Suren it's the wild hairy haggis."

14 † What Price Victory?

Flames sprouted from every tree, lifting their hissing voices in defiance of the drenching rain. All the edge of the forest was in turmoil, men rushing about, fires leaping high, bowstrings humming, as King Kinnemore gave his answer to the call for peace.

Far from the brutal fighting, Prince Geldion sat despondently, his suspicions of his father's feelings for him apparently confirmed. Few prisoners sat in the field near the Prince, most of the soldiers having sworn fealty to the other side. Even now, many of Geldion's men were into the battle, fighting for the Tylwyth Teg, fighting against his father. It was, perhaps, the most bitter pill the troubled Prince had ever swallowed.

And so the fighting that day was even more confusing, with elfs battling men, and men battling men.

Diane, too, was at the front, simply refusing to be left behind again. She rode a white mare beside Gary and Kelsey, the elf leading a wild rush along the length of the battlefield, shouting for men to desert their unlawful King and come to the call of the spearwielder, the new Donigarten. In his shining suit of mail, atop the great stallion, the mighty spear raised high above him, Gary Leger certainly looked the part. But he did not feel the part, did not feel like the reincarnation of that legendary hero. Far from it.

Gary had seen battles in Faerie before, had seen Geldion and a host of his knights battle a sea of goblins in Cowtangle. Indeed, Gary had been in battles, had killed the knight Redarm in single combat. And he had seen atrocities in his own world, on the increasingly graphic evening news, footage of war-torn countries and of the troubles in the cities of his own land. None of that prepared him for this vicious day in Tir na n'Og. The simple fury of the fight, the echoing cries of the dying, the ring of steel against steel, so commonplace that it sounded as one incessant and grating whine, assaulted his sensibilities. He gritted his teeth and rode on, determined to see it all through. This was not the time for weakness, he knew, though it truly revolted him that, in this time of battle, compassion and weakness were apparently one and the same.

Diane was similarly horrified. She had brought both her cameras along, thinking to chronicle the battle. She took only one shot with the Polaroid, though. After that, she used the Pentax, knowing that she would not have to view the result of her handiwork for a long time, not until she and Gary got out of Faerie, at least, where she might get the film developed. That camera became Diane's salvation that horrible morning. Truly a paradox, it made her feel as though she was making an important contribution, while at the same time the camera allowed her to distance herself from the horrible scene. Somehow, watching a man cut down through the eye of a lens was not the same as witnessing it without the transparent barrier.

The fighting went on all morning. With Kelsey leading, cutting a swath through enemy ranks, and with a growing group of Connacht turncoats swelling in the elfish ranks. Gary saw little personal fighting, Diane none at all. But they both were surely a part of that battle, as inevitably scarred as those who limped away from the action covered head to toe in blood—be it their own or the blood of slain enemies.

"We claim victory this day," Kelsey declared long after the bows had stopped humming and the swords were put away. The wails had not ended, though, cries of men and elfs grievously wounded, many still in the scarred area as Tylwyth Teg patrols cut their way through the destroyed tangle, using the screams to guide their steps.

"The enemy has been driven back to the fields, far from Tir na n'Og's borders," Kelsey went on determinedly, though it seemed to all who could hear that the elf-lord wept beneath his stern façade.

Gary nodded grimly, though Diane looked away. She had not learned to accept what must be in Faerie.

Geno, who had spent the day with Mickey as the sole guards over the prisoners, offered no response to the news of victory. The mountain dwarf was untrained in forest fighting, yet tough enough (and deadly enough with those flying hammers!) to keep the score of men on the field in line.

He had been up front for some time now, and had seen the field and heard the results. More than three hundred Connacht soldiers lay dead in the woods, another fifty had been taken prisoner, and three score more had come over to the elfish ranks. But the price had been high. Nearly a hundred Tylwyth Teg were dead or wounded so badly that they would see no more fighting, and the southern border of Tir na n'Og, beautiful even to the dwarf who lived among the great boulders of Dvergamal, would be decades in recovering from the deep scars.

By all accounts, the elfs had scored a victory by a margin of four to one, but Kinnemore could spare four hundred much easier than the Tylwyth Teg could spare one hundred. Kelsey claimed victory, yet his people had surely been decimated, their ranks nearly cut in half.

Kelsey's enthusiasm at his proclamation could not withstand Geno's silent appraisal of the battle. The elf understood Geno's stake in the outcome of the fight for Tir na n'Og, and the dwarf's grim expression spoke volumes.

Kelsey nodded and departed. A new envoy from Kinnemore was expected, now that the wicked King had made his statement with fire and sword. The elf took with him Diane's revealing photograph of their nemesis, and also took with him a grim determination. Kelsey had come to see the world as a larger place than Tir na n'Og. He believed in his heart that the Tylwyth Teg held responsibility for their neighbors' well-being.

But Kelsey realized the devastation of this day, understood that this continuing battle was taking a brutal toll on both sides, and on the forest that served as the battlefield. Kinnemore was losing many good warriors, and was losing precious time while the news of his march inevitably spread to the eastern lands. The longer the King remained bottled up at Tir na n'Og's border, the better prepared his future enemies would become. Even worse, Kinnemore was losing men to desertion, was breeding enemies among his own ranks. That he could not afford, any more than the Tylwyth Teg could afford a prolonged defense.

Kelsey knew what would soon happen, knew that Tir na n'Og would likely see no more fighting, but whatever relief he felt for his kin and his home could not diminish the pain in knowing what would likely befall Braemar and Drochit, and all the folk of the east.

The very next day, the elfish elders signed a truce with King Kinnemore, a pact that included the return of Prince Geldion and any other prisoners.

Kelsey had argued vehemently against the truce, had even revealed the photograph to the elders. They were more than a little suspicious of its origins, since the amazing reproduction was a magic they did not understand. But even conceding Kelsey's point that Kinnemore was not who he appeared to be, was more a creature of Ceridwen's control than they had believed, they would sign the truce and secure the borders of Tir na n'Og.

Let the war for Faerie be fought around their borders, so the elfish elders proclaimed, and if Kinnemore should win out, then so be it. The Tylwyth Teg would survive; Tir na n'Og would endure.

To Kelsenellenelvial Gil-Ravadry, elf-lord and he who reforged the legendary spear of Donigarten, friend of dwarf and gnome, of leprechaun and human, that did not seem enough.

*   *   *   *   *

It took a great effort by Kelsey and Gary, and more than one of Mickey's fine tricks, to keep Geno off Geldion's throat when Kelsey announced the truce. Diane remained at the Prince's side throughout the struggle, shielding him and talking with him.

"Is there so much hate in you?" Kelsey asked the dwarf, the elf's body stiff and straining and his heels digging deep ridges in the rain-drenched turf as the growling Geno bulled on.

"Have you forgotten the pains this miserable Prince has brought to us?" the dwarf replied. "Have you forgotten the fight on the field south of Braemar, where my kin were cut down by Geldion and his soldiers?"

Kelsey had to nod in reply, but he noted something else in Geno's stern tone, something more calculating. The elf smacked the dwarf hard to temporarily break Geno's momentum, then hopped back, standing resolute in the dwarf's path.

"Is that it?" Kelsey said evenly, and the surprising question did more to slow Geno than the slap.

"Is that what?" Geno demanded.

"Are you angry at Prince Geldion for what has occurred, or do you seek a solution now through murder?"

"What are you babbling about, elf?" Geno huffed, but the dwarf, obviously caught off his guard, stood still, gnarly hands on hips. "Give him a weapon, then. I'll fight him fairly!"

"Of course," Gary agreed, recognizing Kelsey's logic. "You want to kill Geldion now to destroy the truce. If Geldion doesn't come out of Tir na n'Og, Kinnemore will renew the fighting, and the Tylwyth Teg will be forced back into the war."

Geno turned a seething glower upon Gary, but he had no answers to the charge. He looked to Kelsey, and saw sincere sympathy in the elf's golden eyes.

"Prince Geldion will be returned, as the elders of the Tylwyth Teg have agreed," the elf said solemnly.

Geno sent a stream of spittle splattering off Kelsey's soft leather boots. "I should have expected as much from a bunch of elfs," the surly dwarf grumbled, and he turned away.

Gary did not miss the clouds of pain that crossed over Kelsey's fair face.

"My people have suffered greatly," Kelsey said, aiming the remark Geno's way. The dwarf turned on him sharply, Geno's blue-gray eyes unblinking. The expression alone rebutted Kelsey's point, said clearly what the elf, in his heart, already knew: with the Tylwyth Teg out of the fighting, the suffering would be greater for those races still standing opposed to the merciless King of Connacht.

"Did ye show 'em the lass's picture?" Mickey asked, more to break the tension than in any hopes of a resolution.

Never taking his eyes from Geno, Kelsey nodded. "They

did not know what to believe," he explained, and he recounted all the doubts of the elfish elders.

"But ye're believing," Mickey reasoned.

Again without taking his stare from Geno, the elf nodded. "And though my people are out of the war, Kelsenellen-elvial is not."

That proclamation did much to soften the surly dwarf's glare.

"Then where do we go from here?" Gary asked, a perfectly reasonable question. "To Braemar, to wait for the new battles? Or back into Dilnamarra, where we try to kill Kinnemore?"

"Not an easy task, if Diane's picture tells the truth," Mickey reasoned.

Kelsey was in full agreement. He remembered the arrow he had put into Kinnemore, a shot that would have killed many men, or at least taken them out of the fighting. Kinnemore, Kelsey recalled, had been more angry than hurt—if hurt at all.

"To the Crahgs," Diane answered unexpectedly, coming over to join the group. All eyes, even Geno's, turned to regard her. "Did I pronounce that right?" she asked.

"It makes sense, doesn't it?" she reasoned against the silent stares. "If King Kinnemore is the haggis, then the haggis must be King Kinnemore."

"Unless Ceridwen merely used the haggis as a model for a transformation of the King," Kelsey reasoned, but Mickey was backing Diane's logic on this one.

"The haggis is older than Ceridwen, by all accounts," the leprechaun put in. "And ever filled with mischief. Me own guess is that Ceridwen would have found an easier time in switching the two than in trying to copy that fiend."

"Exactly," Diane agreed. "And if we go and get the

haggis—King Kinnemore—we might be able to do something about it."

The others had been to the Crahgs and had heard the shriek of the wild hairy haggis, and not one of them, even Mickey who agreed with the reasoning, seemed excited about the prospect of hunting the thing.

"It won't be as bad as you think," Diane assured them, her smug tones telling Gary, who knew her best, that she had a secret. "If the haggis is Kinnemore, the real Kinnemore, he won't be anxious to attack his own son."

Kelsey nodded and even smiled at the reasoning, happy to grab at the offered chance, until he understood the implications of what Diane was saying. His own son, she had said. Did this foolish and ignorant woman expect Prince Geldion to travel along beside them?

"Prince Geldion has already agreed to go along," Diane announced, as though she had expected Kelsey's unspoken doubts all along.

She winced as Geno's spit splashed off her shoe.

"I have agreed," Geldion called from his seat in the clover a short distance away.

"Ye're to go back to Dilnamarra," Mickey said. "As is decided in the truce. If ye do not, then Tir na n'Og'll be full o' fighting again on the morrow."

"And so I will go back," Geldion replied evenly. "I will go back and see this monster that has stolen my father's throne. And then I will leave, explaining that I must scout the eastern road before the army moves on. We will meet in Cowtangle Wood three days hence."

The friends exchanged doubting expressions. They had all dealt with Geldion in that very same forest—Gary, Kelsey, and Mickey had been chased through Cowtangle on two separate occasions by Geldion and his men. They seemed to come to a silent agreement, looking at each other, inevitably shaking their heads.

"He has nothing to lose!" Diane interjected, understanding where the tide was flowing. "Nothing to lose and everything to gain." She looked back to the seated Prince and nodded, and he nodded back to her. "He will be there," Diane asserted, mostly to her husband. "Alone."

Gary paused a moment to consider the claim, to consider all their options. "Cowtangle Wood," he finally agreed, ignoring the skeptical stares of Kelsey and Geno. "In three days."

"Two days," Mickey corrected. "We've got little time before Ceridwen comes free o' Ynis Gwydrin."

Again Geldion nodded. "Then get me back to Dilnamarra quickly, elf-lord," he bade Kelsey. "My King"—his voice was full of biting sarcasm—"will demand a full report, and Cowtangle is a hard ride."

Kelsey looked to Geno, apparently the only one left supporting his doubts. But the dwarf only shrugged as if to say, "What else can we do?"

Kelsey and Geldion soon departed, and Diane rubbed her hands together eagerly, thinking she had solved the puzzle. Mickey and Gary did not doubt her reasoning, but did not seem so elated.

They had been to the Crahgs, the home of the haggis, before.

15 † Too Hot to Handle

Gary leaned the huge shield, Donigarten's shield, against a tree and looked anxiously back to the west, towards Dilnamarra. Gary normally wouldn't have taken the bulky shield, for fighting with it and the great spear was no easy feat. Mickey's offhanded remark that "It'd take a wall stronger than Donigarten's own shield to stop a charging haggis" had prompted Gary's decision, much to the chagrin of the sentient spear.

Dost thou remember thy battle with crahg wolves, young sprout? the spear called incessantly in his mind, and Gary suspected that the spear's reversion to the older dialect was its way of acting superior to him. The spear was referring to a battle Gary had fought in the eastern reaches of these same Crahgs, when a host of wolves had come down after the companions. That had almost been Gary's final battle, mostly because he kept getting tangled up with the long spear and heavy shield in trying to keep up with the darting movements of the swift wolves. *Dost thou remember that this very shield almost sent thee spinning to thy doom?*

Forget the damned wolves, Gary telepathically answered. *We've got a long way to go before I start worrying about crahg wolves!*

The sentiment was true enough. Here they were, still well within the borders of County Dilnamarra, with a hostile army barely a day's march away. And by all reports, the Connacht army would soon be marching down the road from the west, towards Cowtangle. Kinnemore was held up in Dilnamarra, tending to the many wounded and regrouping his forces after the troubles of the battle for Tir na n'Og.

But the King and his men would come soon, Gary knew. Several times this day, he had viewed clouds of dust—small ones, from individual riders, he presumed. The truce had been signed two days before, and, as agreed, Gary and the others had traveled to Cowtangle, about thirty miles east of Dilnamarra, to await Prince Geldion's appearance.

"He is not coming," Geno griped, and not for the first time. "Unless he is at the lead of a cavalry group. Or maybe he is already here, hiding in the woods, waiting in ambush!"

Kelsey seemed similarly cynical, but Mickey, ever the optimist, tried to keep their hopes up, and Diane flatly rejected Geno's assessment.

"Prince Geldion will be here," she asserted every time the dwarf grumbled. "The truth about King Kinnemore wounds him more than anything, and he hates that truth more than he hates you."

Geno didn't show any sign that he was convinced. Nor did the dwarf concede his surly mood when Kelsey jumped up, fitted an arrow, and drew back on his bow. The elf stood perfectly still and silent, and the others, trusting in his keen woodland senses, followed his lead. Suddenly his bow came up, but as the others scrambled for weapons and position, Kelsey eased the string back—and Prince Geldion walked into their encampment, leading a lathered gray stallion.

The small man seemed badly shaken, his oily hair sticking out in back in a sharp cowlick, as though he had spent all the day nervously running his fingers over his scalp. Not only his horse was lathered in sweat; the Prince had been riding hard.

"Who did you bring along?" Geno demanded, not loosening his grip on his hammer a bit.

"You are confused, good dwarf," Geldion replied sarcastically. "This is a horse, not a companion."

Gary wisely bit back his chuckle, remembering that Geno rarely appreciated sarcasm. He heard Mickey cooing softly in Geno's ear, trying to ease the volatile dwarf's hammer down low to his side.

"The army is not far behind?" Kelsey reasoned.

"They will leave in the morning," Geldion answered. "Though scouts have come as far east as Cowtangle. Kinne . . ." He caught himself and looked to Diane, frustration evident on his angular features. "The King," he corrected, spitting the word derisively, "will take his time on the road to Braemar and Drochit, even pausing long enough to send a line around the eastern end of Tir na n'Og, just to make sure that the Tylwyth Teg mean to keep their bargain. Also, he wants to bring some of the smaller hamlets, such as Lisdoonvarna, under his control before he gets to the larger towns in Dvergamal's shadow."

"Foolish," Kelsey remarked. "If Braemar and Drochit are taken—and together they could not resist the army of Connacht—then the smaller hamlets will fall without bloodshed."

"Kinnemore is running shy," Geno reasoned. "His army took more of a beating on the edge of your forest than he, and they, expected. They need to roll over a couple of smaller, defenseless towns to regain their confidence."

Kelsey agreed with the grim assessment.

"The Connacht army will not crush the towns," Geldion put in angrily. "Even more than military confidence, the King needs for the army to believe in the justice of his cause again. We . . . he lost nearly as many to desertion as to wounds in the battle for the forest, and the King knows that he will lose many more if the army perceives the campaign as unjust."

"Not bad having an ear at Kinnemore's side, huh?" Diane asked slyly, aiming the remark mostly at Geno and thinking herself quite clever.

Geldion didn't seem to appreciate the comment, though, and neither did the dwarf.

"I guess that makes you one of those deserters you were talking about," Geno said to the Prince.

"The King is not Kinnemore, so I've been told," Geldion replied. He put a cold look on Diane, as if he was fearful that all of this was an elaborate ruse.

"And I do not believe that I have been deceived," Geldion declared firmly, though his dangerous expression hardly matched that claim. "Thus, I am no traitor to the crown. If Kinnemore was King, and he told me to go to war with the Buldrefolk, I would gladly kill a hundred of your kinfolk."

Geno snorted, half in humor, half in rage.

"I'm thinking that we should be going," Mickey quickly and wisely interjected. "We've a five-day ride to the Crahgs, and an army on our tails."

The group was silent for a long and tense moment, Geno and Geldion locking stares and the rest looking from one to the other, wondering which would strike the first blow. But despite their obvious hatred for each other and their surly dispositions, both Geno and Geldion were pragmatists. The mission before them was more important than their personal squabble, and so they helped break the camp and load the mounts. When the group exited Cowtangle sometime later, out the wood's southeastern end, Geldion rode up front beside Kelsey, with the elf's white Tir na n'Og stallion far outshining Geldion's gray. Next in line came Gary and Mickey, riding the same horse, another of the enchanted forest's tall white stallions (the leprechaun tucked in neatly at the base of the creature's powerful neck), and Diane, on a small and muscled black-and-white mare. Geno took up the rear, walking his brown pony far behind the others, grumbling to himself every step of the way.

"Suren it's to be a long ride," Mickey remarked, nodding towards Geno.

"I don't think so," Diane replied. "Prince Geldion is not really a bad guy—I figure that he's had more pain over what the King has become than any of you."

Gary snickered somewhat derisively. Diane hadn't been with him on his first journeys through Faerie; she hadn't witnessed Geldion's narrow-eyed viciousness or been chased long days by the relentless Prince. She hadn't witnessed Geldion's attack against the men of Braemar and Drochit on the eastern fields, or his presiding over the attempted execution of Baron Pwyll. Even if Diane was totally correct and King Kinnemore had been replaced by Ceridwen with the haggis, Prince Geldion's actions over the last few months were certainly not above reproach, and his loyal-little-son excuse echoed weakly at best.

"You don't know Geldion as well as you believe," Gary said to her.

"Nor Geno," Mickey remarked with a resigned sigh. "Suren it's to be a long road."

Actually, both Gary and Mickey were surprised at how calmly and uneventfully the next five days passed by. With news of war, the roads were deserted, and few traveled anywhere near to the Crahgs in any case. Kelsey and Geldion carried on a running conversation day to day. Gary was truly surprised that the usually judgmental elf could apparently so readily forgive the Prince, considering the recent devastation to Tir na n'Og's sacred border, but when Diane and Mickey put things in a different light for him, that amazement fast shifted to approval.

"He's thinking of the future," Diane reasoned. "What happened at Tir na n'Og wasn't Geldion's fault, but Geldion will have a lot to do with whatever might happen next."

"Aye," Mickey agreed. "Kelsey's putting aside what came before—how could Geldion have known that his father was not his father?"

"I don't know that he deserves a second chance," Gary stubbornly argued. "You remember the chase through the swamp."

"I remember it all better than yerself, like it was yesterday," Mickey said, subtly reminding Gary that while, by Gary's clock, those events had occurred years ago, a span of only a few weeks had passed in Faerie. "But these are dangerous times, lad, and I'm not one, nor is Kelsey, to push away a helping hand."

"Even Geno seems better with the Prince," Diane remarked.

"Hasn't spit on his shoes in two days!" Mickey added hopefully. "And I'm willing to take the dwarf's word that the time when he bumped Geldion into the embers was an accident."

Gary didn't openly argue, but his doubting expression told Mickey that he wasn't as certain of Geno's claim on that smoky occasion. Still, the young man had to admit that things were going better than he had expected when they had left Cowtangle. Geldion had done nothing to provoke any scorn. Far from it, the Prince was going out of his way to excuse Geno's subtle attacks, even while he was patting out the smoldering embers on his scorched behind.

"Prince Geldion has the most to lose," Diane reasoned.

"Geno could lose his home," Gary argued. "And his kin."

"But not his heart," Diane replied.

Gary accepted the logic. This entire episode, all the way back to Kelsey's quest to reforge the spear of Donigarten, and even before that, must now come as a bitter pill to the Prince. On those previous occasions he had been following the will of his Father and King, so he had thought, despite the fact that he apparently believed in his heart that course to be immoral.

Geldion had been deceived into immoral action, and for a man of honor (if the Prince was indeed a man of honor), that could be a more painful wound than any a sword might inflict.

Though they had another half day of riding, the Crahgs were in sight by this time, rolling hillocks, some shrouded in clouds, others shining green under the light of the sun. In looking at them, even from this distance, Gary remembered the paradoxical feelings the place had evoked, a feeling of alluring and tingling mystery, and also one of chilling terror. Mostly, Gary remembered the pervading melancholy, the dreamy landscape that could lure a man off guard to the very real dangers of the place.

With great effort, they coaxed the horses past the first few crahgs. Geno wanted to leave the mounts altogether. He suggested many times that they tether them in a copse of trees and pick them up on the way out, but Kelsey would hear nothing of it. The wild hairy haggis would not leave the Crahgs, but crahg wolves certainly would—and the beasts were known to have a particular liking for horseflesh.

Still, less than two hundred yards from the flat fields and first mounds that marked the western border of the Crahgs, the companions were walking, not riding, pulling their skittish and sweating steeds along behind them. The day was fast fading into twilight, and so Kelsey led them up the side of one medium-sized hillock, a hike of about a thousand feet through thick and wet grass.

The evening grew dark and close about them, and a chill wind came up, biting through their cloaks. Kelsey insisted that they light no fire, and none disagreed. The elf did pile kindling in the center of the camp, and placed some lamp oil and a flint and steel in easy reach beside it—just in case. But Diane in particular wasn't thrilled with their choice of campsite, and wondered why, if they couldn't light a fire, they hadn't found a sheltered vale, or a cave perhaps to spend the chilly night.

"It's the crahg wolves," Gary explained to her, wrapping her in his arms to ward off the cold. "Their front legs are longer than their back, so they don't go uphill very well. If they can't get above their prey, they won't usually attack."

"They will attack," grumpy Geno was quick to put in, and he threw a glare at Kelsey (who was paying no attention). "If they catch the smell of those horses."

With that, the elf turned about, facing Geno squarely.

"But their eyes are usually turned down the slopes, not up," the dwarf conceded, seeing Kelsey's scowl. Geno's blood was up, but he realized that if a fight came, his best ally would likely be Kelsey, and he needed no open arguments with the elf at this point.

"Let us hope that this will be our only night in the Crahgs," Geldion said, and even Geno nodded at the sentiment. "Kelsey said that you would call to the haggis," the Prince remarked to Mickey.

"And so I already am," the leprechaun explained. "As soon as we set the camp, I put some o' me magic into the hill. Nothing'll set a haggis to running like the noise o' working magic. If the beast is anywhere near the western side, we'll likely catch sight of it tonight or tomorrow."

"I still don't know how we're supposed to catch the thing," Geno grumbled.

"If the haggis is Kinnemore . . ." Kelsey began.

"The haggis is Kinnemore," Diane promptly corrected. "And he'll be tamed by the sight of his son."

Geno didn't seem convinced. He picked up a fair-sized rock and bit into it, but his expression soured and he tossed the remaining piece of stone away.

Nor did Gary or Kelsey, or even Mickey, seem convinced. Gary remembered the creature's curious shriek, an ear-splitting cry that sent chills along the marrow of his bones, that stole the strength from his knees. And Mickey remarked more than once that illusions had little effect on the likes of a wild hairy haggis. Only Geldion held out beside Diane's reasoning, and Gary, who felt keenly the loss of his own father, sympathized with the Prince's need to hope.

And so they spent the bulk of that night, huddled against the wind, sitting in a circle as though the light and warmth of a campfire was between them. The horses nickered nervously a short distance away, and stomped their hooves and banged against one another whenever the piercing howl of a crahg wolf cut through the stillness of the night air.

But mostly, it was quiet and it was cold, luring Gary into his dreams.

* * * * *

Gary felt a tapping on his face and opened his heavy eyes. Diane was in front of him, breathing rhythmically. Asleep, and apparently he had been asleep as well. The tapping continued, and it took the groggy man a few moments to understand that it had begun to rain, lightly but with big drops.

It was still dark, though the sky had lightened considerably above the rim of the eastern horizon, a lighter gray area reaching a quarter of the way up into the sky. Around the dozing couple, the camp was stirring. Gary saw sparking flashes as Kelsey struck steel to flint, lighting the piled kindling.

Diane stretched and yawned and came awake as the oiled

kindling caught and threw out a soft light, the flames hissing against the press of rain.

"We're thinking it's the haggis," Mickey whispered, moving near to the pair.

Gary and Diane pulled themselves to their feet, immediately recognizing the leprechaun's serious tones. The horses were crowded together, and though the light was meager at best, thick lather glistened on the sides of the nervous animals, mixing with the streaking droplets of rain. The couple from the other world could feel the tension in the air, a tangible aura, a taste on their lips.

"It is the haggis," Gary whispered, and Diane didn't doubt him.

The hillock was too quiet. Even the horses made not a sound. Geno threw himself to the ground suddenly, putting an ear to the soft turf. Almost immediately, the dwarf's face crinkled with confusion.

"What's it saying?" Mickey asked.

Geno shrugged.

"Who is he talking to?" Prince Geldion demanded.

"The ground," explained the leprechaun.

"The ground?" both Geldion and Diane said together.

"Dwarfs can do that kind o' thing," Mickey replied.

"Be quiet!" Kelsey demanded in a harsh whisper, and Geno accentuated the elf's command by hurling a piece of sod the companions' way. As luck would have it, the flying divot struck Gary, the only one who hadn't said anything.

Geno lifted his head and looked curiously back to the turf, then turned his head around and firmly planted his other ear into the wet grass.

"What's it saying?" Mickey asked again.

"I do not know!" the flustered dwarf admitted. "It's screaming at me—I have never heard the ground so emphatic—but I cannot make out a single word!"

"Perhaps it is the rain," Kelsey offered, but Geno scowled at him.

Gary and Diane, standing side by side, each lurched to the side suddenly in opposite directions, as some burrowing thing plowed between them, just under the ground, making a straight run for the prone dwarf, and for the fire, which was sputtering between it and Geno.

"Geno!" Kelsey called in warning.

Flaming brands and lines of orange sparks went flying up into the night sky. Beyond them, the dwarf lifted and turned his head curiously, then soared into the air as though he had been sitting in the basket of a catapult, spinning out of sight into the dark sky. A short distance farther along, across the top of the hillock where the slope descended once more, there came a tremendous, ground-shaking explosion, and out popped a hunched and hairy form.

"*Ee ya yip yip yip!*"

Diane felt her bones ringing with vibrations; Price Geldion grabbed his stomach as though he would throw up, and Gary Leger, having heard the cry of the wild hairy haggis before, clenched his fist and firmed his jaw, determined to fight away the dizziness and the terror.

Kelsey grabbed up his longbow and rushed about, trying to follow the creature's path. Gary and Diane scrambled for their own weapons, Gary scooping up the spear and Diane hoisting his large shield.

Now is the time for heroes! the proud spear screamed in Gary's thoughts.

"I never would have guessed," Gary whispered sarcastically.

They caught a glimpse of the creature, running clockwise around the fairly uniform slope of the hill. It seemed little more than a large ball of fur, the size of a curled-up man, except that one side of this hairy sphere was cut, practically halfway across, with the widest maw Gary had ever seen, with teeth that looked like they belonged in the mouth of a great white shark. Most curious of all, the creature's left arm and leg were longer than its right limbs, so it was perfectly level as it ran along on the uneven crahg!

"*Ee ya yip yip yip!*" it wailed, and black spots appeared before Gary Leger's eyes. He looked to Diane for support and saw that she was swaying, grabbing at her ears.

Geno landed with a thump and a groan, and bounced back to his feet, pulling out a hammer.

Kelsey cut across the top of the hillock, angling to intercept the haggis, but the beast disappeared suddenly, as abruptly as a fish going under the water.

A mound rolled up onto the hillock's top once more as the creature tunneled as fast as it had been running. The elf leaped to the side, but Geno, still trying to get his bearings from his unexpected flight, never saw the danger coming. Up the dwarf went again, cursing his rotten luck. He tried to turn so that he could launch his hammer towards the running mound, but it had happened too fast, and when he threw, he was already spinning back around.

The hammer shot out to the side, cutting the air right between the wide-eyed, horrified faces of Gary and Diane.

The turf exploded again on the side of the crahg as the haggis came back above ground, and Prince Geldion was there to meet the creature.

"Father!" he yelled, and felt heavy feet run straight up his legs and up his chest. He cried out and tried to throw himself backwards, only then realizing that he was already lying prone on his back, sunk several inches into the soft turf.

The haggis was long gone, taking up its clockwise, circling run around the side of the hillock again. "*Ee ya yip yip yip!*"

Geno landed with a thump and a groan, and bounced back to his feet, pulling out another hammer.

The poor horses kicked and scattered, thundering down the hillside. In the growing gray light of the impending dawn, Gary spotted his stallion, cutting across the path of the fast-running monster.

He started to cry out for the horse, but the words stuck in his throat as the haggis intercepted, barely seeming to shift its angle, moving so brutally fluidly that Gary hardly realized it had leaped off the ground. He heard the impact, though, a sickly, slapping sound as the haggis plowed into the horse's side.

The stallion stopped abruptly and stood perfectly still, and the haggis ran on around the curving mound. Then, to the amazement and horror of all looking on, Gary's stallion fell in half.

Geno pitched a hammer, perfectly leading the fast-running monster and scoring the first hit. The haggis never slowed.

Outraged, Kelsey again took up an intercepting route, but wasn't quite quick enough, and the haggis ran past him and out of his reach before his sword completed its downward cut.

Geldion, pulling himself up to his elbows, saw the creature completing its circuit, bearing down on him once more.

"Father," he said weakly, and he wisely fell back into the Geldion-shaped hole in the ground. The haggis ran right over him, blasting the breath from his lungs and knocking him in even deeper.

Geno and Kelsey scrambled wildly; Gary and Diane simply tried to get their bearings on the dizzying creature.

"Ye got to anticipate the thing's moves!" came a suggestion from high above. Gary looked up to see Mickey, the leprechaun catching the first rays of sun, floating under his umbrella about twenty feet above the top of the hillock.

"Only place to watch a haggis fight," the leprechaun said weakly.

Geno closed fast on the running haggis. He pitched another hammer, but the creature cut an impossibly sharp turn and dove underground.

"Stonebubbles," the dwarf grumbled resignedly as the mound rushed under him, and then Geno was flying again.

Kelsey, off to the side, quickly calculated the haggis's exit point and ran with all speed across the mound, his elfish sword gleaming in the morning light.

"*Ee ya yip yip yip!*" came the bone-shaking shriek as the haggis changed tactics and direction, bursting up out of the ground atop the hillock and bearing down suddenly on Gary and Diane.

Gary's only thought was to save his wife—and her only thought was to save him. They turned on each other simultaneously and slammed together as each tried to push the other from harm's way. Gary was much heavier (and heavier still because of the metal armor and shield), and it was Diane who went flying.

Gary nearly tumbled to the ground, as surprised by Diane's movement as she apparently had been by his. He kept the presence of mind to pivot, though.

Brace! came the sentient spear's warning cry in his head.

Gary lifted the spear, trying to put it in line, and fell aside. The tip only grazed the rushing haggis.

"*Ee yaaaa!*" it wailed, seeming for the first time as though it was in pain.

Geno landed with a thump and a groan, and bounced back to his feet, pulling out another hammer.

The haggis went over the lip of the hillock—and to everyone's amazement, especially poor Gary's, came right back along the exact angle at which it had departed, but now underground.

"Sonofabitch!" stubborn Gary growled, and he planted his feet widely apart, lifted the great shield as high as he could, and slammed its pointed bottom into the turf, sinking it in several inches.

"Uh-oh," he heard Mickey remark from above.

Gary braced his shoulder hard against the shield and peeked around it, his eyes widening in shock as the haggis burst out of the turf, running, flying, right for him.

There came a blinding flash—even the haggis seemed to flinch.

"Ee ya yip yip . . ."

Slam!

Gary knew he was flying, felt the motion and heard the whistle as the air blew through the slitted faceplate of his great helm. He knew, too, that his shoulder hurt again and it felt as if something hard was biting on his arm and side.

He tumbled completely around, his helm falling free. He saw green, shining grass in the morning light, glistening prettily with the wetness of the light rain.

That pretty grass rushed up and swallowed him.

16 ✝ Resilience

It was still raining, and that pitter-patter on his face again brought Gary's conscious mind whirling back from dreamland. He stirred and tried to open his eyes, felt a dull ache throughout his entire body.

From somewhere not so far away, he heard the ring of a dwarfish hammer.

Waves of agony rolled up his left arm, accompanying each note. Gary half screamed, half gasped and tried to roll away, his eyes popping open wide. A strong hand clamped hard on his chest and held him still.

"What are you doing?" the suddenly wide-awake Gary demanded. He managed to turn his head to the left in time to see Geno's hammer go up high once more, then come crashing down, out of his view, ringing against metal. The waves turned Gary's stomach and sent the world spinning dizzily before his eyes. He tried to scream out, but found no breath for it.

Up again went the grim-faced dwarf's hammer.

"No!" Gary protested.

Then Diane was there, gently easing Geno aside (though the dwarf kept his hand firmly on Gary's chest and would not let him turn) and putting her face close to Gary's.

"He has to," she tried to explain.

"What? What . . . is . . ." Gary stammered between gasps.

"It's your shield," Diane went on. She eased Geno's hand away from Gary's chest so that Gary could roll over enough to take in the scene.

Gary's gasps fell away to silence, his breath gone altogether as he regarded his shield, the shield of Donigarten, the strongest shield in all the world. Fully a third of it was gone, the metal ripped away, and what was left had buckled around Gary's arm, bent like the aluminum foil Gary might use to wrap the remains of a Thanksgiving turkey. Gary realized then that, while his previously injured shoulder throbbed with pain, he felt nothing at all along his arm.

Nothing at all.

His gauntlet was off and he stared hard at his unmoving left hand. It didn't look real to him, not at all, resembling the lifeless limb of a mannequin, except that it was so pale that it appeared blue.

"If we cannot get the shield off soon, you will lose your arm," Kelsey said grimly.

"Good shield," Geno remarked, eyeing the flattened end of his ruined chisel—the third chisel he had destroyed in the last fifteen minutes.

Gary was silent for a long moment, considering Kelsey's grim words. He rolled flat to his back again. "Get it off," he said. "Just get it off."

Diane shifted over to be close to her husband, while Geno shrugged and gladly—too gladly, Gary thought—moved back into position.

Again and again, the dwarfish hammer rang out, accompanied by Gary's increasing growls. Finally, after five more minutes that seemed like five days to poor Gary, the dwarf grunted triumphantly and tossed the destroyed shield aside.

Geno was far from done, though. Next he went to work on the arm plates of Gary's armor, twisting and turning brutally, loosening straps and every once in a while giving a solid hit with that hammer and chisel.

Then it was over and Gary lay flat in the rain, closing his eyes and concentrating against the gradually receding pain. Kelsey wrapped his arm in something soggy, which Diane explained as a healing poultice, and Gary only nodded, though he hardly comprehended anything at that moment.

Only the pain.

"Never seen a hit like it," he heard Geno mumble.

"I told ye the haggis was one to be feared," Mickey answered.

"It wasn't the haggis," Diane insisted.

On cue, all eyes turned to Geldion, who had seen the creature up close. "I know not," the Prince admitted helplessly. "If that . . . thing was my father, then it did not recognize me."

"It wasn't the haggis," Diane said again.

Gary had heard that tone before, and knew that his wife had something tangible up her sleeve. He forced himself up on his good elbow, and studied Diane's smug smile.

Gary remembered that last moment before his collision with the beast, the blinding flash . . .

"You took a picture of it," he said to Diane, his tone making the remark sound like an accusation.

Diane chuckled and produced the Polaroid snapshot from her pouch, handing it to Kelsey. The elf said nothing out loud, but his expression spoke volumes. The photograph was passed from hand to hand, from Kelsey to Geno to Mickey.

"Kinnemore," the leprechaun remarked, handing it to Geldion. The Prince's knees almost buckled and he stared at the picture for a long, long while.

Gary felt tingling needles in his arm a bit later, and could move his fingers once more. Diane showed him the picture and explained to him what had happened.

Gary saw the creature clearly in the photograph, a hunched and hairy thing, its left arm and leg nearly twice as long as its right limbs. But the face was not as Gary had seen it. Rather than the hairball with a wide, stretching mouth, it was clearly the face of a man, though still with a mouth that reached from ear to ear.

Gary saw himself in the photo too, peeking around the shield at the flying thing, wearing the most profound expression of terror he had ever seen. Like a missile, the haggis had slammed the shield, Diane explained. And had bitten the bottom piece right off, as Gary had gone flying up into the air.

Apparently the creature had been hurt by the impact, though. With Gary out of the fight and Geldion trampled into a muddy trench, it had almost evened the odds, yet instead of turning back after the others, it had burrowed straight down into the crahg, keening wildly all the while.

"We got back all the horses," Diane went on, and then added in a lower tone, "except yours."

Gary grimaced, remembering the gruesome attack.

"Then we got out of the Crahgs," Diane finished. Gary propped himself up higher to get his bearings. He saw the rolling hillocks a short distance away, and by the position of the sun, a lighter gray area in the heavy sky, he knew that most of the day had passed.

"How's your arm?" Diane asked.

Gary flexed the limb, clenched and opened his hand a few times, and nodded. His shoulder was still quite sore—all his body ached as though he had been in a car wreck—but he felt as though he could go on, knew that he had to go on in light of the photographic confirmation of the haggis's true identity.

He motioned to Diane to help him to his feet.

"What's next?" he asked hopefully of the others.

Kelsey, Mickey, none of them had any answer, and Geldion's responding stare was cold indeed.

"We know now that the haggis is truly the King," Gary reasoned, using that simple logic to try to force them from their helpless resignation.

"Unless your wife is a witch," Geldion retorted suspiciously, "and her magic a deception."

Gary turned a smug smile on Diane. "Sometimes," he answered. "But the pictures show the truth."

"A lot o' good that'll do us," Mickey put in.

"We can't give up," Gary said.

"Maybe we could use the pictures to convince the Connacht soldiers," Diane reasoned. "Prince Geldion could take them back to the army."

Both Kelsey and the Prince were shaking their heads even as she spoke.

"I have come to trust Gary Leger as I would a brother," Kelsey explained. "And thus, to trust in you. Yet, my own doubts about your magic remain. I have watched you with your flashing charm . . ."

"Flashing charm?" Diane asked.

"The thing ye called a camra," Mickey explained.

"And yet I still am not certain of its paintings," Kelsey finished.

"You are asking that I tell loyal and professional soldiers to desert the King they have known all their careers," Geldion agreed. "I could never convince them with such meager evidence."

Diane look to Gary and shrugged, her hands, each

holding one of the revealing photographs, held wide in disbelief. "Meager evidence?" she whispered.

"You're looking at things from the point of view of our world," Gary explained knowingly. "We know what a picture is, and we know how to test it for authenticity. But here, the 'camra' is just another form of magic, and from what I've seen, most of the magic in Faerie is illusion, a leprechaun's tricks. Mickey could produce two pictures that look exactly like the ones from the Polaroid in the blink of an eye."

Diane looked to the leprechaun, and at that moment, Mickey's pipe was floating in the air before his face, lighting of its own accord, despite the continuing rain. The woman gave a loud sigh and looked back to Gary, seeing things in the proper perspective.

"Then we just have to go back and catch the haggis," Gary announced, as though it was all a simple task.

Words of protest came at him from every corner, strongest from Geno (no surprise there) and from Kelsey. Gary eyed the elf skeptically, not expecting such a vehement argument, until Kelsey, in his angry raving, mentioned the dead horse. The Tylwyth Teg were protective of their magnificent steeds, and Kelsey had lost one already to the wild beast.

But Gary remained determined against the tide. "We have to go back," he said firmly. "We'll never stop the war now if we don't catch the real King Kinnemore and reveal Ceridwen's deception."

"And the war will go on without us when we are lying dead in the Crahgs," Geno answered.

Gary started to respond, but fell silent. The dwarf was right—all of them were right. They had met the haggis and had been run out. If not for Cedric's shield, Gary would have shared a fate similar to the one his horse found.

Despite his determination, a shudder coursed along his spine as he pictured himself lying in half atop the wet hillock.

But they had to go back—that fact seemed inescapable. They had to catch the haggis and prove the truth of Ceridwen's deception, or all the land was doomed.

Gary pondered the dilemma for a moment, then snapped his fingers, drawing everyone's attention.

"I saw a movie once," he began, "or maybe it was a cartoon."

"A what?" Mickey asked.

"Or a what?" Kelsey added.

Gary shook his head and waved his hands. "Never mind that," he explained. "It doesn't matter. I saw this show . . . er, play, where a monster was too strong to be held by anything, even steel or titanium."

"What's that?" Mickey asked.

Gary was shaking head and hands again before the leprechaun even got out the predictable question. "Never mind that," Gary went on. "The monster was too strong, that's the point. But in this movi . . . in this play, they caught the monster, and held it, with an elastic bubble."

"A what kind of bubble?" Mickey asked against Gary's shaking head and limbs.

"Never mind that," Gary huffed.

"It might work," Diane agreed, following the reasoning perfectly. "But how are we going to get something like that?"

Gary was already thinking along those lines. "Where's Gerbil?" he asked.

"In Braemar," Mickey replied.

Gary abruptly turned to Geno, his voice filled with excitement and hope. "If I give Gerbil something to design, you think you could build it?"

Geno snorted. "I can build anything."

"On to Braemar!" Gary announced and took a long stride towards the horses.

None of the others took a step to follow, all looking skeptically at Gary.

"Trust me," Gary answered those looks.

Mickey, Kelsey, and Geno glanced around at each other, silently sharing memories of the last few weeks. Gary's ingenuity had gotten them off of Ceridwen's island; Gary's quick thinking had allowed them to escape Geldion's troops in the haunted swamp; Gary's ingenuity had brought about the fall of Robert.

They broke camp and headed out for Braemar, Gary and Diane sharing Kelsey's mount, the elf riding behind Geldion on the gray, and Mickey propped against the neck of Geno's pony.

17 ✝ ACME School of Design

Diane stood wide-eyed, her mouth hanging open. She had been introduced to not one, but two, unusual characters upon their arrival in Braemar. She had met her first gnome, Gerbil Hamsmacker, as expected, and the three-foot-tall, pot-bellied creature was pretty much what Diane had envisioned, even down to his ample beard, orange turning to gray, and sparkling blue eyes. He talked the way Diane thought a gnomish inventor should talk, with long, profound pauses, followed by bursts of rapid sentences all run together, where listeners would then have to sit back for a while and sort them all out. Gerbil was obviously thrilled to see Gary and company, and talked wildly about the shot at Buck-toothed Ogre Pass, the gnome-built cannonball that had toppled mighty Robert and had ensured Gerbil a place of the highest respect—post-mortem, of course—among his colleagues.

Soon after meeting up with his friends, Gerbil called another friend out to meet the companions, one they hadn't expected to see out of his home in Dvergamal, and it was the sight of gigantic Tommy One-Thumb that had so unnerved Diane. His face was childish, dimpled cheeks and a continual smile, and it seemed to fit the kindhearted giant's demeanor despite the fact that Tommy was nearly twenty feet tall, with a foot that could crush a full-grown man flat and hands that could wrap about a human skull as though it was a baseball.

It didn't take long for Tommy to come to like Diane, and vice versa.

But there was little time for pleasantries in Braemar. The town was prepared for war, with most of the farmers from the surrounding fields, a host of dwarfs, and even a contingent of gnomes from faraway Gondabuggan, on hand. More tents were in and about the town than buildings, and the tips of old swords and makeshift spears, pitchforks and huge bardiche axes dominated the scenery in every direction, farmers-turned-soldiers marching in ragged formation.

The friends were well known in Braemar—and so was Prince Geldion. Every smile that turned Gary's way or Kelsey's way inevitably bent down into a profound frown at the sight of the Prince, the man who, in the eyes of Braemar's populace, had accounted for more than a few widows and orphans. He wasn't set upon, no one even challenged the fact that Geldion openly wore that infamous dirk of his, but that was only because of the respect the Prince's companions had rightfully earned.

Kelsey realized how uncomfortable the situation was, though, and he quickly arranged for a meeting between himself, Geldion, and Lord Badenoch, who ruled Braemar and was among the most respected men in all the eastern region.

The others were invited along as well, but Gary, seeing the necessity for all speed, would hear nothing of it. He needed Geno and Gerbil (and he wanted Mickey along), and asked for ink and parchment and a quiet place where they might be alone. They were granted all their requests without question and wound up in an abandoned and ruined farmhouse on the outskirts of the town. The place had been razed in the last dragon raid on Braemar, right before Gary had lured the wyrm into Dvergamal and the gnomish cannon had taken Robert down, and still smelled of soot, but it was light enough in there, since the thatched roof had been vaporized by Robert's deadly breath.

And so the group went to work, with Gary relaying his ideas to Mickey, who produced illusionary images of them on a makeshift table in the middle of the room. As soon as he caught on to Gary's general ideas, Gerbil took over the conversation with Mickey, fine-tuning the basic design into a workable and buildable contraption. All the while, Geno grunted and nodded, scribbling on the parchment, listing the materials and equipment he would need and often interrupting the gnome—whenever the excitable inventor began getting carried away with elaborate and unneeded accessories. Outside the structure, Tommy hovered over them, peeking in over the skeletal stone walls (and often blocking their precious light!).

They got flustered many times, argued more than once, especially Geno and Gerbil. Geno wanted a simple haggis trap, something they could construct in a couple of days; Gerbil's first few designs would have taken a year to build and an army to move. The pragmatic dwarf had the full support of Gary and Mickey, though Gary was truly intrigued by some of the gnome's outrageous designs, and so Gerbil was put under wraps.

The gnome offered up more than a few "Oh pooh"s and at one point stood glaring at the others with his fists tucked tight against his hips and his lips pressed tight into thin lines. But eventually they came to an agreement on the design, the pragmatic friends granting Gerbil one or two of his most easily constructed innovations. Next came a materials list, composed by Geno, and then they were off, scattering to the four corners of Braemar in search of the items and a forge.

*   *   *   *   *

Lord Badenoch was a quiet man, a stately leader of experience and even temperament. Those qualities were put to the test indeed when Prince Geldion entered the man's study!

"He comes not as a prisoner," the Lord remarked, and his face went suddenly stern, grayish blue eyes narrow and unblinking. Badenoch was tall, nearly as tall as Gary Leger, with broad shoulders and perfect posture. His dark brown hair showed signs of gray at the temples, but he did not seem old or frail. Far from it; it was often whispered across Faerie's hamlets that if Kinnemore could be overthrown, Lord Badenoch should be appointed King.

Diane thought him an impressive and handsome man, a combination of vitality and experience befitting a leader. There was a dangerous quality to him, as well, one that seemed on its very edge now, with his most hated enemy standing barely ten feet away.

Geldion, so often placed in a defensive situation, did well to bite back the sharp retort that came to mind. Neither did he match Badenoch's imposing stare, standing quietly to the side and letting Kelsey do the explaining.

"He is not here as a prisoner," the elf answered firmly, "but as an ally. We have new information concerning our enemy . . ." He looked to Geldion and the Prince nodded. "Our common enemy," Kelsey explained to Badenoch, "King Kinnemore of Connacht."

"If Kinnemore has shown himself as our enemy, then he has done so through the actions of his son," Badenoch promptly reminded. The Lord, too, looked to Geldion. "The people of Braemar and of Drochit, and the Buldrefolk, have not forgotten the battle, Prince Geldion," he said grimly. "If more of Kervin's sturdy folk were about in Braemar this day, you would not have made it to my quarters alive."

"Geno Hammerthrower supports our plan," Diane interjected, though she knew that it was not her place to speak. Badenoch's superior gaze fell over her, and she blushed and averted her eyes.

"This is Diane," Kelsey said. "Wife of Gary Leger, who journeyed with him to aid in our cause."

"She is a fighter?" Badenoch asked, and his tone showed no disrespect, for despite the suit of fine mesh armor the elves had given to her and her size (which was large in a land where the average woman barely topped five feet), she did not hold herself as a warrior.

"She is a thinker," Kelsey corrected.

"It was her magic which showed me the truth about my father," Geldion added.

"A witch?" the Lord asked.

"A thinker," Kelsey reiterated. "With a bit of magic about her, no doubt." He looked to Diane and smiled, and the woman, feeling more than a little out of place, truly appreciated the support.

Kelsey's ensuing nod had Diane reaching into her pouch for the revealing photographs, the picture of the haggis-turned-King near Dilnamarra Keep and the one of the King-turned-haggis atop the crahg.

Neither the pictures nor the continuing assurances of Kelsey and Diane, nor Prince Geldion's diplomatic attitude, did much to convince Badenoch of their perspective on the situation. Even if he agreed that Kinnemore and the haggis had been switched, which he did not, he saw little chance that they might gain anything by hunting the King-turned-monster.

Over the last few weeks, though, Kelsey and Gary Leger, Geno, Gerbil, and Mickey had certainly earned Lord Badenoch's trust and respect. There was even a giant walking free in Braemar, trusted despite the reputation of his race simply because he was known as a friend of these companions.

"I do not agree with your assessment," Badenoch announced after mulling over all the information that had been presented to him, after all the pleas and assurances. "Nor do I agree with your apparent trust of this man." Once again, for perhaps the twentieth time in the short conversation, Badenoch and Geldion locked dangerous stares.

They would have liked nothing more than to be alone, Diane realized, to complete their battle and satisfy their mutual hatred once and for all. If Geldion was truly convinced (and Diane believed that he was), then he and the Lord were on the same side in this conflict, but there remained great animosity between the two.

"And I have no men to spare for your desperate plan," Lord Badenoch added, still eyeing Geldion.

"We have asked for none," Kelsey replied.

"Then what do you ask for?" Badenoch said, seeming for the first time a bit flustered. "Then why have you come to Braemar? Why have you brought Prince Geldion before me?"

"To inform you of our designs," Kelsey answered. "The haggis, pretending to be Kinnemore, will soon march east with his army, and battle will likely be joined."

Badenoch grimaced but did not even blink. It seemed to Diane that he had known this already, but hearing confirmation from Kelsey was painful to him nonetheless.

"And the Tylwyth Teg will not come to your aid," Kelsey went on, and now it was the elf who seemed pained.

"I have heard word of the truce," Badenoch replied grimly.

"Not all of Tir na n'Og agree with it," Kelsey said.

Badenoch nodded—that much was obvious just from the fact that Kelsey was now in Braemar.

"I wanted you to know," Kelsey went on. "To know of our plans and to know that I and my companions will not desert you in this dark hour."

"But you will not be there when the battle is joined," Badenoch reasoned. "Your fine sword will play no part, nor will the presence of the spearwielder, whose appearance was said to have made a profound impact on the Connacht army as it battled for Tir na n'Og. Is Braemar any less deserving than your elfish home?"

Kelsey sighed deeply. "I must return to the Crahgs," he explained. "As Gary Leger must. If we are right, we may yet avert this tragedy."

"And if you are wrong?"

"Then we'll return," Diane said firmly. "And we'll fight beside you." She paused and flashed a wry smile, then pointed to Prince Geldion. "Even him," she said. "And more than a few of Kinnemore's soldiers will come over to our side with Prince Geldion among our ranks."

Geldion did nothing to affirm the claim, and proud Badenoch did nothing to acknowledge it. Diane remained solid in her determination, though, and both Kelsey and Geldion were silently glad she had spoken the words.

Kelsey looked to Geldion suddenly, wondering if it might serve them all better if the Prince remained with Badenoch.

"We need him to tame the haggis," Diane remarked, understanding the elf's look.

Kelsey nodded, and realized anyway that leaving Geldion in Braemar might not be such a good idea.

"You may take what materials you need, Kelsenelle-nelvial," Lord Badenoch decided. "I owe you and your companions that much at least. And as for you, Diane, wife of Gary Leger." The proud Badenoch paused and looked intently at Diane, and she rocked back on her heels, intimidated, expecting to be scolded.

"I pray that you may return to Braemar on a brighter day," Badenoch finished. "All of Faerie owes your husband a great debt, and I would be honored if we might meet when times are not so grave." He finished with a curt bow, and Diane, overwhelmed, had no reply.

The three left Badenoch's quarters soon after, and on Kelsey's orders, the elf thinking it wise to keep Geldion as far from the activity as possible, headed for the lonely farmhouse away from the bustle of Braemar.

Gary, Mickey, and Tommy joined them later in the day, reporting that Geno had secured the forge and most of the materials and Gerbil had nearly completed the final designs.

For the road-weary companions, that night and the next came as a welcome reprieve, a time to brush the dirt from their cloaks and allow their tired bodies some much needed rest. But the reprieve was physical only, for none of them could put the coming trials out of their minds, could forget the sheer wildness and ferocity of the haggis and the fact that a hostile army was even now marching their way.

Geno and Gerbil worked right through the night, right through the next day and the night after that. Gerbil made the designs and explained the concepts, such as how to bend the pounded wire into a spring, and Geno, who had well earned his title as the finest smithy in all the world, only had to be told once. When dawn broke on their third day in Braemar, the two half-sized companions joined the others at the farmhouse and announced that the haggis trap was completed.

"Then we're off," Gary was happy to say.

"Just one problem," Geno replied smugly, and even Gerbil seemed at a loss.

"How are we to carry the thing?" the dwarf asked. "It weighs near to four hundred pounds and is too bulky to be strapped onto a horse."

"Oh, good point," Gerbil groaned, and that groan became general.

"Could build a skid for it," Geno went on. "But that will take another day—make it two days because I need some rest!"

The groan went up a second time.

"We're not having two days to spare," Mickey reasoned.

Gary alone was smiling, and eventually everyone focused on him. "Tommy will carry it," he explained when his mirth drew all eyes his way.

A brief moment of doubts and arguments ensued, particularly from Geldion, who hadn't quite gotten used to having an eighteen-foot-tall giant along. But the complaints quieted soon enough, the others realizing that they had few options, and even proud Kelsey had to admit that having powerful Tommy around might not be a bad thing when facing a wild hairy haggis.

They went to the rebuilt Snoozing Sprite tavern for breakfast—all of them, even Geldion, though Tommy could not fit inside and had to take his meal out on the porch. Then they retrieved the haggis trap, and while Gary's eyes lit up as he regarded a tangible material manifestation of his theory, Kelsey and Geldion looked on doubtfully, not knowing what to make of the curious thing.

Its metal frame was box-shaped, thick rods forged together and supported at each corner by metal joists, and supported diagonally on three sides, corner to corner, by crossing rods. Inside this open frame was a second structure, a jumble of wires, metal rods and springs—more springs than Diane had ever seen together in one place! A spring-loaded plate completed the picture, on the front and open end of the contraption. Geno took special pride in this feature, for he had designed and added a particular action to the fast-opening plate.

He nodded to Gerbil and the gnome produced a curious tool, some sort of wrench, and made a simple adjustment to a lever on the side of the box. Gerbil then stepped aside and Geno moved over and grabbed the spring's lever. "Just let the little hairball come at us underground," the dwarf remarked and tugged the lever.

The whole contraption jolted hard as the edge of the faceplate slammed straight into the ground, diving deep beneath the surface.

"Boom!" Gerbil explained happily, clapping his plump little hands.

Gary cupped his hand, blew on his knuckles, and rubbed them across his chest. Diane held back her remarks and let him bask in the glory—even to doubting Kelsey and Geldion, this thing looked like it might actually work.

Lord Badenoch was gracious enough to part with a fine pair of horses, and a pony, for Gerbil decided that he had to go along as well, to see how his design worked out in actual application. Tommy had no trouble in keeping up, even with the bulky box on his shoulder and another sack Geno had given to him tucked under his other arm. The road out of Braemar was clear, with no sign of Kinnemore's army yet apparent, and the group made fine progress back to the Crahgs. The weather was an ally, too, fine and clear and with a comfortable breeze blowing off the Dvergamal peaks.

None of them needed to be reminded that the fine weather would also facilitate Kinnemore's march towards Braemar, and all the way around Dvergamal's southernmost peaks, they kept looking back to the west, looking for a telltale cloud of dust.

It rained on the second day, but the clouds flew away on the third, and by late that afternoon they came again upon the Crahgs. Gary sat atop a brown stallion staring long and hard at the ominous mounds, a look of obvious dread on his face.

"It will work," Diane, on her Tir na n'Og mount at his side, insisted. "The trap will catch the thing and then we'll prove that the haggis is really King Kinnemore."

"And th'other way around," Mickey, tucked in his customary spot against the neck of Gary's horse, added.

"The trap will work," Geno put in, and Gerbil's head bobbed frantically in agreement.

Logically, Gary didn't disagree, but that did little to calm the dancing butterflies in his stomach. He looked from one companion to the others, settling his gaze on Diane.

"It will work," she whispered determinedly.

"Then how come I feel like Wile E. Coyote?" Gary asked, and kicked his horse into a trot to catch up with Kelsey and Geldion.

18 † Frenzy

They went atop the same hillock where they had encountered the haggis previously. Again, fortunately, no crahg wolves or any other monsters were about to challenge them.

"The dragon was flying back and forth on this side o' the Crahgs not so long ago," Mickey reasoned, trying to explain the unusual calm in the dangerous region. "Robert probably sent all them wolves running to the east, deep in their hills."

It was a cheery thought—somewhat. None of the others, certainly not Kelsey, Geldion, or Geno, feared crahg wolves or anything else the Crahgs might throw at them, with the exception of the one beast they had come to catch.

The sun was nearly down as they sorted out their encampment. Kelsey tethered the horses closer to the group this time, while Geno, with help from Tommy, moved about securing the perimeter of the mound. The giant carried the large sack, and took a sheet of metal, perhaps three feet square, from it every few feet. Following Geno's instructions, Tommy jammed the sheets into the soft turf, and the dwarf pounded them the rest of the way down.

"Let the little hairy bug come burrowing at us underground," the dwarf said wickedly and smacked his hammer on top of the next plate in line.

Twilight turned to darkness and the howls of distant crahg wolves came up. All in the camp were nervous; not one of them fostered any thoughts of trying to sleep. Kelsey and Geldion looked to Mickey often, their expressions reflecting their increasing impatience.

Mickey walked all about the mound's top, whispering enchantments under his breath, sending his magic deep into the soil that the wild hairy haggis might hear it clearly. The leprechaun wasn't thrilled about summoning the beast, of course, but his pragmatic side told him that the sooner they encountered the haggis, the sooner they might be out of the Crahgs.

The moon was full and high above them; the calls of the wolves had increased tenfold, and had come closer, sometimes seeming as if the strange-looking canines might be all about the base of the mound.

"Are we to fight a haggis, or all the creature's minions?" Geldion asked nervously after one particularly vocal stretch.

"Let the stupid doggies come up," Geno retorted sharply, his tone revealing his tension. He stalked to the edge of the mound and howled, and when a wolf howled in reply, somewhere in the thick darkness below the mound, the dwarf let fly a hammer, spinning into the night. "Stupid dogs," Geno muttered and walked back toward the middle of the encampment.

Geldion kicked hard at the soft turf in anger, expecting a thousand crahg wolves to rush up in answer to Geno's attack.

"Easy," Mickey said to the Prince, and to all the others. "The wolves'll not come up, not when the haggis is about. We're too much for them, and they know they'll find much carrion after their wild leader's done his work."

"Well put," Geno grumbled sarcastically.

"I mean that's what they're thinking!" Mickey corrected. "How can they be knowin' that we've a trap . . ."

"*Ee ya yip yip yip!*" The cry buried the leprechaun's

thoughts and brought a shriek from Gerbil, and the gnome threw himself face down on the ground.

"What was it? What was it?" he squeaked from under his elbow.

"*Ee ya yip yip yip!*" the cry came again, and the horses nickered and banged together, and Geno hopped in circles, a hammer in each hand, and Tommy, poor Tommy, trembled so badly that he looked like a willow tree caught in the eye of a tornado.

"*Ee ya yip yip yip!*"

"Where is it?" Kelsey demanded, running about and trying to get his bearings on the obviously nearby monster. The haggis's cry echoed off every hillock, resounded a hundred times and filled all the air about them.

Gerbil got back to his knees. "Indisputably incredible," the gnome announced.

"What?" Gary demanded.

"That cry!" the gnome said happily, all his fears apparently washed away. "That cry! Oh, how perfect!"

"Duh?" said Tommy, and Gary and Diane agreed wholeheartedly.

"*Ee ya yip yip yip!*" came the wail.

Gerbil hopped up and down, clapping his plump gnomish hands. "I must find a way to reproduce that!" he squealed. "Yes, in a bottle or a beaker." He looked directly into the blank stares of Gary and Diane. "That sound will keep the rodents from Gondabuggan. Oh, I will get my name on the Build-A-Better-Mousetrap plaque!"

"The Build-A-Bet . . ." Diane stuttered.

"Don't ask," Gary warned, knowing they had no time for one of Gerbil's gnomish dissertations.

"*Ee ya yip yip yip!*"

"There's the bug!" Geno yelped, pointing a hammer over the mound's southern edge. The dwarf growled and fired, then stamped his foot in frustration as the haggis dove underground and the hammer bounced harmlessly away.

Up the hillock the monster charged, churning the ground above it. Full speed, right into the buried metal plate.

The entire mound jolted as though a bomb had gone off, and then there was silence.

Geno hopped up and down and punched his fist into the air in victory.

But then the ground churned atop the mound, on the other side of the plate!

"Duh?" Geno blubbered, sounding a lot like Tommy. Suddenly the dwarf was flying again, spitting curses through every somersault.

Gerbil was fast to the trap, and Tommy too, the giant working to shift the cage in line and Gerbil ready with the faceplate lever.

But the haggis turned abruptly, rushing to the side, towards Kelsey and Geldion. It burst free of the ground and leaped, flying between the two.

Kelsey spun to the side, sword in hand, and snarled as he began his vicious cut.

His arm had barely begun to come around when Geldion intercepted, throwing all his weight against the elf and knocking Kelsey to the ground.

"Father!" he cried after the beast.

The haggis hit the ground and disappeared so quickly that it seemed as if the creature had dived into a dark pool of water. Impossibly quick, too, was its turn, for it came up right under the startled Prince Geldion's heels, launching him into a forward roll.

Geno bounced down, right back in the thing's path. The dwarf's eyes popped wide and he shrieked and dove aside, but reached out with one hand as the haggis zipped past.

"Got you!" Geno cried, his iron grasp locking onto one of

the haggis's legs. But the dwarf's triumph turned to horror as he bounced off behind the wild thing, his "capture" not hindering or slowing the haggis one bit.

"Duh, hey!" Tommy cried, throwing his hands in front of him as the haggis went airborne. The next thing the giant knew, he was laid out flat in the grass, watching the pretty stars and moon, his chest throbbing.

The haggis bounced high after slamming the giant, and plunged down for another underground dive, Geno in tow. The haggis was bigger than Geno, but it was sleeker, and better prepared for its tunneling swim.

The dwarf grunted and ate dirt, and hung in place, his legs and feet the only thing visible above the ground.

And the haggis tunneled off for the edge of the mound, and smack into another of the buried plates, jolting the mound so fiercely that Diane found herself suddenly sitting.

The creature's tremendous momentum took out the side of the mound's lip, and the haggis, suddenly above ground and holding a dented and torn metal plate, sat perfectly still for a moment, apparently stunned.

It shook its shaggy head, its ample lips batting loudly, then let loose another of those bone-shivering wails and ran off into the night.

"There it goes!" Gary called, thinking the encounter ended.

"Here it comes," Mickey corrected, floating up above the camp under his umbrella. "The thing's making straight for the horses."

"Tommy!" Gary called, grabbing at the heavy trap, trying to drag it in line with the approaching beast. Tommy was still staring at the stars and would be of no help. Kelsey came to Gary, as did Geldion, and the three managed to slide the trap across the grass.

Up the hillock came the haggis, diving underground

again and speeding right for yet another of the buried plates.

"Brace!" Mickey warned, but the haggis skidded to a stop right before the plate and popped above ground, gently hopping over the devious barrier.

"*Haaaa, hahahahaha!*" it chided. Its wild eyes darted all about. It looked to the horses and a long tongue flopped out of its mouth, dragged on the ground before licking the thing's lips. Then it seemed even more eager as it regarded the floundering Geno, half-buried.

"*Ee ya yip yip yip!*" it shrieked and disappeared underground, making straight for the dwarf.

Diane was there first, and Gerbil rushed beside her, each taking one of Geno's large boots under their arms and pulling hard. Both flew over backwards, Diane clutching the boot, and it took her a moment to realize that she didn't have the dwarf with her.

She looked back to see the haggis bearing in, the helpless Geno's toes waggling in the air.

"Geno!" she and Gerbil and all the others cried. Sword in hand, Kelsey rushed across, and a horrified Geldion followed, calling for his father, trying anything to calm the monster.

The haggis slammed in; the dwarf grunted and his legs stopped kicking. Then the haggis popped out of the ground, still on the same side of the dwarf, its tongue hanging low and a sour expression on its contorted features.

"*Blech!*" it groaned and again its wild eyes darted side to side, searching for a meal.

Gary heard a whinny right behind him and he turned, then fell away in surprise, seeing a fat pony right where the trap had been sitting.

"Bait it in, lad," Mickey implored him.

The pony-cage whinnied again.

Kelsey charged and cried out, bringing his sword to bear.

He hit nothing but air and grass, though, for the haggis took to tunneling again.

Prince Geldion went for another spinning flight as the hungry haggis sped underneath him, bearing down on the fattest prize of all.

Gary jumped out in front and to the side and plunged Cedric's spear deep into the ground, and the haggis, feeling the strength and remembering the cruel weapon from their last encounter, surfaced and rushed over the angled shaft.

"*Ee ya yip yip yip!*" it cried triumphantly, lifting from the ground, flying for the heart of the fat pony.

Flying straight into the spring and wire cage.

Over and over the heavy cage rolled, off the side of the crahg, settling a dozen feet below the lip.

Triumphant cries became a wail of disbelief as Mickey floated down and yanked the lever, closing the trap's door.

Gary was the first down the hillock, with Geldion and Diane coming fast behind.

"I never knew that Wile E. Coyote hunted the Tasmanian devil," Diane remarked, taking Gary's arm, and the analogy seemed accurate enough, for the haggis went completely berserk, pulling and slamming, biting at the wire and clawing at the thick support beams. Its frenzy stood the cage up on one end, despite Gary and Geldion's efforts to hold the thing steady, and it seemed as if the creature would surely break free.

Tommy came bounding down, but even his great and powerful arms could not hold the cage in place.

"It's not to hold!" Mickey cried.

"Talk to it!" Diane pleaded with Geldion.

The Prince dove to the ground near the cage. "Father!" he called over and over, to no apparent effect.

"Father!"

The haggis stopped its kicking suddenly and focused on

the Prince. A hopeful smile widened across Geldion's face, and he unconsciously leaned nearer to the cage.

The haggis's right arm tore through the mesh and clawed out at Geldion's face, coming up just a few inches short.

"No, I am Geldion!" the Prince protested. "Your son!"

The haggis retracted its arm and a curious expression crossed its face.

"It's trickin' ye!" Mickey warned, but too late, for Geldion, hoping against all reason, again leaned in and the haggis launched its left, and longer, arm and hooked him around the back of the head.

Geldion felt his cheekbone crack under the pressure as the beast hauled him in tight against the side of the cage, but that was the least of his worries with the monster's snapping maw barely inches from his face!

"Stop!" Gary commanded, and he accentuated his point with the point of a spear, sticking the creature in the forearm.

The haggis let go of Geldion and went berserk again, slamming the cage all about.

"I said stop!" Gary roared, prodding at the beast.

"Don't kill it!" Diane yelled, at the same moment that a pained Geldion called for Gary to stick the spear right through the thing's heart.

Gary could hardly aim at any particular point on the spinning ball of hair. Suddenly the creature twisted about, its hands locked around the spear's shaft.

Be strong, young sprout! the spear cried in Gary's mind, and it seemed to the man as though the weapon was terrified.

Gary tried to hold on, but his shoulder ached as though it would pop out of the socket once more, and he got hit more than once in the face from the spear's whipping butt end.

A blast of magical energy exploded from the speartip and

the haggis fell away, dazed, all its hairs dancing up on end.

Gary prodded the spear in tight against the thing's chest. "I said stop!" he growled, poking hard. The haggis sat perfectly still, and slowly, Gary retracted the spear.

"*Ee ya. . . . Ee ya*," the haggis began chanting quietly (quietly for a wild hairy haggis). The creature's wild eyes closed tight, and it swayed back and forth.

"What's it doing?" Gary asked, freeing the spear from the last of the cage's entanglements and withdrawing it altogether.

"Might be that it's . . ." Mickey began, his explanation interrupted by the sudden renewal of howls.

"Callin' the wolves!" Mickey finished. The leprechaun nodded to Tommy, and the giant hoisted the heavy trap. The haggis immediately went into its frenzy again, but Gary poked the spear through the side of the cage and the enchanted weapon issued another stunning blast.

Atop the hill, they found the others, even Geno, to their profound relief, the dwarf standing dazed, his left arm reaching across his chest to hold his other, injured limb tight to his side. Gary had never seen the sturdy dwarf so shaken, a point heightened considerably as the dwarf rocked back and forth unsteadily on his large bare feet.

Geno growled repeatedly upon seeing the haggis, but he made no move towards the beast.

"*Ee ya*," the haggis crooned softly. "*Ee ya*."

"We're off and running fast," the leprechaun said to Kelsey, and a few moments later, they were indeed, with Geno and Gerbil setting the pace, and Kelsey and Geldion taking up the sides and rear, weapons drawn in preparation for any pursuit. Gary and Diane rode on either side of Tommy, Diane talking to the giant, offering him whatever comfort she might, and Gary ready with the spear, prodding the haggis whenever it got too excited.

The wolves did come to the creature's call, dozens of them running in packs to the sides of the speeding group. But crahg wolves were not fast runners (unless they were coming down a hill), certainly not as fast as ponies and horses, and one very frightened giant!

One time a group did get in front of the troupe, but Geno blasted through, and Kelsey and Geldion were up in an instant, the Prince hacking away and the elf setting his deadly bow to action.

The end of the Crahgs was soon in sight, with no resistance between the friends and the open plains beyond, and their escape seemed inevitable.

Apparently it seemed that way to the haggis as well, for the beast went into such a frenzy as they had never seen before, so wild that Tommy tipped over sideways in trying to hold the pitching cage. Gary prodded the creature several times; the spear let off blast after blast of energy. But the haggis would not relent in its insane thrashing.

"Do something!" Geldion pleaded.

"I designed the cage to hold!" Gerbil insisted.

"I built the cage to hold!" Geno added, but neither of the two seemed overly confident in the face of the haggis's incredibly fierce display.

Diane came to understand. "It doesn't want to leave the Crahgs," she reasoned, slipping down from her horse and going as close to the cage as she dared.

"It has no choice in the matter," Kelsey said coldly, and Diane jumped as a rope fell over her shoulder. She looked back to see the other end fastened to Kelsey's steed.

"Tie the cage off," the elf instructed.

Geldion tossed a second rope over and motioned for Diane to tie it to the other side. They were off again soon after, the cage bouncing behind the pulling horses, with

Tommy behind the cage, trying to keep it as steady as possible.

It seemed fitting that the dawn broke just as they crossed between the last two Craghs, and the companions' fleeting moment of hope was torn away by the most agonized and horrifying cry any of them had ever imagined, the scream of a thousand cats dropped into boiling water, of a thousand souls banished to eternal Hell.

"Eeeyaaaaaa!"

19 ✝ A Ray of Light among the Clouds

From a high ridge a few miles to the west of Braemar, Lord Badenoch watched the dawn spread its fingers of light beyond him and across the rolling fields, the sun reaching out to the west. Scores of crows and larger vultures hopped and flitted about, from one corpse to the next.

So many bodies.

Battle had been joined the day before, with Badenoch's forces out on those same fields, hidden behind stone walls or within the many dotting corpses of trees, waiting for the Connacht army's approach. There was no doubt of King Kinnemore's intent; many people, including Kelsey's band, had ridden into Braemar with news that Kinnemore marched east for conquest.

And so Badenoch and the militia of Braemar, along with a small contingent of dwarfs and gnomes, had gone west to meet the invaders. Kervin's dwarfish folk and the gnome designers had worked through two days and nights preparing the battlefield, concealing deadly pitfalls, and laying lines of pickets that could be raised quickly by a single crank.

They had met the enemy head on, with the element of surprise on their side, for Kinnemore hadn't expected the men of Braemar to come out so far from their sheltered mountain dells and meet them in the open fields, where the larger Connacht force held so obvious an advantage. Kinnemore's first ranks hadn't even sorted out the curious sound, the hum of so many bowstrings, before the rain of arrows decimated them. Panic hit hard in the ranks, surprised soldiers at first scattering every which way. When one group had sought shelter behind a stone wall, they had found many more soldiers waiting for them there, poised on the other side of the stones.

The Connacht soldiers were not inexperienced, though, and after the initial shock, they had regrouped into their battle formations and roared across the battlefield, as Badenoch had expected all along.

But something was missing in the Connacht force, Badenoch realized—that element of discipline that had earned them their reputation as the finest army in all the land. They charged as a horde of animals, a bull stampede, straightforward and wild.

In reflecting on it now, in looking down at the corpses strewn across the fields, the Lord of Braemar understood what had been missing. The Connacht army was without the binding presence of Prince Geldion, their undisputed field commander for the last several years. King Kinnemore was likely struggling with too many duties (not the least of which was answering to Ceridwen!), and his field generals, each trying to fill the void left by Geldion's absence, each trying to win the utmost favor of the King, were reportedly fighting among themselves. Badenoch had even been given information indicating that some generals were being executed in the Connacht camp.

At least there was one good point in Prince Geldion's apparent change of heart, Badenoch thought. The Lord of Braemar still did not trust Geldion, and certainly he had no love for the man. All of his encounters with Geldion before the Prince had so unexpectedly shown up in Braemar with Kelsey had been unpleasant and, lately, openly confrontational.

Badenoch looked to his left, to the sparkling snake of a small stream winding through the thick grass. Many soldiers had died there in a group, their right flank terribly exposed when the dwarfs had come out from behind a ridge. Had that flank been left exposed on purpose? the Lord of Braemar wondered. Had one of Kinnemore's generals allowed the slaughter merely for the sake of making a rival commander seem a fool?

The thought sent a shudder along Badenoch's spine; the whole scene sent a shudder along Badenoch's spine. Living in the shadows of wild Dvergamal, the middle-aged man had fought many battles, but he had no taste for war. His heart ached and more than a few tears washed from his experienced eyes, tears for his men who had died the previous day, for the handful of dwarfs and gnomes who would not return to their distant homes. And tears for the Connacht soldiers, helpless misinformed pawns of a ruthless King. Badenoch hated battle even when it was a fight of self-defense against evil goblins or mountain trolls, even when it was necessary.

And the Lord of Braemar never considered battle, man against man, to be necessary.

He had to suffer his emotions alone, though, for his force could not afford to perceive any weakness within him. Despite the slaughter of the previous day, with well over a hundred Connacht soldiers cut down as compared to only two score of Braemar's soldiers, Badenoch could hardly claim victory. The traps were all gone now, along with the all-important element of surprise. The pickets were blunted by bodies, and in the end it had been Badenoch, and not

Kinnemore, who had been forced to withdraw. The Braemar force had given several miles in exchange for a new battlefield, one that Kinnemore and his soldiers were not now familiar with, one that would put the defenders on the higher ground in the foothills of Dvergamal.

Their next retreat—and Badenoch fully expected that there would indeed be another retreat—would put them all the way back into the village of Braemar, with their backs to Dvergamal's towering mountain walls.

And where from there? the beleaguered Lord wondered. Kervin of the Buldrefolk had offered refuge in the mountains, an invitation Badenoch believed he would ultimately be forced to accept. But that refuge would cost his people their homes and their way of life, would separate them from kinfolk across the land, in County Dilnamarra and even in Connacht, and would turn farmers into hunters. And what peace might Dvergamal offer to the weary folk of Braemar? Kinnemore would send scouting forces into the mountains after them, and Ceridwen, when she was free of her isle, would surely give them no rest.

Badenoch looked far to the south, to the distant end of the rugged Dvergamal line. Around that bend, farther to the east, lay the mysterious Crahgs. Somewhere around that bend, Kelsey and Geldion and Gary Leger and their companions hunted for an answer to this unwanted and evil conflict.

Badenoch shook his head and straightened in his saddle, firming his jaw. No more tears washed from his eyes. The Lord of Braemar could not hope for any easy resolution. He had to act based on what he saw before him, had to prepare for this day's battle, and the next.

They would hit at Kinnemore again, and then fall back to Braemar, and from there, Badenoch had to admit, to himself at least, they would accept Kervin's invitation and slip into the mountains, would realign their lives to fit in with the new and harsh realities of Ceridwen's impending reign.

Better that than the price of all their lives should they stay in Braemar. Better that than swearing fealty to Ceridwen's murderous puppet.

*   *   *   *   *

The wild hairy haggis wailed and wailed, kicked and bit at the wire netting until its limbs and mouth bled in a dozen places. Gary's prodding with the spear did nothing to calm it; Geldion's words to soothe his transformed father only sent the beast into greater tirades.

Gerbil and Geno hopped about the cage, inspecting the joints, and both of them shook their heads more than once and wore worried expressions upon their faces.

"It's in pain," Diane observed. She looked back to the row of Crahgs, realizing that the creature's agony had started the moment they had left the hilly domain. Diane remembered what Gary had told her about his imprisonment on Ceridwen's isle, how the witch had cast a spell to keep them in place, to make the surrounding lake as acid to them should they try to leave. Was a similar spell the cause of the haggis's torment? she wondered, and Mickey seconded her guess a moment later.

"More evidence of Ceridwen's spellcasting," the leprechaun said, looking to Kelsey. "If the witch put Kinnemore in the place o' the haggis, then she'd be wanting him to stay in the Crahgs."

Kelsey, too, looked back to the rolling hillocks, his expression grave. He also remembered the imprisonment on Ceridwen's isle, and the spell the witch had used to bind them. The named price of breaking that spell was his very life. What good would King Kinnemore be to him and to the goodly folk of Faerie dead? he wondered and looked back to the cage, where the haggis continued its wild frenzy.

The sun was up in full by this point and the haggis seemed to like that fact as little as it liked being out of the Crahgs.

"Kill it," Geno said to Gary, motioning to the spear. "Just kill it and be done with it!"

Yes, do, young sprout, agreed the sentient spear.

Gary took a deep breath. He feared that he would have to do just that. If the haggis broke free of the cage (and that was beginning to look more and more likely with each passing second), it would probably kill half of them before running back to its hilly home. The thought of stabbing the caged and helpless creature repulsed the young man, though. By all the evidence, this was Faerie's rightful king and no monster. Even worse, this was Faerie's greatest hope for peace, and killing Kinnemore now would do little good for the land.

Gary growled and pushed the spear into the cage.

"No!" Diane cried, but when she moved near him, Geno caught her around the waist and easily held her back. Geldion rushed for Gary as well, but the powerful dwarf's free arm hooked him and stopped him in his tracks.

The haggis twisted and kicked to keep the spear at bay, but finally Gary had the thing pinned, the spear's powerful tip pressed against its belly.

Zap it, like you did to the men in the barn, Gary's thoughts said to the spear.

Plunge me home, the spear replied. *Vanquish the beast!*

"Zap it!" Gary growled and gave the handle a shake.

The ensuing jolt pushed the haggis halfway into the mesh. Gary prodded the spear ahead, keeping pace, keeping the tip pressing on the beast. It looked at Gary curiously now, its hair standing on end, its fingers and toes twitching from the electrical blast.

"Ee ya yip yip . . ." the creature started to wail, and the spear promptly zapped it again.

Then the haggis was calm, suddenly, whimpering and trembling but no longer in its frenzy.

"You're not going back to the Crahgs," Gary said to it calmly. "You're going home, back to Connacht."

The haggis snarled, but the snarl turned into a whimper quickly, the battered creature granting the speartip a great deal of respect.

Geno let go of both Diane and the Prince, and Geldion moved to the side of the cage nearest the trapped haggis and began talking to the creature once more. Gradually, with the haggis seeming under control, Gary eased the speartip away from it.

He looked around to his friends, to Geno, and the dwarf was shaking his head doubtfully.

"That thing starts jumping about again and you kill it," the dwarf ordered. "The cage will not take much more of the beating and I'm not fond of the idea of a haggis running free among the group!"

Gary looked to Kelsey and to Mickey, both of whom seemed in complete agreement.

Geldion's cry startled them all, made Gary clutch tightly to the shaft of the spear. The Prince was not calling out in distress, they soon realized, but in surprise, and when he fell back from the side of the cage, the others began to understand the source.

The face of the haggis seemed less hairy, with clumps of hair falling out before their hopeful eyes. Also, the creature's eyes seemed not so wild, not so animalistic.

"Kinnemore," Diane and Mickey whispered together.

Suddenly, the creature went into its frenzy once again, kicking at the cage near Geldion's face and sending the Prince sprawling backwards. Gary was on it in an instant, his spear prodding through the mesh. The spear loosed a jolt of its stunning energy, then a second, but the haggis ignored them, too consumed by its pain. It thrashed and threw itself against one side of the cage repeatedly, weakening the integrity of the supporting beams.

Tommy grabbed at the iron box, trying to lend it some support, but a haggis arm tore through the mesh and clawed at him.

"It will not hold!" Geno and Kelsey cried. The elf drew out his sword, Geno took out a hammer, and Gary shifted the angle, lining the speartip up for a killing strike.

As the tip neared the beast, though, it suddenly calmed, looking more confused and scared than angry.

"Easy, lad," Mickey implored.

Then the haggis began to jerk violently, and Gary retracted the spear, lest the creature impale itself. It let out a bloodcurdling shriek, a cry of sheer agony, and the companions looked on in disbelief as the haggis went through a series of convulsions and contortions. Bones crackled and popped as the creature's arms shifted, one shortening, the other lengthening until they had become the same length. Then its legs went through a similar realignment. The edges of its wide lips retracted and its face reformed, soon appearing more human than beast. Hair continued to fall from its face and body.

Then it was done, and in the cage, in the place of the wild hairy haggis, sat a naked man of about fifty years, a haggard look on his face and his gray hair standing about in a wild tangle. Deep scratches covered his body, especially on his arms and legs, and his fingers and fingernails were caked with dirt and dried blood from his frantic burrowing.

Prince Geldion fell to his knees and could hardly talk; Gerbil fell all over himself fumbling with his keys to unlock the cage, and Kelsey rushed to get a blanket from his saddlebags.

The cage was too battered for the door to be simply unlocked and pulled open, and Geno had to hammer at the thing for several minutes before freeing the confused and haggard King.

Kinnemore came out and stood straight for the first time in many years, his eyes wide with confusion, his limbs trembling. He wrapped himself in the offered blanket, seeming a dirty hobo awaiting the next train. Gary and Diane looked at each other, neither of them prepared for this pitiful sight. So stood Faerie's King, but could the man even talk?

"We'll stop at the nearest farmhouse," Mickey reasoned hopefully. "And find some clothing more fitting the man. And then we'll get him straight away to Braemar, for a meeting that's long overdue."

Kinnemore looked at the leprechaun and blinked, but said nothing.

20 † When the King Comes Calling

Flames licked the side of the Snoozing Sprite tavern from a dozen different fires. Men and women, even children, scrambled about Braemar, buckets in hand, battling valiantly against the continuing hail of flaming arrows. The grating scraping of steel against steel cut the air as battle joined in a pass west of the town, and the watchman on a ledge along the mountain wall east of Braemar cried out that Kinnemore's army was in sight, to the west, to the south, and to the north.

Lord Badenoch looked forlornly at the one apparently opened trail, a narrow pass running east out of Braemar, deep into the towering peaks of the mighty Dvergamal range. His army had been backed into the town, chased across the foothills by Kinnemore's superior forces. Even dug into the high ground, the militia of Braemar and the handful of dwarfs and gnomes that fought beside them could not resist the overwhelming flood of Connacht's army. They had been forced to break ranks barely minutes after battle had been joined, and Badenoch had declared the fight a rout and had told his men to run with all speed back to Braemar, and to gather together their families and their goods.

Badenoch knew that they could not hold the town from Kinnemore. He and his people would have to take up the offer of Kervin the dwarf and go into Dvergamal. At least, that is what the Lord of Braemar expected that most of his people would do. He would not force their loyalties in this matter. Those who wished to go into Dvergamal would be welcome; those who preferred surrender to Kinnemore would not be judged, at least not by Badenoch.

It all seemed a moot point now, though. Unexpectedly, King Kinnemore had chased Badenoch's retreating force right through the night, and the break of dawn had brought the assault in full on Braemar. Now the Lord knew that he would need to leave a strong contingent of warriors behind, to block the eastern pass and keep Kinnemore at bay. Braemar would lose many men this day, and Badenoch fully expected that he would be among the fallen. And he would lose his village, precious Braemar, to Kinnemore's fires. Tears welled in his wise eyes as he looked upon the scrambling throng of the bucket brigade, people fighting to save their homes.

Fighting an impossible war.

"Tell them to stop," the Lord said to one of his nearby commanders. "Go among the people and tell them to waste no more energy battling the fires. We must be away, on the trail before it is too late."

"It is already too late," came a gruff, but not unsympathetic, voice from the side. Badenoch turned to see Kervin and three other dwarfs rounding the corner of the building behind him, their faces more grim than usual.

"Kinnemore has men on the trail," Kervin explained. "He knew that you would try to run and so he sent riders along the passes north and south of the town."

"How many?" Badenoch asked.

"Enough to hold us at bay until the main force closes on us from the other side," Kervin assured him.

"How do you know this?" the Lord of Braemar demanded accusingly, his voice full of anger. "My watchmen have said nothing . . ."

"The stones told him," answered one of the other dwarfs, and Badenoch quieted, knowing then that Kervin's information was indisputable.

There would be no retreat into the mountains; Kinnemore had them surrounded. Badenoch looked all about helplessly, to the people still battling the flames despite the protest of his commander, to the soldiers running in from the western pass, many of them wounded and all of them carrying the unmistakable look of defeat. How far behind was Kinnemore's army? the Lord wondered.

"Dear Kervin," Badenoch said, his voice barely louder than a whisper. "Then what am I to do?"

"Stonebubbles," Kervin replied under his breath. He sent a stream of spittle to the ground. "Surrender," he said firmly.

Badenoch widened his eyes in surprise, never expecting to hear that word from one of the sturdy Buldrefolk.

"I see few options," Kervin went on determinedly. "They will soon close over us and that monster King will slaughter every person in the town. For the sake of your children, and the helpless wounded and aged, offer your surrender to King Kinnemore."

Badenoch paused for a long moment, contemplating the advice, knowing in his heart that Kervin was right. "What of the Buldrefolk?" he asked. "I doubt that Kinnemore would even accept your surrender, and even if he did, you would be speaking for only a handful."

Kervin snorted, as though the entire line of thought was absurd. "My kin and I will stand beside you—for the time. But we'll offer no surrender to King Kinnemore, not a one of us. He will allow us to go back to our mountain homes—and the gnomes to go to theirs—or we will fight him, every step." Kervin chuckled and spat again. "It will take more than a king's army to keep a dwarf out of Dvergamal!" he insisted, and his wide smile brought a small measure of comfort to the beleaguered Lord of Braemar.

Badenoch nodded appreciatively at his bearded friend, but his answering smile lasted only the second it took the Lord to remember the grim task ahead of him. Kervin's judgment was right, Badenoch knew, though the admission surely pained him. If the stones told the dwarf that soldiers were blocking the eastern pass, then the war had come to an abrupt end. The folk of Braemar could not afford a prolonged battle, could not afford any battle at all.

Badenoch motioned to his commanders, all of whom were listening intently to the conversation with the dwarfish leader. "Coordinate the firefighting," Badenoch explained. "Perhaps the King will accept our surrender and allow us to keep our homes."

In truth, Badenoch had given the commands only to keep his people busy, only to keep them from dwelling on the impending defeat. He doubted that Kinnemore would show much mercy, and knew that he, long a thorn in Connacht's side, would surely be replaced—as Baron Pwyll of Dilnamarra had been replaced.

Badenoch hoped that he would face his death bravely.

*   *   *   *   *

The real King Kinnemore was not as tall as the imposter haggis, but still he towered over Gary, and with the exception of Tommy (of course), Gary was the tallest of the group. He was twice Gary's age, but held himself straight and tall, his expression firm yet inquisitive. He used Kelsey's fine-edged sword to shave, leaving that telltale goatee, and though his clothing remained ultimately simple, it seemed to Gary that this man was indeed a King.

The troupe made fine progress away from the Crahgs, with Kinnemore taking Diane's horse and Diane accepting Tommy's invitation to ride on the giant's shoulder. Gerbil was a bit upset that his cage had to be left behind, but Kinnemore promised the gnome that he would be given all the credit he deserved, by his gnomish kinfolk in Gondabuggan, and by Connacht.

Truly King Kinnemore was in good spirits, ultimately relieved to be finished with his years of torment. His body was sore in a hundred different places, from the transformation and the years of living as a wild beast, but his mind was as sharp as ever, and his determination was plainly splayed across his handsome and strong features.

"I never forgot my true place," he explained to them all. "Even at those times when the savage instincts of my trappings overwhelmed my conscious decisions, I never forgot who I was."

"Even when you split Kelsey's horse in half?" Geno had to ask, just to put a typically negative dwarfish spin on all that had occurred.

Kinnemore took the remark lightly, with a resigned smile, then put a plaintive look upon his son, a look that tried pitifully to apologize for all the lost years. "And I never forgot my son," he said, nearly choking on every word.

Geno, still no fan of Prince Geldion's, wanted to interject another sarcastic remark. He looked at Kelsey before he spoke, though, and the elf, somewhat sharing the dwarf's feelings, recognized the look and gave a quick shake of his head. And so Geno let it go, figuring that both Kinnemore and Geldion had been through living Hell.

Kinnemore rode beside Geldion, talking, always talking. When they made camp, the King listened to Kelsey and to

Mickey, both complaining about the reign of the imposter king, a reign of terror during which every village of Faerie, every hamlet and every secluded farmhouse came to despise the name of Kinnemore. Mickey talked of impossible tithes demanded by Connacht, and of the edicts that declared magic, all magic, the work of evil demons; Kelsey talked of the seclusion of the Tylwyth Teg, of how in recent years, the elfs had come to remain mostly within their borders and had worked hard to keep any who was not Tylwyth Teg out of Tir na n'Og. Geno spoke similarly of the situation concerning the Buldrefolk, though the taciturn dwarf wasn't saying that the new developments, the heightened seclusion from the humans, were a bad thing, and Gerbil explained that the gnomes of Gondabuggan had long ago forsaken the kingdom altogether.

King Kinnemore sat quietly and listened through it all, obviously pained, then turned to Gary and Diane.

"And what of you two?" he asked. "What of the spearwielder and the woman who figured out Ceridwen's most devious riddle?"

Gary and Diane looked to each other and shrugged, not knowing what they might add to the conversation.

"There's not much from Bretaigne," Mickey explained. "The lad and lass're a long way from home."

Kinnemore accepted that readily enough. "And glad I am that you are a long way from home," the King said. "All of Faerie's peoples owe you their gratitude."

"All but Ceridwen," Gary remarked.

"Indeed," agreed the King. "And when this is done, you shall be properly rewarded, and Ceridwen properly punished."

"Just put things back together the way they belong," Diane was quick to respond, echoing Gary's sentiments exactly.

"Indeed," the King said again, and he was pleased.

Gary snapped his fingers suddenly, drawing everyone's attention. "Give him the armor and spear!" he said excitedly, pointing to the King.

Young sprout! the sentient weapon protested.

"Geno can fit it to him," Gary went on, ignoring the whining weapon. "Let Kinnemore look the part of King—that will put the Connacht troops behind him."

None of the others seemed overly exuberant at the suggestion—especially Geno, who wasn't thrilled at the prospect of trying to realign the tough metal. The dwarf had needed the flames of a dragon's breath, after all, to forge the metal of the spear. Kinnemore shook his head doubtfully through it all, and held his hand up repeatedly to stop Gary from going further with the reasoning.

"You are the spearwielder," Kinnemore declared. "And the wearer of Donigarten's armor. And from what my son tells me, you have earned the right many times over."

Gary glanced sidelong at Geldion, surprised that the man would show him any respect at all.

"You are the spearwielder," the King said again, determinedly, "and though you owe your allegiance to a far-off kingdom in the land beyond the Cancarron Mountains, I ask of you now that you remain for the time in Faerie, at my side."

Gary found that his hands were trembling.

"As my champion," Kinnemore finished.

Gary nearly swooned. Once again, he felt as though he was part of something much larger than himself, something eternal and important. He looked around to see Kelsey, Geno, and Gerbil all nodding solemnly, and understood then that he could do much to help the causes of their respective people. Prince Geldion, too, was nodding his head, putting aside his own ego for the sake of a battered kingdom.

Whether or not he could defeat Gary in single combat was unimportant at that time; Geldion had witnessed his own normally loyal soldiers converting to their enemy's cause in the name of Sir Cedric, and he had personally counseled his father to name Gary as champion of the throne.

And then Gary looked to Tommy and Mickey, and to Diane, all beaming—especially Diane—understanding the honor that had just been given to him, sharing his moment of glory.

"I'll do my best" was all that Gary could think of in reply.

Kinnemore nodded and seemed satisfied with that; then he rose and walked away from the firelight, motioning for his son to follow so that they could continue their private conversation.

Gary feared that he would be too excited to sleep, but he did drift off, and slept more soundly than he had in many nights.

*   *   *   *   *

Trumpets heralded the approach of the giant King as he rode triumphantly into Braemar, flanked by a score of armored knights. The pennants of Connacht and Dilnamarra waved in the morning breeze, one on either side of the King, and Lord Badenoch shuddered to think that the flag of Braemar would join that procession when Kinnemore turned north, towards the smaller village of Drochit.

The people of Braemar lined the wide street, cheering as they had been instructed, though halfheartedly, to be sure. Connacht soldiers filtered through the throng, prodding any who did not seem excited enough.

Both Badenoch and Kervin were waiting for Kinnemore in the center of the town, on the wide way between the central building, called the Spoke-lock, and the Snoozing Sprite. They said nothing, silently watched as Kinnemore rode a complete circuit of the town, smiling smugly and turning his head slowly from side to side to survey his newest "loyal" subjects.

Then Kinnemore was before the Lord of Braemar and the leader of the dwarfish contingent.

"I am not pleased," he said from high on his horse.

Badenoch did not reply.

"Your mere presence here wounds me, good dwarf," Kinnemore went on, revealing that his displeasure was not with the Lord of Braemar—at least, not entirely. "I should have thought that you and your kin would have come into the town at the side of the rightful King of Faerie."

"We were already here," Kervin replied sarcastically, "and saw no point in going out just to turn around and come back in."

Kinnemore's features crinkled into a scowl, and a low, feral snarl escaped his tight lips.

"We figured that you would be coming in soon anyway," Kervin went on easily, ignoring the glares of the armored knights, almost wishing that one of those smug humans would make a move against him.

"So be it," Kinnemore remarked, his grim tone hinting that there would be consequences for the actions of Kervin's dwarfs, and for Kervin's treasonous words.

"And what have you to say?" Kinnemore asked Badenoch. "To attack your King out on the field."

"To defend against an invading army," Badenoch corrected.

"Invading?" Kinnemore echoed, seemingly deeply hurt. "We marched to celebrate the dragonslaying, an event worthy of . . ."

"Then why is Baron Pwyll of Dilnamarra not among your ranks?" Badenoch dared to interrupt.

Kinnemore grinned evilly. "The Baron was delayed in Dilnamarra," he replied.

Badenoch slowly and deliberately shook his head, knowing full well that what he was about to say would ensure a noose about his neck. "Baron Pwyll was murdered in Dilnamarra."

"How dare you make such a preposterous claim?" Kinnemore balked.

"Your own son made such a claim!" the flustered Lord of Braemar retorted.

Kervin sucked in his breath; he did not think that so wise a thing to say, and even Badenoch, as soon as he had finished, realized how foolish he had been to reveal that Geldion had been about.

Kinnemore trembled; again came that animallike snarl. He calmed quickly, however, and painted his disarming smile back on his face. "You have spoken with Prince Geldion?" he asked.

"We have heard about the events in the west," Badenoch replied cryptically. "We know that Dilnamarra was overrun, that Tir na n'Og was besieged, though the army of Connacht was handed a stinging defeat at the hands of the proud Tylwyth Teg."

"That is not true!" Kinnemore roared, and he seemed to Badenoch as a spoiled child at that moment, a brat who had not gotten his way. Again he composed himself quickly.

"You should be more careful of your sources of information, Lord of Braemar," the King said. "False information can lead to rash, even fatal, decisions."

Badenoch squared his shoulders and did not justify the remark with a reply.

"So be it," Kinnemore said at length. He nodded to his left, and ten knights obediently dismounted, their armor scraping and clanking noisily. Kervin tightly clutched the axe hanging on his belt.

"Good dwarf," Kinnemore said, noticing the move, "you and your people are without guilt."

"We were on that field," Kervin boldly pointed out.

"You were misinformed," the King reasoned. "By a treasonous lord."

There, he had said it, plainly, and though the proclamation surely stung Badenoch (and condemned him), he was glad that it was finished, glad that the gloating King had put things out clearly on the table.

Badenoch relaxed, even turned to smile at Kervin and to put a calming hand atop the volatile dwarf's shoulder as Kinnemore's soldiers surrounded him.

Kervin returned the look, but the dwarf was not smiling. The only thing stopping him from cutting down the nearest guard was the knowledge that Badenoch had tried to calm him for more than his own sake. If Kervin started something now, then surely his rugged dwarfish kin would join in, and probably half of those men loyal to Badenoch as well. When it was over, Kervin realized, and Badenoch obviously realized, most of Braemar's men, and a good number of the town's women and children as well, would be dead.

So Kervin held his place and his temper. Badenoch was taken away in chains and King Kinnemore addressed the crowd, telling them that they had been deceived, but that he was here now, and peace would prevail and all would be put aright.

As much as the weary folk of Braemar wanted to believe those words (at least the part about things being put aright), not a face in town brightened with false hope.

*   *   *   *   *

"They are in Braemar," Gerbil reported to the group, except for Prince Geldion, later that morning. The gnome, an expected and not out-of-place visitor to these eastern parts, had been riding alone, up ahead, visiting the area farmhouses (though most were now empty). "Word spreads that Badenoch has surrendered."

"Stonebubbles," Geno grumbled.

"A wise move," Mickey remarked. "Be sure that all the town would've been laid to waste if he did not."

"Stonebubbles!" Geno growled again.

"That could make our course easier," Kelsey reasoned, and Kinnemore was nodding his agreement.

"We know now where to find the imposter," said the King.

"But how to get in to him?" asked Diane. "If Kinne . . . if the haggis is in Braemar, then all the town will be surrounded by his army. I'm not so sure that they'll be willing to believe that you're really the King."

Kinnemore nodded to the east, where a lone rider could then be seen, fast flying for the group. "That will be the job for my son," he reasoned. "By all accounts, he is still the commander of the Connacht army, second only to the imposter. Let us see if Prince Geldion is worthy of his heritage."

Diane studied the King hard at that moment, soon coming to realize that Kinnemore did not, for the moment, doubt his son. She was glad for that, for Geldion's sake and not for her own.

"The haggis is in Braemar," Geldion said, bringing his mount to a fast stop before the others. "And Badenoch has surrendered."

"So we have heard," Kinnemore replied.

"Badenoch is in chains," Geldion went on. "And word has it that he will be executed at sunset."

"Big surprise," Mickey remarked.

"What about Kervin?" Geno asked.

Geldion shrugged. "I heard nothing," he honestly answered. "But if the dwarf is still in Braemar, then know that he is not in good spirits!"

"How shall we get in?" Kinnemore asked abruptly, directing the question to his son and reminding them all that they hadn't the time to sit and talk. Even at a swift pace, they would not make the village proper before midafternoon, and if they encountered any delays, then Badenoch would be hanging by his neck.

"I doubt that I will be able to talk us all into Braemar," Geldion, who had obviously been planning that very job, answered. "Not the giant, certainly, and the dwarf and elf . . ."

"All of us," Gary interrupted grimly.

Questioning looks came at him from every side, even from Diane.

"All of us," he said again, not backing down an inch. "We have been through this together, and so together we'll see it through, to the end."

"But lad," Mickey quietly protested.

"Use your tricks," Gary demanded of Mickey. "And you," he added to Geldion, "use your mouth. Tommy's been a horse before, and so he'll be a horse again," he said, referring to the time when Mickey had made Tommy look like a mule so that he and Geno could deliver the reforged spear and armor to Dilnamarra inconspicuously.

"And you'll be more believable," Gary added to Geldion, "if you're surrounded by soldiers when you escort the spearwielder into Braemar."

"Human soldiers," Geldion corrected, eyeing Kelsey and Geno doubtfully.

"So they'll appear," Gary replied without missing a beat. "As will your father. The haggis does not know what happened to you."

"So we're hoping," Mickey interjected. Gary turned to

the sprite, seeming unsure for the first time since he had begun laying out his plan.

"We're not for knowing what Ceridwen's seen, lad," the leprechaun explained. "And what she's telled to her haggis lackey."

"Then we'll have to take that chance," King Kinnemore unexpectedly answered. "The plan is sound, so I say." He looked around at the troupe, affording them the respect they so obviously deserved. "And what say you?" he asked of them all.

"Lead on, Prince Geldion," said a determined Kelsey. "And quickly. Lord Badenoch is too fine a man to share Baron Pwyll's undeserved fate."

Geno grumbled something (certainly less than complimentary) under his breath, but then nodded his agreement.

They were off in a few moments, after the leprechaun worked a bit of his magic, with Diane riding Tommy, who now appeared as a plow horse.

They encountered soldiers an hour later, the back ranks of the Connacht army, settling in for their stay on the fields to the west of Braemar. Whispers went up all about the newcomers, concerns for the appearance of the spear-wielder, and more than one soldier eyed the group intently, fearful of a leprechaun's tricks, perhaps. But not a man would openly oppose Geldion, and he and his escorts were allowed passage.

"Do you know the commander of this brigade?" Kinnemore asked his son quietly as they made their way through the large encampment. The wise King was thinking that perhaps the time had come to enlist some allies. Even if they got into Braemar unopposed, convincing the army that he was the real King, and their leader an imposter—and the haggis, no less—might not be an easy feat. The prospect of a battle within the town seemed plausible.

"Roscoe Gilbert," Geldion replied, and he paused and eyed his father, coming to understand and agree with the logic. "I have trained with him on occasion."

Kinnemore nodded and Geldion broke away from the others, trotting to the nearest campfire to enquire of the field commander's whereabouts.

"Thinking to make some friends?" Mickey, sitting invisibly on Gary's mount right beside the King, asked.

Kinnemore, eyes steeled straight ahead, nodded slightly.

The group did not pass all the way through the encampment unopposed. A line of cavalry galloped around them and stood to block them with Prince Geldion and an older warrior, Roscoe Gilbert, sitting directly before the riding King.

Kinnemore eyed the man directly and slipped back the hood of his traveling cloak.

Gilbert did not blink.

"An incredible tale," the soldier said a moment later, his tone showing that he was not convinced.

"A true tale," Gary replied boldly.

Gilbert turned a nervous glance up and down his ranks. He knew that many of the Connacht soldiers had deserted back near Tir na n'Og, swearing fealty to Sir Cedric. And now the spearwielder was here, right in his midst, with a tale to turn all the world upside down.

"And you have nothing to lose by escorting us," Gary went on, "and everything to lose by not."

"What say you, Gilbert?" Kinnemore asked bluntly. "Do tales of Ceridwen's troublesome interference so surprise you?"

They were off at a swift pace soon after, Geldion and Gary flanking Kinnemore, Diane at Gary's side, and Roscoe Gilbert at Geldion's side. At Kelsey's insistence, Mickey let the illusion drop then, showing the elf, dwarf, and gnome as

they truly appeared (though Mickey kept up Tommy's
façade, knowing that the sight of a giant would unnerve the
sturdiest of soldiers in the best of conditions).

They swept through the next encampments without incident and without delay, Roscoe Gilbert and Prince Geldion
bringing even more soldiers into their wake. By the time
they crossed the western pass, moving into Braemar proper,
few Connacht soldiers had been left on the field behind
them.

Predictably, the entourage attracted quite a bit of attention
as they approached, and most of the people were out and
about anyway, since sunset drew near. Angry whispers
filtered through the crowd; more than one fight broke out,
but the Connacht soldiers were too numerous for the poorly
armed citizens of Braemar to do anything to prevent the
impending hanging.

Those people didn't know what to expect—certainly
nothing good—when Prince Geldion and some of Kinnemore's field commanders swept into the town. The
presence of Kelsey, Geno, and Gerbil, who were all known
to them, and of the spearwielder and his wife, whom they
considered to be allies, brought mixed reactions, some
wondering if the time had come for hope, others thinking
that their supposed friends had either been captured or had
gone over to the undeniable flow of Kinnemore's tide of
conquest.

Kervin, standing by the tree designated as the spot for the
hanging, and Badenoch, even then being led out of the
Snoozing Sprite's wine cellar, his temporary dungeon, did
allow themselves a moment of hope, for they alone among
Braemar's populace knew of the mission to the Crahgs.

The imposter King, standing with his knights in a glade
beside the Spoke-lock, to the side of the hanging tree, did
not know what to make of the entourage, did not know why

Geldion would ride in beside the enemy spearwielder, let alone in the presence of Kelsenellenelvial Gil-Ravadry, that most hated elf-lord.

But Geldion did come in, directly, his newfound friends in his wake and his father, hidden beneath the cowls of a traveling cloak, at his side. Geldion walked his gray right up before the imposter, the Prince's eyes unblinking.

The imposter looked from Geldion to Gary, let his gaze linger long over this man who had become such a thorn in his side, this man who had banished Ceridwen, the imposter's mentor, to her island. Then he looked back to Geldion, trying to find some clue about the unexpected arrival. Why had Gary Leger come openly into Braemar? And why were so many of Kinnemore's own field commanders, and the Prince of Connacht, lined up behind the man?

He waited a long while, but Geldion said nothing, forcing him to make the first move.

"So you have returned," the imposter said at length, indignantly. "I had wondered if you were dead out on the field."

"Not dead" was all that Geldion replied through his clenched teeth.

"Then what is this about?" the imposter demanded. "Have you brought the spearwielder and an elf-lord into my fold?"

"Or have they brought me into theirs?" Geldion said, voicing the imposter's unspoken thought.

"What is this about?" the imposter demanded again, a feral snarl accompanying the question.

"It is about the rightful King of Connacht," said the tall hooded man seated between Geldion and Gary Leger. "And it is about an imposter, a beast tamed by Ceridwen and put in the rightful King's stead." He reached up to clasp the sides of his hood and began slowly drawing it back.

"Kill them!" the haggis roared. Knights bristled; there came the ring of many weapons pulling free of their scabbards.

The friends held calm, kept their composure, and that fact alone bought them the needed seconds.

King Kinnemore pulled the hood from his face. Gasps arose from those close enough to view him, nearly an exact likeness of the man he faced, and whispers rolled out from the glade, down the streets and through every house.

"I am Kinnemore," said the rightful King.

"By whose word?" demanded the imposter. His voice broke as he spoke, guttural grunts coming between each word. Diane and Gary watched him closely, as did Mickey and the others, noticing that his beard seemed suddenly larger and more wild.

"By my word!" King Kinnemore said forcefully, rising tall in his saddle and turning all about so that all near to him could hear clearly the proclamation, and see clearly the man speaking the words. "Trapped by Ceridwen these last years in the body of a beast." The rightful King settled in his saddle and squarely eyed the imposter, who was grunting and wheezing, his mouth widening to the sides.

"While the beast sat on my throne," Kinnemore declared. "While the beast led my kingdom to ruin!"

The knights in the glade escorting Lord Badenoch did not know how to react; none of the soldiers, even those who had come into town in the friends' wake, knew how to react. The battle became, so suddenly, a personal duel between these two men who seemed, physically at least, so much alike.

The hush held for several long seconds, no one knowing where to begin or who should begin.

"Long live the King!" proclaimed Lord Badenoch and he pulled free of the soldiers holding his arms (and they were too overwhelmed to try to stop him) and lifted his chained hands in defiance. "Long live the rightful King of Faerie!"

The imposter tried to say, "Kill him!" but the words came out only as a growl, that same feral, uncontrollable snarl that the true Kinnemore had known all too well in his years romping about the Crahgs. There could be no doubt anymore; the imposter's beard had widened, encompassing all of his face.

He shrieked in rage and pain as his body twisted and cracked, Ceridwen's enchantment stolen by the truth, stolen by the appearance of Faerie's rightful King. The soldier nearest to him made a move, but the haggis slapped the man, launching him a dozen feet across the glade.

Fully revealed, the creature whipped back and forth, eyes wild, maw dripping drool.

Cedric's spear took him cleanly in the breast.

He staggered backwards, clutching at the weapon's shaft, growling and whimpering. Then he fell to the grass and lay still.

No one moved, no soldier put his weapon away, and all eyes turned to Gary Leger, the spearwielder.

The moment was stolen an instant later, when the haggis leaped up and tossed the bloodied spear aside. "*Ee ya yip yip yip!*" it wailed, and all covered their ears—and all in the creature's path fell away in terror as it rushed from the glade, and from the town, down the western pass and farther, running to the southeast, towards its hilly home.

"Tough little bug," Mickey remarked dryly.

"Long live the rightful King of Faerie!" Gary cried, sitting tall atop his stallion. He slid from his mount, recovered the spear, then fell to his knees before the mounted King, bowing his head.

That was all the folk of Braemar, and the weary men of the Connacht army, needed to see. The cry went up, from one end of town to the other, along the mountain passes and through every encampment.

The cry went up for King Kinnemore, for Connacht.

And for peace.

21 † Head On

Gary walked quietly, inconspicuously, down the western trail leading out of Braemar. He had left his armor back in town, glad for the reprieve, glad to be out of the suit, and back there too, talking and singing in the Snoozing Sprite, were Diane and Kelsey, Geno and Gerbil, and all the others. Even without the remarkable armor, Gary was recognized by every sentry he passed and by everyone else walking along the road, most heading back into Braemar for the celebration. Gary's size alone marked him clearly, for the only man in Braemar as large as he was King Kinnemore himself.

The gentle folk granted Gary his privacy, though, only nodded and offered a quick greeting, and soon he was off the main trail, walking down a narrow and rocky path that seemed no more than a crevice cutting between the foothills.

Around a sharp bend, he came into a sheltered dell, almost a cave beneath a wide overhang, where Mickey was waiting for him.

"You asked me to come here to tell me that you were leaving," Gary remarked, having long ago recognized the sprite's intentions.

Mickey shrugged noncommittally. "Would ye have me stay, then? Be sure that all in the town're dancin' and

267

playin', and wouldn't their party be greater if they catched a leprechaun in the course?"

"Kinnemore and Badenoch will grant you your freedom," Gary reasoned. "They owe you that much at least."

Again the leprechaun shrugged. "I been too long with humans," Mickey muttered. "Too long in tricking them and too long in dancing from their greedy clutches. And too long working to set aright things that aren't truly me own concern. I'm back for Tir na n'Og, lad, back to me home that's no longer pressed by an army.

"And so I've asked ye to come out," Mickey went on. "Ye should be thinking of yer own home now."

Gary looked around, a hint of desperation in his darting eyes. Mickey was right, it seemed, but it had all ended so suddenly with the revelation of the true King, that Gary hadn't emotionally prepared himself for returning to Real-earth. Not yet.

"Ye fought the war and now ye're wanting to enjoy the spoils," Mickey reasoned.

Now it was Gary's turn to simply shrug.

"Is it over?" he asked plaintively.

Mickey sighed—it seemed that the leprechaun, too, was somewhat sorry the adventure had apparently come to an abrupt end. "All the folk will rally about the rightful King," Mickey reasoned. "Even Prince Geldion and Badenoch have seen it in their hearts to end their feud."

"I do not believe that it is over," came a commanding voice from behind. The two turned to see King Kinnemore walking around the bend.

"You followed me," Gary remarked.

"I do not think it is over," the King said again, ignoring the accusation. "Not with a witch soon to be coming out of her hole."

"Oh, she's coming out," Mickey agreed. "But not with

much behind her. Ceridwin's power's in those she tricks to being allies, and she's to find few in these times. All the humans'll be together with yerself returned to the throne, and even the elfs and dwarfs'll come to yer call if ye're needing them."

Gary was hardly paying attention to any of it, still perplexed by the appearance of the King. "Why did you follow me?" he asked bluntly, as soon as he found a break in the conversation.

Kinnemore turned a disarming smile his way. "Because I knew the sprite would not remain," he answered. "And I know that you need our good Mickey to return to your own home."

Both Gary and Mickey turned up their eyebrows at that proclamation. As far as they knew, only Mickey, the pixies, Kelsey and Geno, and a few other of the Tylwyth Teg knew of Gary's true origins, with everyone else merely thinking that he had come from the far-off land of Bretaigne.

"I guess he's the King for a reason," Mickey said dryly.

Kinnemore chuckled at that. "I had many dealings with Bretaigne in my first years on the throne," he explained. "Before the witch interfered. I know a Bretaigne accent, and know, too," he added, looking straight at Gary, "when I do not hear one."

"Fair enough," Mickey admitted.

"And I have entertained visitors from your world before," Kinnemore went on. "Thus I know that you may soon be returning, and thus have I watched closely your every move, even following you to this place."

"To say goodbye?" Gary asked.

"To ask that you remain," the King replied. "For a time."

"Oh, here we go again," Mickey whispered under his breath as Gary squared his shoulders and assumed a determined expression.

"The witch will soon be free," Kinnemore declared. "And she does indeed have allies," he added, shooting a quick glance at Mickey. "The mountains of Penllyn hold goblin tribes and great clans of mountain trolls."

"She'll not come out with them," Mickey reasoned. "Not in an open fight. Never has that been Ceridwen's way."

"Perhaps not," the King conceded. "But Robert is no more, and the witch will not surrender her designs."

"You want to go after her?" Gary stated as much as asked, his tone skeptical and bordering on incredulous. Gary had been to Ynis Gwydrin before, and the memory was not a pleasant one.

The King didn't flinch a bit as he slowly nodded.

"Oh begorra," Mickey muttered.

"Now would seem the time," Kinnemore said. "Ceridwen and her powers are locked upon an island, and our army is already assembled on the field. We can deal Ceridwen a blow from which she will be years in recovering, cripple her to the point where her mischief will not be so great."

"Why're ye needing Gary Leger?" Mickey wanted to know.

"We are not," Kinnemore replied to the sprite, though he never took his unblinking gaze off Gary. "But would it not add to the legend? And would not the presence of the spearwielder serve well the morale of the soldiers? Do not underestimate the power of emotion, good sprite. Why, after all, did Ceridwen try to prevent the reforging of Donigarten's spear?"

"Now, how're ye knowing all of this?" Mickey asked.

"I guess he's the King for a reason," Gary answered, mimicking Mickey's earlier tones.

"She feared the emotions inspired by the reforged weapon," Kinnemore said, answering his own question. Again he put an admiring look directly on Gary Leger. "And rightly so, so it would seem."

Gary held the King's gaze for a long moment, then turned to regard Mickey, the leprechaun sitting on a stone and shaking his head, and lighting his long-stemmed pipe.

"I want to stay," Gary said.

"I knew ye would," Mickey replied without hesitation.

"And you, too, I ask to come along, good sprite," Kinnemore said. "And by my word and Gary Leger's arm, not a man will bother you."

"It's not the men I'm fearing," Mickey whispered under his breath, thinking of the huge mountain trolls, and worse, of the witch herself, as mighty an enemy as could be found in all of Faerie. Despite all of that, though, Mickey knew that Kinnemore's reasoning was sound. Robert was gone, and without the dragon to balance the power, they had to work hard and fast to keep Ceridwen in check.

Mickey just wanted to know why he, a carefree leprechaun used to romping in the secluded meadows of a sylvan forest, kept getting caught up in the middle of it all!

*   *   *   *   *

Gary knew that there was something big, probably a mountain troll, crouching around the tumble of boulders. When he paused and concentrated, he could hear the monster's rhythmic breathing, barely perceptible against the steady breeze that blew over Penllyn this day.

The armored man turned back to his companions and nodded; the four of them, Gary, Diane, Tommy, and Mickey, had played out this same routine three times already in the five days of fighting since the Connacht army had entered the mountainous region around the witch's island home.

Diane, more than any of them, held her breath now. She still hadn't quite gotten used to the spectacle of a mountain troll. They weren't nearly as big as Tommy, only twelve feet tall, but they looked like the stuff of the mountains that gave them their name. Their skin was a grayish color, sometimes tending towards brown, and their heads were square, faces flat, like a big slab of stone. They wore little clothing, and needed no armor with their thick skin; and whatever hair they had, on top of their heads, across their massive chests, or anywhere else, typically stuck out in clumps, like small bushes among the rocky sides of a mountain. No, trolls weren't as imposing as Tommy, and certainly the spectacle of the giant had somewhat prepared Diane for the enemies she was facing now, but she doubted that she would ever be comfortable seeing one of the dirty monsters, even a dead one.

Gary rested back against the stones and took a deep, steadying breath. He lifted his mighty spear in both hands, took another breath and adjusted his too-loose helmet, then rushed around the bend, shouting wildly.

The troll leaped out at him, club in hand, but the man, expecting the resistance, had already begun to backpedal.

Around the bend came the pursuing troll, and its square jaw surely drooped open in surprise when it found an eighteen-foot-tall giant waiting for it!

Tommy's uppercutting fist had barely begun its ascent when it connected squarely on that jaw, and by the time the troll broke free of the giant's swinging arm, the dimwitted evil brute was several feet in the air, and rising as rapidly as the fist. The troll slammed down against the rounded top shoulder of the boulder tumble, cracking its thick head, and slid slowly down the side, unconscious at least, and probably dead.

"There's another one, lad!" Mickey squealed from his high perch on a ledge against the mountain wall behind the main group.

"Behind you!" Diane added, rushing to Gary's side.

The young man spun on his heel, thrusting desperately with his spear, scoring a solid hit in the rushing troll's belly. The brute roared in agony, but could not stop its charge, further impaling itself, and running Gary down.

Tommy turned to try to catch his tumbling friend, but Mickey yelled again, and the giant spun back just in time to take a hit from yet another troll's whipping club. Tommy grunted, not really hurt, and responded with a punch that crushed in the troll's face.

But two more trolls stood behind that one, each delivering a solid whack against the giant's thick arm. And another troll came in from the back side of the boulder tumble, bearing down on Diane, whose short sword surely seemed shorter still facing the likes of a twelve-foot-tall, nine-hundred-pound troll!

Diane shrieked and stabbed, scoring a glancing hit. Her heart stopped as the troll's great club swished across, but to her ultimate relief (and amazement) the monster somehow missed her cleanly. Not stopping to consider her fortune, she struck again, and a third time, each stroke of her elfish blade drawing a line of red blood on the massive creature's torso.

The troll responded with its club, and again missed badly. It snorted in disbelief and kicked with its huge boot—and missed again, overbalancing in the process so that when Diane wisely snuck in under the high-waving foot and jabbed at the knee of its lone supporting leg, the monster fell heavily to the stone.

Diane rushed around near the monster's head, slashed at grasping troll fingers—which, for some reason that Diane could not understand, were grasping at the empty air three feet to her left—and dared to dive in close, poking hard at the fallen behemoth's throat.

She scored a single hit, and dove away desperately as the

suddenly wheezing monster began to thrash and kick. The troll grasped at its torn throat, bubbles of blood and spittle coming out through its fingers. Its shin slammed against a boulder and sent the stone flying; its foot slammed straight down, cracking the stone beneath it.

"More, lass!" Mickey called above the tumult, and Diane nearly fainted away when she looked back around the boulders to see half a dozen more mountain trolls rushing down the path behind the boulder tumble, bearing down on the group. She called for Gary, and saw that he had slipped out from under the dead troll, but was working hard (and futilely) to free up his impaled spear.

Diane looked to Tommy, just as the giant caught a handful of troll hair in each massive hand and, ignoring the clubs pounding hard against his sides, slammed the brutes' heads together with a resounding *crack!*

Diane winced as Tommy slammed the heads together repeatedly. The clubbing stopped after the third or fourth smack; the heavy clubs fell to the ground.

"Six of them!" Mickey called.

"Run away!" was Gary's sound advice. He finally tore free the spear, but slipped on the wet, gore-covered stone, falling hard to his back.

Diane was beside him, helping him, urging him to his feet.

Trolls swarmed about the boulder tumble, spiked clubs in hand, with only poor Tommy to block their way.

Tommy, and a hail of arrows.

Horns sounded from every trail, and scores of Connacht soldiers, led by Prince Geldion, followed the volley, shouting for Sir Cedric at the top of their lungs.

It was over before Gary had even found the opportunity to strike another blow, all six of the new trolls joining their five comrades in death.

"How did you know?" Gary asked Geldion when all had settled.

"Credit the King," the Prince explained. "He did not approve of your little band running off to fight on its own."

"We've been doing that since the war began," Diane interjected.

"So my father knows," replied the Prince, "and so, he believes, does Ceridwen. The witch understands the implications of the war, and knows that the spearwielder is an important target. He would not let you go out on your own, though you believed that to be your course."

"Thank him for us all," Diane remarked.

"I guess he's the King for a reason," both Mickey and Gary said together, sharing a knowing wink.

Gary looked at the fallen trolls—nearly a dozen more in this encounter alone. And similar battles were being waged all across Penllyn, with Kinnemore's army, bolstered by Lord Badenoch and the forces of Braemar, rousing the trolls and goblins from their filthy mountain holes, scattering them to the wastelands to the east, and killing those that did not flee. By all reports nearly five hundred mountain trolls had been slain, and perhaps ten times that number of goblins, the unorganized and chaotic tribes proving no match for the teamwork of the skilled and trained soldiers.

In five short days, the heart of Ceridwen's ragtag forces had been torn out of her mountain stronghold.

Gary wished that Kelsey might have witnessed this. And Geno! Yes, he decided, the sturdy dwarf would have liked to walk over the bodies of so many dead trolls and goblins. But neither had chosen to make the trek to Penllyn, not now. Kelsey was off to Tir na n'Og to report on the monumental happenings and to advise his elders in their dealings with the rightful King, and Geno had simply decided that he had been too long from his forge and his backlog of work.

They would have enjoyed this rout, Gary knew. They would have applauded every battle, knowing that the land of Faerie would be a better place when Penllyn was purged.

And so, with grim satisfaction, Gary Leger looked over the newest battlefield, and Ceridwen looked over Gary Leger, the frustrated witch fuming, feeling positively impotent. She could not yet go free of her island, could not even send forth her magic to aid the monsters in the mountains. And the one contingent of monkey bats she had sent flying out from Ynis Gwydrin had been met by a seemingly solid sheet of arrows, most of the strange-looking monsters falling dead in Loch Gwydrin before they had even cleared the lake.

She had lost Kinnemore, and had lost her hold on Connacht and the army that came with that hold. And now, before her very eyes, the remnants of her last force, the mountain trolls and goblins that she could always manipulate or force under her control, were being swept away.

Positively impotent.

It was a feeling that the mighty witch did not enjoy.

"Geek!" she screamed, and the spindly-armed goblin, who had been standing only a foot behind the witch, jumped so violently that he left one of his shoddy boots sitting in place on the floor.

"Yesses, my Lady," he grovelled, falling to his knees and slobbering kisses all over Ceridwen's beautiful shoes (and at the same time, trying to quietly manipulate the boot back on his smelly foot). The goblin had been beside "his Lady" for many years and knew that this was no time to give Ceridwen any excuse to vent her rage.

The witch pulled her foot from the goblin's spit-filled grasp, retracted the leg, and kicked Geek hard in the face.

"Thank you, my Lady!" he squealed, and she kicked him again, closing one of his eyes.

"Did you send my messenger?" the witch demanded.

Geek looked at her quizzically—and promptly got kicked in the face a third time. Of course he had sent the monkey bat—Ceridwen knew that he had sent the monkey bat!

A single thought overruled the goblin's confusion: No time to give her an excuse!

"Yesses, of yesses!" the goblin squealed. "It flied off last night, it did! It should be close to Giant's Thumb . . ."

"Oh, shut up," Ceridwen grumbled and kicked the goblin square in his smiling face one more time.

"Yesse . . ." Geek started to reply, but he wisely realized that answering that command was directly contrary to that command. With a whimper, he rolled out of kicking reach and cowered on the floor. After a few minutes he dared to look up again, and saw his Lady standing by the tower's window, staring out to the east, to the mountains and beyond.

Ceridwen was more calm then, finding a measure of composure in the knowledge that she was not sitting idly by, that she was at least taking some action to aid in her cause.

But even then, standing safe in the bastion of her evil power, a castle that she had owned longer than the memory of any living man, the witch realized that she might be playing her final card.

*   *   *   *   *

At the end of that fifth day, bold King Kinnemore set his camp on the very banks of Loch Gwydrin, in plain sight of the witch's crystalline castle. Assured by Mickey that the witch could take no personal actions, magical or otherwise, beyond the boundaries of her place of banishment, the King, still carrying the scars of outrage from his years running wild in the Crahgs, thought it fitting to push the witch to the edge of her sensibilities, to taunt her in every manner that he could find.

To that end, he set his soldiers to singing, loud and clear, the ancient songs of proud Connacht.

Diane was charmed by the magical sight of Ynis Gwydrin—and the witch's castle was truly an enchanting vision—but Gary Leger, who had been to that island and that castle, was not alone in his trepidation of simply being in view of the place.

Even Mickey, who constantly assured Gary that the witch was fully bound to her island, seemed on the edge of his nerves. So great was their fear of the witch that Gary and the other soldiers were honestly relieved each morning when they left the encampment, and the sight of Ynis Gwydrin, and went into the mountains to hunt giant trolls.

Those trolls were getting harder to find, and by the third day of the Loch Gwydrin encampment, the eighth day of the assault on Penllyn, only a single small skirmish occurred, and that with a handful of goblins that surrendered before the Connacht bows thrummed from the release of the first arrows. That same day, when the sun was at its highest point, King Kinnemore declared Penllyn secured.

"And a good thing," Mickey remarked to the King shortly thereafter. "The witch'll be walking free in just two days, by me guess, and we'd be a smarter bunch to be gone from the mountains before she can start her mischief."

"Off and running," Gary agreed.

King Kinnemore said nothing, just turned a longing stare out towards the crystalline castle. In ages past, Ynis Gwydrin had been the seat of goodly power in Faerie; Kinnemore's own ancestors had presided over their kingdom from the place that Ceridwen now called home.

"Don't ye even be thinkin' it!" Mickey spouted, recognizing the gaze, and the wish behind that gaze. The leprechaun's outburst brought a number of looks—Geldion's, Gary's and Diane's included—sharply on him. One simply did not talk to a King that way!

But Kinnemore gave a short laugh and nodded his head in agreement. "We came to Penllyn to cripple the witch," he said. "To steal her means of mischief, or at least, to steal the army she might conjure to deliver that mischief. Penllyn is secure, excepting the island fortress, and Ceridwen will be a long time in recovering from the wounds we have inflicted."

"And from the alliances you have forged," Gary put in.

Again, King Kinnemore nodded his head in agreement; then, to Gary's profound relief (and the leprechaun blew a sigh, as well) the King gave the orders to break down the camp.

The tents were almost down by midafternoon, and the four friends hoped that they would get several hours of marching before setting the next camp (though Tommy, who had spent many fairly good years serving Ceridwen on Ynis Gwydrin, looked to the isle more than once, his expression almost homesick).

Geldion came to the group then, his face grim. "Lord Badenoch rode in," he explained, "just a few minutes ago. He sought a private audience with my father."

"Are ye feeling left out?" Mickey asked, not quite understanding the Prince's sour expression.

"There are rumors that an army approaches from the east," Geldion explained. "A vast host. Robert's old minions, come to the call of Ceridwen."

"Lava newts," Gary whispered.

Diane eyed Gary, and then Geldion, nervously. She remembered Gary's tales of the dragon's mountain castle, of the lizardlike guards that served and protected mighty Robert.

"We will hold the mountains against them," Geldion said determinedly. "Our position is one of strong defense."

"For a day and a half," Gary put in.

"Until the witch flies free," Mickey added grimly.

22 † Preemptive Strike

Gary, Diane, and Mickey were beside King Kinnemore, Geldion, and Lord Badenoch before dawn the next morning, on a high plateau that peeked through the towering mountains and afforded a view of the eastern plains.

The sun broke the horizon in their eyes, dawn spreading its lighted fingers across those plains, but all the companions saw was a dusty haze, and a darkness so complete beneath it that seemed as if a foul lake or a great, black amorphous blob was rolling out towards them.

"Thousands," King Kinnemore remarked, and for the first time, he seemed to doubt the wisdom of coming to Penllyn.

"Tens of thousands," Badenoch corrected. "Eager to serve a new leader, eager to anoint Ceridwen as their god-figure."

"We could fight a retreating action out of Penllyn," Prince Geldion offered. "Nearly half our force is mounted, and should be able to flank any spurs of lava newts that rush out to challenge our flight."

"And then where?" the King asked. "Back to our homes? Back to Connacht and Braemar? Which town will Ceridwen likely strike against first?"

"Braemar," Badenoch was quick to put in, for his village was the closest to Penllyn, with the exception of Connacht itself.

"Connacht," Kinnemore corrected. "Ceridwen is outraged. She will come straight for the throne, straight for my heart."

"Connacht's high walls will . . ." Geldion began, a snarl of determination accompanying his words. But Kinnemore cut him short with an upraised hand.

"Connacht's high walls will offer little protection against the witch's magic," the King answered. "Ceridwen will open the holes through which her wretched army might flow."

"We will kill five newts for every man!" Geldion promised.

"And even so, it would seem that we would still need ten times our number of men," the King answered. But Kinnemore, despite the grim words, did not seem despondent, seemed, in his own way, at least as determined as his volatile son.

"What are you thinking?" the perceptive Diane asked him bluntly.

"Ceridwen comes free tomorrow," Kinnemore replied. "Today she remains on her island." He looked directly at the woman, the set of his eyes showing that he spoke in all seriousness and with a clear mind. "Her small island."

"Oh begorra," they heard Mickey grumble.

That clued in Gary to the leprechaun's suspicions, a guess that he shared. "You're going after her," he said to the King, his tone making the statement sound like an accusation.

Kinnemore didn't flinch. "My son will command . . ."

"I'm going with you!" Geldion interrupted.

Kinnemore paused for a long moment and studied the Prince. Geldion had been fiercely loyal all his life, even against his own better judgment, because he had believed that the haggis was truly the King. Kinnemore had heard this above all else when his field commanders and old friends spoke of his son. It wouldn't be fair now, Kinnemore realized, to force Geldion to remain behind, even if he believed that Geldion was the best choice to handle the impending battle with the lava newts.

He bobbed his head, just slightly, and Geldion returned the nod.

"Lord Badenoch," the King said, turning the other way to face the proud man, "it would seem that I am without a commander."

Always conscious of protocol, the man did not verbally respond, just came to a straighter posture.

"And so I give you the command of Connacht's army," Kinnemore went on. "And in the case that we do not return, I give to you the crown of Connacht. Wear it well, good man, for if we do not return, then surely your first days as King will be filled with difficult decisions."

Badenoch unexpectedly shook his head. "In this I must refuse," he answered, and more than King Kinnemore gasped in surprise.

"You have a commander," the Lord of Braemar explained. "And though I applaud Prince Geldion for wanting to accompany you on this most important mission, I fear that his judgment is skewed, and his wisdom is altogether missing."

"You speak words that could be considered treasonous," Kinnemore replied, but there was no threat in his inquisitive tone.

"So they would be, if they were not true," Badenoch said. "The mission to Ynis Gwyndrin is of utmost importance, but so too is the coming battle. Our armies must fight well now or be destroyed, and scattered from the mountains. While flattered by your confidence, I must admit that I am not qualified for what you have asked. I have never directed a force a quarter as large as the army of Connacht, nor am I familiar with the training and tactics of your soldiers."

"Surely there are commanders . . ." Kinnemore began to reason, but Badenoch was adamant.

"I have witnessed your army in action without the leadership of Prince Geldion," he firmly replied. "They were not an impressive force."

"I wish to go to Ynis Gwydrin," Geldion said through gritted teeth, for he could see that his chance to accompany his father was fast slipping away.

"Yet you are needed here," Badenoch answered. "To direct our combined forces in a battle that might well determine the future of our land. I understand your preference, and applaud your loyalty and courage. But you are a Prince of Faerie, and if you are ever to properly ascend to your father's throne, then you must learn now that your personal preferences are of little consequence. To be a leader, Prince Geldion, means to understand the needs of your subjects, and to put those needs above your personal preferences."

Gary, and everyone else, gawked in disbelief. Lord Badenoch had just put this tentative and so new alliance to a difficult test by speaking to, scolding, Prince Geldion publicly. But the Lord of Braemar's words had been honest, and undeniably wise, and even Geldion, showing no outward signs of any impending explosion, seemed to understand that.

King Kinnemore started to respond, but paused and put a thoughtful look over his son.

Geldion glanced around to all his companions, his expression revealing that caged and hungry look that had typified the volatile Prince's behavior for the last few years. That expression changed to resignation, though, and then to open acceptance. Gary, and especially Diane, saw that clearly, saw that Prince Geldion had just passed the first true test of this new kingdom.

It seemed to Diane that at that moment, the boy-Prince had become a rightful heir.

"With your permission," Geldion said to his father, "I will excuse myself from the trip to Ynis Gwydrin. I will do as you first instructed me, and lead our forces to victory over the invading lava newts." Geldion paused and glanced at Badenoch, who was trying to remain regal, but could not completely mask his widening and approving smile.

"Fare well, my father," Geldion said, fighting hard to keep his voice from cracking. "And, I pray you, keep safe."

"Here it comes, lad," Mickey whispered as both Geldion and Kinnemore slowly turned Gary's way.

"I'm going with you," Gary, the King's appointed champion, remarked before Kinnemore could even ask.

"And I am, too," Diane promptly added.

Behind them, Mickey groaned, and Gary smiled, knowing that the sprite, too, would accompany them. Gary had come to fully understand Mickey McMickey, and he had confidence that the loyal leprechaun would stick by his side through any darkness.

Kinnemore accepted Gary's offer with a determined nod, then looked from the man to his wife.

"She goes," Gary said, his even tone offering no chance for debate.

Again the King nodded, and thought that Gary's trust in his wife was a very special thing indeed.

The encampment near Loch Gwydrin bustled with activity soon after, the soldiers putting down their weapons and taking up hand axes, pegs, and ropes. Tommy was most effective, running from the sandy banks repeatedly, returning each trip with an armful of huge logs that could be cut and strapped together into barges.

Gary, ordered by Kinnemore to keep his armor buckled on, Diane, and Mickey remained with the King during the construction, lending silent support to the determined yet obviously troubled man. Kinnemore had little to say those hours, even when Diane proclaimed that his son would one day make a fine King.

Mickey wasn't so sure of that; neither was Gary, who had seen the other side of Prince Geldion, but neither said a word to contradict the claim and both hoped that Diane was right.

The boats were completed soon after noon, a flotilla of fifteen barges that could each carry between seven and nine soldiers, in addition to those rowing. They were squared boats, just strapped logs, really, but Gwydrin was not a large lake and the isle, nestled in the shadows of towering cliffs, was only a few hundred yards from the shore.

Kinnemore quickly determined his forces. It would take four men to properly navigate each raft, and all but one of the barges would return to this bank, ready to ferry more men across if the need arose or if they could be spared by his son. That would put approximately six score soldiers on Ynis Gwydrin with the King and his champion—or champions, because Diane was playing the role as well as Gary. Kinnemore picked the leaders of that small force from the few friends he remembered from the days before Ceridwen had stolen him away, the few soldiers who had been strong enough to remain in their beloved army despite the unruly reign of the haggis. The King, in turn, let these leaders select the men who would accompany them, and then the rest of the boat-builders, some three hundred soldiers, were dismissed, to return to Prince Geldion for further orders.

It was all done quickly and efficiently, without a hitch— except for one.

Tommy put a perfectly plaintive look over Gary, the giant understanding that none of the barges would support his bulk. Tommy had walked across this lake before (once even carrying Gary and his companions), but even the not-so-bright giant seemed to understand that he would not be allowed to go this time.

"You have to get back to Prince Geldion and Lord Badenoch," Gary said cheerily, trying to put a positive spin on things. "They'll welcome your strength in their fight!"

Tommy shook his head. "Tommy go back to the island with you," he replied. "Tommy wants to see the Lady again."

The giant's tone made Gary and Mickey exchange nervous stares. Ceridwen had not treated Tommy badly in his years on the island, had served somewhat as a surrogate mother to the orphaned giant, and if Tommy held any remaining loyalty to the witch, he would surely make King Kinnemore's mission more difficult.

"Tommy remembers," the giant said determinedly. Again Gary and Mickey looked to each other. "Tommy remembers what the bad lady did on the one mountain."

"The one mountain?" Diane asked.

"Giant's Thumb," Gary explained, and both he and Mickey were more at ease then, knowing that if they could not convince Tommy to remain behind, the giant would at least be a complete ally in this venture, even if their goal turned out to be the death of Ceridwen. Ceridwen had turned on Tommy, had nearly killed them all on the slopes of Giant's Thumb, before Gary had put the mighty spear into her belly, banishing her to Ynis Gwydrin.

Still, Gary thought it important to convince Tommy to go to Geldion and Badenoch. The powerful giant would no doubt be much more helpful in the coming large-scale battle than in the tight confines of the witch's castle.

"You can't even stand straight in most of the rooms," Gary reasoned. "If you go with us to the island, you'll have to just wait outside the castle while we go in after Cerid-wen."

The giant's expression became an open pout.

"But if you stay here," Gary continued hopefully, "you'll be able to help out in the fight. And they'll need you, Tommy."

The giant continued to pout as he considered the words. "Tommy does not like his choices," he remarked at length.

"Neither did Geldion," Diane put in. "He wanted to go along with his father, but he knew that it would be better for everyone if he stayed behind. That's what we have to do now, Tommy. Think what's better for everyone."

The giant stubbornly shook his head, but in the end, he agreed, and after pushing off all of the barges (and what a fine start that was towards the island!), Tommy waved goodbye to Gary, Diane, and Mickey, gave a determined nod, and followed the departing soldiers into the mountains.

*   *   *   *   *

Prince Geldion sat atop his horse, the same gray he had used on the two trips to the Crahgs, on a high ridge at the head of a valley that opened up to the fields east of Penllyn. When he and Badenoch and their closest advisors had first come to this spot, after Geldion had left his father, Geldion had thought this a magnificent view.

Soon after, all he could see was the encroaching doom, the lava newt army swarming across the fields like the shadow of a dark cloud.

"Too many," Badenoch whispered at his side.

Geldion eyed the Lord directly.

"I agree that we must catch them between the spurs, in this same valley," Badenoch went on. "But I fear that they are too many to even fit into this valley."

Prince Geldion couldn't find the conviction to disagree. His first plan of defense for Penllyn had been simply designed. They would try to lure the lava newts into the mountains through a few select areas, most notably the valley before him, where the defenders might concentrate their forces enough to stall any advance. To that end, Geldion's cavalry and a single, imposing giant were even now slipping out of the mountains south of the approaching force in an attempt to strike at the lava newts' southern flank. By all accounts, the lava newts were running and not riding, and thus should pose little threat to the swift force, for the soldiers were not out to engage on any large scale, only to herd.

Prince Geldion was betting that the lava newts, so anxious to get to Ceridwen, thinking that they would do better against horsemen in the rough mountain terrain than on the open fields, and thinking that they would do better to avoid the giant at any cost on any terrain, would hardly slow to deal with the minor inconvenience of the cavalry. Likely, their forces would slowly shift to the north, putting them more in line for the rocky spurs and the valley, the designated killing field.

All reports thus far showed that Geldion's guess appeared to be on the mark. The lava newts were sliding inevitably north, giving ground to the cavalry and running with all speed from Tommy. That gave little measure of comfort to the tactical-minded Prince, though, for he feared that Lord Badenoch's assessment that, like a flood, the newts would simply swarm over the hills, through all passes, guarded and unguarded, might prove painfully true.

"Every group is ready, my Prince!" one of Geldion's advisors said determinedly, and Geldion nodded, not doubting the discipline of his warriors, or of those men from Braemar.

"Then tell the archers to bend back their bows," Lord Badenoch replied, and motioned back towards the eastern end of the valley, where the lead runners of the lava newt force had nearly entered.

They spotted the cavalry contingent a moment later, tiny figures out on the wide field, working hard to keep the line shifting. Horsemen rushed in and out for quick hits and quicker retreats. Geldion (and the others too) winced as one horseman rode down a newt too far out from the line. But the soldier's horse tripped up as it pounded over the fallen monster, and though the man managed to keep his seat and keep the horse upright, the stumble cost him precious moments. Before he could bring his mount back up to a gallop, a group of newts rushed over him and, by the sheer weight of numbers, brought him down. Other horsemen tried to get in to help their fallen comrade, but they were inevitably driven off by scores of the vicious lava newts. Tommy rushed in and scattered the newts, but the soldier was lost by that time.

Crying out in their hissing voices, beating their clubs and swords against shabby shields, a huge bulk of the lava newt force thundered into the valley.

Badenoch looked to Geldion, but the Prince sat calm. "Let them come," Geldion said softly, more to himself than to the Lord, trying to keep his calm and his patience.

Half the valley was full of newts, and lines of the lizardlike humanoids filtered up the rocky spurs, and no doubt along many of the trails north of this position.

Still Geldion waited. Their moment of complete surprise would be short; the Prince knew that he had to make it as effective as possible.

Most of the valley was filled with darkness. Lava newts flowed out from many angles, along climbing trails, most of which led nowhere.

Finally, Prince Geldion nodded and the soldier to his left put a horn to his lips and blew a single, clear note.

Up came the roar of the Connacht and Braemar forces. The humming of half a thousand bowstrings echoed from the mountainsides, and a wall of arrows cut the air with a great rush and whistle.

The newts continued to pour into the valley; screams of pain grew around their hissing war chants. Arrows flew as thick as locusts, and few answering shots came up from the valley floor.

Along those trails exiting the valley that did not abruptly end, the leading newt soldiers found themselves suddenly in combat—and usually in the worst possible attacking position along the ledge. Ringing steel joined the thrumming of bows, and screaming newts plummeted from high ledges, crashing in among the dead on the valley floor.

In all their years, in all their battles, neither Geldion nor Badenoch, nor even the professional soldiers flanking them, had ever seen such a massacre. The devastation was horrendous, the valley floor fast blackening with the writhing forms of dying newts. In one section along the southern wall, Geldion's soldiers even set off a small avalanche, crushing a hundred newts under tons of rock.

But a thousand newts swarmed over that area immediately after the tumble had ended.

All across the valley, and in those passes to the north, the line of the invaders seemed endless, two replacing every one that died, and four to replace those two after that. The archers continued to rain devastation on the newts, while those soldiers holding the strategic ledges methodically cut down their opponents one after another.

Even so, the newts made progress to complete the filling of the valley. Even so, every time a soldier on any ledge was defeated, valuable, critical ground was lost. And those newts that had gotten into the foothills along the northern passes were coming fast, flanking the defenders.

It went on for a solid half hour, lava newt bodies piled high, but the tide began to shift, the ratio of losses began to even out.

"Well fought," Lord Badenoch remarked to Prince Geldion when the two came to a new vantage point, one farther back as all of the Connacht army had been pushed. Geldion studied the older man. Badenoch's sentiments seemed true enough, but the man's tone revealed a sense of utter hopelessness.

"I know how you are feeling at this moment," the Lord of Braemar explained. "For I felt the same when my army came out onto the fields to battle the forces of Connacht. The tactics were impressive, and we have killed the newts at ten to one, or more. But they, and not we, have the soldiers to spare."

The grim words rang painfully true to Geldion as he looked down at the now-distant valley, its floor writhing with the black mass of lava newts who had not yet even seen battle. All along Penllyn's eastern edge, north, and even south of the Prince's position, was now in the hands of the enemy.

Geldion looked over his shoulder, back to the west, to the higher and still-open trails filled with defensible positions. But Geldion's expression was not a hopeful one, for he feared that he and his soldiers would soon have nowhere to run.

23 ✝ Terms of Surrender

They were met on the beach of Ynis Gwydrin by the witch's ragtag island forces, goblins mostly, but some other races, including more than a few humans who had spent years in Ceridwen's captivity and did the witch's bidding only out of fear of reprisal. Undisciplined and untrained, the island defenders went in a mob towards the first barge that skidded aground near the beach, swarming like ants, and those soldiers on that barge were sorely pressed.

But the soldiers of the other craft, including Gary and Diane, came ashore with relative ease. Mickey used his tricks to aid in the confusion near the first barge, making men appear where they weren't and sending goblins splashing to the surf after wild swings that hit nothing but air. And Gary led the charge of the Connacht infantry, all of them calling, "Yield to the spearwielder!" with every running step.

They formed into a wedge as they cut into the island mob, with Gary at its tip. Donigarten's spear flashed every which way, cutting down goblins. As the monstrous ranks parted, Gary came upon a human soldier, a filthy wretch of a man.

But a man nonetheless.

"Yield!" Gary screamed, jabbing the spear's deadly tip near the man's belly. "Yield!" Gary desperately hoped the man heeded the command, desperately hoped that he would not have to kill another human. His sigh of relief was sincere when the enemy threw down his makeshift club and fell groveling to his knees, whispering "Sir Cedric" repeatedly.

The wedge cut on, soon linking with those soldiers caught on the barge. The witch's forces swarmed around the lines, hoping to encompass the entire group, but as they went wide of the Connacht soldiers, they presented wonderful targets for the battery of archers waiting patiently further down the beach.

By the time the goblins had passed that rain of arrows, the back edges of the wedge had come together, turning the formation into a defensive diamond, and though Ceridwen's forces still outnumbered and had surrounded the invaders, the skilled Connacht troops were now fighting back to back, with no weaknesses in their line.

Gary, still the spearhead of the group, swung them about and pressed in from the beach, and like the prow of a fast ship, that corner of the diamond sailed through the sea of enemies.

"Above!" came more than one cry, and one Gary recognized as Diane's voice. All those soldiers, Connacht and island forces alike, who were not engaged looked up to see a black swarm coming out one of the crystalline castle's high towers, a line of monkey bats, screeching and beating their leathery wings. Even worse, out the castle's main door came two huge shapes, mountain trolls, armored head to toe with heavy metal plates over their thick hides and carrying swords taller than Gary, with enchanted, glowing blades as wide across as a strong man's leg.

The Connacht soldiers closest to the trolls rushed in fearlessly, scoring vicious hits with their fine swords. But the weapons seemed puny things next to the brutes, and were turned aside by the two-inch layer of metal armor.

The trolls swept across with their huge swords, cutting

through shields and armor and men alike, cutting a swath of devastation in a single swipe.

Gary understood his duty here, knew that he alone carried a weapon that might get through the trolls' plated armor. He broke from the formation, running across the sand—and those minor island troops that saw him coming worked hard to get out of his way!

You must not let them maneuver about you, the sentient spear telepathically instructed. *Position, brave young sprout, will see us through!*

Gary didn't consciously answer, but was nodding his agreement as he came up on the first troll. He swerved far to the side and winced as the troll slashed its sword, sending an unfortunate Connacht soldier flying through the air. Then Gary came in hard, jabbing the spear against the side of the troll's leg. Sparks flew as the speartip connected on the heavy armor plating, and as Gary had expected (as Gary had prayed!), the mighty spear, the most powerful weapon in all the world, poked through.

The troll roared; its leg buckled sideways. It didn't tumble immediately, but roared again in absolute agony as Gary yanked the spear back out and ran on, out of the stumbling thing's reach.

Back near the water, Diane, standing with a handful of infantry as guard to Kinnemore and to the archers, heard the cry and noticed Gary's daring actions. Her heart skipped more than a few beats as she watched her husband rush around the wounded troll, cut between it and its other gigantic companion.

"Mickey!" she called, hoping the leprechaun might in some way help, but when she turned, she saw Mickey behind the battery of kneeling archers, as intent as they on the approaching flock of monkey bats.

As one, the archers fired, and so did the leprechaun,

casting a spell to make every arrow appear as ten. Barely a dozen of the three score monkey bats took any hits, and only half of those were fatal, but all of the group went into a frenzy, dodging illusory and real bolts, slamming against each other, and spinning desperate maneuvers from which they could not recover.

The archers quickly readied and fired again, but before their next volley was even away, Mickey's continuing line of arrow images had the monkey bats scattering. A few more took hits and tumbled from the sky; the rest broke ranks and flew off in every direction available to get them away from Kinnemore's nasty soldiers.

The wounded troll tried to turn about as Gary darted behind it, and that movement, pivoting on its torn leg, brought a resounding crack as the monster's knee snapped apart. Down it went in a spinning tumble, dropping its sword and clutching at the leg. A swarm of Connacht soldiers, following the lead of the spearwielder, of their King's champion, fell over it, hacking mightily and mercilessly.

Gary, bearing down on the next troll, hardly noticed the brute behind him, had his focus straight ahead. He clutched the spear in line, one hand balancing the shaft, the other near the weapon's butt end, and put his head down as though he meant to run the weapon through this troll's leg as well.

Up went the troll's sword and the beast lurched forward, bending to cleave the puny charging human in half. More than one soldier coming behind Gary cried out, thinking the man surely doomed, but Gary skidded up short and straightened suddenly, and his back hand rushed forward, hurling the spear straight for the most dumbfounded expression Gary had ever seen.

The troll cut across with its sword, trying to parry, and for a moment, Gary thought it had somehow knocked the spear aside. But when it all sorted out, there stood the beast, somehow still clutching its sword, hands out wide, and with the back portion of the spear's shaft protruding from its neck, angled up under the brute's chin.

The sword fell to the sand and the troll reached up with both hands behind its square head, weak fingers grasping at the spear's other, more deadly end.

It fell forward, and Gary did well to scramble out of its way.

The fight was over in the span of a few minutes, with dozens of goblins and a few of Ceridwen's men lying dead in the sand, many more of the humans huddled on the ground in surrender, and many more of all the monsters and humans running wild, scattering in terror along the beach.

It took Gary and a half dozen men a long time to shift the dead troll about so that Gary could pull free his bloodied spear, and by the time he had the weapon back in his grasp, Diane, Kinnemore, and Mickey were again at his side.

The King said nothing, but his admiring expression showed that he had gained new and greater confidence for this man he had named as his champion. Gary knew that Diane, too, was proud of his actions, but her sour look only revealed her disgust at the carnage on that bloody beach, and at the pieces of gore that Gary had to wipe from his magnificent weapon.

The skilled Connacht soldiers soon had the beach, all the way to the crystalline castle, fully secured, with an area set up for their wounded, and another for the prisoners.

King Kinnemore gathered his leaders together and bade them to sweep the island clean of opposition. Then he hand-picked a group of soldiers to accompany him and Gary (and Diane and Mickey—and the leprechaun wasn't too thrilled about that!) into the castle to parlay with the witch.

Kinnemore allowed Gary the honor of rapping on the huge doors of the castle, and Gary wisely did so with the butt end of his spear. Sparks flew and a minor explosion erupted as the weapon connected with the door, and Gary was thrown back several steps and would have fallen to the seat of his pants had not two Connacht soldiers caught him by the arms and held him steady.

"A minor trap," the embarrassed man said, and he was glad that he wore the great helmet so that the others, particularly Diane and Kinnemore, could not see that his hair was standing on end.

With a determined grunt, Gary went back to the door and pounded it again, even harder. "Little witch, little witch, let me in, let me in!" he called in his best big-bad-wolf voice. He turned to Diane and winked through the faceplate of his helm. "Ceridwen doesn't have any hairs on her chinny-chin-chin," he said, trying to make light in the face of his true fears.

Those fears were fully revealed when the door unexpectedly swung open, and Gary jumped right off the ground and gave a yell.

Geek the spindly-armed goblin stood eyeing the man curiously.

"We have come to speak with Ceridwen!" King Kinnemore declared, stepping past his unnerved champion.

Geek nodded stupidly. "The Lady will see you," the goblin announced, and his confident, evil chuckle—even though he was so obviously vulnerable and overmatched—made more than a few soldiers look to each other nervously, as did Gary and Diane and Mickey, all wondering if they were walking right into the proverbial spider's web.

But in went King Kinnemore, fearlessly, and the others were obliged to follow.

*   *   *   *   *

The Connacht and Braemar armies fought well, continuing the slaughter that had begun between the rocky outcroppings of the great spurs on the eastern edge of Penllyn. But the vast lava newt force could not be stopped, made its inevitable way to the west, taking one trail after another and pushing the defenders back on their heels.

Geldion and Badenoch each saw fighting that afternoon, each bloodied their weapons and took many minor hits. Most devastating was Tommy One-Thumb, the giant pounding away whole groups of lava newts at a time. But when Geldion and Badenoch came upon Tommy, sitting behind the lip of a high ridge overlooking Ynis Gwydrin, they knew that the giant, like an honest reflection of their entire army, was nearing the end. Tommy was truly exhausted, and his resigned look spoke volumes for the Prince and the Lord of Braemar, who knew that they could not win.

Gradually the human army had contracted, coming together on a high and flat plateau in north central Penllyn. The well-organized lava newts were all about them, particularly on the lower fields to the north, preventing them from fleeing the mountains and running back to their towns.

Prince Geldion blamed himself, thinking that he should have hit at the newts repeatedly, but with the ultimate design of fleeing the mountains.

"We could not afford that course," Lord Badenoch promptly reminded him. "The mountains offered our best defense, better than the walls of Connacht."

"And how many soldiers will run free of Penllyn?" Geldion asked sarcastically. "And what shall Connacht, and Braemar, do without their armies when the witch comes free?"

With no comforting answer, Badenoch shrugged and eyed the black host encircling his force, the ring growing ever tighter.

The lava newts continued to show skill and discipline. Those on the east, west, and south of the plateau dug into defensive positions, for the trails were narrow and treacherous from those approaches, and easily defended by the soldiers on the higher ground. The host in the north gathered in increasing numbers, filtered together in a vast swarm. Their run to the plateau was open, though uphill, and the human defenders would be hard pressed by lines a hundred abreast.

Like a thunderstorm, the lines broke, and with a singular, hissing roar, the lava newts rolled towards the cornered humans.

"Fight well," Badenoch said to Geldion, and from his tone, the Prince understood the further implication: Die well.

*   *   *   *   *

King Kinnemore knew nothing of the battle as he walked along the maze of the crystalline castle's winding and mirrored corridors. The lava newt force would be held at bay on the eastern edge of Penllyn, so he hoped, and thus he had devised the terms of surrender, including the reversion of Ynis Gwydrin to the rightful King of Faerie.

With their common understanding of the powerful witch, Gary and Mickey thought the King's plan grandly optimistic and based on presumptions that simply did not hold true where wicked Ceridwen was concerned. Neither said anything, though, or showed their fears, for Kinnemore was more determined than any person either of them had ever seen.

And he was the King, after all.

They met Ceridwen in a bare, octagonal room, its walls, floor and ceiling mirrored so that it took each of them several moments to get their bearings. The witch, beautiful and terrible in a black silken gown, seemed completely at ease, standing barely a dozen feet from her greatest adversaries.

"You know why we have come," Kinnemore said to her, his voice steady. If the King was intimidated, nothing he did, nor the tone of his voice, revealed it.

Ceridwen cackled at him.

"Your surrender will be accepted!" Kinnemore demanded. "The truth is known, evil witch, throughout the land. And ever was the truth your greatest bane."

Again the witch cackled hysterically. "The truth?" she chided. "And what do you know of the truth, foolish man? Is it not true that your pitiful son is even now being overrun in the mountain passes? That your pitiful army, so undeservedly proud, is now in full flight from a host of lava newts that have come to my call?"

Both Gary and Diane eyed the witch curiously, then looked to each other. Beyond what Ceridwen was actually saying, which was disturbing enough, the witch's lips seemed to be moving out of synch with the words, like a badly dubbed movie.

"What do you know of the truth?" the witch boomed in a voice that was not Ceridwen's, in a voice that was powerful and deep, grating and demonic in its pure discord.

Kinnemore began to reply, but the words were caught in his throat as the witch began to change. A third arm, black and scaly, burst from the creature's chest; writhing tentacles grew out of her hips, slapping the floor at her sides.

"What do you know?" the beast roared again, from a head that was now monstrous, fishlike, with a gaping, fanged maw and needle-sharp spikes prodding from the forehead.

Kinnemore fell back a step, Mickey whined, and Gary and Diane couldn't find the breath to utter a sound. Neither could the five escorting soldiers, though they remained loyal enough to their King to draw out their swords.

"Be gone!" the King managed to call to his escorts, but when he and they turned about, they found only another unremarkable mirror where the door had been.

"That might be a bit harder than ye think," Mickey whispered.

* * * * *

Geldion centered his front line, arrows flying over his head from behind, cutting devastation into the lava newt ranks. The Prince only shook his head, for the black tide was barely slowed, the monsters merely running over their dead and wounded without regard.

A hundred feet away, Geldion could see their slitted, reptilian eyes, gleaming eagerly, immersed in the thoughts of the killing that would soon begin.

But then another volley of arrows hit the lava newts, a greater volley than had come from behind Geldion, and this one coming, not from in front of the approaching horde, but from the west!

"Tylwyth Teg!" screamed one soldier, and it was true. Riding hard along the western trails, their white mounts shining in the light, their bows humming in their hands, came the minions of Tir na n'Og. Behind them charged the remaining men of Dilnamarra, a group whose eyes were set with such determination as can only be inspired by great sorrow.

And from the north, from behind the horde of lava newts, came a second force, a greater force, such a host of Buldrefolk as had not been seen outside of Dvergamal in a dozen centuries. Geno Hammerthrower and Kervin were at their lead, and beside them, Duncan Drochit, and behind him, the brave soldiers of the town of the same name.

Great gnomish war machines rolled across the rough ground to either side of the dwarfish force, hurling stones and flaming pitch and huge spears into the midst of the suddenly scrambling lava newts.

Prince Geldion did not miss the moment. "Ahead!" he cried to his men. "Fight well!"

Lord Badenoch echoed that call, and this time, there were no dire, unspoken implications in his exuberant tone.

Kelsey, his bow spewing a line of arrows, rode hard and fearlessly. Unlike in the battle for Tir na n'Og, the elf saw a definite end to this fight, a conclusion from which all the goodly peoples of Faerie would benefit. He had left Braemar hopeful, but with the knowledge that the witch would soon be free and the misery could certainly begin anew. To Kelsey's surprise, he had found a host of elves marching east on the road outside of Dilnamarra, along with the remnants of Dilnamarra's militia and those soldiers the phoney King Kinnemore had left behind to guard the town. The word of the imposter haggis and the return of the true King had spread faster than Kelsey's ride, and already, the people of Faerie had seen the opportunity presented them.

And so the elf had been thrilled, but not truly surprised, when his force had swung to the south, a direct line towards Penllyn, and had found another army—the men of Drochit, a strong contingent of gnomes from Gondabuggan, and a force of sturdy dwarfs five hundred strong—marching south from the Dvergamal line, paralleling them on their way to Penllyn.

The lava newts were not nearly as chaotic and self-serving as the goblins and trolls and, under the guidance of iron-fisted Robert, had trained for large-scale battles. But now they were caught by surprise, nearly surrounded and with death raining in on them from the front, from the side, and from behind. They tried to swing their lines about, to regroup into tighter defensive formations, but they were too late, and the elfs and dwarfs, gnomes and humans fell over them, cutting their force piecemeal.

Many numbered the dead of the men that bloody day. Many elfs, who should have seen the dawn of centuries to come, would not, and many of the sturdy Buldrefolk were taken down, but not a one before he took down a dozen newts with him. The only unscathed force was that of the gnomes, and not a single name would be added to the plaque of *Fearless Gnomish Fighters*, as with all gnomish awards a posthumous honor, from the fabled battle of Penllyn. The lava newts did not know what to make of the huge gnomish war machines, and kept clear of them. The closest any gnome came to serious injury was when an upstart young female by the name of Budaboo strapped flasks of volatile gnomish potions around her waist and, desperate to get her name on that plaque, and perhaps even to win the posthumous Gondabugganal Medal of Honor, launched herself from the basket of one catapult. Budaboo had the good fortune (or misfortune, from her perspective) of sailing into an area near a friendly giant with soft hands, and Tommy promptly caught her and carried her back to safety. Later tales of the battle claim that Budaboo's ensuing, "Oh, pooh!" was heard above the clamor of the fighting, above the trumpets and the cries.

None of Gary's friends fell that day. Among them, only Geno took any hits at all, and the dwarf, with his typical stoicism, shrugged the wounds away as inconsequential. And when the battle was ended, the lava newts were scattered and beaten. The call of Ceridwen had been silenced by the thunder of armies joined.

24 ✝ At the Heart of Darkness

The thing was huge, half again taller than Gary and as wide as three large men. Eight limbs, all dripping slime, protruded from it: two scaly legs, four long arms ending in clawed fingers, and two tentacles, waving teasingly, with suction rings along their length and tipped by a cudgel of thick bone. Was it a creature of the water, or of the earth? Gary wondered, trying to find some perspective, trying desperately to put this most awful sight in a proper viewpoint. The monster's wide mouth gulped in air, but below the face, where the torso widened, were rows of slitted gills, and, though this room had been dry, a large puddle grew around the feet of the monster.

"Not water," Gary whispered to himself, shaking his head. He had met a demon before, in this very castle, and had defeated the creature, but that fact did little to bolster Gary's confidence now.

Courage, young sprout, the sentient spear, sensing the man's failing sensibilities, imparted.

"Not water," Gary whispered again, and he ignored Diane's ensuing question at his side. He watched another ball of slime elongate to hang low on the creature's forward arm, then splatter to the floor. This was a creature not of earth and not of water, he decided, a creature of sludge, of the eternal torments of Hell or the Abyss, or some other awful place.

Gary was not the first to muster the courage to charge. Two of the five soldiers who had accompanied him and the King to this room burst from the line, crying for their King and waving their swords.

A tentacle whipped across low, catching one man on the side of the knee and dropping him to the floor—where he hit the slippery slime and slid in close to the monster. Before he could even shift his body around, the fish-demon slammed a heavy foot atop him and ground him mercilessly.

The other soldier stumbled in the slime, but held his balance and even managed a swipe with his sword. The weapon hit the creature's arm, but did not bite deeply, sliding down the slimy limb. A clawed hand caught the man by the wrist and jerked him forward.

Where the monstrous maw waited.

In charged Kinnemore, Gary, and the other three soldiers. Diane drew out her small sword, but hesitated, understanding that they would need more than simple weapons to win out. She glanced all about the room, searching for a door, searching for a clue, and noticed Mickey, shaking his head helplessly and fading away into invisibility.

The monster kicked the man under its crushing foot aside, and he slid all the way across the room to slam hard into the base of one mirror. The other man, his shoulder torn away, was thrown to the side, where he fell without a sound, too far gone to even cry out in agony.

Both tentacles met the charge. One hit a soldier on the side of the face, and he went down, his consciousness blasted away. The other whipping limb took out the feet of a second man, then continued on into Gary.

Gary had seen it coming, though (mostly because the first

victim had cried out as he tumbled away), and he dropped to one knee and angled his spear in front of him to catch the brunt of the blow. He had been stopped, but with a deft shift of his weapon, he made certain that the dangerous tentacle stayed with him and could not impede his other companions.

That left only King Kinnemore and a single soldier moving in close to the monster. As its front limb reached out for them, both scored solid hits with their swords, and the arm dropped free to the ground, where it writhed of its own accord in the slime.

On charged the two, between the fish-demon's side arms. The King's sword slammed hard against the thing's gill, opening a new and deeper slit. An arm clamped around him, though, and hugged him tight, and he worked desperately to keep the chomping maw from his face and neck. He looked back for his accompanying soldier, but saw the man stopped cold, for the monster had grown a new limb, where the arm had been severed—and this one more resembled a spike than an arm, a spike that had impaled the surprised charging man!

Gary worked the spear fiercely in front of him, twisting and turning to keep the tentacle from retracting so that it might strike at him again, or strike at the man lying stunned on the ground not so far away.

Then Gary's breath was stolen away as the second tentacle smacked hard across his back, a blow that he believed would have cut him in half if he had not been wearing the armor. He felt himself sliding inevitably backwards as the second tentacle, its suckers clinging fast to his armor, moved away. As soon as he broke clear of the first, Gary kept the presence of mind to jab ahead with his spear, snagging it and pulling it along, as well.

"I'm with ye, laddie!" Mickey cried, coming visible right

beside Gary, stabbing at the tentacle locked on the man's back with a puny knife.

"Use your tricks!" Gary yelled, stunned to see Mickey in a physical fight.

"And what use might they be against a demon?" Mickey asked sarcastically. The leprechaun's undeniably sharp knife dug in again on the tentacle, but Mickey seemed to Gary to be a tiny mouse nibbling a fat length of hemp rope.

Gary called to the man on the floor, told him that his King was in dire need. But the man could not rise, could not find his sensibilities enough to even know where he was.

That left Kinnemore battling alone in close, smacking his sword wildly against the fish-demon's head and torso, though the weapon, fine as it was, seemed to have little effect. The monster spat forth a line of slime, right into the King's face, blinding him. And then Kinnemore was yelling in agony, for the slime was based in acid.

Diane went down to her knees at full speed, slid across the wet floor as though it was ice, with her sword pointing straight ahead and angled up, braced in both arms. She hit the fish-demon in the armpit, the elfish sword plunging in right up to its hilt.

A hot green liquid spewed from the wound, and Diane wisely fell back. Her eyes widened in horror as the hilt of her sword fell to the floor, and she found that the blade had been melted away.

The fish-demon was fully capable of fighting multiple battles. Though it roared in pain from Diane's solid hit, and though it was still engaged with King Kinnemore, its tentacles worked in unison against Gary, pulling in opposite directions, one secured to Gary's back (and seeming hardly to notice the leprechaun's repeated strikes), the other tugging at the impaled spear.

"Hit it!" Gary screamed to his weapon, fearing that the

spear would be pulled from his grasp. The spear complied, sending a burst of energy from its tip into the tentacle.

Gary inadvertently punched himself in the chin, under his great helm, as the tentacle whipped in a frenzy. He somehow managed to hold on, though, and the spear blasted again, and a third time. The tentacle danced wildly, but without control, its muscles reacting to impulses that did not emanate from the fish-demon's brain.

Gary heaved up with all his strength, then reversed his grip and slammed spear and tentacle against the floor, the sharp edge of the mighty spear cutting through and free of the monstrous limb. Then Gary spun about, knocking Mickey face down in the slime and jabbing hard at the second tentacle, scoring a brutal hit.

"Ye're welcome," Mickey muttered dryly.

The fish-demon wailed and hurled Kinnemore to the floor, where he lay crumpled in the slime. Diane, weapon-less, thought of going for his fallen sword, but discounted that avenue and grabbed the King by the collar instead, tugging hard. Surprisingly, the King resisted, even slapping Diane's hand away. Half-blinded by the acid, battered and bleeding in several places, Kinnemore went for his sword.

He forced himself to his feet, coming up right in line with the fish-demon's maw, and managed a solid slash across that wide mouth, taking out two fangs and sending lines of bright blood into the creature's mouth.

The maw snapped forward; Kinnemore snapped his sword in line to block and scored a wicked hit.

But that blade wouldn't stop the powerful monster, and as it broke through, teeth gouging into Kinnemore's chest, only Diane's tug at the King's back stopped him from being bitten in half. Both Diane and the King fell back, and so did the fish-demon, for the sword was stuck painfully into the roof of its mouth.

Diane found her breath hard to come by as she looked around at the King's garish wound. Kinnemore smiled weakly at her, as if to say that it was worth the attempt, then slipped from consciousness. Diane couldn't secure her footing on the floor, but the slime worked in her favor, allowing her to drag the King quickly.

Soon she passed Gary, who was still hacking away, and Mickey joined her, and together they got back to the place where they had first entered the room.

Gary regained his footing and, finally free of the sticky tentacle, covered the retreat. He struck repeatedly with the mighty spear, at the tentacles, at a reaching arm, at the bulk of the beast whenever it ventured too near. Still, Gary didn't see where he and his friends might ultimately run. Diane searched frantically along the spot where they had entered, but it seemed just a mirror now, with no handles or hinges.

Not so far away, one of the soldiers started to rise.

"Stay down!" Gary cried to him, for the man was obviously dazed and in no position to defend himself.

The soldier apparently did not hear, or did not comprehend the meaning, for he continued to rise, and almost made it up to his feet.

Almost.

The fish-demon whipped a heavy tentacle across, the bone cudgel slamming the rising man on the back of the neck and launching him into a flying somersault. He flew into the nearest mirror and crashed right through, falling into a shallow alcove amid the shards of crumbling glass. He continued to groan and to stir a bit, but could not begin to extract himself from that mess.

Overwhelmed by rage, Gary charged ahead, thrusting the spear in vicious and effective overhead chops. As with Diane's sword, the mighty spear plunged into the monster's torso, but the spear, unlike the sword, could not be damaged, could not even be marked, by the green acidic gore.

Gary blindly struck repeatedly, growling every time his weapon hit something substantial, but soon his fury played itself out. He had backed the fish-demon halfway across the room, but now it was the creature that was advancing. Gary slashed the spear across in front of him, parrying the lunging limbs and the prodding spike.

There were too many angles, though, too many limbs and weapons from this unearthly beast. Gary saw a tentacle soaring at him from the left, down low, noticed out of the corner of his eye the other tentacle, fast flying in from the right, up high.

"Oh, no," he muttered, and he jumped and tried to curl into a ball, feeling like a double-dutch rope skipper on the local playground.

He got clipped on the heel and the opposite shoulder, the momentum of the heavy blows sending him into a double spin, sending his loose-fitting helmet flying away, before he crashed down to the floor. He heard Diane calling, heard Mickey calling, but all he saw was the fish-demon leering, smiling at him as it began its advance once more.

Gary fought to regain his footing, tried to rationalize that the fight was going better than he could have hoped, that he had scored many serious hits on his monstrous opponent.

But when Gary looked to those wounds for encouragement, his heart fell away, for all the wounds were fast mending, closing right before his eyes.

He muttered a hundred denials in those next few seconds, a hundred pieces of logic that told him this could not be. But it was, and his words were truly empty. Gary was still muttering when he felt the butt of his spear tap the mirror at his back, when he noticed Diane and Mickey flanking him, their expressions as hopeless as his own.

Reacting on pure survival instinct, Gary spun and slammed the spear into the mirror. The glass broke apart, but though the companions had entered through this very area, they found no door behind the break, just another shallow and unremarkable alcove.

"Search it!" Gary cried to Mickey and he spun back, whipping his spear across just in time to deflect a tentacle swipe from the closing monster.

The fish-demon roared and charged suddenly, and Gary and Mickey and Diane all cried out, thinking their doom upon them. Simply because she had nothing else to possibly do, Diane lifted the Polaroid and snapped a picture—and the blinding flash stopped the fish-demon in its slimy tracks.

Gary didn't miss his one chance. He leaped out from the wall and plunged the spear deep into the monster's chest. The fish-demon fell back, off the tip, and responded with a tentacle clubbing that staggered Gary and almost knocked him from his feet. The monster was in a slight retreat, though, giving Gary the time to recover.

He heard a winding noise then, and turned to accept the other flash, the one that could be fit atop the Pentax, from Diane. He saw that Mickey was in the newest cubby by then, but the sprite was shaking his head, finding nothing that gave any clues to a door.

Full of determination, but not of hope, Gary advanced on the monster. One of the other soldiers was up again, wounded but willing to fight, and with sword in hand. He and Gary shared a nod, then advanced.

A tentacle slammed the soldier, but he caught it and went with it, holding fast with one hand while hacking away with his sword.

Gary spun to the other side, his spear intercepting and driving away the second tentacle, and then he charged straight ahead and scored again with yet another solid overhead chop.

"How many can you take?" Gary snarled defiantly at the fish-demon and struck again, then leaped back and twisted frantically to avoid the rushing monster and its front limb that had become a deadly spike.

He avoided the hit, but lost his footing, slamming heavily to the floor. And when he managed to look up, there was the demon's maw, barely a foot away, too close for him to bring the spear to bear. Gary didn't know if the "ready" signal was lit on the back of the flash or not, and didn't have the time to look. He just thrust the small box forward and pushed the button.

The flash did fire, and the fish-demon bellowed and fell back, allowing Gary to scramble to his feet. The spear-wielder backpedaled, and winced as the outraged monster gave a tremendous snap of its engaged tentacle that sent the poor soldier spinning across the room.

Then Diane was beside Gary, though he was far from Mickey and the fallen Kinnemore. She had no weapon, though.

Just a photograph, a picture of the room that revealed, in the light of the flash, a slender silhouette behind one of the mirrors.

Gary lifted the spear over his head, prepared for the fish-demon's final charge, the one he knew he and Diane could not hope to stop.

On came the beast; Diane stuck the picture in front of Gary's face.

It all happened too fast for Gary to truly sort it out, but the one thing he held above all was his trust in Diane, and when she called for him to "Throw the spear!" he understood her meaning perfectly.

With a primal scream, Gary shifted and heaved the spear

to the side of the demon, past the demon. It hit a mirror and dove right through, and cracks widened around the hole. Shards of glass fell clear, and there, in the alcove, stood a stunned Ceridwen, Donigarten's spear deep into her chest. She grasped at its shaft and tried to scream, but no sound would come past her trembling lips.

Gary and Diane were watching the fish-demon, though, and not the spear's flight. The monstrous beast bore down on them, seemed to fly straight for their hearts. They huddled together and cried out, certain that their death was upon them. But like the mirror covering Ceridwen, the fish-demon suddenly split apart into black shards and fell away to nothingness.

And then the room was strangely quiet, eerie, with Gary and Diane standing at each other's side, holding each other, in the slime and the gore and the devastation.

"The laddie got her again!" yelled Mickey McMickey, the most welcome voice and words that Gary Leger had ever heard.

25 † The Torch Is Passed

"Name her place, lad!" Mickey called excitedly. "Send her away before it's too late."

Gary was mesmerized by it all, by the so sudden shift in the events about him. He gawked at Ceridwen, her form becoming an insubstantial shadow, fading around the spear (which was stuck fast into the wall behind her).

"Name her place!" Mickey cried again. "If ye do not, then she'll be bound again to Ynis Gwydrin, bound again to this very castle, and the fighting will begin anew!"

That grim possibility shook Gary from his daze. He thought for just a moment. "Giant's Thumb," he announced in a loud and clear voice. "I banish you to Giant's Thumb, evil witch, where you shall remain for a hundred years!"

Mickey nodded, but his cherubic smile was short-lived. There was a hoard of treasure in Giant's Thumb, the leprechaun realized, a hoard that, with Robert dead and the lava newts away to Penllyn, was all but unguarded. The leprechaun gave a resigned sigh, admitting to himself that Gary, with his limited knowledge of Faerie, had chosen well. The lad had indeed beaten the witch again, stuck her with the only weapon in all the world that could hurt her.

But whatever feelings of victory Gary, Diane, and Mickey might have felt were washed away as soon as they considered the room about them. Two of the five soldiers lay still in pools

315

of blood, one of them obviously dead and the other three, even the one who had stood to fight beside Gary in the final moments, grievously wounded.

So was King Kinnemore, his face burned, one arm broken, and a deep wound in his chest.

The defeat of the witch also returned the door to the strange room, and Gary ran off to gather the other soldiers together, to find help for the wounded, and to find news of the fight in the mountains. Diane and Mickey remained behind, and Diane knew enough about first aid to realize that King Kinnemore was in a very bad way.

*   *   *   *   *

Prince Geldion bit back tears and bravely firmed his jaw as he knelt beside the cot, staring at his father.

Kinnemore managed a weak smile and lifted a hand to gently stroke his son's cheek.

"'Tis not fair," Geldion whispered. "I have only recently found you."

"What is fair?" Kinnemore replied between shallow breaths. "Better this fate than what I was presented. Better that I have lived to see my kingdom restored and to see what a fine man my son has become."

Geldion's eyes misted at that. "I wish to know you," the Prince protested. "I wish to know your joys and your sorrows. To learn from you."

Kinnemore slowly shook his head. "You do, my son," he whispered.

"I am not ready . . ."

"You are," the King interrupted forcefully, and the exertion cost him his strength. He fell deeper into the cot, his muscles relaxing for a final time. "You are," he whispered, barely audible, "my son."

Gary and Diane, Mickey and Kelsey and Geno, and all the leaders, dwarf, elf, gnome, and human, gathered in the anteroom to the King's chambers (in what had been Cerid-wen's chambers when the witch ruled Ynis Gwydrin) when Geldion came out.

"The King is dead," the Prince said quietly, though his expression had told all before he ever uttered the words.

Gary looked all around, not knowing what to expect. Would Geldion become King? Would Badenoch and Duncan Drochit, and particularly the Tylwyth Teg, accept this man who had been so complete an enemy?

"A fine man was your father," Kelsey offered, and he privately nodded to Gary. "Let none question his wisdom or his courage."

"To King Kinnemore," Lord Badenoch said, drawing his sword and lifting it high in salute, a movement that was repeated all about the room.

Diane saw her opportunity and did not let it pass. She wasn't sure of Faerie's customs in this regard, but guessed that it was pretty much along the lines her own world in ages past. She moved beside Geldion, took his hand and lifted it high. "The King is dead," she proclaimed. "Long live the King!"

There ensued a moment of the most uncomfortable silence, even Geldion seeming confused as to how he should proceed, as to whether anyone would second Diane's bold claim.

Gary put a stare over Kelsey, green eyes matching gold, the man silently reminding the elf how crucial this moment might be for all the land. Whatever Kelsey's feelings for Geldion, whether or not the elf was convinced that this man should rule, the Connacht army would surely remain loyal to Kinnemore's son.

Kelsey returned Gary's stare for a long moment. "Long live the King!" he said loudly, shattering the silence, and more than one person in that room, new King Geldion included, breathed an honest sigh of relief.

The first days of the new King's rule met, and even exceeded, the hopes and expectations of the leaders of the other towns and races. Geldion proclaimed that Ynis Gwydrin, and not Connacht, would become the new seat of power, and that the island, and all of Penllyn, would be open and welcoming to any of Faerie's men, elfs, dwarfs, and gnomes.

To Lord Badenoch, who had been perhaps Geldion's staunchest detractor, the new King offered the Dukedom of Connacht, and when the Lord, loyal to his dear Braemar, politely declined, and when Duncan Drochit, equally loyal to his own town, also declined, Geldion begged that both men provide a list of candidates who might properly fill the most important position. It was an offer that surely brought the confidence of many camped in Penllyn, including the Tylwyth Teg, all glad to know that the new King would not put a puppet in Connacht's seat.

That only left one position open, and Gary Leger alone was surprised by Geldion's next offer.

"Your friend, Baron Pwyll, died a hero," Geldion said to Gary one night on the quiet beach of Ynis Gwydrin. The lights of a hundred campfires flickered in the distance, on the shore across the still water.

"Aye," agreed Mickey, the leprechaun standing at Gary's side and doodling in the sand with his curly-toed shoe.

When Gary did not reply, Diane hooked her arm in his, offering him support.

"The people of Dilnamarra have come to expect excellence from their leader," Geldion went on. "The good Baron . . ."

Gary's skeptical stare stopped Geldion momentarily,

reminded the new King that he and Pwyll had not been the best of friends while Pwyll was alive.

But Geldion nodded in the face of that doubting expression, and silently admitted the truth. Things had changed, so it seemed, and Geldion pressed on. "Perhaps Baron Pwyll's detractors were misinformed," he admitted. "No man has known a finer moment than Baron Pwyll. He stood on the platform in Dilnamarra, surrounded by enemies, and spoke the truth, though he knew the words would bring about his death. I pray that I might find such courage should the occasion arise. I pray that I might be as much a hero as Baron Pwyll of Dilnamarra."

The sentiments seemed honest enough, and Gary found himself placed in the middle of a test, much as Kelsey and the others had been placed when Diane had first proclaimed Geldion as King. Gary let go his anger then, completely, and put aside his judgments. Through all the turmoil, Geldion had been loyal to his father, or to the monster he had believed to be his father; in remembering his own dad, how could Gary honestly claim that he would have done differently? And now Geldion had lost his father, as Gary had lost his, and the new King was standing strong and honestly trying to do what was right.

Gary's glower faded away.

"I am in need of a Baron," Geldion went on, seeming to understand that he had gained Gary's confidence. "A man who will command the loyalty of the beleaguered people of Dilnamarra. A man who will guide the rebuilding of the town after the grave injustices they have suffered."

For the first time, Gary understood what was coming.

"I offer Dilnamarra to you, spearwielder," Geldion said firmly. "To the slayer of Robert, the man who has acted on behalf of Faerie's goodly folk in all his days in the land. I offer it to you and to Diane, your wife, she who solved the riddle of the haggis and saved Faerie from a darkness more terrible than any the land has ever seen."

Gary and Diane looked to each other for a long, long while.

"They'll be needing some time," Mickey whispered to Geldion, and the two slipped away, leaving the couple alone on the dark and quiet beach.

*   *   *   *   *

He thought of the good he might do, the improvements to the political system and the general welfare of the common people. He felt like an American colonial, who might bring the idea of democracy to a world full of kings, who might draft a document based on his own Constitution. He and Diane could stay for a few years, perhaps, then return to their own world, where by that world's reckoning they would only have been gone a few days.

How tempting was Geldion's offer, to Gary and to Diane.

Then why? Gary wondered when they were back in a glade in Tir na n'Og just a couple of weeks later, waiting with Mickey and Kelsey for the pixies to come and begin their world-crossing dance. Why were they going back?

Both Gary and Diane had come to the same conclusion, separately, that they could not, should not, remain in Faerie. For all the thrills it might offer, this was not their world, not their place, and they both had families back home. And they had been summoned by an even more insistent call, a call that emanated from their own hearts. Gary had come to terms with the loss of his father now. In the fight for Faerie, in what he had seen pass between Geldion and Kinnemore, the young man had come to remember and dwell on not his father's death, but his father's life. He had come to terms with mortality, and knew then how to beat the inevitable. His answers would not be found in Faerie, but in his family.

Gary and Diane had decided that the time had come for

them to have a child, and they could not do that in Faerie—how could they go back to their own world and possibly explain the new addition?

So it was not with heavy hearts that Gary and Diane said their goodbyes to Geno and Gerbil and Tommy at the border of Dvergamal. And it was not with heavy hearts that they stood now in Tir na n'Og, waiting to go home.

"Ye're sure, lad?" Mickey asked, drawing the man from his private contemplations.

Gary could tell from Mickey's tone that the sprite approved of the decision. The leprechaun had hinted several times during their journey back to Tir na n'Og that too much needed to be done in Gary's own world for him to even think of staying to help with Faerie's problems. Indeed, Gary got the distinct impression that if he remarked that he had changed his mind now, Mickey would likely try to steer him back towards his original choice. Kelsey seemed in full agreement. As much as the elf had come to trust and love Gary, and as much as he had already come to respect Diane, Kelsey still thought of them as outsiders, as people who belonged to another place.

"It's been an amazing few . . ." Gary stopped before he said "years," remembering that, by Mickey's terms, all of this incredible adventuring had occurred in just a few short months. "It's been an amazing few months," he corrected with a private chuckle. "So how many others have come over for a similar experience?"

"Faerie's always wanting another hero," Mickey explained cryptically.

"So is my own world," Gary replied. He looked at Diane and shrugged. "Not that I'm anything special back there."

"It's a tough place to get noticed," Diane agreed with a resigned smile.

"But we have to go back," Gary asserted to Diane and to

Mickey. "I'd be willing to return—we both would—but let's keep it one adventure at a time."

"It's more mysterious that way," Diane explained. "If we stuck around long enough for the people to get to know us, they'd probably become a bit disenchanted."

Gary, Diane, and Mickey shared a chuckle at the self-deprecating humor.

"I do not believe that," Kelsey interrupted, the elf's tone even and serious. "Their respect would not lessen with familiarity."

Gary, who knew Kelsey so very well, understood how great a compliment the elf had just given to him and his wife. He turned to Diane and she was nodding, fully comprehending.

That satisfying moment was lost when the melodic call of pixie-song wafted through the night air. As one, the companions turned to see the ring of glowing lights, Gary and Diane's ride home.

With a nod to Mickey and Kelsey, and not another word, for they both knew that if they dragged this out, they would not have the strength to continue, the two walked over and stepped in.

"Remember, lad and lass," they heard Mickey call, his voice already sounding distant, "the bridges to Faerie are in yer mind's eye!"

Then they heard the surf pounding below them, and awoke in the early morning hours amid the ruins of a castle in a lonely place on the Isle of Skye known as Duntulme.

† Epilogue

"The bridges to Faerie are in your mind's eye," Gary muttered.

Diane looked up from her book. "What?" she asked, putting her mouth close to Gary's ear so that he could hear her over the drone of the 747's engines. As usual, the two found themselves sitting over a wing, with no view and the loudest noise.

"What Mickey said," Gary explained. "The bridges to Faerie are in your mind's eye. What do you think that means?"

Diane sat back and folded her book on her lap. She hadn't really considered the leprechaun's parting words in any detail, too consumed by the journey back to her own world and by the implications of all that she had witnessed. Like Gary on his first journey, like any who had gone over to Faerie, Diane found the foundations of her own world, and of a belief system that had guided her through all her life, severely shaken.

"Mind's eye?" Gary whispered.

"Maybe Mickey was saying that the bridges remain, and you'll be able to see them," Diane offered.

Gary was shaking his head before she ever finished. "Mickey's been saying that the bridges are lessening—look at the woods out back of my mother's house. That place was a bridge to Faerie, once upon a time."

Gary sank back into his seat, his expression sour, lamenting.

"Maybe the bridges are what Mickey was talking about when he said that your world, that our world, needed fixing," Diane offered.

Gary looked at her quizzically, doubtful but intrigued.

"Really, do you think you can make some major changes in the course of our world?" Diane asked. "Five billion people in structured societies—what, are you going to become President or something?"

Gary started to say, "It could happen," but realized that he was beginning to get more than a little carried away. In Faerie, he was the spearwielder, the wearer of Donigarten's armor, champion of a King. In this world, he was Gary Leger, just another guy going about his life, trying to get along.

"So what do you think he was talking about?" Gary prompted, thinking that Diane had a better grasp than he did on the reality of it all.

"The bridges," Diane decided after a short pause. "Mickey laments the passing of the bridges, and he wants you to make sure that they don't all go away."

"That would make our world a better place," Gary quietly agreed, resting back more comfortably in his seat. Diane smiled at him and went back to her reading.

A few minutes later, Gary popped forward, drawing Diane's full attention. "That's it!" he said excitedly, and too loudly, for he noticed that several nearby passengers had turned to regard him. He huddled closer and spoke more quietly as he continued. "We can show them," he said. "We can tell them and we can show them, and we can make them understand."

Diane didn't have to ask to figure out who this "them" that Gary was talking about might be. He was speaking of the general populace, speaking of going public with their adventures, perhaps even with the pictures of Faerie that Diane had brought back with her. Her doubts were obvious in her expression.

"We've got the proof," Gary went on undaunted. He nodded to Diane's travel bag, the one holding the cameras and the revealing film.

Diane looked there, too, and shook her head.

"They're unretouched Polaroids," Gary protested.

"Of what?" Diane asked bluntly.

Gary mused that one over for a moment. "Of the haggis," he said finally. "We've got a picture of the haggis in the King's clothes."

"That should get us on the cover of one or two tabloids at least," Diane replied sarcastically. "Maybe even on a daytime talk show, right next to the London werewolf."

Her sarcasm was not without merit, Gary fully realized. The most remarkable pictures they had were shots that could be easily faked, were images that didn't even compare with the ones in the lower-budget science-fiction movies.

"Mickey wouldn't have said it if he didn't have a reason," Gary huffed, growing thoroughly flustered. "There's a key to this somewhere. I know there is."

"Your imagination," Diane answered suddenly.

Again Gary looked at her quizzically.

"Your mind's eye, don't you see?" said Diane. "The bridges to Faerie are in your mind's eye."

"We didn't imagine . . ."

"Of course not," Diane agreed before Gary could even finish the argument. "But maybe what Mickey was talking about, maybe the reason we're losing the bridges to Faerie, is because we, as a world, are losing our ability to imagine."

"The bridges to Faerie are in your mind's eye," Gary uttered once more, the words coming clear to him then.

Diane leaned in close and whispered into Gary's ear. "And maybe we can open up someone else's mind's eye," she said.

Gary knew what she meant, had the answer sitting in his desk drawer in his apartment in Lancashire, Massachusetts, in the form of a book written by a man who had opened up Gary Leger's imagination. Maybe, just maybe, he and Diane could do the same for some other potential adventurer.

It was a seven-hour flight back to Boston's Logan Airport, and by the time the 747 touched down, Gary had the first chapter plotted and ready for the keyboard.